THE FOUND JAR

Praise for Jaycie Morrison

Basic Training of the Heart

"There are some great WWII lesbian romances out there, and you can count *Basic Training of the Heart* among them. It's well worth a read, and I look forward to seeing what's next in this series."—*Lesbian Review*

Heart's Orders

"I am so enamored with this awesome story! While I was reading this book I got so caught up in the struggles the characters faced—I felt as though I was experiencing all of the angst, confusion and elation right along with them. There is one thing that I know for sure; this story is going to stay with me for quite some time. These strong-willed women are truly unforgettable, and they will capture your heart and attention from the first page."—*Lesbian Review*

"Jaycie Morrison has captured the mood of an era really well in these novels, and the determination of the women who have signed up to the WAC to not only do a good job but to forge a place for themselves in the world…The romances are sweet and gentle, the mood is soft focus despite the harsh realities of the time. An excellent follow up in the Love and Courage Series, I look forward to book three."—*Lesbian Reading Room*

By the Author

Basic Training of the Heart

Heart's Orders

Guarding Hearts

The Found Jar

Visit us at www.boldstrokesbooks.com

THE FOUND JAR

by
Jaycie Morrison

2020

THE FOUND JAR
© 2020 By Jaycie Morrison. All Rights Reserved.

ISBN 13: 978-1-63555-825-8

This Trade Paperback Original Is Published By
Bold Strokes Books, Inc.
P.O. Box 249
Valley Falls, NY 12185

First Edition: December 2020

THIS IS A WORK OF FICTION. NAMES, CHARACTERS, PLACES, AND INCIDENTS ARE THE PRODUCT OF THE AUTHOR'S IMAGINATION OR ARE USED FICTITIOUSLY. ANY RESEMBLANCE TO ACTUAL PERSONS, LIVING OR DEAD, BUSINESS ESTABLISHMENTS, EVENTS, OR LOCALES IS ENTIRELY COINCIDENTAL.

THIS BOOK, OR PARTS THEREOF, MAY NOT BE REPRODUCED IN ANY FORM WITHOUT PERMISSION.

Credits
Editor: Barbara Ann Wright
Production Design: Stacia Seaman
Cover Design by Tammy Seidick

Acknowledgments

As always, I appreciate the entire Bold Strokes Books team and their unflagging patience and attention to detail. Special thanks to Barbara Ann Wright, whose humor during the first edits was a great source of encouragement, and whose replies to my whining 1:00 a.m. emails helped keep me sane—or whatever semblance of that state exists for authors these days. I'm already preparing my "feelings" for the next one. And to Stacia, the last, best line of defense against errors. You rock!

Getting two books out in one year was a dream come true. Unfortunately, I picked a nightmare year to achieve it. To those folks I didn't get to visit with at Pride events or the GCLS convention or any of the other canceled outings—I miss you and hope to see you next year! And kudos to all those who have made do with online events as we work our way through a new (hopefully temporary) normal. And, like all of us, I owe boundless gratitude to the "essential workers" without whom even our bizarre pandemic lives would not be possible. Consider this a virtual hug.

My gratitude to those who beta read, or beta talked, through the early stages of this story, and to Julie R, who did an amazing job of helping with my proofs. And to my writing group: Kimberly, Janeen, Millie, and Avery—your humanity and dedication are a weekly inspiration. Thanks so much for letting me join in.

To my wife, whose love and support never fails—
whether I'm in lazy writer or crazy writer mode.
All the love in every story is for you.

And to Marti, whose encouragement was the earliest guide
on this path and whose longtime friendship has been with me
every step of the way. Sorry to keep you waiting for your
California book, but someday…

Chapter One

Vacation? Me? No, thank you. Almost never and not now and especially not there. You'd think my friends would remember how I'd always refused similar invitations in the past. A poor swimmer, too much water made me uneasy. Moreover, boats terrified me. It was an irrational fear, but I'd readily run off the rails with Amtrak or even risk a no-frills airline crash before I'd set foot on a boat. So the idea of traveling to the Outer Banks of North Carolina—islands, for Christ's sake!—was supremely unappealing.

Plus, I had writing to do, the kind of work that needed large doses of solitude, which meant that living three months nose to tail and elbow to asshole, even with folks I rather liked, seemed extremely ill-advised. I'd come to believe that distance, or at least frequent absences, was the second-best social lubricant for such associations, next to alcohol. When it came to more personal relationships, I'd had such things well under control for the last few years.

Every couple of months or so I'd wander down to a bar in the Village and drink enough to end up in a bathroom stall or an alley or someone's back seat or, when she was really something, a moderately priced hotel room. I needed the liquor to loosen the mental restraints of my strict upbringing, and the short-lived satisfaction of my body reinforced exactly what I already knew. Pleasure was fleeting. A clever line or an interesting mannerism sometimes made its way into my work, but that was all I kept.

I was generally comfortable, except for a nagging sense that there must be an expiration date on such behaviors. I hadn't acted on my true sexuality until the ripe old age of thirty-two, and my shelf life probably wasn't long. But since nothing enjoyable in my life had lasted for long, there would be no surprise if this was the case as well. Once

I'd understood that I could have sex—and orgasms—without love, it was easy to stay on that path. Safe had been my default mode since childhood, which was one reason why I'd been willing to vigorously ignore the attractions to women I'd been feeling for all those early years.

My friends often mistook my restraint for an utter lack of feeling, something I'd never bothered to deny. But when I tried rejecting their two-couple summer holiday invitation on the grounds that I'd be a fifth wheel, they counted that I'd be a much-needed spare. I shook my head as I wrote another brief decline to the email, reflecting that it took me almost as long to warm up to a new place as it did to new people. I'd been buffeted by change enough that it was never something I sought.

I'd married a man at age twenty-four after completing graduate school and failing to find a job. Jackson told me he found my "patrician features" appealing, apparently not recognizing I'd cultivated the detached, somewhat haughty expression to keep people away. I quickly learned that what I did during the day was of little concern to him, as long as he came home to dinner, a clean house, and some occasional—if not routine—sex upon request. Those simple demands and Jackson's own aloofness had me briefly convinced things between us might work out. But after I'd been thrown in with his cronies' wives for a time, their talk of the latest appliances or the difficulty of finding good help gave me visions of thousands of brain cells crying out as they died sedentary, slothful deaths. I began passing the time by taking my private, unspeakable memories and reframing them into somewhat more satisfying narratives, becoming what Mel later called a closet writer.

I met Melanie Daniels at one of Jackson's work parties. She was there ostensibly to represent her father's company, but in reality, she was scoping out the women. Once I convinced her that I wasn't available sexually, we began a great conversation which continued over coffee the next day. Mel seemed to accept that I would be an intellectual conquest rather than a physical one, and I found myself oddly enthused about becoming friends with a lesbian. When I hesitantly revealed my writing habit, her reaction was exactly what I'd feared: she wanted to read my work. After another week of cajolery and the encouragement of one wine in the park afternoon, I handed over a series of my short stories.

"Damn, woman," she said after reading them. "You're even more disturbed than I suspected." When I bit my lip, she shook the printed pages, adding, "This shit will sell like hotcakes. I'll be your agent... and we need to get you an editor." Three years later, I'd had modest success and good reviews on the short story collection and one novel I'd published in the genre we called horror romance. Things went bump in the night in more ways than one but strictly between men and women. The succeeding three years brought two more books and deep gratitude that my readership continued to grow after my divorce. But since I wasn't altogether certain they would still accept me after my vision of a love interest transitioned to that of another woman, I continued to write them as men.

Mel remained my publicist-agent-cheerleader and primary asskicker, and I'd continued to ignore her occasional bouts of possessive flirtatiousness, realizing that her personality contained elements of classic narcissism. Mel had her talents, but she needed frequent praise for her abilities and achievements, and she would do her damndest to get whatever she wanted, while everyone else had to go along to get along or get out of the way. I could accept the notion of being your own number one but preferred not to be anyone else's.

June, Mel's current bedmate, seemed to understand their arrangement perfectly, though perhaps what she truly comprehended was Melanie's enormous trust fund income. Or she took her cues from our mutual friend William, longtime partner of Walter, renegade artist son of a restaurant chain billionaire. Both men were terrific guys, who we referred to as the Fabulous W's—always said with love. The four of them comprised my entire personal business unit: promotion and design, business and art work. Improbably, we'd also become friends over the years. And unlike the women I slept with, my friends persisted.

Even after I'd used my work excuse to turn down their idyllic summer trip, June messaged me on Facebook and sent photos of a gorgeous house and picturesque beach located outside a small town called Windsom Edge. Walter texted to assure me that his culinary skills—admittedly outstanding—would be the highlight of the trip, while William, who was secretly my favorite, called, promising to be my measure of sanity.

"If things get too crazy, I'll take you somewhere peaceful and leave you for a while. Or we can just go get loaded." He never failed to make me laugh.

For her part, Mel informed me I looked "like shit" and insisted

I needed to get some color besides rarely-see-the-sun white. "Those circles under your eyes make you look ten years older," she groused. "Don't you ever sleep?"

Since I had no intention of discussing my nocturnal issues with anyone, I put her off by suggesting that authors of horror stories were supposed to look like the walking dead. She dismissed my attempt at humor, countering with a guarantee of privacy and quiet. I vacillated. She continued her vigorous sales pitch for a change of scene by unkindly pointing out the depth of my current writing rut. When I countered with a solid defense of routine, she cautioned me that a boring life could lead to boring writing. I had no answer for that. I wasn't even sure if it was true, but it worried me. I put her off and made a list of requirements. I would drive my own car. I would have my own room and bathroom. Everyone else needed to understand that for me, this was a working vacation, and if the mood struck—day or night—I would be writing and was not to be disturbed.

"Look Emily, everyone knows you're a heartless, demanding asshole," Mel said during our next call. "We just want to be able to parade around with someone famous occasionally. Or is it occasionally famous?"

I was much further from famous than they were from parading, but they'd taken to calling me Famous Author—or simply FA—after my first novel had been published. Ultimately, everyone agreed to everything, and my summer plans were set. I knew I should be thankful these relatively decent people wanted to spend time with me, so when we all met at Mel's to sign the contract on the place, I brought champagne to celebrate my caving in.

As promised, I was given the only room located downstairs in our rental, which should have been ideal. What I got when I opened the door to my retreat was the overwhelming smell of mildewing decay, a tiny crab-like creature that scuttled under a loose baseboard when I turned on the light, a complete lack of windows or ventilation, and the disturbing awareness that the bathroom fixtures were in the same space as my bed and dresser. I hurried upstairs to voice my displeasure, but everyone else had already settled in, obviously pleased with the views and furnishings.

I pulled Mel aside. "This isn't going to work for me. Have you seen that hovel down there?"

"Yeah," she said turning from June's display of tiny lingerie with a sigh. "It's pretty bad, I agree. But how about if you sleep on the couch and write outside on the deck? You can share our bathroom. And I'll cover half of your rent."

I was already shaking my head. It didn't surprise me that she would offer money as a quick fix to any given situation, but my concerns couldn't be solved that way. My insistence on seclusion was only partially work-related. To my thinking, people could be friends without knowing *everything* about each other. Certainly my nightmares were my own affair. I was about to launch into "I didn't want to come on this trip in the first place" in my bitchiest tone, when there was a firm tap on the outer door. We turned to see a middle-aged, somewhat heavyset woman wearing a dark blue smock over her plain white shirt and black skirt.

"Excuse me," she said, somewhat differentially but not timidly. "I'm Mrs. Janser, the housekeeper for this property. I stopped by to make sure everything was in order."

"The downstairs room is not in order," I said before Mel could act like everything was fine, letting my one chance to get this situation fixed walk away.

"The downstairs room is not inhabitable," Mrs. Janser clarified, her voice irritatingly calm. "I've told the realty company that for the last two years, but they continue to list it incorrectly."

Both Mel and I stared at her for a few seconds with our mouths slightly open. Finally, crossing my arms, I said, "Look, Mel, refund my money, and I'll head back to the city. The couch might be okay for a night or two, but it certainly won't work for twelve weeks."

"No way. We want you here," Mel said. "Besides, they won't refund at this point. They might exchange for another property, but I'm sure there's nothing else available." I knew this group could easily cover my share of the rent, but Mel was notoriously cheap for a rich bitch, and the W's would follow her lead.

"Nothing of this size," Mrs. Janser agreed. "But the Guest House up the hill would certainly be comfortable for one or two persons. If you'd agree to that couch for a night or two, I'm sure we could make it presentable, and you wouldn't be far away."

"Guest house?" Mel and I said together.

Mrs. Janser gestured, and we followed her down the stairs and to the road behind the house. She pointed to a painted wooden structure. "That's the Guest House. It's not on any of those rental websites, but I know the owner, and I'm sure he'd be willing to rent it for a twelve-week period. He just doesn't like messing with short-term folks."

Mel looked at me. "That might work, don't you think?"

"I'll have to see it before I make a decision." I didn't want to appear ungrateful, but I wasn't going to jump blindly into something that could be every bit as bad—or worse. I'd had that experience before.

Mrs. Janser inclined her head approvingly. "Of course. Nine o'clock tomorrow morning?"

She'd let her voice rise ever so slightly, but I knew it wasn't really a question. "Fine. Thank you."

At the appointed hour, I huffed my way up the hill to the Guest House, having declined Mel's rather insincere offer to accompany me. She'd roused herself to see me off, but I suspected the gesture was more out of guilt than friendship, or more likely, the scent of the coffee I'd made had done it. Everyone else was sleeping in after they'd partied late, celebrating the arrival of their extended vacation. I'd tossed and turned until morning, having all but decided to return to the city no matter what. I felt I owed Mrs. Janser the courtesy of a look at the place, sure I could easily find a reason to decline. I'd be back in my own apartment by late that night.

Halfway along the sandy path, the gently rolling sounds of low tide breakers made me look down at the water. A mild breeze brought in fresh salt air as the morning sun warmed the day. I sipped my coffee, a little surprised to find myself enjoying a scene so different from my usual circumstances. Even the sight of distant boats, dark specks bobbing and clanging softly out on the rolling blue waves, didn't make me uneasy for once. It occurred to me that after being moved steadily east since my birth and early childhood in Oklahoma, I'd now made it all the way to the Atlantic Ocean. Each of my life's jarring permutations had taught me to care less and less about what anyone else thought. I'd learned that no matter where I was, there was nowhere to hide from the flaws of who and what I was. By the time I'd come to New York for college, I had a clear plan of defense—physical distance, emotional suppression, and personal secretiveness.

Sighing, I looked at the Guest House. From my hard lessons about getting my hopes up, I knew better than to make an exception for this arrangement. But the warming sun and fresh salt air convinced me to allow a tiny space for being pleasantly surprised...maybe.

Up close, the house looked taller. It was a pale, somewhat

weathered blue, with white trim around the windows. Like most of the houses along the coast, it was two stories, with the living quarters on the second floor. But this place wasn't on stilts, and I supposed this was because it was farther from the water. The full ground floor had no windows and appeared to be used for storage. The deck above jutted out over the edge of it. A late model, slightly rusted Honda already sat there. Mrs. Janser must have seen me coming because she met me at the foot of the stairs.

"You'll be the one to say, of course," she said, "but if you can't get your money back, I'd think this wouldn't be a bad second choice." She gestured at the downstairs door. "The owner tells me there could be parking space there, but if you want it cleaned out, the cost will be on you."

"I'm fine outside," I answered, trying not to divulge that it wouldn't be more than a few hours at this point. "I'd rather avoid any extra expense."

She nodded, and I followed her cautiously up the stairs. To my surprise, they seemed well-built and solid, leading to a peculiar sense this home had once been someone's much loved refuge. It would have been much more like me to imagine it as the scene of some grisly crime, but before I could work out the inconsistency, Mrs. Janser opened the door and motioned me inside.

"I've only had the place open for a few minutes," she said, and I sniffed, catching some mustiness in the air but no scent of mildew or rot. A small stacked washer and dryer were set into the wall on my immediate right and covered with a louvered slide. Past that was a modest-sized second bedroom with a half bath. "Most use this as a child's bedroom or an office, although there's a small second living area on the back of the house which could work for that as well," Mrs. Janser explained. The rest of the layout was compact but well thought out. Dustcovers kept me from fully assessing the upholstered furniture of the main living area, which looked out on large windows. Across from there was a full, galley style kitchen. "There's no large dining area like in your friend's place," Mrs. Janser said, gesturing to the small table with four chairs by the window. "But all the cookware and six place settings with glassware are included."

I gave the kitchen a casual glance. The fridge and oven appeared relatively new, but the dishwasher looked ancient. Not that it mattered. Mel and Walter were the cooks. I'd lived on cereal, canned soup, and takeout for years.

The master was surprisingly large with a king bed, and the en suite bathroom had obviously been updated, as it offered a tub and shower along with two sinks.

"Linens?" I asked.

She shook her head. "It's been too long since someone's been here. But if you're interested, I'll talk to Mr. Guest about providing them."

I squinted at her, putting two and two together. They called it the Guest House because of the owner's name, not because it had been used for company by some other, larger place. "Or he could reduce the price by what it costs me to buy new, and I'd leave them when I go."

She pursed her lips. "We could try that."

I walked through the place one more time, trying to imagine it at different times of the day and at night. The door to the deck pushed open easily, and I caught my breath as I looked out to the breathtaking view of sparkling water beyond. The day was calm, making the line between the sea and sky almost invisible, but the immensity of it seemed inspiring rather than threatening. With some surprise, I realized I could do this. I'd long ago stopped asking the universe for anything, having reaped only anguish and disenchantment early on. How odd that I would come to this place and get everything I wanted…in terms of accommodations, at least.

"You'd be looking down on your friends." Mrs. Janser's voice held a hint of amusement as she gestured at the group rental house—known as Reefside—which was slightly to our left.

"And they'd hate that," I agreed, smiling.

At the approaching sound of a small engine, she excused herself and made her way outside. When a blue scooter, larger than the typical Vespa knockoff, stopped in front of the Guest House, she greeted the rider, who removed a helmet in a splash of sunlight before glancing at me with a face partly covered by dark glasses. Mrs. Janser began speaking, and the rider's head swiveled around to her. Curious, I made my way downstairs.

"…told you to wait until 10:00," Mrs. Janser was saying.

The rider looked at the sky, glasses still on. "I thought it was close to that."

When I came into view, she tucked the shades into her faded black T-shirt, revealing a tanned, youthful face and sparkling light brown eyes. Our gazes met, and she brightened and gave a little wave. Her open, pleasing appearance seemed completely free of pretense or affectation. "Hi."

THE FOUND JAR

I waved back automatically, and the rider broke into a wide, effortless smile. She had a beautiful mouth, full and sensuous. Mrs. Janser sighed emphatically, but I was too absorbed to care. Living in New York City for over ten years, I found the sight of someone so vulnerably friendly almost shocking. "Mrs. Harris, this is my daughter, Rebekah...uh, Becka."

"Beck," the rider corrected, not losing her grin as she favored me with a slight eye roll suggesting infinite patience, not irritation. Mrs. Janser harrumphed.

I didn't usually enjoy these sorts of familial interactions, but with Mrs. Janser's overblown annoyance fixed on her daughter, I felt free to join in a closer inspection. The left side of Beck's sun-bleached hair was shaved close, while the top was grown out to chin length and combed onto the other side. One long, thin braided piece trailed several inches farther down her back. She wore faded cutoff jean shorts, and the T-shirt was emblazoned with the name "Tuffy's," along with the image of a mynah bird. Since it was the beach, I decided to be casual in my reply. "Hi, Beck. Please call me Emily."

"Emily is a great name," she said with much more enthusiasm than younger types usually showed. "Do you know of Emily Dickenson, the poet?"

I couldn't help smiling. "I do. As a matter of fact, I was named after her."

Beck clasped her hands together. "That's great. I was named after Rebekah in the Bible. Right, Mama?" She turned to me again. "*Nomenclature* was my word of the day about a week ago. That applies to this conversation, doesn't it?"

Mrs. Janser's lips stretched thinly. "I'm sure it does, Becka. But Mrs. Harris has more important things to do than discuss family history or vocabulary terms with us."

"Sorry." Beck dismounted her scooter, looking chastened.

"Not at all," I insisted, wondering if she was studying for the GRE. "As a writer, I'm interested in names and where they come from."

Beck blinked, looking from me to her mother and back. "Did you say you were a writer?"

That personal detail had slipped out while I'd been fumbling for something to erase her forlorn expression and restore that smile again. "Yes," I said. "But contemporary stuff. Nothing cultured, I'm afraid." I'd found that trying to describe my peculiar blend of horror and romance was too complicated for an introduction.

Beck shook her hands as if drying them, clearly trying to channel her excitement. "That's the coolest thing I've ever heard." She looked at her mother again. "Mama, have you ever known a writer before?" Mrs. Janser's expression matched the chill in her voice. "Not that I know of, Becka. I don't have time for that kind of nonsense." The enthusiasm vanished from Beck's face, and Mrs. Janser turned her gaze on me. "No offense, ma'am, but we are a simple, working-class household."

"I understand," I said, easily translating Mrs. Janser's comment. She didn't approve of anything as fanciful as fiction or probably even higher education. Beck was staring at the ground. After a few seconds of uncomfortable silence, I cleared my throat. "Well, I should be going. Please tell Mr. Guest I'll take the place for twelve weeks. And I'd appreciate it if you'd ask about the linens."

"I'll do that, Mrs. Harris." Mrs. Janser was starting up the stairs.

"It's Ms.," I said, not ready to walk away. She kept going, but that was fine with me. "It was nice to meet you, Beck."

The young woman's head came up, though her smile had significantly less wattage. "It was nice meeting you too, Emily." She ventured a step closer and dropped her voice to a whisper. "I'd read your book anyway if I could. But I sometimes have trouble concentrating on stuff that's real complicated." She absently rubbed the side of her head as she spoke.

I nodded sympathetically. "But you've read Emily Dickinson, I take it."

"A friend read her to me. Mama didn't approve because she thought—"

She was cut off by her mother's voice calling from the doorway. "Don't keep the lady, Becka. You need to get on in here and get started on this kitchen."

"Sorry." Beck started toward the stairs.

"Don't be." A strange desire to run my fingers across the shaved part of her head as she passed by made me react with unusual cordiality. "Maybe we'll get to talk again sometime."

She turned back, her brows raised hopefully. "Could we really?" When I didn't respond immediately, her expression flattened. "Here's the thing. It's okay if you said that because you were just trying to be nice. But if you didn't mean it, I'd rather know."

I was quite sure I'd never seen anyone beyond their childhood years display their emotions so clearly. I wasn't sure what to make of it, but curiosity won out. "Sure we could."

Her full smile returned, and I couldn't help but respond in kind. After a few seconds, she murmured conspiratorially, "I'll be here by myself tomorrow if you want to come by and...like...check on my work."

"I'm certain I will," I said in the same tone.

She bounced on her toes, apparently pleased with our agreement, before turning and running up the rest of the stairs.

I walked briskly back to Reefside, feeling like working for the first time in several days.

After a productive afternoon of writing, during which my friends left me alone as requested, we gathered for dinner at the big table in the dining room. We'd just poured some wine when there was a knock on the door. Mrs. Janser looked in and, seeing the wine, an expression of righteous satisfaction crossed her face. It made me wish we were smoking dope or having an orgy or something more shockingly worthwhile.

"Mr. Guest agreed to a one-time ninety-five-dollar discount on your linens," she said. "That would be towels for both bathrooms and one king and one twin set of sheets. Would you like for me to shop for you?"

"No, thank you, Mrs. Janser," I answered, rising to the challenge. "I'll run into town tomorrow and see what I can find for that price." I feared being punished for my heathen intellectual ways with non-absorbent towels and scratchy sheets.

"Suit yourself." She shrugged and, after a few seconds' hesitation, added, "Mrs. Harris, could I speak to you privately for a moment?"

Luckily, no one had had enough wine to make them hoot suggestively at such a request, and I joined her on the deck after shutting the door.

"Mrs. Harris—" she began, but I corrected her again.

"It's Ms. Or Emily, if you prefer."

"It's about Becka," she started again, sparing us both any title, but gaining my full attention. "She wouldn't stop talking about you while we were working earlier, but I'd like to ask you not to indulge her interest. Maybe I've kept her sheltered, but she's easily impressed, and too much outside influence would only be distracting. I'm sure you understand."

I wasn't sure I did. Dismissing the brief gratification of Beck's regard, it sounded like we were talking about a child rather than a young woman. I knew some mothers were overprotective, though that certainly hadn't been my experience. Or not once my sister was gone.

"I'm here to work, and to enjoy some time with my friends, Mrs. Janser. I don't anticipate causing any such disruption." Her stern expression relaxed, making me wonder if Beck's enthusiasm would likewise dampen if I failed to show tomorrow. But if there was more to her mother's concern, I should deal with it now. "But is there some issue I should be aware of? Because if the place won't be ready in time, I may need to make other arrangements—"

"Oh, no, that's not what I meant. Beck has been working with me for years now and is perfectly capable of doing this kind of job. It's just new situations that can unsettle her." I raised a questioning eyebrow, and she added, "People have taken advantage of that, so I want to make sure she's safe." She looked away and sighed. "She doesn't even remember the one time she was outside of Windsom. That makes her somewhat naïve about the ways of the world." She turned back to me and her tone hardened. "For her own sake, it's easier if she stays that way."

The phrase "for her own sake" had always rubbed me the wrong way, and it sparked a mental rerun of my very brief impression of Beck. She struck me as young, maybe a bit innocent, but not gullible. She knew that people sometimes said things they didn't mean, and from my point of view, that was all you needed to deal with them successfully. I'd also experienced what it was like to find out important things much later in life than you should have simply because you'd been taught to be afraid. "Shouldn't that be her choice?"

"I know Becka doesn't want to leave Windsom. This is her home, and she's comfortable here."

And it had been comfortable being married…until it wasn't. How much more genuine would my life be if I'd had the courage to act when it was called for? "Comfort isn't everything," I murmured.

She frowned. "For someone like Beck, it is." I opened my mouth, ready to continue the argument, but she cut me off. "Look, not that it's any of your business, but there was an accident on her father's boat when she was ten. A piece of equipment broke, and a pulley hit

Becka on the head. It knocked her unconscious, and if she'd gone into the water, she would have drowned. The injury was so severe that she got airlifted off-island for rehabilitation. Once she got back to school, they put her in special classes with kids who were never going to get any better, even though her brain function was steadily improving. She was due to start fifth grade when I gave up on them and started homeschooling her. Since one of her big problem areas was finding the right words, I gave her a lot of work on vocabulary and reading. She worked hard at verbal skills and still does. Now, I'm sure I wasn't the best teacher, and I had to work too, so she spent a lot of time with her daddy on the water again."

I took a moment to absorb all this, suppressing a shiver at Mrs. Janser's description of Beck's boating accident. My agitation must have been obvious because she added, "Oh, Beck wasn't ever scared. I don't think she remembers anything that happened the day she got hurt. But they discovered that she had a real knack with anything mechanical. I think she repaired or reconditioned about every piece of equipment on that stupid boat. Then, come ninth grade"—she caught herself and stopped for a few seconds—"the point is, even though Becka has a hard time learning new things, she's always been very friendly and trusting around people. At least until she has reason not to be. It's been hard enough for her to understand that some folks here will always give her a hard time. So it wouldn't be prudent for her to…socialize…with someone from out of town. I'm sure you understand."

I wasn't normally this intrusive, but now I was truly curious. "How old is Beck, Mrs. Janser?"

She sighed again, this time in defeat, like someone who knew their argument was about to be lost. "She's almost twenty-six."

I tried to hide my shock. I'd have thought her in her early twenties at the most. "My God, how can she not be aware of the world outside of Windsom? Sooner or later, she'll have to deal with people and things beyond this place." I knew I sounded harsh, but I couldn't let her "ignorance is bliss" defense stand.

Mrs. Janser sniffed disapprovingly. "You're entitled to your own opinion, I'm sure, but Beck is my daughter, and I'll expect you to grant me the same courtesy." I strongly suspected if she hadn't been working for us, her request would have been a lot less polite.

"Of course," I answered, and we nodded good-bye to each other.

"What was that all about?" Walter asked, watching me take a substantial drink of my wine after I returned to the group.

"I think I've just been told to stay away from her daughter," I said, holding one hand innocently in the middle of my chest.

"She must be an excellent judge of character," Mel said from the kitchen.

I smoothed my eyebrow with the appropriate middle finger while Walter and William laughed.

Chapter Two

When I started writing full-time, which also involved meeting strangers and reading aloud in public, I'd invented a separate author persona to go with my penname. M. E. Leigh was a strong, capable woman with a definite rebellious streak—a rule breaker with a heart of gold—the exact opposite of who I truly was. So it was more like Leigh than Emily to make a stop at the Guest House on her way into town the next morning. Beck's scooter was the only vehicle parked outside, and I momentarily wondered if that transportation was her choice or if her mother didn't trust her with a car.

Stop it. Seeing everything about Beck through the lens of someone with questionable capability was probably what her mother wanted from an outsider like me. I hopped up the stairs, opening the door quietly as I took in how much had already been done inside.

Newly cleaned windows shone over tidy sills, and the plantation shutters had been wiped. The upholstery appeared vacuumed, while the wood pieces shone with polish. Hearing the dishwasher, I looked in the kitchen. Beck was facing away from me, earbuds dangling from her ears and disappearing into her back pocket. The tinny music was likely coming from a cell phone, suggesting her world was already somewhat bigger than her mother knew. Wiping off the inside of a cabinet, she was dancing, and I didn't need stereophonic sound in order to appreciate the moves. I stood for almost a full minute, admiring the motions of her body, the perfect flows and actions of arms and legs and the entrancing bump of hip, shake of shoulders, and bob of head. I'd been in enough bars in recent years to recognize a good dancer when I saw one, and Beck was more than good. She was fantastic. A highly inappropriate thought entered my head before I could stop it. *If she moves like that while cleaning the kitchen, she must be great in bed.*

Fully aware I needed to put the brakes on that kind of thinking, I called out, acting as if I'd just entered. She jumped, pulling the earbuds out and stuffing them into her pocket in a practiced motion. Focusing on me, she breathed out with obvious relief. "Oh, Emily. You startled me."

"I'm sorry, Beck." I gestured at her pants. "But your secret is safe with me."

Color rose in her cheeks, making her even cuter. "I don't mean to be defiant. Mama doesn't seem to understand music makes the time go faster when I'm working by myself. I only get the free kind, but there's always something I like."

"I understand. I love to listen to music while I'm traveling. Or audio books." At her frown, I elaborated. "I bet you'd like the way professional voice actors bring the story to life."

"You listen to them while you're driving?" When I nodded, she seemed to be trying to imagine such a thing before her expression became worried. "I might never get out of the driveway once I turned it on. Or people would honk at me because I'd be stuck at a stoplight, listening."

I smiled. "I've been known to drive a few extra miles out of my way to finish a chapter. But you can also load stories on an iPod or phone and listen to them inside when you're not doing anything else."

"Oh yeah. That would be cool." Her eyes grew distant, and I could see she was entranced by the idea. Abruptly, her gaze shifted back to me. "Seems like most good things cost money."

I shrugged apologetically. "Maybe that's what gives things their value."

She stood quietly, as if lost in thought. "But not people. Do you think human beings are mostly good or mostly bad?" she asked after a few seconds, looking at me intently.

Wow. Talk about an abrupt transition. Beck apparently wasn't much for small talk, which suited me. My awkwardness at parties or with any groups where I didn't know many people often led me to blurt out similar questions…or say absolutely nothing for hours. "I think most people have the capacity for either. Some act based on how they're brought up, which means they may think they're doing the right thing, when in fact, they're harming someone else." I could tell she was listening intently, and I added, "In other cases, people behave based on the situation they're in. They may say they believe in something

The Found Jar

but find themselves acting very differently when they're in a particular circumstance."

"Like what?" She cocked her head, taking a step toward me.

My usual reaction would have been to take a step away. I liked space between myself and others unless I knew them well, but the intent look on her face seemed only about our conversation, so I stood my ground. Not wanting to get overly cerebral, I said, "Someone might say they're opposed to bullying, for example. But will they have the courage to stand up if the person being picked on is a stranger, and their friends are doing the harassment?"

Beck eyed me thoughtfully. "Have you ever been in a situation like that?"

I wasn't sure which part of my scenario she was referring to. "One where I had to stand up to a friend?"

She shuffled her feet. "One where you were being bullied."

"Yes, I have," I told her. "And you?"

"Yeah. But I'm lucky because I have some friends in Windsom who will stand up for me." I nodded, and she glanced down the hill. "Are those people in Reefside your friends?"

"Yes. Business associates and also friends." I wasn't sure why I'd made the distinction, but it seemed important.

"But you can count on them?" She seemed genuinely interested in my decision on this matter, but oddly, I didn't feel pressured—simply compelled to think deeper than I usually did about such things.

"Yes," I said again after a few extra seconds. "I'm sure I could."

"I'm glad." She seemed satisfied with my answer. "It's good to have people you can count on."

"I agree." We smiled at each other for a few seconds, and I had the strangest feeling we'd settled something meaningful between us. When Beck's pants began to buzz, my thoughts went south again as she dug her hand into a tight pocket. She had a really, really nice butt. Positive she didn't want me as her designated lecher, I barely dragged my gaze up to her face in time.

"Yes, Mama?" She shrugged and did that quick eye roll again. "Yeah, twenty minutes should be about right…Yes, I have…Okay, thanks." By the time she was putting her phone up, I was already moving away. "Sorry, Emily," she called, following me. "I'm on the clock, and Mama's bringing me lunch."

I stopped at the low table across from the second bedroom which had a tall, open glass container on it. I was sure it hadn't been there when I'd viewed the house with Mrs. Janser. Gesturing at it, I said, "Do your services include decorating?"

Beck grinned. "That's your found jar. It's a very important part of becoming a beach person."

Becoming a beach person wasn't on my agenda, but I was intrigued. the idea was an interesting one. "And what do I do with it?"

"Everyone finds stuff when they go beachcombing, or they get souvenirs from local activities. So this becomes like a physical diary, and whatever you want to remember or you think is pretty or seems important, you put it in there. But the thing is, when it's full, or when you leave, you only get to keep one item. The rest you have to return to the ocean to let someone else find."

I tried not to smirk, thinking it wasn't likely I'd find even one thing to take with me. I wasn't a collector, and wandering around in an area I didn't know was definitely not my style. "Fair enough," I agreed. At the door I turned back. "Oh, I've got to find a place to buy some sheets and towels. Any suggestions?"

She directed me to a locally owned linen shop in town, as opposed to one of the national chains out on the highway, and the clerk who helped me could have been the owner, given the time and care she took helping me. As she totaled my purchases, she asked, "And may I ask how you came to find us?"

"A local young woman who's doing some work for me sent me here," I said as I signed the credit card pad. "Beck Janser."

"Becka Reynolds, you mean?" the woman asked.

I couldn't imagine more than one Beck in a town this size—or anywhere, really—so I nodded. "Yes, I suppose. I don't know her all that well. I first met her mother, so I assumed…"

The woman leaned toward me in the way of a typical small-town gossip. "Her daddy was lost at sea, and her mama remarried a few years later. But Erik Janser never adopted Becka, though I can't imagine why not. I'm sure a sweeter child never drew breath, and I can say that because I have three of my own." She laughed and handed me a large sack. "Anyway, after a few years, we all kinda got the impression Becka was just as glad, so I guess it all worked out. She's a fine young woman, in spite of that hair. You tell her Maggie said hi, and thanks for your business."

I left the store musing over the odd experience of learning something personal about Beck from a stranger. The image of her father dying in a tiny boat on that deep, foreboding sea made my fear feel legitimate, and I shivered. Briefly, I speculated on what her stepfather must be like, given his refusal to adopt his wife's child. I wondered if her mother's protectiveness of her daughter extended to him as well.

❖

A day later, I'd finished my walk-through and signed the lease. In possession of the house key and Mrs. Janser's business card, I waved as my friends arrived to inaugurate my cozy summer habitat. Everything shone like new, and they oohed and ahhed appropriately.

"It's so weird how this all happened," June gushed, "but I have a really good feeling about this place. I think it's going to be great for you."

I was feeling unusually affectionate and gave her a quick side hug. "Thanks, June. I think so too."

We finished three bottles of wine with the freshly made shrimp gumbo they'd brought and enjoyed relaxed conversation. When Walter commented on the found jar, I repeated Beck's explanation, and everyone except Mel nodded appreciatively.

"If this is such a big deal, how come we don't have one?" she groused. "This whole trip was my idea, you know."

I caught William's eye, and a look of silent understanding passed between us. Someone else had been the center of attention for too long. Assuming her usual role as peacemaker, June assured Mel they would find a container to use right away, and the party began to break up.

I bid my guests good night after they assured me they could find their way by the light of the full moon. Apparently mollified by the certainty of getting her own jar, Mel called, "Don't forget us," over her shoulder.

"How could I?" I called back. "You still owe me money."

I listened to their laughter and watched them disappear among the plants on the dunes between our places. Cleanup was quick, and I happily unpacked, sorting my things into the well-designed spaces and inviting furnishings. I knew I'd sleep, and even if I dreamed, it wouldn't matter. I was here in my own place where the distant sounds of the ocean would drown out my calls for help that would never come.

❖

So exhausted my hands were shaking, I hit a wrong key twice before successfully punching the number from Mrs. Janser's card into my cell phone. "Mrs. Janser?" I blurted as soon as the line was answered.

"No," the voice said. "This is her daughter. May I help you?"

Beck. I recognized the voice now and smiled at her obvious effort to be formal and proper. She and her mother had probably practiced that reply a lot. For some reason, this notion helped calm me. "Hi, Beck. It's Emily Harris, the lady who rented the Guest House. We met a couple of days ago." I was glad I didn't sound like a panicky idiot.

"The writer?" Her voice was almost breathless, and I was ridiculously pleased.

"Yes, that's right."

"Hi." She sounded genuinely excited. "How was your first night?"

"Well, actually, that's why I'm calling." I was relieved to not have to broach the subject myself. "There were some horrible noises that seemed to be coming from the downstairs area last night, but I wasn't about to go looking by myself in the dark." Hoping to add some levity and not sound totally gutless, I added, "We all know what happens to women who investigate sounds like that in the movies."

There was a slight pause. "I don't think I do know," she said finally. "But I don't like to see people get hurt if that's what you mean."

Okay, time to get to the point. "Yes, well, bottom line, I can't tolerate those terrible sounds every night, so I was hoping your mother could come by and check on the situation."

"But the thing is, Mama has already gone to work across the sound. She won't be back till dinnertime."

I sighed. I would need to start for the city well before then if this couldn't be worked out. The thought of repacking and doing that long drive made me ask, "Well, could you come? I need to figure out if I can stay here. And I'm not going into that garage by myself."

"Sure." She sounded excited by the idea. "I can be there within an hour."

"Good. Thank you."

"Okay, bye." Beck disconnected.

It occurred to me this was the second time I'd deliberately violated Mrs. Janser's veiled request to stay away from her daughter, but in fairness, this time, I hadn't done it intentionally. I was confident she'd be placated if Beck coming over ultimately meant I'd be able to remain in the house and pay rent through the summer rather than heading out after only one night. Especially after all the work they'd done getting the place ready. I went to change out of my pajamas and spent a few minutes at the bathroom mirror, hoping to look a tad less like the Captive Wild Woman when Beck arrived.

When I heard her scooter, I hurried downstairs with the house flashlight. Beck had just taken off her helmet and sunglasses and was smoothing down her hair. Something about her disarray made her look cuter than the last time I'd seen her. When she grinned and said hi, I couldn't help smiling back, even though I primarily wanted to get this matter resolved and get to work.

"Thank you for coming. I hope your mother won't mind you're here."

"Oh no. I called her and explained what was going on. She said I had to leave as soon as we figured out what the sound was." Her eyes drifted away from my face. "She said I mustn't make an annoyance of myself."

Her phrasing made me wonder if *annoyance* was another word of the day. More importantly, I didn't like her being made to feel that way about her mere presence, so I gave her shoulder a quick, awkward pat. "I'm sure you would never do that. In fact, you're doing me a huge favor by getting here this quickly." I grimaced and pointed at the side door to the bottom half of the house. "And by being willing to go into that garage."

Beck lifted her head and squared her shoulders. "Which I am." She took the flashlight and walked to the door. I followed, and she looked around, surprised. "Are you coming in too?"

"Maybe," I answered hesitantly. I held out my cell phone. "Someone has to be prepared to call 9-1-1."

She snorted derisively. "You haven't met our sheriff, have you?" When I shook my head, she turned the doorknob. "In this situation, he'd be behind both of us."

The door creaked as she pushed it, and I caught a puff of cool, stale air. She pushed her head and half her body inside and stilled. I could feel the blood rushing through my veins. She looked at me from the darkened space. "I hear something," she whispered. "Some faint squeaking sounds, and there's some movement."

Another step and she disappeared into the gloom. I stood for about five seconds, before—mentally kicking myself the whole time—I followed. Once my eyes adjusted, I could see Beck's form a few feet ahead. She turned toward me with her finger to her lips. I stopped and listened. She was right about the sound, but along with the squeaks, I heard something else…a faint rumbling.

"What is it?" I whispered after a few seconds, unable to stand the suspense. I made a mental note to lessen the amount of time my characters suffered through similar scenes.

"I think I have a sense of where to look, so I'm going to turn on the flashlight," she murmured softly.

I tensed, sighting the doorway and preparing to run. 9-1-1 could wait until I got outside. There was a click, and a beam of light swept across the far edge of the room, which was apparently under my bedroom. Nestled in some rags in the corner was a cat, purring loudly as she curled around what appeared to be five mewling babies.

"Kittens!" The awe in Beck's voice was unmistakable. I laughed weakly, feeling relieved and more than a little foolish…until her hand found my forearm and slid down until it wrapped around my palm. What followed was a shock that even the warmth of her skin didn't diminish. Holding hands wasn't something I did. Gestures like that were silly romantic moves that had no place in my life, but I remained frozen in place, unable to pull away. She turned to me, joy evident on her face. "New life."

I only nodded, still sorting through my reaction alternatives. Jerk my hand away? Ask her to let go? Squeeze her hand gently in response and get upstairs as quickly as I could? Beck turned back to the feline family. "Most likely, what you heard last night was her delivery cries and maybe the babies fussing for milk at first. I'm sure it won't happen again." She indicated the mother cat with her free hand. "They say having children is painful. Have you ever had any?"

"Uh, no," I replied, trying to sound casual.

"Would you ever want to?"

If someone else had asked, I wouldn't have considered answering such offensive prying, but I sensed a fundamental innocence accompanying the gentle contact of her hand. Beck wasn't someone trolling for dirt; she was simply and genuinely asking about me. Oddly, there was something about her I instinctively trusted. I swallowed to give myself another few seconds. "No, I don't want to. What about you?"

The mother cat stirred restlessly, and Beck turned the light off, whispering again. "I think we should go. She might not be used to people, and we're disturbing her."

Still holding my hand, she led me outside. When she let go, along with my great relief, I experienced an odd awareness of the loss of connection. I stood squinting in the bright morning light for a moment, enviously watching Beck slip on her sunglasses. "What should I do now?" I asked. "Call animal control or something?"

She studied me thoughtfully. "You could do that," she said. "Or not," she added after another second.

"Or not?" I echoed. "But what will happen to them if I don't?"

"Nothing."

"What do you mean, 'nothing'?" I hated this parroting thing, but Beck wasn't being particularly forthcoming.

"They'd get to grow up here instead of in a tiny cage while their odds of being adopted dwindles and the likelihood of them being killed increases." She gestured at the garage. "At our shelter, once the kittens are weaned, the mama probably won't last another week."

"But wouldn't I have to feed them if they stay here?" I asked urgently. "I mean, I don't know the first thing about taking care of cats."

"No pets, either?" she asked, and I began feeling defensive.

"I travel a lot." That wasn't the reason, but she didn't need to know the details. "What about you?"

"No, but I'd like to. To both questions. I don't have any say right now because I still live with my mama and her husband, but someday..." She trailed off, looking out at the ocean.

I waited, but she seemed to have forgotten we were in the middle of a discussion. "Beck?" I asked, keeping my tone mild.

"I'm thinking about a report one of my homeschool friends did," she said, still facing away. As I struggled to connect the dots of the conversations, she turned back to me, adding, "It was about cats. I'm pretty sure I remember how to take care of them. I can look stuff up too, but it sometimes takes me a while to understand it."

We were standing in the full sun, and sweat was forming along my brow. "Look, I can't put two thoughts together at the moment. I hardly slept at all, and I haven't had any coffee. Is there a café in town that's any good?" As if on cue, her stomach growled, and at her embarrassed blush, I began to laugh. I was accustomed to eating alone, but she wasn't the worst company. "If you'll navigate, I'll drive. And breakfast will be my treat to thank you for saving me from that vicious mother cat and her obviously murderous kittens."

"So you'll be staying, right?" she asked, lifting her glasses to fix her honey-colored eyes on me. Of course, this was all about the rent. Feeling slightly deflated, I nodded. "Then I'll show you the grocery store after breakfast, and you can stock up for the next week or so."

"Including cat food?" I asked, my tone playful. If I hadn't been watching her, I would have missed the hopeful expression that disappeared quickly. *This is someone who's accustomed to disappointment but hasn't yet become totally jaded.*

"The thing is, I don't know you well enough to know if you're teasing or not," she said after a few seconds. "Do you find it hard to know what people really mean sometimes?"

For one wild second, I thought to tell her my never-fail strategy for dealing with people: if you expect the worst, you'll never be disappointed. "Yes, often," I said, making another quick decision. "Okay look, I'll buy the cat food if you'll come take care of whatever they need. I don't want to be responsible for them in any way, and I don't want to be disturbed when it's feeding time, so you'll have to come and go quietly. If you don't think you can manage those conditions, I'll have to call animal control."

Beck grinned that infectious smile and put out her hand. "Deal."

We shook, and this time, her touch wasn't such a shock.

Accompanying Beck to the local diner—whose unimaginative name was the Edge—proved to be more of a social event than I'd anticipated. It seemed like half the people inside greeted her, and those who didn't gave me the long appraising looks that a stranger got in a small town. At a nod from the hostess, Beck moved to sit in a booth on the far side of the room, waving or saying hi as we went and not making any effort to introduce me, which was fine. But the big-bodied, long-faced waitress who approached our table didn't waste any time getting the details.

"Who's your pretty friend, Becka?" she asked, slapping down two menus.

"This is Emily," Beck said, apparently confident a last name wasn't needed. "She's staying in the Guest House for the summer."

The big woman cocked an eyebrow at me. "That a fact?"

I nodded and managed a smile. "Beck and her mother did a wonderful job getting the place ready. They really helped me out of a jam."

Apparently, I'd given the right answer because the woman's face softened. "Yes, Beck and her mother are fine people. And that place has been needing some TLC for a while now. Glad you got the ball rolling, Emily." She gave the full pot she carried a gentle shake. "You folks want coffee?"

We both hummed in assent, and after she filled our cups, I read the tag on her shirt and thanked her by name, something I never would have done in the city. Barbara gave me a wink before departing, saying she'd give us a little more time. I sipped carefully, watching in amusement while Beck added milk and honey to hers. Suppressing a moan of appreciation for the strong, hot brew, I could barely acknowledge the favored choices she pointed at on the menu. Beck took small sips as her gaze casually scanned the other patrons. Eventually, she said, "Barbara is a super nice person, but by this afternoon, everyone in here and all their friends will know who you are. Saves time, don't you think?"

Small town life indeed. I had to laugh in agreement.

Beck's face turned serious. "But here's the thing. If you ever come here again, be sure and ask for her section. You can count on her to take care of you."

We ordered, and Beck pulled a small notebook from her back pocket. "Let's make a grocery list while we wait."

It seemed rather invasive to tell someone I barely knew about my particular eating habits, but Beck slowly wrote out my requests without comment. "Why aren't you working with your mama today?" I asked when the list was done.

"I have class later this afternoon," she answered. "Over at the community college."

I was pleased to hear she was a student. Maybe I'd misjudged her mother's attitude toward higher education. "I loved college. Sometimes, I think I'll go back. What are you majoring in?"

"I'm not majoring at all. I'm only taking a class that interests me." She looked slightly guarded, as if anticipating some negative response.

"Even better," I said when Barbara had taken our orders after topping off our coffees. I liked this place already. "No point in wasting time and money until you figure out what you want to do."

She sniffed. "Our community college is good, but it's kinda small. I bet you went to a big school." At my nod, she said, "Will you tell me what that was like?" The pure curiosity in her expression encouraged me to give the tourists' version of life at CUNY. Her jaw dropped when I quoted the enrollment as over 275,000 students. "That's like, four times as many people live on this whole island." We both glanced over as the bell over the door jangled, but Beck turned away quickly, her face almost slack as a group of young men entered.

"Look, Randy," I heard one of them say as he nudged his buddy. "Your favorite dyke retard is here."

They were moving in our direction when Barbara intercepted them, the two plates she was carrying tilting threateningly in their direction. "Counter service only. You boys know the rules."

Everything got very still for a moment before the tallest one said, "Oh sure, Barb. We know." The group moved away from us, positioning themselves on stools in front of a man who stood wiping the counter on the opposite side of the dining area. Barbara delivered our food, patted Beck on the arm, and left without a word. I wasn't sure what to do, so I began eating. When I looked up, Beck was pushing her food around aimlessly, her face a study in dejection.

"May I ask you a personal question?" I asked. She shrugged, her focus still on her plate. I pointed at the sunglasses dangling from her shirt front. "Are those prescription?"

"What?" She looked up.

"Your sunglasses. Did you get them from a doctor?"

"No. From the drugstore. My mama read an article that said people with eyes like mine should wear protection when they're outside to help prevent glaucoma."

She did have beautiful eyes. Sometimes the color seemed almost amber, sometimes closer to hazel.

"I asked because when I first started kindergarten," I said, "I'd been diagnosed with what they called lazy eye. It was like my eyes didn't work together because one of them needed better nerve stimulation along the pathways to the brain. To help strengthen the lazy one, I had to wear a patch over the good eye every day." I took in a breath, aware I had her rapt attention. "When I arrived at school wearing the patch, I thought I looked like the coolest pirate ever. But some kids didn't share my opinion. They teased me mercilessly, calling me Cyclops or Shockwave." I paused, stunned how the distant hurt of those months still echoed, though what had happened with my sister Abby a few years later was so much worse. Remembering my purpose, I forced a smile. "Lucky for me, summer came, and the patch came off. I started first grade with different kids, and no one called me names after that."

Beck examined my face intently. "Is everything okay now?"

"Yes, I'm fine."

She nodded, but her glance fell. "My mama used to tell me the bullying would stop someday, but it hasn't."

"And I'm sure she told you people who talk that way are doing it because they're threatened by you."

Obviously puzzled, she scratched the side of her head. "Threatened?"

"Sure. Even someone without perfect vision could see you're devastatingly darling. And we've talked enough for me to know 'retard' is something that couldn't possibly apply to you, besides the fact that it's a completely uncool thing to say."

I wasn't foolish enough to think a few compliments or a stranger's story could offset what had probably been years of insults, but I was pleased when she blushed and took a bite of her pancakes. We finished our meal in silence, and Barbara swung by to fill our cups once more and drop off our check. I was leaving a generous tip when an elderly man stopped at our table. White-haired and slightly stooped, when he gave me a friendly grin, I saw his glance was clear and sure.

"You're not gonna miss class today, are you, Becka?" His poised voice was strong. A professor emeritus, perhaps?

She grimaced briefly but shook her head. "No, sir, Mr. Howell. I've only got one errand to run, so I'll be there."

He looked to me as he gestured at Beck. "One of my best ever, this one. You should see her—"

She stood quickly, interrupting. "But we need to get going if I'm going to be on time. See you this afternoon, Mr. Howell."

He didn't seem offended his conversation was cut short. He patted her shoulder affectionately, and she smiled at him. I grabbed my purse and followed her quickly departing form, throwing him a quick wave. At the door, I heard the boys at the counter making loud comments obviously meant for Beck.

"Couldn't spell cat if you spotted her the c and the a."

"I'm gonna get my hedge trimmers and fix that hair, first chance I get."

"Looks like there's a new sugar mama in town. Someone better tell Peyton."

I glared in their direction, but Beck pulled me out onto the sidewalk. Putting on her sunglasses as we walked to my car, she gestured down the street. "The grocery store is three blocks that way."

Someone else's reluctance to talk was easy for me to understand. Very few people had respected that trait in me, and I was determined to give Beck all the space she needed. She knew her way around the store, and our purchases didn't take long. Other than a wry grin when she loaded the cat food onto the bottom of our cart, she remained focused on our task. After a quiet drive and two trips up the Guest House stairs, everything was loaded into my kitchen pantry.

She shuffled her feet, not meeting my eyes. "Thanks for breakfast. Sorry it got kinda weird."

There were dozens of things I wanted to say, but I settled for, "Will you come by tomorrow to check on your kittens?"

She nodded. "It'll be early since I have to work with Mama tomorrow. Maybe we should put the food downstairs so I won't disrupt you."

Strangely, I didn't feel her presence would be a bother, but I agreed, and she carried the bag back to the garage. I followed with the flashlight, and we looked at each other for a second before she cracked open the door again. The kittens were sleeping, and the mother cat was gone. Beck put the food on a wooden chair whose cane seat was partially rotted away.

"How did the mother get out?" I asked.

"Probably the same way she got in. There must be a loose board or gap somewhere. I'll look tomorrow, but we shouldn't fix it until the kittens are grown."

"When will that be?"

She shrugged. "No sooner than eight weeks, but I'd rather wait ten to start adopting them out, just to be sure."

We returned to the sunlight, and Beck handed me the flashlight. I could see she was still upset, so I replied with a submissiveness totally out of character for me. "I trust your judgment. We'll do whatever you think is best."

She hesitated, blinking against the sunshine. "I think you're an unusually nice person, Emily," she said finally. "One of the nicest I've met in a long time. I'm glad you're here, and I hope you enjoy your summer."

She was turning away to get on her scooter when I stopped her with a hand on her arm. "Thank you, Beck. And I appreciate all the work you and your mother did to make this place good for me." I moved my hand away before I went on. "I don't usually spend this much time with one person, but I enjoyed today."

"Did you really?" She smiled shyly, and I warmed inside at the change.

"I really did."

Her glance flitted to my face and away again. "Maybe we could do it again sometime? Breakfast or some other meal?"

I felt my internal brakes come on. It had been a long time since I'd gone too far, been too nice, but that was obviously the case here. "Well, I have a lot of work to do, Beck. So I can't—"

"I've made a pest of myself, haven't I?" That wasn't exactly what I was thinking, but it was close enough that I said nothing. "Mama was right," she muttered to herself, putting on her glasses before pulling on her helmet. "She's always right about stuff like this." She started her engine and flipped down her visor, further shielding her face. "Maybe I'll see you around sometime."

I knew she wouldn't hear any reply, so I simply nodded, and she rode away without a second look.

Chapter Three

My new beach life got blissfully quiet after that. The unfamiliar tidal sounds and smells were surprisingly calming, easing my usual daily agitation into a more relaxed state. From my perch on the hill I saw occasional beachcombers wander past, but Windsom Edge was far enough away from the more populated areas that tourists rarely made it this far. I enjoyed my solitude but was pleased when Mel checked on me a couple of times—always without calling first, of course—and we made vague plans to go see a movie sometime.

I'd dropped the book of matches I'd gotten at the diner in the found jar, but they remained alone. I didn't venture to the beach or explore the town but sat in the morning or late afternoon sun on the deck and napped during the heat of the day without dreams of strangers in the dark. I worked when the mood struck me, forgoing my stricter city schedule, feeling as if time had become more circular than linear.

When a glance at the calendar one morning reminded me that I hadn't heard Beck's scooter for almost a week, I began to worry. Had she decided not to take on the responsibility of the cats, or had she simply forgotten? I took a break from my writing and did some research on brain injuries. For a mild concussion, total recovery was common within three months. But occupational-physical therapy, speech-language therapy, psychological services, and social services might be needed for a traumatic brain injury, which seemed to fit Mrs. Janser's description. Though recovery of most or all brain function was possible in time, an individual could have problems in social situations, including not understanding nonverbal signals and lack of awareness of abilities. The website also described possible intellectual obstacles, and difficulty with focus and forming new memories, along with being slower at processing thoughts. However, the acuteness of these complications varied. Given that she'd remembered me when I'd called, and based on our conversations, it seemed to me that Beck was functioning well, certainly far above what the boys in the diner had unkindly called her.

True, she was a bit distractible, but I was that way too, at times. I suppose the way she took my hand in the garage was impulsive, but her excitement at the kittens could certainly be reason enough. I read on, wondering if she'd experienced any of the depression, anxiety, or mood swings that were also listed as potential emotional troubles. She certainly didn't lack empathy for others. The article added that frustration, sadness, and feelings of loss were also common later in recovery, especially when the injured person became aware of their long-term issues.

I closed my laptop, feeling deeply touched by that last sentence. Perhaps Beck and I had a connection of experience beyond kittens at a beach house. I was always aware of my long-term situation, though sadness and loss barely touched the surface of my emotions. With effort, I brought myself back to my original concern. Nothing I read had indicated Beck would be less likely to follow through on a task for which she felt confident, which she had seemed to be. So why hadn't she come back?

Sighing, I grabbed the flashlight and started down the stairs, apprehensive about what I'd find in the garage. Visions of a starving mother huddled beside her dying babies made me hesitate at the foot of the stairs. When it registered that the door to the garage was open slightly, my apprehension ratcheted up. Was this Beck's neglect or had someone…or something…else made their way inside? I forced myself forward, trying to shake off the image of mangled, half-eaten bodies, when the rising and falling of a voice made me freeze. Edging closer to the opening, I strained my ears to understand the sound over the noise of the ocean. After a few seconds I began to sense a repeating cadence, a kind of rhythm. Holding my breath, I put my face to the crack and peeked in.

Beck was sitting, her body in profile, singing as she stroked the mother cat on her lap. Now I could hear the tune clearly. "And if that mockingbird don't sing, Daddy's gonna buy you a diamond ring. And if—"

I sagged against the door frame with relief, thinking I had clearly spent too much time reading my own disturbing work. The old wood creaked loudly, and they both looked around. The mother hissed and jumped off Beck's lap, disappearing into a dark corner of the garage, but my attention was riveted on the blood already gathering on the deep cut the cat's back foot had gouged into Beck's leg.

Beck said, "Ouch," at the same time I said, "Oh shit."

Something about our mismatched chorus made us both laugh. Beck stood. "Hi, Emily. It's nice to see you again."

"Hi, Beck. I'm sorry I frightened the cat. I came to check because I didn't hear your scooter." I hadn't seen it either, come to think of it.

Her eyes darted away from my face. "I didn't want to disturb you, so I left it on the road and walked here."

That had to be a quarter of a mile away. Guilt over the way our last conversation ended resurfaced. "Oh, Beck, I never meant—" A fat trickle of blood oozed down her leg. "Why don't you come upstairs and let me put something on that scratch?"

She gave a quick glance. "It's not a grievous wound. I can take care of it at home."

Smiling at what I assumed to be another word of the day, I said, "I know you could, but it's partly my fault. Come on, and we can talk for a while. You can tell me about your progress with the mother cat. It seemed like she's taken to you."

She took a step toward me and hesitated. "Are you sure?"

"Positive. In fact, if you say yes right now, I'll throw in a cup of coffee."

Her face fell. "Oh no, I couldn't do that. Mama said I shouldn't have let you buy me breakfast the other day."

I stepped out into the daylight, gesturing for her to follow. "Maybe that's something else we need to talk about." She cocked her head. "Have you always told your mother everything?" I was undoubtedly venturing into ill-advised territory, but the words were out before I could think better of it.

"No," she said flatly, her expression somewhere between defiant and contrite.

"And why didn't you?"

"Because Peyton said it wasn't any of her business. It was just between us." I could see a blush creeping up her neck.

"And is it still that way?" I asked, making sure no hint of criticism crept into my voice as I recalled that name. The boys at the diner had said something about Peyton, and I thought the new sugar mama comment was intended for me. Could there be some illicit romance lurking in Beck's life?

"Yeah, sometimes," she mumbled into the ground.

"Well, maybe our friendship could be that way too, sometimes. Just between us."

She looked back up, her eyes shining. "So are we friends now?"

My big mouth had walked me right into that. Though I didn't know what saying yes would mean exactly, I couldn't very well say no, given the direction I'd taken things. "Would you like to be?" I asked, hoping there might some neutral territory.

"Very much," she said, her gaze fixed on me, and her voice deeper with certainty. What was I supposed to do with this young woman, who was cute and sexy and clueless at the same time? I couldn't help smiling even as I thought, so much for neutral.

Moments later, I was mortified to discover I had no first aid supplies of any kind in the house. I started a new grocery list and supplied Beck with a washcloth to clean her wound with soap and water. Afterward, she held a fresh paper towel to it until the bleeding stopped. "I have a kit in my scooter," she assured me. "I'll get a Band-Aid there."

I held out two bowls. "Cereal? As a consolation prize?"

Beck looked side to side. "Just between us, right?"

"Absolutely." I added a banana and was about to juggle as much as I could carry out to the deck when Beck said, "Wait," and pulled a beautiful lacquered tray from one of the tall floor cabinets. I tried not to be embarrassed she knew my kitchen better than I did.

While we ate and had our coffee, she told me about the cats, how she was sure the mama was someone's pet at some point because she was sweet once she trusted you, and how the kittens should have their eyes open any day now. "It'll be fun when they get old enough to start playing. I've seen some kitten videos. They'll get to be really cute." Her smiled faded. "Mama says all babies are cute so the adults will love them and take care of them. Does that mean they wouldn't otherwise? Like, if there was an ugly one, it would die?"

She touched her hair self-consciously, and I felt a rush of sympathy. My sister Abby was the one they'd called beautiful. Obviously, Beck had suffered through more than her share of belittling and ridicule with no one to defend her. "No, I don't think that's what it means at all. I think what your mother meant is that all parents think their children are beautiful. But that's not why they love them. They love them because they're part of them, and they hope it's the best part. They love them because..." I paused, trying to merge the explanations of a series of counselors and dozens of self-help books, all of which I'd ultimately rejected. What did I truly believe? That not all parents knew how to love their children? That things could happen that were so terrible that any chance of nurturing was torn away and only trauma remained? Beck watched my face calmly, and when I opened my mouth to speak and closed it again, she put her hand on top of mine.

"It's okay, Emily. You don't have to explain everything to me. The thing is, bad stuff happens, and no one really knows why. But you somehow keep going and one day, it's not as bad, and after another day, it's a little better still. That's all." As I stared at her with my mouth slightly open again, she flashed that gorgeous smile, adding, "And someday, if you're lucky, you'll get to have coffee and cereal with a friend."

I sat, trying to decide how to feel about her philosophy while she put our breakfast things on the tray. "You cooked, so I'll clean up. Then I have to go."

"I cooked?" I asked faintly, rising after a few seconds to follow her into the kitchen. "I don't think cereal and coffee is real cooking."

She had the dishes already in the dishwasher and was giving the counter a quick wipe. "Thank you for having me here," she said without turning. "I'm glad we're friends now, 'cause I like talking to you."

The braided piece of hair swayed across her back as she moved, and I had a vision of her dancing in this space before. Ignoring the voice in my head screaming, *don't don't don't*, I ran my hand down it. She went completely still, and I said, "I'm glad too, Beck. I think you're a very interesting young woman." I could hear her breathing, but when she didn't move or speak, I knew I'd overstepped, and I hated myself for it. Not wanting to face her rejection, I turned toward my bedroom. "Thank you for taking care of the kittens. Please let yourself out."

I couldn't believe I'd been so foolish.

❖

A few days later, footsteps pounded up the outside stairs. Too fast for Mel but maybe one of the W's. I saved my work and turned away from the computer at the knock. "Come in."

Beck stood in the doorway, beaming. "They're open. Come see!"

I didn't move for a second, and her expression began to waver, fading as if she was second guessing herself. *Go. She's giving you a break. Take it.* "Sure, okay." I reached for the flashlight, but she shook her head.

"You won't need that. I replaced the bulb in the overhead light."

"Oh. Well...good." When had stupid become my default?

She gestured impatiently. "Come on." I half stumbled on the third stair, and she turned, grabbing my arm to steady me. "They're blue, you know?"

"What are?" I asked as she pulled me in the door of the garage.

"Their eyes. But they won't stay that way."

A bare bulb in a ceiling fixture illuminated the area. The mama was nowhere to be seen. The babies mewed and crawled over each other, sniffing their surroundings but not roaming very far. I hadn't realized their fur had different colors. Beck let go of my arm and carefully picked up an orange kitten who was farthest from the group. "We're not supposed to handle them too much, but I do want them to get used to my scent." She cuddled it against her chest for a second before returning to my side. "Do you want to hold it?"

She pushed the kitten toward me, and I took it automatically. The tiny body curled against me, meowing with a high, thin sound. I touched its rounded head carefully, amused by the look of its tiny ears plastered close.

Beck was grinning happily. "It likes you."

I laughed. "How can you tell?"

"Because if they don't, they'll hiss like the mama did."

Damn. I hadn't even thought to ask. "How is your leg, by the way?"

"It's fine. I told Mama it happened in class, so she wouldn't be mad about me bothering you again."

Shaking my head, I said, "That wasn't a legitimate excuse, Beck. In what class would you get hurt like that? Knife Fighting 101?" She frowned and looked away. I wanted to slap myself. It was probably the best she could come up with given her...limitations. How insensitive could I be?

"You'd better let kitty rejoin its siblings," she said almost sadly. I did. She petted each of them briefly and turned toward the door. Gesturing at the wall, she added, "Here's the switch for the light, in case you ever need something in here."

After watching her ride away, I gave myself a serious talking-to. What was I thinking, letting this stranger hang around? All right, she wasn't a complete stranger, but I was supposed to be working, not playing with kittens and killing time with some young eye candy. Beck was a complication, and that was something I definitely didn't need.

I didn't see her for three days, though I did hear the scooter coming and going. Every morning, I braced myself for a knock on the door while I practiced my prepared speech about boundaries and how things needed to be, even with friends. I should have been relieved when there was no contact, but for some reason, her absence made me edgier. I'd just gotten out of the shower when I heard someone calling me. For one second, I thought it was Beck, and a wild fantasy played in my head about what would happen between us when I appeared in nothing but a towel. Then Mel's voice bounced into the room.

"Movie tonight, Em?"

My work hadn't been going particularly well. Maybe I needed some time away. "Sure," I called from behind the door.

"We can do dinner first if you can be ready in an hour."

"No problem. I'll come to Reefside in forty-five minutes."

June had done her research, and we arrived at the Seagoer, which was certainly the most expensive restaurant in Windsom Edge. But the food was excellent, and William and Walter knew how to keep the conversation moving, updating us all with the latest news and internet gossip.

As we strolled the street toward the movie theater, I caught sight of a familiar figure across the street. Beck was standing with a group of three young people, two scruffy-looking boys and one girl whose face I couldn't see but who was currently on the receiving end of one of Beck's terrific smiles. A sensation rippled through me and, uncommon as it was, I recognized it right away…envy. I needed a second to clear my head, so I stopped and pretended to adjust my sandal, motioning the others to go on. After a few seconds, I heard music blasting from a passing vehicle. I straightened in time to see a classic muscle car careen over to the curb in front of the group.

"Hey, Peyton," a male voice called out over a break in the music. "Why are you hanging with those losers? Come ride to the beach with us."

In the time it took me to focus on Beck's group, the girl had already distanced herself and was leaning onto the car, chatting with the boy at the window. She had that saucy, somewhat sleazy look that might be considered desirable during a girl's first bloom, but that generally faded into base tawdriness within a few years. Beck had turned away, so I couldn't see her reaction, but I could practically feel her aching for what she didn't have and couldn't offer. Interested as I was in the idea of Peyton being a girl, I was more concerned with Beck's hurt.

Crossing the street before I had time to reason myself into inaction, I called Beck's name loudly enough that everyone turned, something I ordinarily worked hard to avoid. I concentrated on her face, and when her brows rose in wonder above the hint of moisture in her eyes, I felt completely vindicated.

"Emily?"

There was so much emotion in the way she said my name that I hesitated. Recovering, I continued, reaching to touch her bare shoulder for a quick moment before shaking myself past the awareness of her solid, tanned arms. "Hi, Beck. Sorry to interrupt your evening. We're in town to see a movie, and I thought I recognized you." *Don't babble. Get to the point. Any point.* "Listen, would you have time to do another grocery store run with me tomorrow? I hate shopping, but you were so quick and good at it, it was almost painless."

For a few horrifying seconds, I thought she wasn't going to answer. Finally, she blinked and said, "I'd be delighted," and I let my gaze wander to her friends in relief. "Oh," she said, recovering further. "These are my buddies, Brick and Jonesy. This is Emily. I work for her sometimes."

Each of the young men nodded, mumbling something that might have been "ma'am" before looking away again. I was careful not to look in Peyton's direction, but I heard the slam of a car door accompanied by a swell of muttering. Time to cut and run.

"Great. I'll see you in the morning. Enjoy yourselves." I tried to include the boys in my vague wave, and crossed the street, finding Mel waiting for me.

"How do you know that baby butch?" she asked. "She's not my type but quite the hottie in her own way." June was a half block ahead with the guys.

"That was Beck, Mrs. Janser's daughter," I answered, ignoring the full-throated insults and slurs now originating from the muscle car.

As the engine revved to a nearly painful level, Mel shot the finger in their direction, and the car screeched away. "The one you were supposed to stay away from?"

I felt a twinge of guilt, remembering how I'd talked to Beck about not telling her mother everything. "Uh, yeah." Mel grinned suggestively and artfully dodged the elbow I aimed at her midsection. "Shut up. You know me better than that."

"Even if what happens at the beach…"

I was grateful we caught up to the others so she could leave off the end of the cliché. I gave her a meaningful look, and she cocked her head to let me know she was letting me off the hook...for now.

❖

Thunder woke me before the nightmare could, but the storm quickly moved inland, leaving a soothing, steady rain behind. I got up, invigorated, and had been working for several hours when I heard the scooter engine. I watched through the window as Beck hopped off, fastened her slicker to the seat of her machine, and ran into the garage. How could I have ever doubted her devotion to those cats?

Smiling, I poured some coffee for her, fixing it the way she'd made it before. It was an oddly domestic feeling to know how someone else took their coffee and certainly wasn't something I'd known about any of my recent lovers. Of course, Beck wasn't in that category, though I'd thought about her more lately than anyone else I'd been with. The sound of her steps on the stairs shook me from that strange progression of thoughts.

I opened the door before she could knock, grinning at her use of a small board as an umbrella. "Why did you leave your slicker on your seat?" I asked.

"Hi, Emily." She grinned when she looked at my movie ticket keeping the matches company inside the found jar. I could tell by the way her nose lifted that she smelled the coffee, and I handed her the mug. Her eyes went wide. "This looks perfect. How did you know?" My smile froze after she took a sip, her sound of approval rushing into me like the sea breeze off the warm sand.

I turned away, busying myself with putting away the milk and the honey. "Those of us who drink it black have time to notice the production made by you who are less pure." I hoped it was clear I was joking and added, "Like in the diner the other day," so she'd remember.

"I don't like riding with a wet seat," she said.

For a few seconds, I couldn't imagine what that meant, until it clicked that she'd answered my question about the slicker. "So how was the rest of your evening?"

Beck gave a noncommittal shrug. "Peyton came by later like she sometimes does." She turned toward the ocean with her coffee. Unable to see her face, I couldn't read her mood.

"Is she your girlfriend?" I blurted after a few seconds, surprised at my own curiosity. Normally, other people's personal business held no interest for me.

"I used to think she might be." Her voice was pensive and pained. "Now I think it's just about the sex."

I gave a little cough, grateful I hadn't been drinking at the moment. She didn't seem to notice.

"Sometimes, when we go out, she leaves with someone else. It used to hurt, but lately, it doesn't seem to matter as much. When we first started having sex, I hoped more would happen between us. Here's the thing: I'd like to have a steady girlfriend, but I've always known that Peyton has sex with guys too. But when she told me I'm the only one who can get her off, I thought that might mean something. Now I think it's not enough."

I recognized Beck's phrase about "the thing." She used one of two varieties of the saying when she was serious. I found it interesting that she would make a distinction between having a girlfriend and someone to have sex with, since to me they were the same. I was also astonished she would speak openly about something so personal. I found myself divided between wanting this conversation to stop there and saying enough to at least let Beck know I was on her side. I took in a breath. "It sounds like she's using you."

Beck's head ducked. "That's what Mama told me. She doesn't care that Peyton's a girl, but she doesn't like the way she treats me. She wants me to stop seeing her."

I'd have to revise my opinion of Mrs. Janser yet again. "But you haven't."

She sighed. "It's not that I'd mind being alone. But it's hard to walk away from someone who says she needs you…even if it's feigned."

Absently noting another word of the day, I considered how deliberately I'd avoided exactly that kind of entanglement. The realization that Beck had a soft heart didn't come as a complete surprise, but it increased my awareness of what I lacked in that department. I was about to suggest we leave, but she spoke again, her back still to me. "Have you ever been in love, Emily?"

Oh no. We were definitely not going there. "Listen, we should get moving," I tried, moving to the counter to pick up my purse.

"Yeah, I don't think I have either."

I stopped, nonplussed. Where had that come from? "I didn't say—" I started, but she kept going as if I hadn't spoken.

"You can tell, you know, because people that are, they get a look in their eyes and want to tell you how wonderful it is. And people that used to be, they get a different look and tell you how they want to feel like that again. And then there's the rest of us. The ones who don't have a clue what we're supposed to feel or even where to find those feelings. Or how to tell the difference between love and anything else that makes you feel good for just a little while but kinda bad afterward."

Speechless, I watched her take another sip. I'd had that exact thought and had said something like it to Mel once on a drunk and disappointed evening. She'd told me I was wrong, that love found everyone eventually, and they would know when it did. Judging from her track record of cohabitation, she found it on a regular basis. But it hadn't found me. And apparently, it had missed Beck as well.

"I suppose that's why I don't write normal romance novels," I said quietly, almost to myself.

Beck chuckled, and when she did, I did too. She turned, her eyes bright. "I used to think normal was the best thing a person could be. I like hearing you don't see yourself that way either. It makes me feel better."

All I could say was, "I'm glad."

"Me too." She finished her coffee and rinsed the cup before putting it in the dishwasher, another behavior that reminded me of myself. "Where's your list?"

I flipped my hand. "Only normal people make lists," and we both laughed again.

Despite the gloomy weather, we were in high spirits during our trip around the grocery store, buying off-brands and the occasional odd item—like pimentos—for no reason other than our continued rejection of normalcy. The store was considerably more crowded, and Beck reminded me it was Memorial Day weekend, which meant the busy tourist season was about to begin. Still, I felt light and comfortable, buoyant with the ease of the day in spite of its serious beginning. But when we got to the checkout area, Beck shook her head when I tried to steer us toward the checker who had just opened her lane.

"I know that girl," she whispered. "She's mean. She'll charge you twice for the same item and argue when you try to tell her. She especially does that to black people, like our neighbor Regina. We figured out she'd be less likely to do it if we only bought, like, ten items at a time because it would be obvious that something was wrong if you had ten items on the belt and fourteen charges on the receipt. Now if Regina needs a lot of things, I come with her, and we divide her list so each of us gets half."

As much as I admired Beck's heroic solution, I wondered why they didn't seek a more permanent resolution. "Why don't you tell the manager? That's stealing, and she should be fired."

Beck began walking our cart toward a male cashier with one other person waiting in his line, still keeping her voice low. "The manager is her daddy. He wouldn't take Regina's word or mine over his darling daughter."

But before we reached the other checkout, a reed thin man with an equally thin mustache approached at a quick walk. Beck muttered something I didn't hear as the man hooked his bony fingers around the front of my cart, pulling as he fawned, "This way, please, madam. Carla can get you right now."

I followed, stumbling at the sudden change in direction. Beck had taken a step away, but when he turned to give me another appraising look, his glance found her. We stopped abruptly. "Rebekah." His voice was cool. "Are you shopping for something?"

"No, Mr. Dirkens, I was—"

He cut her off, his tone hardening. "You know the rules. No loitering. Our customers don't want to be bothered by shiftless young people who are out looking for trouble."

"Excuse me," I jumped in, uncharacteristically assertive. "She isn't loitering. I'm a visitor in town, and she was helping me find my way around the store."

"Welcome to Windsom Edge, madam. I'm sure you'll have a lovely stay, and you are welcome anytime. But let me caution you against being taken in by any of our more, ah, unsavory characters. If there's something you need while you're here, my daughter Carla would be more than happy to help you." He gestured at Beck, his voice hardening. "It's certainly not necessary for you to be bothered by someone with such an unfavorable reputation for divisiveness."

Nothing in my previous experiences with Beck made me believe that was truly the case, but his malice shocked me mute as we resumed our forced march to Carla's checkout lane. The girl there greeted me with a gleeful smirk that indicated she'd heard it all. After her father gave her a nod and departed, I looked around for Beck. She stood on the spot where Mr. Dirkens had seized my cart, her shoulders slumped and head lowered as if wilted by shame. I couldn't see her eyes. Would they be pleading for help like Abby's had been that horrible night, and if so, would I fail her as well?

I straightened as a wave of resolve shot through me. Ignoring Carla's sniff of disapproval, I went to Beck, squeezing her shoulder gently. "Come on, Beck. Let's finish our shopping."

She shook her head, her gaze still downcast. "It's okay, Emily. You go on, and I'll get a ride back later."

Even from our one small point of connection, I could feel that her entire body was stiff. Soft heart, I reminded myself and said, "But I need your help. Please?"

I felt her relax slightly but she still didn't meet my eyes. "You do? Really?"

"Yes, really. You empty the cart, and I'll pay. The sooner we get that done, the sooner we can go home." I'd have to think about my use of *home* later.

"Yeah." When she looked up, her expression was almost fierce. "Let's get out of here."

I was so glad to see her rallying that I did too, giving her shoulder one more squeeze before letting go.

Beck placed our purchases on the conveyer belt as if she were playing a game of Tetris. Every item was tucked neatly in beside another with no wasted space. Carla rolled her eyes at me, but when I didn't respond, she turned her attention to Beck.

"And what have you been doing with yourself this summer, Beck-y?"

She shrugged. "Working. Class. The usual."

The bag of Sun Chips fell over, and when Beck reached to straighten it, Carla caressed the length of her arm. "I haven't seen you around campus this semester. Are you just in Mr. Howell's class again?"

Beck barely nodded, withdrawing her hand quickly. "How's Eddie?" she asked, and there was something new in her voice, caution.

Carla leaned closer. "Gone to the mainland for a bachelor party this weekend. Why don't you come by and we can…catch up?" Her voice dropped to a whisper. "Peyton doesn't have to know."

When Beck paled and started to shake her head, I decided enough was enough. "Look," I made a point of reading her nametag, "Carla. Maybe propositioning customers is your form of *personal service*, but Beck is working for me this summer, and between that and her class, she doesn't have time for any of your nonsense." Thanks to Beck's warning, I'd seen her scan the ham, the most expensive item I'd bought, twice. "Now let me ask you something. If I call that nice manager over here, and we go through these items again, is my final tally going to be the same?"

"Uh." While Carla made a show of looking over the screen, Beck took a step closer to me. When I gave her a quick glance, I could see she was fighting a grin. "I...uh. Oh, I see my mistake."

She rang up a deduction, and I smiled sweetly, swiping my credit card through the slot. "Thank you."

Beck caught her preparing to put the heavy bag of cat food on top of the carton of eggs and bananas on the bottom of a sack. "I'll take that," she said, deftly standing both bags side by side in the cart. She was right. Carla was mean.

It was still sprinkling as we loaded the car, and we didn't speak as we pulled onto First Avenue. At the stop sign leading to our beach road, I shifted to look at her. She was staring straight ahead, her expression blank. Without thinking, I reached over and did what I'd wanted to do since the first time I'd seen her. I ran my fingers across the close-cropped part of her hair. Her eyes closed, and my vision blurred.

In my mind, we were standing face-to-face. I was braless, and my button-up blouse was undone. My other hand glided through her longer hair, and I pulled urgently, guiding her beautiful mouth to my bare breast, my erect nipple already anticipating the warmth of her lips. She sucked gently at first but in perfect time with the pulse between my legs. When teeth grazed my hard flesh, I felt the first curl of orgasm in my belly.

A horn honked behind us, and I jumped back to reality. Where the hell had that come from? Shocked, I withdrew my hand and pulled away from the sign. Have you lost your mind? I asked myself, still feeling the flush of arousal. After a deep breath, I whispered, "I'm sorry."

"For what?" Her eyes were still closed. "That's the nicest thing that's happened to me in a long time."

Me too, I thought, aware I was thinking of something completely different. It made no sense to apologize for my secret fantasy, and as for the touch that sparked it...I should have known better. I did know better. I'd already overstepped once but apparently hadn't learned my lesson. I took another moment to gather my wits, finding something else to speak about. "No, I...I should have spoken up to that manager."

Beck took in a breath. "Mother says we shouldn't let others' behavior affect how we act." She turned her head to look at me, her eyes alive again. "But I thought I was going to bust out laughing when you were schooling Carla."

"My friend Mel would advise you to stay away from straight girls." She'd said as much to me dozens of times.

"I'm not sure you should call them that," Beck said. "I've read sexuality is a continuum or like a bell shape. Smaller numbers on the extremes with most people fitting in an increment along the way."

I stared at her for a few seconds as another unexpected burst of wisdom caught me off guard. Beck had such an unusual take on life. Instead of taking the opportunity to disparage people who had been cruel or were using her, she found a way to defend their choices and attempted to understand their behaviors. I agreed with her assessment of sexuality, however, so I said, "That's probably true. And it's none of my business."

"Carla was the office helper who took me around on my first day back in public school," she continued as if I hadn't tried to ease away from the conversation, her words muffled as she turned to look out the window. "My papa had passed on, and Mama said I couldn't be homeschooled anymore. It was a hard time for me, and Carla acted nice, at least when it was only the two of us. She showed me all the make-out places in the building, and one day I found a note in my locker saying to meet her in one of them after school. When I got there, she asked me flat-out if I was a dyke, and when I said yes, she kissed me. Before long, it turned into more. We hooked up off and on that year, but I knew it wasn't serious. It was just something to do, a way to blow off steam. She said we'd get together over the summer, but the few times I saw her in town, she was always with some other kids, and she acted like she didn't know who I was."

We arrived at the Guest House, but she made no move to get out. I cut the engine and waited.

"By our senior year, I hardly ever saw her and never heard from her at all, and I was okay with that. But then we had a Halloween hop. Brick likes to dance as much as I do, and we were on the floor a lot. The next school day, there was a new note. I didn't go. A couple of days later, another one. I went, telling her no in person. She didn't like that and threatened that if I didn't go along, she'd tell everyone I came on to her. I said I didn't care if she did. She started to cry, telling me how lonely she was and how none of the people she hung out with were her real friends. She said how much she missed me and how she wished I was in a class with her so we could sit together. She talked on and on about how we should leave Windsom after graduation, move to the big city together, and all the while, she was touching me in a way she hadn't done before. I got...persuaded.

"For a while, it went on like before. Later, I learned she would talk bad about me to her friends. But a couple of months before graduation, I heard she and Eddie Quast were engaged. Eddie was in my reading class. I liked him. So I refused to see her again. After that, I started getting mean looks from a lot of kids. Guys would run into me on purpose, knock my books away, gross stuff would show up in my locker. Typical bully stuff, I guess." She worried at her lip. "Funny, but Eddie never said a thing, never acted any different. He's a nice guy, and I hope she doesn't talk bad about him." She sighed. "Carla was wrong for asking me over, wasn't she?"

"She was wrong for a lot of things."

The soft rain continued to fall, muffling the outside world from us like a blanket. After a long moment, Beck said, "Abnormal is the opposite of normal."

My resolution not to touch her again collapsed at the sound of pain in her voice, and I wrapped my hand around her forearm. "So is extraordinary."

When she moved her gaze from where we touched to my face, she was smiling. "Yeah?"

"Yeah."

Chapter Four

It was still raining after we'd put away the groceries, but Beck declined my unusually generous offer to drive her to class. "I rode over here, Emily," she reminded me. "And as long as I don't have a wet seat, I'll be fine."

"There's no wet seat in my car."

She grinned. "I wouldn't be too sure."

I turned away to hide my blush, unwilling to contemplate if the double entendre was intended or if this was a weather-related observation. After the sound of her engine died away, I fretted around the house. Everyone had their hard-luck stories, including me. Why should I care what one twenty-something had gone through? I wrote stories of death in gruesome circumstances, of those who partook in murder and mayhem and those who tried to avenge the lost. Any romance was an afterthought, something added to keep the pages turning for those poor folks who hadn't known what they were getting into. I made a pot of coffee, sat at my computer, and wrote the most horrific scene I could imagine. I was shaking when I finished but told myself I'd simply had too much caffeine.

It wasn't totally dark, but it would be soon. I grabbed a flashlight after I put on my raincoat and made my way toward Reefside, hoping company would lift my mood. Only a few lights were on, but Mel's car was there. I knocked, pressed my face against the glass, and waited. I was desperate enough to knock a second time, though I suspected they wouldn't answer. I'd already turned away and was three stairs down when the door opened. June stood in a T-shirt I recognized as Mel's, and possibly underwear, though I wasn't sure. The annoyed expression on her face changed when she saw me.

"Hey, stranger. What are you doing out in this weather?"

I laughed shakily. "Honestly, I have no idea. I suppose I was wondering what was going on tonight."

She scratched her head and yawned. "What time is it?"

I looked at my bare wrist. When had I taken my watch off? I tried for a smile before stepping away. "Probably time for me to let you guys enjoy your evening."

She reached for me, and I let myself be pulled inside. "No, no, no. Mel and I took a nap, but it's time to get up. Let me rouse the guys too. It's always party time when the famous author is in the house."

I didn't remember the walk back. My last clear memory was of June, her pretty face close to mine, asking, "Are you sure? You're kinda loaded. You could stay here, you know?"

Apparently, I'd declined her offer, and then William, ever the gentleman, was helping me open the door. "You'll get to bed all right?" he asked.

By way of answer, I kissed his cheek and stumbled into the house.

I was under the covers in my childhood bedroom, and that man was in the room. I knew it by the fetid, rank scent of him and by the way my insides twisted. The subconscious, animal part of me recognized him and had awakened me for fight or flight. Fight? Not me. Abby would, but I'd never been a fighter. Fear, coppery and sharp, flowed through my systems. Don't look. Don't look and it won't be true.

He had Abby. And his hand was over her mouth as he held her close against his body. "Not a word," he snarled in my direction, "or I'll come back for you."

My sister's eyes were begging for help. I opened my mouth, but no sound came out. I tried to gather air into my lungs, but nothing happened. The door was closing. I had to do something. With supreme effort, I forced myself upright as a scream ripped the air. Mine? Abby's?

I blinked uncertainly against the roiling remnants of fear in my gut. Then I ran instinctively to the bathroom of the Guest House where I heaved up dinner and entirely too much to drink, well aware I'd never be rid of the shame and the self-loathing, no matter how long I vomited.

❖

For the next three days, I wrote like a woman possessed. When Mel came by, I ignored her knock until the worry in her voice brought me to the other side of the still-locked door.

"Please go away, Mel. I'm fine, but I'm working right now, and I don't want to be distracted."

"Are you sure, Em? You sounded all kinds of crazy the other night."

Shit. I had no idea what I might have said. "Look, call it creative license, okay? Now beat it so I can make us both some more money."

"Okay. But call me tomorrow, understand?"

I didn't call, but she left me alone. Once or twice, I might have heard Beck's scooter coming or going, but nothing else penetrated the fever of my concentration. By the end of the third day, I'd drafted a new ending which I liked much better and had smoothed over several rough spots in the story. I wasn't finished, but I was closer. I'd fallen asleep at my desk with my head on my arms, when I was roused by the sound of soft tapping. Acting on autopilot, I opened the door to find Beck looking like everything young, healthy, and vibrant. When the smile on her face faded to something resembling worry, I knew I must look bad. I stepped away, intending to close the door, but she stepped forward at the same time, sniffing the air as though searching for something.

"Hi, Emily." Her usual greeting was quieter than normal. "Have you been sick?"

"I'm fine, Beck. I've been working a lot, and I wasn't expecting company." That hint was probably too subtle, but I thought I'd try.

"I wasn't expecting to have today off, but I do. I thought you might like breakfast and a grocery store run." She gestured down the stairs, beaming again. "We're going to need more kitten chow soon. Have you seen them lately?"

Those damn cats. I tried to keep the irritation out of my voice. "I haven't, but look...if you're going, why don't you grab a few things for me? Whatever you think I'd like." A quick glance around failed to turn up anything resembling my purse. "I'll pay you when you get back."

Her face fell. "I guess I could do that." She glanced toward the dirty dishes littering the kitchen. "But wouldn't you like to have coffee and some breakfast? It might make you feel better."

"I feel fine," I snapped, my temper giving evidence to the contrary. "Look, why don't you ask one of your girlfriends out to breakfast?"

The corner of her mouth lifted, and her eyes took on a mischievous glint. "I thought I *was* asking one of my girlfriends out to breakfast."

If I'd been anywhere near my normal, quasi-social state of mind, I would have laughed at the idea of Beck flirting with me when I could have been a character in *Creepshow*'s "Weeds" story. Or I could have been charmed by her obvious attempt to lift my spirits. But part of me was caught in the disturbing world of my fiction, and the reminder that I wasn't anyone's girlfriend seemed a painful jolt of reality. "I would recommend you ask one who'd actually have sex with you."

For a few seconds, she simply looked at me, all emotion gone from her expression. "Here's the thing, Emily. If you don't want to go, just say so."

I replayed our conversation as best I could. She was right. I'd never specifically said no. She already turned to go, disappointment obvious in her slumped posture. "Look, Beck, I…" I trailed off, not sure of what I would say in my defense. I simply became a bitch when I wrote too long? I hadn't recovered from the latest round of nightmares, and I didn't think I ever would?

She wasn't stopping, and my stomach soured even more. I'd acted like one of those sick kids who tore the wings off butterflies, damaging a beautiful thing for no reason. "Hey, I'm sorry." I caught her at the door, my hand on her shoulder. She stopped but didn't turn. "Listen, I'm not really—" In mid-sentence, my stomach growled loudly.

"Not really hungry?" Beck filled in, and I caught the slightest hint of humor in her tone.

I managed a chuckle as I tried to remember when I'd last eaten. And what? Cereal? Ice cream? Nothing particularly nutritious, I was sure. "I'm not suitable for the public at the moment, and it would take me an hour to get ready. You don't want to spend your day off waiting for me."

Beck still hadn't turned, but she straightened slightly as if breathing in some faint hope. "But the thing is, I'm really good at waiting."

Sighing, I assessed the situation. I could say no now, nicely, and Beck would forgive me for my earlier rudeness because she was like that. But in an hour, I would be hungry, and my pantry and fridge were certainly empty or close to it. Fine. "If you're sure you don't mind…"

She turned, and we were closer than I'd realized. Her hand came to rest on my waist, its warmth matching her smile. "I honestly don't. You're so worth it."

You're so wrong, I almost said, but I didn't want to see disappointment on her face again. What I wanted was to take another step and put my head on her shoulder, drawing her sweetness inside me to do battle with the dark. "I'll try to hurry," I said, stepping away quickly.

"I'll be here."

I was pleased with myself when I walked into the living area, calculating it was less than forty minutes. Beck looked up from the small kitchen table where she was sitting with a glass of water, the notebook I'd seen before, and a pencil. Her expression suggested clean hair and makeup had brought me several steps along the *Creepshow* makeover.

"Wow. You look very nice," she said, shoving the pad into her back pocket as she stood.

I became aware that the mess I'd made in the living area and kitchen had been cleaned. I glanced in the direction of my work desk. I regularly left myself notes in a variety of ways, from Post-its to shredded napkins, and any disturbance in my disorganization could take me hours to recover. Thankfully, everything looked exactly as it had.

"I didn't touch anything over there," she said, following my gaze. "I know a work in progress when I see one."

"Thank you," I said. "And you didn't have to clean up."

She shrugged. "It's what I do. It comes naturally, I guess." Moving quickly into the kitchen, she added her glass to the dishwasher. "I didn't want to use the hot water while you were in the shower, but I'll run this now, if that's okay."

Had her mother taught her to be so considerate? Or was that something else that came naturally? "That's fine." Once I heard the old machine grind into life, I held out my keys. "Can you drive a car, Beck? I'm still feeling a bit shaky."

She looked at me with wide eyes. "Sure, I can drive. Or you can ride with me on my scooter."

No fucking way. "Maybe some time, but for now, I'd prefer doors and a windshield."

"Got it."

It didn't take long for me to relax into the ride. Sunglasses on, Beck handled the car skillfully, driving with the same care and thoughtfulness she seemed to apply to everything else. She was polite but not passive, navigating confidently but not recklessly. The perfect chauffeur. I couldn't help wondering what she saw herself doing in five or ten years. Surely not still cleaning houses. I started to ask before catching myself. It was none of my business, and I certainly wasn't in the mood for her random version of twenty questions in return.

We pulled in at the Edge diner where we'd eaten before. It was late enough for the breakfast crowd to have thinned out, but I stopped at the Please Seat Yourself sign, waiting for Beck to suggest a place. She touched my lower back lightly, but her warmth penetrated my blouse. Without consciously meaning to, I leaned into her.

"Let's take that same table by the far wall," she murmured.

"Show me," I replied, walking slowly, feeling her steer me with that touch. I'd seen her dance by herself, and now I had the sense of how she'd be as a partner. Really, really good. After we sat, I reached across the table and touched her hand as she toyed with her empty coffee cup. "Thank you for talking me into this. You're the best kind of friend to have."

An adorable pink crept across her cheeks. "Thank you for agreeing to come. Do you mind me saying I've missed talking with you?" She turned her hand so the tips of her fingers grazed mine. Although calloused with work, they felt warm and wonderful. I shook my head in answer as the sensation reverberated through me.

Luckily, Barbara chose that moment to make an appearance. She beamed at Beck and began clapping. "We are so proud of you, honey. You're gonna put this place on the map." The counterman was clapping too, and he yelled, "Go get 'em, Becka!"

A few other people scattered around the diner joined in the applause, though some seemed as confused as I was. Beck's hand had made its way into her own lap, and the slight blush that had been present earlier had become a full-blown reddening of her tanned face. After blinking furiously for a few seconds, she waved at the man across the way and grinned at Barbara. "Thanks, Jack. Thanks, Barbara. You remember my friend Emily? We're in serious need of coffee and one of your great breakfasts."

Barbara nodded at me and said, "Sure thing, honey." Turning over our cups, she looked to Beck. "I bet your mama's about to bust a button. You tell her to come by soon so we can brag on you together."

"Okay," Beck said, paying careful attention to smoothing her napkin in her lap.

Barbara poured our coffees and left menus. Beck was studying hers as if it contained the secrets of the universe.

"Do you want to tell me what that's all about?" I asked.

Beck shook her head, not looking up. "Let's eat."

"Which means you'll tell me later?" I pursued.

She shrugged, not meeting my eyes. "If you honestly want to know."

Which of us would be the judge of that, I wondered? We ordered, and after a few minutes of quiet coffee drinking, Beck asked again if I'd seen the kittens lately. When I said no, she began to describe their most recent behaviors and appearances. She'd named them all, of course, and spoke as if I was well acquainted with them as individuals. Her animation brought me back to my earlier train of thought. "Have you ever thought about being a vet? Or at least a vet tech? That way you could be around animals all day."

She sighed. "I used to say I wanted to do something like that. But it's a lot of schooling, especially reading and stuff. Besides, sometimes vets have to deal with sad things, like animals who are really sick and won't ever get better. I wouldn't like doing that."

It was in my head to say that even the best things had some sadness with them, and that was something we all had to deal with, when the hypocrisy of my philosophical offering struck me. Who was I to tell anyone about dealing with sadness? Our food arrived, and I looked over to see Beck studying me closely.

"Now, this is on the house," Barbara announced. "Yours too, Emily. You were in here with Beck before, so we know you're not a fair-weather friend."

"Oh, Barbara, no," Beck protested, but the waitress gave a dismissive wave before topping off our coffees and leaving.

"What did you do?" I asked, genuinely intrigued.

"What made you unhappy just then?" Beck countered.

"I was thinking how ridiculous it is for anyone to give advice to someone else."

"Why is that sad?"

I sighed, knowing I could never explain. "Don't you think it is?"

She didn't reply for a while. We ate in silence. Our plates were nearly empty when she said, "I don't know how to answer you because I'm not sure I agree. Some people give good advice. Others are good at taking it. And there are probably a hundred shades of in between. I suppose the sad thing would be if you had a giver paired with not a good taker, or vice versa." She held up her last strip of bacon as if considering it seriously. "Don't you love it that we have a phrase like *vice versa*? It's Latin, you know."

And just like that, I was laughing. Sharing word play was one of my favorite pastimes, and no one else I knew enjoyed it. "Did you know the German word for cell phone is 'handy'?"

From there we moved on to idioms in both English and other languages. Beck pulled the notebook from her pocket and wrote down a few of my favorites. She contributed some I hadn't heard, including "He that makes himself an ass must not take it ill if men ride him."

"Did you first hear that from your mother?" I asked, still chuckling.

"No, from my papa." She tried to smile, but her eyes had turned sad. The combination was such that I almost couldn't catch my breath. How did she not have a serious girlfriend?

Tables at the area around us were beginning to fill in, and I realized it must be lunch time. Our game came to an end, and we began our shopping in the produce aisle, where she admired the fresh asparagus, telling me of a favorite recipe.

"Some people say casseroles are poor folks' food, although Erik is about as impoverished as it gets, and he's real picky. He won't eat asparagus." She blinked, and a hopeful expression replaced the brief unhappiness. "But if you like it, I could fix it for you tonight."

"Only if you'll stay and eat it with me." Seconds later, I was mentally kicking myself. I'd already spent more than enough time with Beck. Why had I asked her to stay? I wasn't social like that, but something in me warmed to her presence. *This could be trouble.*

Before I could put my mind to finding a way out of my invitation, Beck had put the asparagus in the basket after nodding to a tiny old woman who was waving vigorously. We stood in the checkout line without speaking. Thankfully, Carla was either not working or on break, and her father was nowhere to be seen. I closed my eyes on the ride home, grateful Beck wasn't the kind of person who felt obliged to make small talk. After we arrived at the Guest House and put the groceries away, she stood at the counter with her back to me. "That lady in the grocery store was Mrs. Parrish, my first art teacher. She taught me a lot." Her voice was quiet. "But she never could stand up to those kids."

Even from behind, I could sense her working to keep her emotions in check. I imagined she was experiencing unwelcome memories of cruelty at the hands of her classmates. Our youthful experiences hadn't been that different, in some ways, and I understood very well how a person's reactions to present circumstances were shaped by lingering childhood sorrow.

Was that commonality why Beck seemed to be the exception to my antisocial tendencies? Not once on the drive home had I worked on a reason for her to leave. Instead, I'd pondered how there were moments when she was incredibly open, and other times, she was completely closed. I was never as open, but what was I longing for at those times when pain closed me into a tight fist? Was the certainty that I didn't deserve comfort the reason I shied away from most friendships, let alone the caring touch of a lover? As sure as I was of my own guilt, I was equally convinced Beck deserved whatever consolation I could give her. I moved behind her, resting my hands lightly on her shoulders. "I think I'll nap first and work before we share our dinner. Thanks again for getting me out of the house."

I felt her inhale deeply, as if it was the first full breath she'd taken since the grocery store. "Thanks for hanging out with me, Emily. I'm going to make that recipe and go check on the cats. I'll be as quiet as I can, but if you've decided you don't want my company, I'll leave when I'm finished. Then you can eat whenever and with whoever you like."

I squeezed and dropped my hands to her shoulder blades, rubbing lightly. "I know how mean kids can be. And it hurts no matter how tough you are." I was running my hands along her arms, enjoying the way her body felt. I should have stopped, but if I moved away now, it would seem strange.

"I'm sorry you know about that," she said, half turning. "Sometimes, I get the feeling you got hurt badly, and I hate that for you."

I did move my hands away then. "Feel free to lie on the couch if you want to. I'm going to nap in the bedroom."

❖

I didn't think I'd drop off with someone else in the house, but the domestic sounds of utensils against bowls and the soft closing of cabinet doors gradually lulled me to sleep. The slant of sunlight looked like late afternoon when I awoke, dressed, and wandered out into the den. The house smelled wonderful, and my stomach growled appreciatively when I opened the oven, admiring the bubbling casserole Beck had made. At the sound of an exclamation followed by a loud crash from the garage, I slammed the oven door and moved quickly onto the deck.

"Beck?" I called over the railing. "Beck, are you all right?"

When no answer came, I pulled on my shoes and hurried down the stairs. A dozen things went through my mind: Would she or her mother sue me if she was injured? Did she have medical insurance? Was there a hospital near here?

The light was on, but I couldn't see her as I stepped into the musky room, urgently calling her name again. As I took another step, I heard a moan and a shuffle. A faint voice from the far corner said, "Yeah, Emily, I'm okay," and I moved in that direction. Beck was picking herself off the floor; all around her was a tumble of boxes containing what appeared to be ancient paperwork. The kittens cowered in the far corner, and the mother cat was nowhere to be seen.

"I found a door," she said, brushing dust and shredded cardboard off her clothes. She gestured, and I saw it, a regular-looking door with a rusty doorknob.

"Where does it go?"

She looked up, and I followed her gaze. "I figure the room we're in is about half the size of your house. This door must lead to the other part." Rubbing the side of her head, she looked apologetically at me. "I'm really sorry about the mess. I swear, I wasn't going to go in there without your permission. I was trying to move these boxes that were blocking it so we could get it open if you said it was okay."

Did she think I was mad? "As long as you're okay, I don't mind you looking. But should we ask Mr. Guest first?"

She frowned, eyes darting from side to side as she considered the question. "Maybe we could call Mama and see what she thinks."

I couldn't have explained why I balked at that suggestion. I'd been willing to revise my opinion of Mrs. Janser on more than one occasion, but for some reason, I didn't like the idea of turning to her for this.

"You know, I'm renting the house. The whole house. I don't see why I couldn't go anywhere on the property if I wanted. There were no restrictions in our agreement." To be honest, I didn't recall much about the rental contract, other than signing it.

Beck lifted her shoulders. "Okay. Let's take a look."

Let's? Somehow, I hadn't seen myself in the role of co-take-a-looker. "Are you sure you feel like it?" I stalled.

"Oh, sure." She grinned and rubbed her head again. "I've had way worse than that little bump. Do you have that flashlight?"

"No, I didn't bring it."

"It's okay. I've got a small one in my scooter. Wait here."

I followed her out, having no intention of staying inside that nasty, feline filled garage by myself. While she went to her scooter, I walked around the back side of the garage, a place I had never been or even thought about. There I found one huge, thick slab of wood, wider and taller than my arm span, with a heavy-duty handle on each side. There were wheels at the top mounted on a track; the piece was obviously designed to slide open. The only problem was a large padlock holding the door in place. I heard scuffling from inside and called to Beck.

"That door in here is locked," her muffled voice told me.

"Come around here and see this," I replied, and she joined me, gawking at the size and design of the door.

"Wow," she said, eyeing the building above. "This must open into the same area as that door inside."

"What do you suppose is in there? Maybe we'd better rethink this. Someone seems to have gone to a lot of trouble to keep it locked up."

Beck grinned at the worry in my voice. "I think you spend too much time with your scary stories."

I was about to snap a response about her being overly naïve, when it occurred to me that the likelihood of this being a recent torture chamber or ancient burial site was probably rare. At the worst, it held something like musty old records of shady business dealings. I gave Beck credit for knowing what there was to be worried about in Windsom, so I was willing to trust that the elusive Mr. Guest wasn't some psychotic killer. Instead, I responded with my best Wicked Witch of the West cackle and said, "We shall see, my pretty. We shall see."

Beck's laugh made me glad I had chosen that response. "I was twenty years old before I could watch that movie and not be terrified of those flying monkeys," she said.

"What do you mean?" I asked. "I'm still terrified of them."

Now we were both laughing, and it felt good. The sun had lost its scorching heat and was gently sinking into evening. It must have been high tide because I could hear the ocean even from behind the house. I let myself enjoy the moment, admitting that Beck's company added to, rather than detracted from, my pleasure. Before I could spend any time considering what to do about that, one of the kittens appeared from around the side of the house, making its way cautiously toward us.

"Hey, Carrot Top," Beck crooned softly, crouching and rubbing her fingers together. "What are you doing out here?"

The creature mewed, and I observed how its fluffy orange head and white body did give it some resemblance to the entertainer. I tried to remember what the rest of them looked like, wondering if all their names were so aptly chosen.

"This one's always been the troublemaker," she told me, waiting as the kitten approached her hand. "First one out of the box, first one to try the dry food, and it looks like he's the first one to…Hey!" She was looking up from where she squatted, in line with the large door. "This lock isn't fastened to the other side. It's only closed on itself. Look!"

I moved to her other side, examining the area. She was right. I'd seen that the lock was closed and had assumed it was threaded through the hasp on the other side. But it wasn't. Beck had collected the kitten, who was purring in her arms.

"What do you think?" she asked excitedly. "Don't you think the two of us can push this open?"

Just because you can, doesn't mean you should. My Aunt Sharon's frequent advice echoed in my head. But we'd never gotten along all that well. "Sure. As long as you'll fend off anything weird that comes jumping out of there."

"That I will, my lady," Beck drawled, flexing her muscles like a bodybuilder. The thing was, she had great definition in her biceps, and my stomach clenched. In many ways, she was the total package—sweet, kind, generous, and very well-built. In a bigger city, she would have had girls crawling all over her. Here, she had to settle for her dysfunctional girlfriends and one terribly messed up writer's fantasies.

"Okay, I'm in."

"Yes!" She pumped the air with her fist as she returned the kitten to the other side of the garage, pushing him into the room with a gentle swat on his behind. Returning, she took a position near the lock. "Can you pull while I push?"

I looked at the far side of the door. She was putting me farthest from where the opening would be, where I'd be safer. Had she sensed my uselessness, my desperate cowardice? I moved resolutely, pretending confidence as I grabbed the handle on my side. "Say when."

"On three."

At her count, I pulled with all my strength, determined to redeem myself as much as possible. Whether from our combined efforts or because it wasn't really stuck, the door moved with relative ease, though it did make a loud screech. At the end of its track, the movement stopped abruptly, and I slid unceremoniously onto my butt. I looked to Beck, expecting her to at least ask if I was okay. Instead, she was staring, spellbound, into the opening.

"Oh wow," she mouthed, stretching a hand out into the opening.

Chapter Five

"What's in there?" I asked, getting to my feet. When Beck didn't answer, I moved tentatively toward her, brushing myself off and listening to the strange, heavy clinking sounds that got louder as I stepped closer.

"Metal." Her voice was almost reverent.

I peered in where the swath of fading light illuminated the area. Two or three lengths of thick iron chain swayed gently from the rafters, and what looked to be pieces of cars—bodies and engine parts and things I couldn't possibly identify—were scattered around the space. "Was this some kind of repair facility?"

She didn't answer, stepping inside and running her hands over a discarded fender. "I wonder..." Her voice trailed off as she looked around slowly, her eyes taking inventory. She bent and picked something up.

"Wonder what?" It was getting hard to keep the hint of annoyance from my voice. She was acting unusually goofy, as if we'd discovered hidden gold or something. Plus, I was hungry and becoming concerned our dinner was going to be overcooked.

She focused on me. "Would you mind if I asked Mama to speak to Mr. Guest about this? Maybe he'd be willing to sell me a few pieces for a reasonable price."

I shook my head. "This is junk, Beck. What could you possibly want with it?"

She motioned me outside and pulled the door shut, wincing at the screech. "WD-40," she said. I wasn't going to guess what that meant. I simply looked at her until she added, "That will fix the squeak."

She started toward the front of the house, but I put my hand on her arm. "You haven't answered my question. Why are you interested in that scrap?"

Her expression was difficult to read. The sunset was all but gone. "Well, uh, it has to do with what the people in town were talking about."

My annoyance vanished, and I took a step closer. "Good. Tell me."

Her gaze lowered, but the corner of her mouth turned up in a tiny, shy smile. "I'm a finalist for the Presidential Arts Foundation Award."

I blinked. "In what field?"

Her head wagged side to side as if she was embarrassed to tell me. "I do metalwork."

"Like sculpture?"

"Yeah, sometimes. Or hangings or series and sometimes kinetic pieces. A little of everything, I guess."

I slid my hand down her arm and took hold of her fingers, turning them toward what fading light remained. Two had small, healing cuts on them, and the roughness I'd thought was from her cleaning work could very well be from her artwork instead. "So you're an artist," I said, a new insight falling into place about her. No wonder I couldn't see her cleaning vacation houses for the rest of her life. Now my imagination jumped to envisioning her name all over the art world, her work for sale in fine galleries and displayed outside of skyscrapers or in parks.

"Well, I—"

"How did you learn to do metalwork?"

"Remember Mr. Howell? You met him at the diner that first time?" I nodded, remembering the aged man and his comment about "Becka" being one of his best ever. "He's my teacher, my mentor, and he's taught me everything I know about metal. The man is an incredible talent and one of the best people I've ever met. I started taking classes from him a couple of years ago and—"

"A couple of years ago? And you're already a finalist for PAFA?" Anyone remotely connected to the arts knew of this prestigious award. It was intended to encourage and reward those who had graduated high school but were not yet out of college. There was a category for literature, but by the time my first book was done, I'd been much too old to apply. My voice rose. "I can't believe you've been with me all day, and you're just now telling me." Something else clicked. "Is this why you unexpectedly got today off?"

She shifted uneasily. "Yeah, 'cause the thing is, for your final entry, you have to submit something brand-new. You can't use stuff from your existing portfolio. So Mama gave me today to work on some ideas, but

I haven't been able to think of anything. Plus, metal is expensive. But that stuff in there? I think I could figure a way to use it that might be really cool."

"Do you have any pictures of your work? Like on your phone?"

She shook her head. "Nah. The camera on my phone doesn't work." She held out what looked to be a well-used second-generation iPhone. "Mama used to take pictures of my early stuff, but she had to sell her camera a couple of years ago. She's not real good at using her phone. Plus, she's always busy with work or taking care of things at home. I had to use Peyton's phone to send in my portfolio for the PAFA entry."

I wondered if the troubled expression that had settled on her face was because she'd made reference to her family's financial state or from her mention of Peyton. Ignoring that, I started up the stairs, pulling her behind me. "I want to see them. Would you show me your entry?"

She shook her head, her tone as glum as her appearance. "Emily. You don't have to pretend like you're interested."

I rounded on her. "I'm not pretending. I'm...I'm absolutely thrilled for you, and I...I like knowing this about you. It's really, truly extraordinary, Beck."

A full-on smile returned. "You think so, huh? And you haven't tasted my cooking yet."

I swatted her arm. "Maybe if you'll talk to me some more about your work while we eat, I'll be doubly impressed."

Dinner was delicious, and while she put off showing me her submission—or maybe she simply had a hard time believing I genuinely wanted to know—once she began to talk about metalwork, I was more than impressed. I was enthralled. It was shallow of me to let the fact that I now saw her as an artist alter my opinion of her this way. But maybe it simply confirmed what I'd suspected—there was much more to her than first appearances would suggest. Before I knew it, she had me talking about my work, about writing and the joys and challenges it had brought me. We'd finished dinner and pushed the plates aside, leaning toward each other as we spoke, the intimacy between us growing.

Beck gestured animatedly over my description of "finding the zone" when I wrote. "That's it exactly," she said. "It's like a whole other place and this world..." She trailed off.

"Doesn't even exist," I finished.

We nodded at each other in complete understanding, and I wondered if this was what I heard people describe as meeting someone with whom they clicked. I looked away, breaking the connection. This wasn't a date, and click or no click, there couldn't be any more to our relationship than casual friendship. When I looked back, her eyes had filled with tears.

"What's the matter?" I asked, reaching for her hand.

She held her other hand over her mouth as if she didn't want me to hear what she said. "I'm not going to win that award, and everyone's going to be so disappointed."

I shook my head. "You can't say that, Beck. I'm sure your work is excellent. But in any case, you have to wait for the judges to decide."

"It's not that," she whispered, eyes downcast. "I won't have a chance. There's a big problem."

Footsteps thumped on the staircase, and Mel burst in the door. "I've been calling you for hours. You're going to miss the fireworks."

I frowned, trying to recall if I'd taken my phone off mute after my nap. Windsom Edge offered Saturday-night fireworks as a regular summer thing at the beach. They were brief and singularly unimpressive, in my opinion.

Mel's head tilted in our direction. "Why are you holding hands with that cleaning chick?"

Beck flinched as if she'd been slapped and moved into the kitchen where she started clearing our dishes.

"Damn it, Mel." I snarled. "Don't you ever knock? And I'll have you know—"

Beck cleared her throat, and when I looked over, she shook her head slightly. "Would you like me to put this in the refrigerator?"

Mel strode into the kitchen, sniffing at our leftovers with interest. "Whatcha got there, Spike?"

I groaned, not sure how to explain Mel's annoying practice of calling other butch women by names like Spike or Mack or Jake.

"I made this for dinner," Beck said coolly. "Would you like some?"

"Sure." Mel rarely refused a meal, though it was too early for her to have eaten dinner. She and June maintained a New York dining schedule no matter where they were. "It smells great. And I love poor folks' food like this. Reminds me of Maydee, the first family cook I remember." She grinned at me. "So you found a dyke who cooks and cleans too? No wonder you were holding her hand."

"God, just shut up, will you?" I was embarrassed for myself and for Beck, whose expression gave nothing away. I joined them in the kitchen. "Look, she can warm this herself," I told her as she prepared a generous portion for Mel. "It's getting late, and you probably need to go home."

She shrugged. "Yeah." I watched her move away. At the door, she turned. "Three hundred degrees for about fifteen minutes or until it bubbles."

"Got it," Mel answered, fiddling with the oven.

Beck's light steps descended the stairs. I fought the urge to catch her before she left and say...what? How much I'd enjoyed the evening? Or the whole day? How sorry I was that Mel was such a jerk? That I wondered why she was so shy about her nomination for the PAFA and mostly, what was the problem that had her this upset? My gaze fell on the coffee table. There were two new things in the found jar—a silver bolt and a terribly rusted piece of engine—both obviously contributed by Beck from her junk metal find.

Mel's voice broke into my thoughts. "I know you like lowballing, but this is pretty far down, even for you. But hey, go kiss her good-bye if you want to."

Although I resented her description of both of us, what bothered me most was that my mind went immediately to what kissing Beck would be like. "Fuck off, Mel."

❖

My nightmare that night was different. It was better, in the sense that it wasn't based on something real. Plus, I didn't wake up screaming, though I was sweating and shocked. Beck and I had been in a workroom of sorts, filled with all kinds of tools and indistinguishable materials. It could have been the garage downstairs, but it was different in the way that dreams are. She was closer to the door, pulling on something when a large pile of sand and debris showered onto her, and she was trapped and struggling. It was all too heavy to move, and I was desperate to find anything that would free her. She was trying to tell me something, but as her breathing became labored, her voice became softer and softer, as if she was moving away from me. I was terrified she was dying, and I wasn't doing enough to help her.

Then Mel was beside me, saying, "You'd better kiss her good-bye now, for sure."

Wide awake, I made my way to the bathroom before wandering restlessly around the living area. On a whim, I went out on the deck. The night was warm, and there was no moon, making the stars seem unusually bright. I sat in a chair and listened to the ocean, not thinking of anything in particular, which was nice. Big city living had been my choice since adulthood, and it had always suited me, but I hadn't missed my small apartment yet, because the Guest House was a lovely, comfortable place. At home, the air could be filled with the noise of horns and sirens and people's voices at all hours, but the charm of this quiet life in more natural surroundings was easy to see. I could go to the beach sometime, not that I would swim, but maybe to walk along the shore. It was silly to be so close and not experience sand between my toes at least once.

I closed my eyes to imagine my seaside exploration and was struck by a surge of apprehension. Who was I kidding? Unlike Abby, I wasn't the adventurous type. I'd never been to the ocean before and had no idea of what to avoid or what to look for. Didn't people drown in rogue waves or get stung by venomous creatures? I knew it wasn't wise to spend time researching the various dangers of coastal regions because I'd seek out the most frightening, gruesome events that could happen. I needed a relaxed, knowledgeable, local guide. Beck's face came into my mind, and for once, I lingered in the vision.

Beck had a sweetness about her I found almost irresistible, and her lack of sophistication made her seem authentic, rather than inelegant. Her enthusiasm about taking me to the beach would be contagious. Would she take my hand again? I chided myself for such a silly thought. The important thing was, a walk would give us time to talk privately about whatever was bothering her about the PAFA. Smiling to myself, I resolved to plan it at the next opportunity. When dawn woke me, still on my chair on the deck, I was amazed to find myself completely unharmed by a portion of the night spent out-of-doors. I took it as an omen that trying something new might be a good thing.

❖

For each of the following days, I only heard Beck downstairs briefly, and each time, she was gone before I could catch her. Finally, I hurried to the deck after she arrived and called to her as she left the garage. Head tilted up, face partially covered by sunglasses, she looked much like she had on the first day we'd met.

"Come up for some coffee," I offered, but she shook her head.

"Thank you, Emily, but I can't stop. I'm working extra hard for the next few weeks."

"Are you working on your project for PAFA?"

When I saw her head droop, I anticipated not liking her reply. "No. The thing is, I need to make some money first."

I didn't want to ask why from such a distance when she was in a hurry. "Please wait there for one second," I called as an idea came to me. I could pay her to be my beach guide. Not a lot but hopefully enough to make it worth her while. I slipped into my sandals and rushed downstairs. "I have a proposition for you," I panted when I reached her.

She'd tucked the shades into her T-shirt again, and despite the weariness and stress on her face, I also saw open admiration. "It's nice to see you," she said. I'd forgotten I was wearing only a T-shirt and underwear, and she smiled as her gaze made its way down my legs and back to my braless breasts. "Especially so much of you." I blushed, tugging ineffectively at my shirt. "And if your proposition includes you wearing that outfit again, my answer is yes."

"Beck!" I acted shocked, though I was secretly pleased. "What would your mother say?"

"My mother likes you," Beck said. "She'd probably ask what I was waiting for."

Not sure what disconcerted me most, her continued flirting or the idea that her mother liked me, I chose to go with the latter. "She does?"

"Uh-huh. She says you must be a very nice person to put up with me *and* a bunch of squalling felines."

I'd never been crazy about the cat idea, true, but I didn't like hearing that her mother put her in the same league. I put my hand on her arm. "Can you come for dinner some time? I've missed talking to you."

She covered my hand with hers and took a step nearer, her expression wistful. "I've missed you too, Emily. I can't tell you how much."

Clearly, I'd gone overboard in trying to convince her. I carefully pulled my hand free, using a more offhand tone. "But look, I understand you're busy. I am too, so I don't want to keep you. Just, you know, think about a day and tell me what works. It could be next week, if that's what you need to do."

"Or the week after that? Or the next? Or next month?" she asked in a voice that almost choked.

I nodded. "Sure. It's no big deal," and she looked away.

"Yeah. Of course it isn't."

She went to her scooter without another word, put on her specs and helmet and rode away. Well, shit. Was she being moody, or had I been unthinking in how I amended my invitation?

❖

A week later, I was working on a short story to go in a fundraising anthology for one of my favorite book events. Normally, I didn't take time for smaller scale jobs, but I was restless and between projects, waiting to hear about the last round of edits. It seemed like Beck was coming and going more quickly than before. Sometimes I didn't even hear her scooter, and I wondered if she was walking here like before. I fretted over it—debating whether she was angry or simply rushed—but I was determined not to seek her out again. I'd begun running out of food, so I'd bummed dinner with the gang at Reefside twice before I finally convinced June to make a grocery store trip with me.

As we drove past the diner, she asked, "What do you think that place is like? A typical greasy spoon?"

"No, it's pretty good. I've been there twice."

She raised an eyebrow. "Really? By yourself?"

I felt my face redden. "Uh, no. With Beck."

"Who's Beck?"

Either she and Mel didn't communicate much, or she was trying to play dumb. Or not playing. "She's the daughter of Mrs. Janser, the one who cleans for the rental company. The one who came by Reefside to talk to us after we got here."

"Wait. The daughter you're supposed to stay away from?"

I laughed. "Yeah, but I think we're over that now. Beck said her mother likes me." What was wrong with me? I never spilled my business like this and certainly not to June who was the newest addition to our group and the one I knew the least.

"So you're seeing her now?" June asked as we pulled into the grocery store parking lot.

"I'm definitely not seeing her." I waved and reached for my door handle. "It's a long story involving kittens."

"Kittens!" June practically squealed. "I love kittens." She turned to face me. "Tell me everything."

I didn't argue. Mel had told me dozens of times how June was the most stubborn woman she'd ever met once her mind was made up about something. As I talked, I felt increasingly bad about not having been much of a friend to Beck, certain that she would have sought me out if the situation was reversed. "Let's hurry and get our shopping done. I want to be there in case she comes by tonight."

We were on the last aisle when a familiar figure stacking cans on an endcap caught my attention. I grabbed June's shoulder. "That's her," I whispered urgently. "That's Beck."

She pulled the cart away from me. "Tell me what else you need. I'll head toward the checkout when I'm done. You go talk to her." She peered down the aisle. "I love her hair. She's so cute, Emily. Are you sure—"

I handed her my list and pushed her none too gently in the opposite direction. "I'll see you outside."

Beck's face was set with concentration, but her movements were sluggish with fatigue. As I approached, she misjudged the angle of a can, and it toppled to the ground, rolling away from her. She lunged to catch it, tripping on the box she was pulling from. Her shoulder hit the ground, and she groaned aloud, rolling onto her back.

"Beck," I called, moving quickly to kneel beside her. "Don't try to move yet. Rest a minute."

She peered up at me. "Emily? What are you doing here?"

"I should ask you the same thing," I said, smiling. "This is about the last place I thought I'd see you working."

She closed her eyes, reaching over to rub the injury with her other hand. "I know. But they pay fairly well just for stocking."

"How much?" I asked.

"How much what?"

"How much do they pay?"

"Nearly ten dollars an hour."

Her voice was lethargic, her eyes still closed. I was pretty sure she was falling asleep right there on the floor. The store intercom crackled to life. "Rebekah Reynolds, report to Mr. Dirkens's office immediately."

Beck sighed and looked up. "I have to go. I'm sure he wants to tell me how much he's going to deduct from my pay for that dented can."

I looked at my watch, doing some quick calculations. "I'll pay you fifty dollars to take the rest of the day off."

She struggled to a sitting position. "What?"

"Fifty dollars if you'll come back to my place and talk to me until dinner. I won't make you cook if you think you could stand a pizza." I wasn't about to make one from scratch, but I'd seen June put three frozen ones in her buggy, and I was hoping I could beg one from her.

She frowned at me as if trying to work out a complicated problem. "Why would you do that?" I hesitated, not sure how much more to say. There weren't many shoppers in the store, but those who passed were giving us second and third looks. Beck struggled to her feet when I faltered. "It doesn't matter. I can't take your money, Emily. It wouldn't be right."

"Yes, it would. Because I should have found you sooner and straightened this all out. Friends are people you can count on, remember? And you're my friend."

She looked away. "Am I? Even if it isn't time for our no-big-deal dinner yet?"

I ran my hand across the close-cut side of her hair, and her eyes closed again. "You know that wasn't what I meant. I was trying to make things easier for you. It sounded wrong because you're tired and upset. I'll tell Mr. Dirkens you've injured yourself, and you won't file for workman's comp if he gives you the rest of the afternoon off. But only if you'll come home with me. Please say yes."

She took a breath, and her fatigue seemed to lift slightly. "Okay. I don't want your money, though."

"Don't worry, I'm going to make you earn it," I suggested, and she smiled tiredly.

June was remarkably restrained as I guided Beck to the car. After introductions, she offered to let Beck sit between us. She declined, though, and stretched out across the back seat. She might have been asleep before we got through town.

I drove to Reefside, assisting June with her groceries and getting a frozen pizza for my trouble. The fact that Beck didn't wake and insist on helping was further evidence of her exhaustion. When we reached the Guest House, she slept until I had everything put away and returned to the car to wake her gently.

"What time is it?" she asked, rubbing her face.

"Time to come inside," I said, helping her up the stairs. I led her into the guest bedroom as if that had been my plan all along. It wasn't, but I could see she was in no condition to talk. She lay on top of the covers with a groan, and I slipped her tennis shoes off before I left the room. At my desk, I worked on my short story with more success than I'd had since I started. Four hours later, I put the pizza in the oven and made a salad before going to wake her.

"How about some dinner, Beck?" I asked, touching her cheek. "We've got pizza."

"I had the best dream," she rasped, eyes still closed. "I dreamed Emily came into the store and made me go home with her."

"That wasn't a dream, sweetheart." I stopped abruptly, shocked by the endearment. I'd never called anyone those kinds of names. They always sounded stupid and fake. But maybe not this time, as I imagined Beck's heart really was sweet, not absent like mine.

Her eyes opened, and her lips stretched into a cool, lazy smile that made my pulse jump. "I actually knew that." She stretched languidly and spoke through a yawn as she glanced out the window. "I'm sorry I slept so long. I sure haven't been earning my salary."

June's earlier admiration of Beck had reinforced what I'd thought for some time, but seeing her relaxed and unguarded like this, I was reminded she was quite an attractive package. Despite the signs of fatigue, her pale brown eyes were warm, and the sight of her body stretched out on the bed sent my mind in decidedly inappropriate directions. I forced myself to look away, though I didn't want to. "It's fine. We won't start you on the clock until after you eat." I gestured. "You know there's the small bathroom in case…" I stood, making my way to the door. I heard the bed creak, and Beck's soft voice was right behind me.

"Emily." I turned and was drawn into a close embrace. With her face against my ear, she whispered. "Thank you."

It had been months since someone touched me like that, maybe longer. And then, in all likelihood, it was only Mel. I generally didn't go in for hugging, or kissing for that matter. In the quick jumble of my sex life, it was more about getting to the point. I knew I should pull away, but I didn't want to hurt her feelings. I wanted her to feel comfortable enough to talk to me. So I let myself unwind a bit, let my body soften against hers. I put my hands at the indention of her waist, aware of the slight swell of her hips below my touch and murmured, "You're welcome." We stood like that for a few more seconds before I added, "I should get the pizza before it burns."

She let go without a word, and like the first time she'd held my hand, I felt the loss of contact acutely. I should ask Mel if she'd discovered any gay bars in the area. I definitely needed to work off some tension.

We discussed the merits of various pizza toppings during dinner, and she assured me there was a local pie that was "absolutely the best there was." I reminded her that my wide samplings of New York pizza meant her selection would have a lot to live up to. We both had a beer, and Beck told me something I'd already surmised: she rarely drank. She looked away and muttered something about "him" drinking enough for all of them, and I supposed she was talking about her stepfather. After a few seconds, she cleared her throat and stood, reaching for the empty plates. I surprised her by taking her arm and pulling her out to the deck.

"I can deal with those later," I said as we sat. "We need to talk."

She didn't pull away, but I could feel her tense. "About what?"

"About whatever the problem is that has you in such a state that you're not working on your PAFA entry. Instead, you're running around like a chicken with your head cut off, doing menial jobs and worrying us all while you risk your health." Her head dropped. "Beck, look at me." Slowly, reluctantly, she did. "I know we haven't been friends for very long, but I care about you. And whatever it is, you can tell me."

"But I don't want to," she whispered. "I don't want anyone to know."

"I understand how that feels. I absolutely do." Something in my voice must have made her look over at me. Disregarding her scrutiny, I waved away my revealing remark. "But sometimes, talking to someone makes it better. Or clearer, at least."

She lowered her gaze again. "It's probably too clear. That's the problem."

I turned in my chair to face her. "Tell me, Beck. I'll do anything I can to help."

She sighed. I waited. After a minute, she stood and walked to the railing. I gave her a long minute before I joined her. We looked out at the water, almost black under the starlight. She sighed again. "Here's the thing. You know there are pages and pages of rules in the PAFA contest?" I nodded. This was government related, after all, so a long, complicated form made sense. "Well, Mama and I had been going over them, and I left the papers in my room. Peyton came over later that night, and I guess she read them when I was in the bathroom. She... she made a video of us, you know, having sex." She turned to me, a pleading expression on her face. "I didn't know, Emily. I swear I didn't."

I put my arm around her shoulder. "I believe you, Beck."

She shuddered and leaned into me. "One of those rules is about not having 'inappropriate, lurid, or illegal material' out on social media. When the news came about me being a finalist, my mama was real excited, telling everyone in town, and naturally, Peyton got wind of it. Now's she threatening to post the video all over the internet."

I took in a breath, trying to work through the scenario from Peyton's side. Why I was able to identify with the villain in any situation was an easy answer but not the most important thing now. That Peyton must be a petty, small-minded bitch was the starting point. The question was, why would she not be satisfied by being on the arm of the PAFA winner? Perhaps she thought Beck had no likelihood of winning. No, she presumably saw it as being like the lottery; at least they had a chance, right? And she could claim the status of the muse—or if she was too stupid to know what that was, the inspiration—for Beck's work. True or not, Beck wouldn't correct her. I was missing something. "Why would she do that?"

Beck turned away from me, staring out at the water again. "She's mad at me," she said after a few seconds.

"Why?"

"Because we haven't been spending time together recently."

I'd become accustomed to these kinds of conversations with Beck. Normally, pulling every little detail out of someone would make me crazy, or I simply wouldn't care enough to try, but somehow, I didn't mind with her. "Why not?"

I felt her hand cover mine, though she was still looking away. "I haven't felt like being with her. Because I'd rather spend time here."

I felt a warm surge of pleasure at the unspoken "with you," but pushed it aside. So Peyton was angry. Hell hath no fury, and all that. I sighed but didn't move my hand. "And what does she want?"

"She wants a thousand dollars." Her voice had been quietly resigned, but it rose as she ran her free hand over her face. "A thousand dollars? She might as well say a million. I've been working like crazy for nearly a week, and I barely have two hundred saved up. At this rate, it won't matter if she posts it because I won't have an entry ready by the deadline, and everyone will wonder why. I don't know what to do, Emily."

In the starlight, I could see tears shining in her eyes. I hurt for her. "Listen, we'll figure something out. I just need some time to think." Her shoulders slumped. I suspected she was hoping for an instant solution. "Have you seen this video?"

"No, she wouldn't let me see it. She only played it over the phone, but I could hear the sound."

"Did she…uh…say your name?"

"Yeah, a lot. And there was more to it than that."

"Like what?"

She looked out at the water. "I really don't want to say."

"Look, if I'm going to help, I need to know everything. I don't want to start on a plan and get blindsided by something I didn't expect."

She put her head in her hands. "Sometimes she like to pretend things. Like she's my teacher or we're hostages somewhere." I hid my smile. That didn't sound so bad. "But that time she wanted to act like she didn't want to have sex, and I was…like, forcing her." *Shit.* I could see where this was going. "I told her I didn't like that game, but she swore…she said she'd get me off this time if I would."

Wait, what? *This time?* I blinked, confused. "You mean, she doesn't usually, uh, reciprocate?"

Beck sniffed, looking up. "She says I'm the butch, and butches aren't supposed to want that."

"Oh, Beck. You know that's not true, don't you?" I was getting madder and madder at this Peyton chick, and I was going to make damn sure she got her due.

"When you're with someone, do you always—" She broke off, rubbing her face again.

"Assuming they want to, yes." I needed to change the subject. "All right. Peyton recorded you acting like you were forcing her? And in the end, she gave in?"

Beck ducked her head. "After she was, you know, finished, she said she'd never been so turned on."

I thought some more. What she'd likely do was cut her final admission and post only the pretend rape. "Maybe we need a lawyer," I mused, thinking of getting a sworn affidavit that the video was false.

"What?" Her eyes went wide. "Why? Am I in trouble?" Her voice shook with fear. "I can't afford…Emily, I'm scared of going to jail. I couldn't, I won't—"

I grabbed her by the shoulders and pulled her to me, worried she was going into a full panic. "Listen to me, Beck. Are you listening?" I felt her nod against me. "No one's going to jail, understand?" I paused, the nucleus of an idea forming. "Unless it's Peyton."

❖

I didn't have to explain much to get the Reefside gang on board with my plan. I didn't go into the details of why, only that my young friend was being blackmailed by this horrible person, and I wanted to help. Ultimately, they all confessed to a degree of boredom and readily agreed to take part. I set my other writing aside as I worked on our script, doing everything I could think of to ensure the outcome I wanted, plus maximum embarrassment for Peyton. Other than asking Beck about Peyton's class schedule, I was careful not to involve her in any way.

Mel's narcissistic streak meant that while she wouldn't have simply loaned Beck eight hundred dollars, having a part in our plot meant she'd gladly spend a chunk of that amount on official-looking documents, badges, and uniform rentals. Her Halloween parties were the stuff of legends, and this crazy scheme was just her style.

"I think this is the sweetest thing I've ever heard of someone doing," June said after our last rehearsal. I think she meant it was the sweetest thing she'd ever heard of me doing. "And don't forget, you're bringing her for dinner when this is over." I couldn't ever see that happening, but I smiled and nodded.

We put our hands together like some sort of randomly dressed athletic team and chanted, "Don't let the bitch win."

Chapter Six

I'd been too nervous to find a place to hide and watch the action, but by the time the cork popped on our third bottle of champagne back at Reefside that evening, I thought I had the whole story. The short of it was, the plan had worked perfectly. June was charming and completely convincing as the college employee who pulled Peyton from her classroom. State trooper Mel had apparently put the fear of God—or jail—into the girl. And William and Walter had played good attorney, bad attorney, using the perfect amount of push and pull until Peyton handed over her phone and the only copy of the video was downloaded onto the newly purchased iOS drive and then deleted, along with all of her other content.

The single gaffe had come when Mel called William by the name we'd used for Walter. Peyton questioned it, but William had smoothly covered by telling them that "even the court clerk makes that mistake from time to time."

From beside me, Mel scowled at the reminder of her mistake, her sulky tone almost ruining the celebration. "You're the one who forgot the damn money."

Part of the plan had been to charge Peyton with two hundred dollars in "fees," an amount which would double what Beck had made during her extra work. I waved dismissively, practically giddy as I held the cork from the previous bottle. "That was icing on the cake. We got what we really needed."

Wanting to overcome her resentment as they teased about her goof, I reached for Mel's knee, giving it a squeeze. "You were wonderful." I gestured at them with my glass. "All of you. I can't thank you enough. Honestly. This was absolutely perfect."

Everyone began talking again, rehashing their roles in the Colossal

Coed Caper, as William had dubbed it. June tapped my shoulder. "When are you going to tell Beck?"

"More importantly, how am I going to tell her?" I replied, my celebratory mood turning to unease. "I mean, what if Beck is in love with that girl and wants to make up, to forgive her?" The words tasted strangely ashy in my mouth.

"Too bad, so sad," Mel sang. "Spike is all yours now, Em." I began to protest, and she laughed. "Oh wait, that's right. I forgot. You don't want her. You just don't want anyone else to have her." Disregarding my pained gasp, she stood, taking June's hand. "Come on, baby. Let's go look at some dirty videos." She wiggled the iOS flash drive.

"Mel, no." She could say whatever she wanted about me, but I couldn't stomach the idea of her watching illicit images of Beck. I rose, reaching for the device. "Not that video."

"Why the hell not?" She held it behind her, out of sight. "I paid for it, didn't I?"

I hated it when Mel got this way. She was a loyal friend who'd pulled me from my self-absorbed world on many occasions. After financing this whole adventure without questioning my motives, she'd turned into the egotist whose own wants were paramount, leaving nothing but malice for anything standing in her way. Once her focus turned to *I*, *me*, and *mine*, anyone else's feelings were a distant whisper. To my surprise, June came to my rescue.

"Emily's right, babe." Her voice softened. "We wouldn't want other people looking at our videos." The W's looked away as she leaned into Mel, whispering something that was clearly intimate. She pulled on Mel's arm and slipped the flash drive from her hand. Handing it to me, she murmured, "Let's go visit some of our own greatest hits instead, okay?"

And just like that, the party was over. I thanked the W's again, and we said good night. Most of the buzzy thrill I'd felt earlier was gone, but a pleasant feeling of satisfaction remained. I had good news for Beck, and though I wasn't exactly sure why it mattered so much, it did. I would figure out how to tell her in the morning.

The walk from Reefside to the Guest House was becoming as routine as if I'd stopped off at my neighborhood grocery, and I smiled when I found I was still holding a champagne cork. I put it in the found jar alongside the metal and the matchbook.

❖

As it turned out, I didn't tell Beck, though I truly intended to. I woke early, anticipating her morning arrival, but the scooter engine had barely shut off before she came rushing up the stairs, shouting my name and waving her old phone. Heads close, we puzzled over the "unexpected" message from Peyton offering a sincere sounding apology and a promise that no video would be posted, along with a rather touching good-bye. Beck was incredibly happy, and I decided anything I could say about the Colossal Coed Caper would only diminish her joy.

"Will you miss her?" I asked, still feeling that odd twinge of insecurity over what we'd done.

Beck's expression was unusually tough to read, and she looked at me for a long time before she spoke. "I'd rather have a constant friend like you than a sometime fake lover like her."

I was so relieved, I felt as if my insides inflated. We smiled at each other for a moment. Then she said, "You have to come see the kittens. They're getting bigger, and they're really fun to watch."

Watch? Did they do dramatic reenactments of significant historical events or perform interpretive dance to popular show tunes? I sighed dramatically but let myself be taken downstairs to the dusty garage. Beck flicked on the light, but they'd clearly heard us coming and were ready for breakfast.

She called, "Morning, babies," and the noise level increased to what I imagined feeding time at a zoo would be like. Their repetitive, plaintive meows sounded like desperate cries, but once they were fed, they went relatively still, the complaining replaced by contented purrs. I could see none of them had missed a meal recently. The multicolored, plump little furballs were obviously eating well out of their weight class.

"Is the mother still around?" I wouldn't have been surprised if she'd abdicated her responsibilities since Beck was doing such a good job.

"Oh yeah. She'll be by to eat at some point." She pointed, and I saw another bowl of food on part of a bookshelf the greedy babies couldn't reach. Yet.

Beck finished her duties and came to squat by my chair. "I've been thinking about this a lot," she said, sounding serious.

"Thinking about what?"

"Which of these kittens you might like best."

I stood. "Oh no. You will not get me to keep one of these beasts. You can forget that noise right now."

Beck waved her hands placatingly. "Not to keep. Just to play with while they're here."

"Why would I want do that?"

"Come on." She eased me back into the chair. "You have to admit they're cute."

I shook my head. "I don't do cute. I'm a horror novelist."

"Horror romance, isn't it?" She grinned. "That means you have a soft side buried in there somewhere. And I know the perfect gal to bring it out."

I raised a brow. "Oh, you do, do you?" The greedy pack had finished eating, and one or two were quietly cleaning themselves while the rest were flinging their fluffy bodies wildly at each other or at some unknown enemy among the ruined furniture. While it was true that they weren't quite as bad as I made them out to be, and I did have to laugh when two of them approached each other with samurai-style wrestling moves, I had no desire to get any closer.

Beck had other plans. She moved among them for a moment before returning, holding a sleek white kitten who was eyeing me curiously. "This is Sugar. I named her that because she's sweet. She's the quiet type who can usually be found reading in the corner or doing tai chi alone."

I would have laughed, but she deposited the kitty on my lap, and I was afraid it would scratch me if I moved. "Beck…"

"Relax, Emily. Pet her. Like this. Gently but firmly." She ran her hand across the cat's head and side and tickled her under the chin. Sugar bowed beneath her touch, and I felt a kind of electricity, as if Beck were touching me instead of the furry creature in my lap. "Try it," she said, oblivious to my reaction. She took my hand and placed it on Sugar's back, where the motor of her purring added to the odd thrumming inside me.

I jerked my hand away, and the kitten gave me a look. Her startling green eyes appraised me coolly, and I wondered if she found me lacking. You know how to pet a girl, I thought, chuckling to myself at the thought. Beck was watching, so I moved my hand carefully along Sugar's delicate frame. Her fur was softer than I expected, and after a few seconds, she settled into my lap like we'd done this before. I was stunned.

What I hadn't told Beck was that, in my experience, animals didn't like me. Strays that would eat out of other people's hands would run from me. The lion at the zoo who had lain for hours in the sun, entertaining my eighth-grade class, had abruptly gone into its private area when I'd approached. Even house pets, for whatever reason, wouldn't come around me or would only tolerate my attention for a few seconds. Eventually, I'd given up and decided I didn't like them either.

I ran my fingers to the tip of Sugar's thin tail and back onto her head. She rubbed her chin against me, closing her eyes as if it was the best thing she'd ever felt. I admired her perfectly formed but delicate body. "She's small."

"She's the runt," Beck said softly. "Probably the last one born. I used to have to feed her separately because she ate slowly, and the others would get her food."

"But she's okay now?" I asked as she began kneading the leg of my shorts. There was a sharp point of claw every now and then, but it didn't really hurt.

"Yeah. She's okay now." I could hear the smile in Beck's voice, but I didn't look over. "She likes you."

Yeah, right. I knew where this was going. I dropped my hand. "Please take her," I said, still not looking at Beck.

"Sure." She moved to us. "Come on, Sugar. Go play with your brothers and sisters."

The cat made a tiny meow in protest, reaching toward me with a dainty paw. I looked away as Beck put her on the ground. "Hey," she said, her voice light as she led me toward the door. "Would you mind if we looked in on the metal supply in the next room? I'm starting to feel like working again, and I want to remember what's in there."

Beck puttered around for a while, talking to herself about the various pieces. I settled on a small patch of grass in the shade and watched, feeling pleased with myself, as if her progress toward this prize was my own. The day wasn't too warm yet, and there was a nice breeze coming off the ocean. After a few minutes, I stretched out on my back, enjoying the few fluffy clouds drifting by. I had a strange sensation like I'd done this before, though I couldn't imagine when. I closed my eyes and envisioned Abby lying on my right, pointing at a cloud. I hadn't pictured her this way since I was eleven, that horrible year after she'd been taken. There had been several frightening months in foster care where her pretend visits were my only comfort. After my Aunt Sharon came to claim me, I'd believed she would be my savior. That was my last encounter with belief or saviors.

"That looks like a kitten," my imaginary Abby said. I saw no resemblance in the cloud's shape, but I certainly wasn't going to tell her that. A sound to my left distracted me. I turned and opened my eyes. Sugar meowed softly from close to my face. "Abby," I whispered. "Is that you?"

Sugar pushed her fuzzy cheek against my chin, purring loudly. I reached out a tentative finger. My sister would have loved this kitten. She'd had such a kind and loving heart. Nothing like me, I thought, choking back tears.

"Beck," I called, trying to keep my voice low so it wouldn't startle the cat, though she seemed content to rub against my hand. I heard an answer from inside the garage, though I couldn't make out the words. "That white kitten is out here."

"Huh?" After a few seconds, her head popped out from the doorway. "Oh, hi, Sugar. It's okay. They've all been out a few times, but Mama always rounds them up again. She doesn't think they're ready for the great outdoors, but a few minutes while we're here won't hurt. We'll put her in when we go up."

I sat up, feeling unnerved. "Are you getting hungry?"

"Yeah, kinda," she answered absently, still looking into the garage. After a few more seconds, she looked back as if seeing me for the first time. "Oh, Emily. I'm sorry. I dragged you out of the house without warning, didn't I? I'm a terrible guest. Let me fix breakfast to make it up to you." She stepped out and began to shut the door. The loud squeaking sound made Sugar jump, and she scooted into the other garage door.

"WD-40," Beck muttered to herself, slapping her own leg sharply. "I told you that last time."

I stood and went to her. "Beck," I said softly. "There's been a lot going on since last time. You need to give yourself a break on the WP-120 or whatever it is."

"I just get so mad at myself when I forget stuff like that. It's what stupid people do."

"Everyone forgets things, Beck. It's perfectly normal."

Her words were the slightest bit hesitant. "I thought we had rejected normal."

"True," I agreed. "I should have said, all users of HD-75 forget things from time to time."

"WD-40." She pronounced the name slowly, sounding almost like a commercial. "It lubricates, penetrates, and protects."

I opened my mouth to make a smart remark like "Exactly the attributes you want in a girlfriend," but thought better of it. Beck must have thought I was confused because she added, "It makes things work more smoothly and not make noises like that."

"I see." I took her arm, walking her slowly toward the stairs. "Perhaps they would like to sponsor your first showing." I gestured as if reading a banner. "WD-40 presents: The Wonderful Works of Beck Reynolds."

She leaned into me lightly. "I'm terrified at the idea of a show. What if people don't come? Or what if they do, but they say terrible things about my work? What if it's all a flop, and I've totally been wasting my time making trash?"

"You can't think like that," I said firmly. "Listen, I'm always nervous before a signing, and I've done quite a few of them. I'm still scared I'm going to make mistakes when I'm reading, and I worry they won't like my story."

"Really?"

I nodded. "The worst part is I usually can't eat that day, and I get even shakier when I'm hungry."

We'd reached the foot of the stairs. "Is that a hint?" There was a twinkle in her eye that made me grin.

Normally, I kept my inner Southerner at a great distance, as some New Yorkers would think that accent marked me as stupid and an easy target. In this case, I was careful to exaggerate my drawl, not wanting her to think I was mocking her. "Heavens above, Beck Reynolds, I wouldn't dream of suggesting anything so impertinent."

The smile on Beck's face faded, replaced with a slight frown, making me suspect her word of the day practice hadn't gotten to that one yet. "Race you," she said before I could think of what to do, and dashed up the steps.

She made us lovely omelets, and I supplied the coffee. We both ate hungrily, with scant conversation, and she made short work of our dishes, though I offered. Having noticed that she cast repeated glances downstairs, I asked, "Did you want to do some more in the second garage?"

"Yes, if you don't mind." She looked at me hopefully.

"Of course I don't mind, silly. You can go in there anytime you're here. Once you get your W-2 on that door, I probably won't notice."

Beck laughed. "WD-40, Emily," she repeated carefully. "W-2 is for taxes. Even I know that."

I looked at her for a moment. "Would you do me a favor, Beck?"

She nodded solemnly. "If I can, I will."

"You can do this, I'm sure. Will you please try not to talk badly about yourself? For example, don't say things like *even I know that* or accuse yourself of being stupid. It makes me sad to know you think less of yourself, because I don't. I think you are an exceptional person."

She looked away. "But the thing is, those thoughts are already in my head, and they just come out sometimes."

"I know. I know how it is to have bad things in your head. But you have to let them go. Or make them go. Don't live with them as if they are the truth."

She looked back at me. "Is that what you do?"

I took in a breath. "Not very well, most of the time. But I'll try harder if you will."

She looked into my face for what seemed like a long time before holding out her hand. "Deal."

We shook. Not letting go, she leaned in and kissed me on the cheek, a quick, soft peck. "And I think you're exceptional too," she whispered in my ear and walked out the door.

I was standing in the same spot, trying to figure out how to react, when I heard the second garage door squeak open. Unable to decide on anything else, I went to work on my short story. It was going a little differently than I expected, as sometimes happened in writing, and I barely heard the door closing some time later. Then Beck called, "Bye, Emily," and the scooter roared away.

It was early afternoon and getting to be hot, so I decided to take a nap.

❖

It shouldn't have come then, but it did. It had been a nice morning, and I felt good. But I never could figure out what triggered the dreams: my mood, the company I kept, drinking or not drinking, or the phase of the moon. I only knew the ones about Abby were seasonal, occurring during the warmer months, like the real thing had. But this wasn't quite the same as the usual.

It started earlier in that dreadful evening, as Abby and I were getting ready for bed. The room we'd shared was decorated with animals, jungle images on one wall, ocean life on another, forest life, and so on. Abby was going through a phase where she'd pretend to tame the animals, and sometimes the lion or the bear would bite her. At that point, she'd want me to bandage her imaginary wound, and then she'd sleep with me in my twin bed instead of in her own. She usually fell asleep promptly and slept soundly without a lot of thrashing about, so I really didn't mind, but I always acted like I did. She'd been pleading with me in that pitiful but not serious way that always made me change my mind, when our mother came in. Abby turned to her, begging to sleep in my bed, but she said no. Mother usually babied Abby, but that night she'd said Abby needed to sleep on her own like a big girl.

So we were in separate beds. She was pretending to read aloud from the book in her arms. Her voice morphed into a popular song from the radio—"Another Lonely Night"—until it gradually fell quiet. I had a flashlight because I loved books, and even the long summer days didn't give me enough time to play and read. But I'd fallen asleep with the flashlight on, and now it had burned out. The room was too dark for me to see what was making that sound, although I felt a sense of growing panic in expectation of finding out. Perhaps the tooth fairy had made a wrong turn and was going to leave some money by mistake?

Abby made a complaining sound as if something had awakened her too, and she said, "Daddy?"

Our father was out of town on a church retreat. Abby knew that but had likely forgotten in her sleepy state. I shook the flashlight vigorously and tried it again, confused when a weak beam of light illuminated... not him but Beck.

Except it was Beck as a man. "Abby makes you sad, so I'm taking her away. That was our deal."

"No," I screamed, sitting up. "No, no it wasn't," I repeated, hearing my own voice, still trying to stop them. Shaking my head, I came fully awake.

I went to the bathroom and splashed water on my face before sitting at the kitchen table, trying to make sense of it all. These nightmares were never warnings. It was too late for that. One therapist had told me it was my mind trying to rationalize something which didn't and wouldn't ever make sense. Another had said it was my emotions needing to be released, and once I had done that, the dreams would stop. By "emotions," I was sure she meant guilt, but I could never be released from that, no matter what kind of deal I'd made with Beck.

Not meaning to, I thought of her sweet kiss and quiet words when I'd asked her not to think badly of herself. That had to be the most hypocritical thing I'd ever said. Even though there were times when being with Beck made me feel different, like someone who could be loving and lovable, being alone again made me face the hard truth. She didn't know me at all. And it was time to stop pretending I could be her friend, or whatever I'd been doing. I'd be gone soon enough, and I wasn't worth her time.

I got a glass of wine and went to my computer to read over what I'd written. It was stupid, sappy, romantic drivel, full of crappy sentiment and not at all like my work. First order of business: delete. I wiped out the whole file, even emptying the trash icon. Then I set about instilling serious vices and faults into those same characters while torturing them with doubts and the inability to successfully affect any change in themselves or in the world around them. Much more my style. Much more me.

❖

"Emily."

Someone was shaking me. I lifted my head from my arms, sucking the drool from the side of my mouth. I'd fallen asleep at my desk and probably had a keyboard imprinted on half my face.

"Are you okay?"

Was that Mel? *Shit.* As my consciousness returned, I vaguely recalled having finished that bottle of wine and opening another. My head was pounding, and my stomach burned. *Fuck fuck fuck.* Why couldn't she just leave me alone? "What time is it?" I croaked.

"It's kinda late. I was at a bonfire down the beach with some friends, but I left and walked over this way to…you know, to get some air. I saw your lights were on. I knocked, and when I didn't hear anything, I got worried."

Not Mel. Beck. *Oh God, no.* Mel had seen me in worse shape than this plenty of times. Beck had not. I looked around blearily. It seemed like every light was burning.

"Have you eaten anything tonight?" she asked. Her tone carried genuine concern, something I didn't deserve. There was nothing but a trail of misery behind me, and Beck's presence only reminded me of all that was lacking. My whole family had fallen apart, and it was all my fault. That same cowardice that had ruined our lives was still a part of me. Nothing I did now could change my past, and nothing she could do would transform my present. I wanted no part of her compassion. I snapped.

"That's none of your fucking business, is it?" I snarled, shaking off the hand that still rested on my shoulder. "And I don't need a goddamned nursemaid, thank you. Especially one who doesn't even know what *impertinent* means."

Beck's expression altered, and she stepped away, looking defensive. "I looked it up. It means intrusive or presumptuous. Or rude," she added pointedly.

Exasperation flared at her impudence, a verbal challenge I wasn't prepared for. I struck out with a typically blunt reaction. "Fuck off, Beck. I mean it. Get the fuck out of here and stop bothering me all the damn time. I don't need you, and I don't want you around anymore, understand?"

She took two more steps away and blinked, before leaning back toward me. "Why? What did I do? Emily, I'm sorry if I made you mad about something." She paused a few seconds as if thinking. "Is it because I kissed you? I just meant it as—"

"Shut up," I screamed, which only served to make my head pound harder, making me angrier. I closed my eyes against the pain and spoke through gritted teeth. "God, are you so fucking brain-damaged you don't understand what I'm telling you? Leave me…the hell…alone." Turning away to avoid her face, I pointed out the deck door. "And get those goddamn cats out of here soon, or I swear I'm calling animal control."

I didn't hear her move across the room, but her voice was farther away when she spoke. "I need two weeks on the cats," she said quietly.

"Two weeks and every damn one of them better be gone." I swallowed and brushed my hand over my mouth, trying to pretend that the roiling in my stomach wasn't happening, that the sweat gathering along my hairline was coming from the warmth of the evening. The bile of self-loathing rose in my throat and I swallowed audibly, knowing I was going to lose it soon.

"Thank you." I waited until she closed the door before I opened my eyes and stood. My balance was shot, and I had to grab the edge of my desk to keep from falling. The wave of dizziness finished off what was left of my control, and I barely managed to take two steps toward the kitchen before I crashed to my knees and emptied my stomach onto the tile floor. Finally, I fell onto my side, and the coolness on my face felt nice. I would have rejected the comfort of it, but the stench I'd created made up for it. Partings were tragically easy, weren't they? And unbearably impossible to forget.

❖

June came to my rescue—yet again—when I called the next morning, begging her to bring over some ginger ale and crackers. She bustled in like Suzy Homemaker, opening the windows and doors to air the place out and mopping the floor. I'd done my best with paper towels, but that had been all I could manage before I passed out again on the couch.

"It's official," I moaned. "I'm dedicating this next book to you. Maybe the next three books."

"So…" She pressed two aspirin into my hand. "Do you want to tell me what caused all this?"

I shook my head and regretted it immediately.

"Mel is worried about you," June said, sitting on a vacant space on the couch. "And so are the W's."

"But you're not?" I asked, through slitted lids. Why did the sun have to be this freaking bright?

"I was considering writing it off as artistic temperament." She patted my leg. "But I think there's something else going on. Something more personal."

"My work is very personal," I muttered. "At least it is to me."

She said nothing, and I lay there, hoping she would think I'd gone to sleep. I felt her get up, heard her in the kitchen again. A cabinet closed, and the can opener whirred. A pot scraped onto the gas burner. I drifted until I felt her leaning over me.

"Here's some tomato soup. Can you sit up and eat a little?"

Mine was a delicate stomach, but it seemed to recover fairly quickly. "Okay." I groaned to a seated position. I blew on a spoonful and slurped. It tasted surprisingly good.

"Will you answer one thing?" June asked.

I should have known there would be a catch. No one was that nice. "Mmm," I replied, hoping I sounded noncommittal.

"Is this about Beck?"

I choked on a sip. Beck. Oh my God, the things I'd said to her.

Coughing, I dropped the spoon into the bowl. There were a dozen ways I could have ended our friendship, but I had chosen to be needlessly unkind. She was well rid of me, but it might take a while before she figured that out. Until then, she would be hurting, and it was all my fault.

June rose and went back to the kitchen. "I thought so. Whatever she did, I'm sure she's sorry. Or whatever you did, you can always undo it."

"Not always," I mumbled, but she was busy putting the leftover soup in a container and rinsing out the pan.

She stood at the door, watching me for a minute. "Sometimes you have to give people, including yourself, a second chance." She gestured at the soup bowl on the coffee table in front of me. "I'm leaving that in case you want some more later."

But I knew I wouldn't. No second chances for me.

❖

Would I ever feel normal again? For days, I couldn't seem to find an appetite for anything, though I forced down the rest of the soup that evening and was ridiculously grateful to find another can in the pantry. Mel and I hadn't spoken since the Colossal Coed Caper, which already seemed like a lifetime ago, but I knew her advice would be "hair of the dog." I had no interest in it, however. I considered officially giving up drinking but concluded I was too much of a weakling to make that kind of commitment. Eventually, I was able to eat some cereal with berries that were about to go bad and later, a salad. But the very idea of red meat seemed revolting. Was this how one became a vegetarian? You simply woke up one day and couldn't stand the thought of eating animal flesh?

Additionally, my typical restlessness was now overridden by the capacity to sleep at any time. In the mornings, I made a point of staying in bed until Beck's scooter had gone. When I heard her in the evenings, I would go and take my shower. I was ashamed for her to see me, and I didn't want to tempt myself by accidentally catching a glimpse of her. Her routine gave an odd structure to my day that otherwise seemed ungrounded and almost pointless. I reread the short story and hated it more than the first version. I trashed it as well and decided not to try again, sending my regrets to the event's founder along with a vague excuse about my health. Her reply was more than gracious and only made me feel worse. I spent an hour on social media, which I rarely did, and found it as insipid as ever. I checked in with my editor, but she wasn't ready to send my second round of revisions.

"Start something new," she suggested. "You always have something perking in that scheming mind of yours."

But the fact was, I didn't. I was as blank as a new canvas and every bit as boring. Just like my life. Perusing my e-reader, I found nothing in my library that interested me. The library. That was an idea. I needed to ask Beck where... *Shit.* I could have found it on the internet, but instead I went back to bed.

A few more days passed, and Mel called. I think she knew I wasn't okay, but in typical Mel fashion, she ignored the elephant in the room since it didn't belong to her. "Why don't you come to dinner?" she suggested after an awkward silence. "The W's bought like, a dozen fish to fry. You can take some home to have later too." I knew this was as close to a peace offering as I was going to get. And though the idea of fish didn't completely turn my stomach, the idea of company did. I declined politely with some lame excuse about starting a new book and not wanting to interrupt the creative process. I'd probably made a similar excuse to her a dozen times over the years, but she seemed to sense that this time, I was lying.

"We miss you," she whined. "And June is sure you're not eating well."

"I'm fine, Mel. And tell June thanks for her concern. I'll be over again before long."

There was another pause. "How's Spike?"

Something tightened inside. I struggled to keep my voice neutral. "I'm sure she's fine. We haven't spoken lately."

"Trouble in paradise?"

I let out a breath. "Mel, you can be a real pain in the ass, you know?"

"I know." After at least five seconds of silent contrition, she added, "But you still love me, right?"

Sighing, I looked outside. In spite of it all, Mel was a friend, and I didn't have many of those. With her typical bullishness and lack of thorough planning, she had brought me here, giving me a taste of how different my life could be from the day-to-day in NYC. It was gorgeous outside. Sun and a warm ocean breeze filtered through the screen door.

The air smelled like...it smelled like Beck, goddamn it. "Yeah, but I gotta go." I swallowed around the lump in my throat. "Let's talk in a couple of days."

She was saying okay or good-bye or something else as I clicked off the call.

I went out and stood on the deck, letting the sun warm the empty space inside me. I considered going to walk on the beach, visualizing how the last of a wave rippling over my toes or watching the changing patterns of sand and light could be very therapeutic. But earlier, I'd planned on having Beck take me, and now I couldn't imagine doing it without her. For a moment, I let myself feel how much I missed her and how I missed who I'd been when I was with her. How had she found her way inside my life so quickly?

There were people I'd known for years who had never gotten as close to me as Beck had. For a few shining moments, I'd let myself believe that I could change. That someone...Beck...could make me into a better person simply by being who she was. No magic. Just the companionship of someone truly good to bring out a better version of me. Regrettably, I'd chosen the easy way out, the rut, the return to selfishness and isolation and fear. Though they seemed out of place here, that rendering of myself fit perfectly in my daily life in the city. And along with already being there emotionally, I'd be going there physically soon enough. I sighed again and went inside, automatically sitting at the computer, though there wasn't anything I was working on. I closed my eyes, going back to the image of sun and sea and sand... and Beck. In a tiny corner of my mind, I raised the question: was there a story I could write even if I would never live it?

Chapter Seven

I began by deciding to write under a slightly altered version of my real name, Emily Harrison. Leigh's following wouldn't know what to think of a storyline like the one I had imagined. Plus, the idea of becoming "real" appealed to me in a Velveteen Rabbit kind of way. It took several false starts to find my narrator's voice...my new voice... but I finally found the tone of an optimistic pessimist, someone who wished for the best but wasn't surprised by the worst. I worked on balancing my speaker's hopes and fears, making it clear her character could go either way. Part of the tension would be the way events pushed her in one direction and then the other.

Sometimes I saw more of myself than in any of my previous work, but it was Emily, the aspiring romantic, rather than Emily, the disillusioned, bitter loner. I'd always planned my plots before I'd started, but in this case, I wasn't sure where I would end up. In some ways, that was too realistic as well. All I knew for sure was that I wanted the readers to root for my character to end up on the side of hope, even though I personally wasn't there. It was the hardest thing I had ever done, especially as the influence of my guide on this journey had already begun to wane.

It had been almost two weeks since my meltdown. My new story was going surprisingly well despite my long list of personal regrets, including what I'd said about the cats. I wanted to leave Beck a note telling her not to worry because I wouldn't call animal control, but I doubted she'd believe me at this point. I wouldn't have.

One morning, I thought I heard a car door instead of Beck's scooter. By the time I was dressed and at the window, the aging Honda was leaving, and I couldn't make out the driver. There had been rain the previous evening, but it had stopped, so there didn't seem to be a reason why Beck would drive her mother's car. Unless her seat had gotten wet, I thought, smiling to myself. That had been a fun day, hadn't it? I remembered how she'd spoken openly about her life. She'd given freely, and I'd done nothing but withhold and withdraw. Would I ever find the courage to become a different me in real life? I squared my shoulders. First things first. I went back to work, careful to stay in my new persona, trying to channel my secret muse as I wrote.

That evening, I was surprised when I heard the car door again and hurried to the window. It was definitely Mrs. Janser's form shuffling into the garage. Why? Where was Beck? I pushed away the taste of panic, telling myself she wasn't hurt; she was busy. Working. Inspired. Preparing her piece for the PAFA. I thought of the second garage space full of metal. I didn't think I'd heard that door, but perhaps she'd applied the WD-40, and it had become silent. Lost in my considerations, I didn't notice Mrs. Janser had come out until she was glancing up at the window. I'm sure she saw me duck away, and I was horribly embarrassed to think how that looked. Had Beck told her of our falling-out? I almost laughed to myself. *Falling-out?* What a chickenshit way to say it. Had Beck told her I'd become the bitch from hell who had cut her to the core, so she'd resolved to never speak with me again? Better, or rather, more honest. The car drove off.

Early the next morning I awakened to a sharp rapping on the door. I stumbled out of bed, nowhere near prepared for company, and whoever was there was going to hear about it. Mrs. Janser's eyes went first to my disheveled appearance and then to the mess behind me. It was impossible to tell which she disapproved of most. I put a hand to my hair self-consciously before admitting the damage was done and there was nothing to do but see what she wanted and close the door promptly.

"Yes?" I asked, as coolly as possible.

"I'm sorry about the time, Mrs. Harris. I wouldn't bother you, but we're in something of a situation here, and I'm afraid I have to ask for a favor." That familiar touch of haughtiness in her voice was absent as she spoke.

"Yes?" I repeated. Somehow, I'd gained an advantage here, and I wasn't going to give it away.

She cleared her throat. "There's been an accident," she began, and I gasped.

"Not Beck?"

"No," she said quickly. "Her teacher, Mr. Howell. But Becka is very close to him, and she'd like to stay with him in the hospital for now. He doesn't have any next of kin around here."

I remembered the friendly senior man from the diner and how warmly Beck had spoken of him later. I hoped no one else had been hurt. "But he'll recover, won't he?"

She looked down. "They don't know yet. It's touch and go right now."

Oh God. *Poor man. Poor Beck.* I put my hand to my chest. "What can I do?"

She took a breath and met my eyes again. "Without Becka to help me, I won't have any spare time, and I was wondering if you could manage to feed the cats for a couple of days." I opened my mouth, but before I could speak, she held up a hand. "You should know that before this incident, she had been working day and night to find homes for them. Several have already been adopted. There are only three left now, so it's less work than it was."

"Three and the mother?"

"No, three kittens. They've been weaned, so she found a home for the mother." She stopped and seemed to be holding her breath. I realized she was waiting for my answer.

"Is Sugar—" I cut myself off. It didn't matter. "Of course I'll do it. And please tell Beck that..." I trailed off. There was no much to say, but none of it was for Mrs. Janser to hear. "Please tell her I'll suspend the deadline until things are more settled with Mr. Howell."

Relief washed over her face, but she maintained her formal posture. "Thank you, Mrs. Harris. That will be most helpful, believe me."

"Do we need more food?" I asked, having tried and failed to recall how long it had been since I was last at the store.

"I brought a small bag, but it will be gone soon. So yes, you'll need some before long. But you'll make it through this morning and tonight."

"About Mr. Howell...do you have any idea how long..."

She shrugged. "It's in God's hands."

Too bad God couldn't take on these kittens along with the rest of the world, but I supposed that was a lot to ask, especially when you no longer believed in him. "Fine."

She nodded. "I thank you, ma'am. Becka surely didn't want me to talk to you, but I've racked my brain, and you were the only one I could think of who could take this on." She turned to start away, but I caught her arm.

"So she doesn't know you've asked me?" She shook her head. "Has she been working on her project for PAFA?" She shook it again. "Did she tell you about what we found in that second garage?"

"What?"

I asked her to wait while I pulled on a pair of jeans and tennis shoes. I didn't want to wander around all that rusty metal in my sandals. I guided Beck's mother to the back garage where she cocked her head at the large door in the back. "I didn't even know this was here," she said.

"Beck and I didn't either," I said, wincing at how chummy it made us sound. "But look."

I pulled, and the door opened without a sound. Clearly, the WD-40 had been applied. Mrs. Janser gaped at the junk inside. "Becka must have loved this," she murmured.

"She did. And she was going to ask you to call Mr. Guest to see if she could purchase a few pieces from him. I take it she didn't do that."

"No. She's acting the way she does when she's upset. When we're not working, she stays in her room, not talking or eating much, using those earplugs to listen to that music she thinks I don't know about."

I closed my eyes and swallowed, trying unsuccessfully to shield myself from the image of Beck dancing in my kitchen. When I looked, Mrs. Janser was rummaging in her purse. She pulled out a small figure and handed it to me. It was a little bigger than two large paper clips and made from them as well. It stood on short legs and crow's feet, its rounded body a complicated maze of unwound paper clip pieces painstakingly intertwined. The head sat directly on the body, with wiry hair sticking out in all directions. On its chest, where the heart would be, was a tiny hinged door. I looked at Mrs. Janser in wonder. She gestured, and I opened the door. The inside was empty. I felt the sting of tears.

"She's made one of them every day for the last week or so," she said, turning for her car. "Why don't you keep that one?" I couldn't answer. At her door, she added, "I'll call Mr. Guest. He's a nice man, and he likes Becka, but he does love a dollar too. Maybe he'll be reasonable about this. Maybe it's what she needs."

I raised my hand as she drove away. I held the figure tightly and went in to see the kittens. They were sleeping. When I saw Sugar curled in the middle, I scrubbed at my face, forcing my unshed tears away. Heartless people like me didn't cry.

❖

While I waited for June to come over, I wondered if Beck knew a litter of kittens was also called a kindle. Recalling our word games, I could admit that wasn't all I missed. I wanted to see that smile again and hear her voice. Other than Abby, I'd never missed someone physically, but thinking of Beck gave me a deep yearning. I'd thought of calling her, but we'd never exchanged numbers. I'd written several drafts of an apology note, but the words felt flat. Ultimately, I resigned myself to wait, certain I'd see her at least one more time and could throw myself on her mercy.

What I'd said to her was inexcusable, but in my usual gutless way, I tried to think of an explanation that might prompt her to forgive me. First, I'd been drinking, which had been an easy and frequent justification for almost any insensitive behavior in my past. I could tell her that I'd given it up...so far. It was also true that I was known to speak sharply at times, and those close to me had learned to take it with a grain of salt and were more than capable of giving as good as they got. Maybe my only friends were people who had their own emotional shields for our banter, or maybe they were just as callous as I was, but I knew very well that Beck had no such defense, especially against my harshness. I'd been drawn to the fact that she was nothing like them, nothing like me, but then I'd been terribly cruel to her, and had unnecessarily forced her hand about the kittens. Would it matter to her if she knew how sorry I was? Could I find a way to convince her that I didn't want to be that person, at least not to her? I dreaded the notion that I might have exhausted the essential kindness she demonstrated in every encounter, and that there was no chance of a reprieve. But I knew I'd try for one, if I ever got the opportunity.

June uttered a barely suppressed squeal upon seeing the remaining kittens, and they momentarily stopped their play. She wanted Sugar, but I told her she was spoken for. I didn't know why. I had no intention of keeping her, and letting June have her would give me the opportunity to see her from time to time, but the words were out before I knew it. After playing with them, June consoled herself by agreeing to take the other two. They were both calicos, which I had learned meant they were likely female. One had a perfect white face and legs with just a smattering of black and brown on her back and tail; the other was completely, asymmetrically mottled. I teased that she could name them Before and After. She countered with Lucy and Ethel, which made me laugh, the first time I'd done that since my horrible outburst at Beck.

"Thelma and Louise?" I suggested.

"Xena and Gabrielle," she said, and knowing Mel's taste, I nodded sagely.

Thrilled to have them spoken for, I agreed they could stay with me until everyone was ready to leave. June promised to come by regularly to get them accustomed to her.

Several days later, I was doing the evening feeding when Mrs. Janser's car drove up.

"Mr. Howell seems to have turned the corner," she said with no preamble. "He's gonna be okay, so Beck wanted me to tell you she'll take over the feeding again, starting tomorrow."

"There's really no need," I said. "It hasn't been that much of a chore with only three of them. And I found homes for the two calicos."

Mrs. Janser's face creased into a genuine smile, and I thought, this is a first. "That's wonderful. Beck has been worried sick about those three. Says she asked everyone she knows and plenty of folks she don't. Who did you get to take them?"

"One of my friends over at Reefside," I told her. "They'll be extremely pampered, I assure you."

"Oh, I'm not worried. You could drop them off a pier at the marina as far as I'm concerned. But you know Becka…" She trailed off.

"Yes," I said quietly, wishing that were still true.

"So there's just the white one left?"

I nodded. "I'm sure she'll find a home. Please tell Beck not to worry."

She looked toward the garage. "I have some other news too. Mr. Guest is willing to let Becka have all that metal junk for two hundred dollars. She made that much a few weeks ago when she got a bee in her bonnet to work two other jobs. For the life of me, I couldn't figure out why at the time, but I guess the good Lord guided her mind so that she has the money for this material now."

"Perfect," I said, wishing I could have seen Beck's face at the news.

"Well, I thought so too, but she didn't seem at all excited about it. She barely glanced at me and went back to making them paperclip men." She ducked into the car before holding out a small figure. "Here's the latest version."

The basic look was the same, but instead of standing with the hinge on its chest, this model was kneeling, gripping a piece of a broken heart in each hand. The jagged edges looked as if they would never fit together. My hand was shaking, and I looked away, blinking rapidly.

"Becka's my only baby," Mrs. Janser said softly, "though I know I ain't been the world's greatest mother."

"At least you're here," I wanted to say, unwillingly recalling the last time I'd seen my own mother. *She could be dead for all I know.* I associated guilt and loss and pain as the price for being in a family, maybe even when a child was grown...or gone. "I don't think that's true, Mrs. Janser. Beck loves you very much. She speaks of you in the best terms."

"Right now, she don't hardly talk at all, but I know these critters she makes are not about me. She was like this when her daddy passed, real still and all inward facing, you know? This time, she must have been hurt some other way." She sighed. "I know this is contrary to what I said to you before, but if there's anything you can do to help her get through this, I'd consider myself in your debt. I'd hate for her to let the chance at that prize go, but that's not something I can make her do."

As I tried to focus on the last part of her statement instead of the first, I realized she had no idea I was the one who'd hurt her daughter. She was waiting for my reply. "No, it isn't," I agreed quickly. "And I can't make her do it either. But maybe with Mr. Howell getting better, she'll be ready to start again."

She sighed. "And if not, I guess she can try again next year."

Possible but not likely. But I didn't offer anything more. What was there to say?

❖

After spending much of the next two days cleaning every nook and cranny of the house, I rewarded myself by accepting Mel's offer of crab cakes that Saturday night. I'd readied myself for company and the questions they might ask, but everyone seemed to be on their best behavior, and little by little, I relaxed. Since June had obviously been circumspect about sharing my issues, I thought I should return the favor.

When we had a moment alone, I asked, "Have you told anyone about Xena and Gabrielle?"

She grinned and pulled me outside to the deck. "Not yet. But I went over to play with them this morning. I'm sure they recognized me. They're so cute! I can't wait to take them home." My stunned expression must have made her say, "Not that I'm ready to leave yet or anything."

"Oh, sure, I know," I said casually, but now I wondered…should I just go?

As if summoned, Mel joined us and handed me a check. "Here's your money back from the rental for this place. I'm sorry it took me this long. I honestly forgot."

She'd probably been trying to figure out why I was upset and had finally recalled she owed me money. I totally believed it had slipped her mind. Wealthy people rarely remembered details like that. Now I could square my bank account and basically break even. Did that mean it was time to cut my losses and go? "Thanks. And no worries, okay?"

"So we're good?"

"You bet." I gave her a quick hug, and we went in to dinner. I passed on the wine, and of course, the Fabulous W's called me on it. "What's up, FA?" William asked. "Trying to avoid rehab?"

I nodded seriously. "According to your mother, it was pretty rough."

Walter cackled wildly, and it was on.

"That's because she had to sleep with your mother while she was there," William retorted.

"Not sleep is more like it, according to my mother. Apparently, your pillow princess snores."

This went on for several minutes. Mel interjected a shot or two, but June merely looked on, a tiny crease between her eyes. Everyone in the room knew William and I were estranged from our families, so any mother jab was perfectly legal.

The rest of the meal was uneventful except for me passing on dessert. Now Walter, who was always battling his weight, started in. "What gives, Em? Are you on some kind of deprivation diet or what?"

"You do look like you've lost weight," June said quietly, and everyone concurred.

"Hard work and clean living," I said mildly, addressing Walter. "You ought to try it sometime."

"No, thanks," he sang. Turning to William, he pinched the inch around his belly, asking, "Liposuction or lap band?"

"Neither, baby," William said flatly. "You know I love every ounce of you."

Mel pretended to gag while I made kissing sounds. It felt like old times, and I left with a spring in my step, remarkably pleased to be sober. Strange it had taken me all these years to figure out I might have been using alcohol in a problematic way. It made sense now that I thought of it. Over the years, I'd been prescribed all kinds of drugs for my anxieties and sleeplessness, but none of them had ever worked well enough to warrant the fog and weirdness they caused. Since alcohol was generally available in all the social situations I dreaded, I'd used it to ease my way in and out of everything from large parties to small get-togethers to sex. Drinking never completely blocked out the voices of my past, but I had thought it made them—and me—more tolerable. Maybe neither of those things was true, but these weren't the people to ask. And even if this abstention was only temporary, perhaps I at least needed moderation to be my goal. After all, I wasn't in my twenties anymore. Right now, it didn't bother me how bland and boring that sounded. I just felt better about feeling better.

The Sunday morning knock on my door didn't find me hungover, nor was the house a wreck. I wasn't made up, but my hair had been combed, and the coffee was on. And when I opened the door, I was very, very glad.

"We're sorry to bother you, Mrs. Harris. I know you must think all we do is ask for favors, but this time, we're here to strike a bargain." Mrs. Janser was talking to me, but her focus was on Beck, who stood partly behind her as if hiding behind her ample torso. "Becka, would you explain the details of our proposal to Mrs. Harris?"

I had a feeling Beck's mother had prompted her like this a hundred times over the years. And Beck had probably reacted exactly the same every time, with a deep breath expelled with a huff. Before she could speak, I opened the door wider.

"Please, won't you both come in and sit down? The coffee's about ready if you'd like some."

Beck was still wearing her sunglasses, but I could tell that her glance didn't make it to my face before she bit her lip and shook her head. But her mother had already stepped inside. She looked back and gestured. "We've been invited in, Becka. What do you say?"

"No, thank you," Beck mumbled, and her mother rolled her eyes. I almost laughed, thinking this scene was nearly the opposite of when we'd met.

Mrs. Janser was watching Beck as if she might take a loss of eye contact as a chance to make a break for it. "I'll take some of that coffee, Mrs. Harris, thank you. I'll fix my own in a minute, but my daughter and I are going to have a quick word while you get whatever you want."

I put my hand on her arm, and she looked over at me, startled. "If you'd go ahead and fix yours, Mrs. Janser, it might save us some misunderstanding if I spoke to Beck first."

"Don't talk about me like I'm not here." Beck was still looking away, but her tone was full of resentment.

"You're right," I said. "Will you speak with me for a moment, Beck?"

She gave her head a half shake again, but somehow, it ended with a half shrug that left me hopeful. Mrs. Janser opened her mouth, but I squeezed her arm and gestured toward the kitchen. She drew away slightly before taking my cue. Once she was busying herself with the coffee, I stepped nearer to Beck, who flinched at my approach. I swallowed hard, knowing this would be my one chance.

There had been so many things I'd fucked up in my life, things that could never be fixed. As an adult, I'd never believed in crap like destiny or fate, but maybe getting a new start with Beck would put me on the path to possibilities beyond who and where I was. It seemed terribly important to look her in the eye, so I carefully removed her sunglasses. I pressed them into her hand, wondering if she'd missed that touch as much as I had. The gesture was so unexpectedly intimate that we were both speechless for a second.

I recovered first and spoke with all the urgency I could muster, relying on the experience of several thirty-second book pitches. "I don't have time to begin a sufficient apology for what I said to you, and I can only imagine how you feel being here after how terribly I acted. There's no excuse for my behavior, and I'm not trying to make one, but I want you to know I haven't had a drink since that night. And I'd give my left hand to go back in time and undo every single, reprehensible second. But whatever it is you're here for, I'm so, so glad to see you again, and though I know you couldn't possibly forgive me, if there's any way forward for us, I very much want to try our friendship again. Please come in and have some coffee. Please?"

Beck studied my face as if trying to determine my sincerity. With anyone else, I would have wilted under such scrutiny or been defiantly angry, but I knew I had it coming. If this look was the worst I got, I was getting off ridiculously easy. After what seemed like an eternity, she took one step past me over the threshold and stopped. "Place looks nice," she said.

I felt like I could breathe again. "Thank you," I said with genuine appreciation. We both knew I wasn't talking about the compliment. There were no further pleasantries as we all sat with our coffees.

After everyone drank, Beck cleared her throat and began what must have been a prepared speech. "My teacher, Mr. Howell, is doing better, but he'll be going to a rehab facility before he goes home, and then it may be months before he can return to work. The school has canceled his classes, and they're going to take advantage of his absence to redo some of the facilities in the art department. That means everyone has to get all their stuff out. Everything." She paused for a second and looked at her mother, who nodded encouragingly. "Our house isn't much bigger than this, with no yard I could use."

"My husband uses what little space we have to practice with his air rifle," Mrs. Janser explained.

"And sometimes his pistol," Beck added, but her mother shook her head.

"Not lately, Becka. Remember what the police said last time?"

Beck glanced at me briefly, perhaps waiting for a comment. I said nothing, though internally, I cringed at the idea of this man with a gun at Beck's house. She went on. "So we'd like to propose we rent out your second garage space to store my stuff. There will be finished and unfinished projects, raw materials, and tools." It sounded like we were back to the prepared speech, and I was ready to say yes, but she wasn't done. "But here's the thing. We can't pay you with money, because Erik doesn't get much in disability, and we pretty much need every dollar for our house payment and bills."

So the man with the gun also didn't work. This picture wasn't getting any better, but I kept my expression neutral. "I know times are hard."

"There's plenty that have it worse," Mrs. Janser said, with more than a hint of defensiveness. I inclined my head reassuringly.

"If you agree," Beck continued carefully, "I would pay with light housekeeping twice a week and one big cleaning a month. Cooking up to two meals a day. I'd do the grocery shopping and whatever other errands you need run. You don't need to be here when I'm here. Once we set the schedule, you can leave me instructions and go visit with your friends or see a movie or walk on the beach, and I'll be on my way as soon as I finish." I hid my smile at that, already planning to trade a cleaning session for a beach visit with her. "I'm aware this arrangement will intrude on your privacy, but I am quick and careful, and I'll be glad to provide references if you'd like to see them." I felt disheartened that she was addressing me as if we were meeting for the first time, but considering my previous outburst, she might feel like she didn't know me at all.

I would have agreed immediately, but something told me it would be insulting if I didn't ask any questions or counteroffer in some way. "What will you do with your things when I leave?"

"I don't know," Beck said. "We hope to figure something else out. Or maybe Mr. Guest will let me leave the stuff if I clean for him."

I gestured toward the garage. "Do you plan to work on your project there as well?"

"No. I'm not working on that right now. I just want to store things."

"Then my answer is no," I said. I heard Mrs. Janser breathe in, and I knew I was taking a big chance. But something had to push Beck back into her art, and I was willing to be that something, especially since I suspected I was at least part of the reason why she'd quit working in the first place. "You'll have all those materials, and I'm sure there will be room for you to work once you get everything organized." Beck was shaking her head, but I leaned toward her, and she froze. "I could get anyone to cook and clean. But I want to have a soon-to-be famous artiste working for me. I want to be able to say I knew you when."

A tiny grin lifted the corner of her mouth, and her gaze warmed. "When what?"

"Don't be smart, Becka. You know what the lady means." Her mother's voice was sharper than I'd heard it in some time.

"Sorry," she mumbled while it crossed my mind what an absurd thing it was to say "don't be smart," though I knew the phrase well. My Aunt Sharon used to say it to me all the time, and in typical contrary teenage fashion, I'd go and do my darnedest to be exactly that: smart.

"Say you'll try, Beck," I said, catching her eye again. "That's all I ask. If you can't, I'll understand. I've had writers' block for weeks now, but in my experience, you just have to keep at it."

Beck closed her eyes, probably to stop looking at me. She took in a breath and after another pause, blinked slowly. "I'll try," she said quietly.

Mrs. Janser looked as if she might kiss me. I gave a slight shake of my head. Making too big a deal of this would ruin everything. "Okay, then. Would you like me to write up our agreement on my computer? I can print us each a copy so there's no misunderstanding."

Beck nodded, and her mother corrected, "Use your words, Becka." Back to normal, I guessed.

"Yes, thank you," Beck said, and I was pleased she didn't sound terribly sullen.

"When are you going to start bringing your things?" I asked.

"My husband's friend is coming to jump his truck," Mrs. Janser said, standing. Beck followed her lead. "We'd better go give them a hand. Is sometime this afternoon all right with you?"

"I'll be here," I said, walking them toward the door.

Beck pulled out her phone as her mother went onto the stairs. "There's no landline here. Could I call your cell phone if there's any delay?"

"Don't worry. Whenever you can get here is fine," I replied, not realizing it sounded as if I didn't want to give her the information. Watching her expression shutter again, I caught my mistake and reached for her phone. Keying in my number, I said, "Call me now, so I'll have yours." She pushed a button and strains of "I'll Be There for You," from the TV show *Friends*, started to play. I couldn't have been more embarrassed. The person calling me wasn't usually there when my phone rang. "Oops. Guess I'm stuck in the nineties."

She giggled, and it felt like having a cool drink of water on a hot day. "I used to watch that show with my papa. He seemed to think it was really funny, but I think I was too young to get most of the jokes."

"Becka, do you remember what we talked about?" Her mother called from the stairs, and her sweet, open face closed down.

"Sorry," she said and moved toward the door.

I caught up and turned her toward me, leaning as close as I dared as I whispered, "Please don't be. I can't tell you how much I missed you, and how much I'm looking forward to talking with you again. This"—I gestured between us—"is like the best gift I could have gotten."

I could see she wanted to say something more, but her mother made an impatient sound from outside, and she turned away with another shrug. "Okay."

I didn't care. It was enough. I hugged myself when they were gone, grateful no one was around to see me, and laughed. She was coming back to me. *Back to our friendship.* That was what I meant.

❖

She called about eight o'clock that night. "I'm sorry to have kept you waiting all this time, but it's not going to happen. Maybe next Saturday if you're free?"

"That would be fine, Beck. But is there a problem? Can I help?"

She sniffed and didn't answer for a second. "Erik's buddy brought beer. I kept thinking they were going to stop after a couple, but they didn't. Neither of them is driving anywhere now. They're inebriated."

Fairly sure that word of the day had been used more than once, I sighed. "Would you like to come over sometime this week? Look at the space again?"

Another pause. "I would, but it's high season. Mama and are I working dawn to dark," she said finally.

"Oh, sure." I wanted to say more, but it was too soon. "Then I'll... I'll see you next Saturday."

"See you next Saturday," she echoed softly.

I clicked off and rubbed my eyes. I moved around the house, picking up the few dishes I'd gotten out. When I finished in the kitchen, I walked slowly toward the second bedroom as if drawn by some magnetic force. Thinking about the man with the gun who drank and didn't work, I assessed the furnishings: a twin bed, dresser, and small chair. I paced the distance to the master bedroom. Could I do this? Could I not? I hadn't lived with another human being since my marriage and hadn't had the least desire to do so. It wasn't simple desire that was motivating me now, either, but my mental state was almost too chaotic to analyze. I wanted Beck safe. I needed to protect myself and my secrets. I liked her company well enough, but I required solitude for my work. If there was a compromise in there somewhere, was it one I wanted to find?

❖

About two o'clock on Saturday, I heard the sound of a laboring engine accompanied by loud rattling and clanking sounds. I walked out to the deck in time to see Beck jump out of the truck bed where she'd barely fit amidst the equipment and pieces of metal of various shapes and sizes. Her friends, the two boys I'd met downtown, got out of the cab. Beck leaned in the driver's window and said something, and the engine shut off. She directed the boys to the far side of the garage, and they began pulling out the car parts, stacking them neatly along the far side of the building where they would be out of sight. I was as excited as a child on Christmas and ran to see.

Beck must have heard me coming because she met me at the foot of the stairs, blocking my way. "You need to stay up there," she whispered urgently.

"But I can help. And I want to see your work."

She shook her head. "No. You wouldn't be a help."

My gut twisted. She was shutting me out. For some reason, I'd lost what minor progress we'd made earlier. "Beck, listen—"

She put her hands on my shoulders and gave me a little shake, her expression more serious than I'd ever seen it. "No, you listen to me. It needs to be this way." She glanced anxiously toward the truck. They'd backed in until only the first part of the hood was visible from the driveway along the far edge of the house. "Please, Emily. I don't want him to know I know you. And I really don't want him to know you live here. You can help later, okay?"

Realization hit me. She was doing everything I hadn't done. Protecting someone she cared about from the man with a gun who drank and didn't work. And I had to let her. "All right. But come up if you need anything."

"I will. Thank you."

The relief on her face made me want to hold her, but instead, I put my hand on her cheek for a second before going into the house. I paced for an hour and a half, hating that I couldn't even watch from the deck. But when I heard the truck's engine, I ran to the window. Beck saw me and waved as they pulled away. I waited until the sound was gone before I went to look. The scrap metal was still outside, sorted into stacks with some method I couldn't decipher, and the large door was closed again. I was toying with the idea of opening it, of sneaking a quick peek at the pieces inside, when I heard Mel's authoritative voice.

"Yo! What's going on over here?"

Sometimes she had a protective streak too, I realized, which was probably one of the reasons why we'd stayed friends all these years. "Hey!" I came around the side of the house and waved. "That was Beck storing some stuff here."

She looked at me with brows raised. "Paradise restored, huh? So what is this, prelude to a U-Haul?"

"It's not personal stuff. It's…work stuff." I tried to guide her away from the garage, but she didn't budge.

"Work stuff? Like cleaning supplies?"

I sighed. With Beck here more regularly and hopefully working, it was going to come out sooner or later. "No, work stuff like her art. She does metalwork."

"No shit. Is she any good?"

I shrugged. "I haven't seen anything she's done. But she's a finalist for this year's PAFA."

"Damn." I could practically hear the wheels turning as Mel transitioned from skeptical friend to agent before my eyes. "Does anyone represent her?"

"I don't know, but I doubt it. She's extremely private about her work. Give her a chance to settle in here before you go charging at her like a bull in a china shop."

She ignored my comment and looked over at the garage. "So her stuff's in there? Don't you want to see it? Let's take a quick look, so I'll know if she's worth my time or not."

It was funny how the path could be much clearer when someone else showed it to me. I stepped possessively in front of the door. "No, Mel. I'm not going to violate her trust on the first day."

"What, you're going to wait a few days and then violate it?"

I pulled on her arm, and she moved away reluctantly. "I'll ask her if she has an agent if you want me to."

"Would you? That would be great. I don't think she likes me."

I poked her in the ribs. "It would help if you called her by her actual name."

She sidled away from me, rolling her eyes. "Yeah, yeah. When is she coming back?"

"Probably not for a few days."

"But you'll ask her?"

I shook my head. "Mel, no one else is going to steal this kid away from you, okay? Do you see a bunch of agents crawling around here?

THE FOUND JAR

This isn't New York City. Let me mention it when I think the time is right." I batted my lashes. "Trust me?"

She laughed. "Fine. But come to dinner with us tonight. June's found a restaurant she wants to try over in Portsend, and we can kick off my birthday week in style."

Chapter Eight

It hadn't occurred to me that with July underway, I'd have to prepare for Mel's tradition of extreme birthday-ing. She usually expected to start celebrating the week before and continue through the week after. I often teased that she didn't have a birth day, she had a birth season. In the city, plenty of people would come and go during that period, but out here, I'd be expected to take on the best friend end of the daily honors. I suspected June would make up for the lack of extra faces with lots of activities all over the island. I stifled a sigh.

"Sure. Sounds fun." We finalized the plans, and Mel glanced at the second garage one last time before she left. I decided to have the unusable lock removed and purchase a new one. I was looking for a local locksmith online when my phone rang. It was Beck.

"Hi, Beck," I said cheerily. "Is everything okay?"

"Uh, yeah, everything's fine. I just…uh…I wanted to tell you how much I appreciate you letting me use that space, and I wondered if… uh." She cleared her throat and took a breath. "The thing is, the college is having a summer dance next weekend, and I bought the guys tickets as a thank you, and I thought, well, maybe you'd like to go too?"

I felt my face break into a smile. It was totally in character for Beck to have forgiven me so quickly. "Are you asking me out, Ms. Reynolds?" I drawled teasingly.

"No, I meant…" There was a pause. "Would it be okay if I did?" she asked quietly.

I remembered my commitment to Mel and her upcoming events. "Oh Beck, I can't. I—"

"It's fine," Beck said abruptly. "I don't know why I asked when I would have been surprised by any other answer. I'll see you tomorrow."

She ended the call before I realized what had happened. In the next five seconds, I replayed how I'd answered the question about the dance, understanding she would have heard me turning down any and all opportunities with her, as if I was withdrawing when she attempted to do something nice, as I'd done every other time. Shit. I tried to call her back, but the phone went to voice mail before announcing the mailbox was full. Shit shit shit. I needed to get ready for dinner but vowed to clear the air with her tomorrow.

But at dinner, June whispered she needed me to help finalize some of Mel's celebration activities. "Let's go to breakfast at that diner in town tomorrow, and we can talk."

"The W's too?"

"Of course. We need all the fabulous we can get."

Despite my less than sunny mood, I had to laugh at that. "I'm glad you came along this summer, June. You're a great addition to this group."

"Hey!" Mel's attention had shifted to us, and she leaned across June's other side. "Stop hitting on my girl. Bring your own next time."

I doubted if she meant it—meant either comment, really—but I raised my hands in surrender. June turned from Mel's line of sight and winked at me. "Eight tomorrow," she mouthed, and I nodded.

I was shuffling into the kitchen to make coffee the next morning when I heard a sound outside the door. I couldn't imagine June was this early. I peeked out the window to check and saw Beck sitting on the step, leaning on her elbows with her head back and eyes closed, soaking in the soft, early morning sun like a budding flower. Sugar was curled on her lap, purring contentedly. Warmed by the vision, I smiled and opened the door. They both startled, and Beck got to her feet quickly as Sugar struggled in her arms.

"Sorry," Beck said quickly. "I hope I didn't wake you. I was waiting to cook breakfast like we agreed." I noticed the grocery bags by the door.

"Listen, you don't have to—"

Sugar meowed, and Beck gestured with her head. "Let me take her down to the garage."

"Please, come on in when you're done," I said. "Get yourself some coffee but don't start on breakfast yet. I need to jump in the shower before we talk."

She was sitting on the deck when I came out, the groceries already put away. The pot of coffee was untouched. I made her a mug and took it out. Her glance lingered for an extra second before she looked away. "No, thank you."

I was definitely getting the cold shoulder. I tried to tease her into it. "Beck, I'm not going to drink this crazy mix. You might as well."

Standing, she shook her head. "So did you not want breakfast?"

"No, I'm going to the diner with June and the guys. We have to plan some things."

"Fine. Lunch? Dinner?"

"I'd like to talk to you about the schedule." A horn honked downstairs. *Damn it.* "Can you stay for a couple of hours until I'm home?"

"No. I have to go to work with Mama as soon as I can. I'll leave your supper in the fridge with instructions."

"Could you come and eat it with me?"

She sighed. "I don't think so, Emily." The horn honked again. I went to the edge of the deck and waved. When I turned back, she'd gone inside.

I got my purse and stopped in the kitchen where she was opening a container of mushroom soup. "I hope you'll change your mind." I went to stand behind her, putting my hand on her shoulder and squeezing gently. "We have a few things to clear up."

She lowered her head and shook it slightly. I walked toward the door, thinking I'd talk to June about what to say to make it better. "I'm not sure I can count on you," I heard Beck whisper as if to herself, and the pain in her voice made me ache almost as much as the words themselves. I'd hurt her more than once, and now I had no idea if the relationship between us could be fixed or how to go about it. In my casual encounters, it had been easy to let someone go without a backward glance. To return to friendly terms with Beck, it was clear that something would have to change. What, and more importantly, how, I had no idea.

❖

June was completely absorbed in planning for Mel's birthday week, and the W's added wonderful suggestions for other activities. Unlike me, they'd obviously done some research about the area, and we had the whole week planned out in no time. A 4x4 SUV ride to see the Corolla wild horses, Jet-Skiing, and climbing a lighthouse were among the activities, along with lots of food, drink, and an evening at *The Lost Colony* play. It all sounded wonderful, except for the fact that I'd be gone pretty much all day, every day, which meant no time to speak with Beck. I tried not to fret, but Walter, ever observant, called me out.

"What's wrong, Emily? Did you want us to include a fishing charter?"

I knew the first question was serious, though the second was not, so I sighed dramatically. "I simply can't believe you've left out a visit to the Wright brothers museum. I was sure it would be at the top of your list."

Walter's mother's idea of a vacation had always been planned around what she viewed as important, which meant the things she'd been taught in school. "If we could have seen the World's Largest Thermometer or Cadillac Ranch instead of strictly authorized museums, those trips would have been infinitely better," he'd often said. As a result, Walter's taste ran to those quirky or environmental sights he'd never gotten to see as a child. I suspected *The Lost Colony* would have been out if it hadn't also been theatrical.

"I've seen it. I could reenact the highlight for you if you like." He spread his arms and flapped his lips, making a motor-like sound for as long as his breath held. "Twelve seconds. One hundred and twenty feet. That's pretty much it."

We were all laughing, and June said, "Be sure and do that for Mel later. We can't let her feel she's missed out."

As we walked to the car, I noticed a locksmith shop across the street. "Would you mind if I run in here for a minute?"

William was already checking out the antique store next door. With a glance at Walter, whose eyes gleamed enthusiastically, he said, "Go ahead. Take your time."

I handed over the key I wanted copied, and the clerk directed me to the aisle with locks. June followed me into the shop, wanting to know about Beck. Since she'd been very sweet with me, I decided not to hedge too much on the question. I told her there had been a misunderstanding but I hadn't yet had time to fix it. I felt marginally better just having expressed my concern and thanked her for asking.

She nodded. "That's what happens when you get in a serious relationship. You find at least one friend you can talk to about it."

"Well, I wouldn't call mine a serious relationship, but I still appreciate you lending an ear."

I settled on a large lock with three keys and arranged for someone to come out and cut the old lock off. As I paid for my purchases, receiving the copies in a small, separate envelope, she asked, "Who's that one for? Us?"

"Uh, no. It's for Beck. I'll be gone a lot this week, so I thought..."

As I trailed off, June smirked and rolled her eyes. "Not serious, huh? Whatever you say, FA."

❖

When I gave Beck her key the next morning, I thought she'd be pleased, but she only shrugged and put it in her pocket. I'd met her at the door, and because I was already running late. I could have left it with a note, but I wanted to see her face. Her cool disinterest hurt, and I brushed past her onto the porch, looking over my shoulder. "I thought this would make things easier for you."

"I thought it was making it easier on you," she replied, and I flushed.

"I won't be home for dinner either, so don't bother making anything."

She worried at her lip as she looked around. "Should I clean?"

I was about to tell her I didn't care what she did, and then I thought about PAFA. "Why don't you do some work on your project? That was part of our deal too, if you'll recall."

For a second, her eyes flashed, and I knew she was angry at me. "Yes, I'm cognizant of that fact," she said through gritted teeth.

"Good. I'll expect you to make some progress on that today. You can show me in the morning before I leave." I wasn't halfway down the stairs before the door slammed behind me. Fine. I was okay with mad. Mad was something I knew how to deal with. My relationship with Aunt Sharon had featured a lot of anger...on both sides. I'd much rather Beck be mad instead of sad. I knew I was pushing her, but I was convinced that doing so was right in this case.

The next morning, I was dressed and waiting with coffee made when Beck let herself in. In the first instant, her expression lit up in a way I recognized from when she used to be glad to see me. Then her expression emptied, and she looked away. I swallowed the loss that rose in my throat and smiled.

"Good morning. Get yourself some coffee, and let's go downstairs."

She jammed her hands into her pockets and stuck her chin out a bit, as aggressive a posture as I'd ever seen her take. "No point."

I kept my voice neutral. "Why not?"

"Because I couldn't do any work yesterday."

"Is that because you didn't feel like it? Simply couldn't find the inspiration?" I stood. "You know, Beck, making art isn't always thrilling. Sometimes it's grinding it out and refining and polishing until it turns into something magical."

"Gee, thanks for the great piece of advice, Emily. I sure would like to try that approach, but I guess I'll have to wait until you decide to take that new lock off the door." She walked into the kitchen and began pulling cookware out of the cabinet.

I blinked. Shit. I hadn't remembered what I'd arranged about the new lock. When I'd given Beck the extra key to the house, her aloof attitude had made me forget to tell her. I let out a breath. "Okay, wow. Now I feel like a total idiot."

To her credit, she laughed. A short, somewhat angry sounding laugh, but still. "I know we're not on the best of terms, but I didn't want to believe you would do that to me on purpose."

"Oh God, no, Beck. I'd never...I...I'll get you a key for the lock too. Hang on a second." I found my purse and rummaged for the set that came with my purchase. I carried them into the kitchen in my palm. "Here's an extra one for your mother. Or whoever. You know, just in case." She reached for them, and I held on for an extra second. "I wish I had more time, but I can't get out of these commitments. I'm truly sorry, Beck. For everything. Do you believe me?"

She looked into my eyes. "Why did you put the new lock on?"

"Two reasons. After you left your work here, my friend Mel came over to see what was going on. She's an agent, you know. Well, she acts as my agent anyway. She wanted to see your art to decide if she wanted to represent you." Beck stiffened and drew her hand away. "I told her no, Beck," I said quickly. "But I know Mel, and I wanted to secure things a little better."

After a few seconds, she nodded and took the keys. "What was the other reason?"

I couldn't look away, though I wanted to. "Me. Simply sliding open that door, especially with the WD-40 on it, was temptingly easy. But having to unlock it first and thinking of doing it without your permission reminds me you have the right to your privacy."

There was a tiny lift at the corner of her mouth. "You remembered about WD-40."

My phone buzzed. I didn't have to look to know it was Mel or

June asking where I was. "I'm sorry, but I have to run. I don't need dinner tonight either, so same deal, okay?"

"Sure." Her voice had turned flat again. I hated it, but I didn't have a second to spare.

"Listen, since we're getting a later start tomorrow, maybe we can have breakfast together about eight? And you can show me your work, if you feel like it." I took a step closer, watching her carefully. "I'm not trying to pressure you, Beck. But I want to know you haven't given up, that you still want to compete for the PAFA."

She looked away and shifted uncomfortably. "The thing is, I'll need a couple of days to get organized."

"Of course." I was dying to ask what the deadline was but didn't. It wasn't my business, but I was hoping since the rules required a new creation for this final stage, perhaps the time allotted was more generous. My phone buzzed again. "Let's talk some more in the morning, okay?" She nodded again slowly, and I squeezed her arm before dashing down the stairs.

The night at Jackie's Famous Buffet and Lounge had gone on way too long, especially since I still wasn't drinking. This made me the designated driver, which seemed to give everyone license to drink even more than usual. But it also meant I couldn't very well leave them, tempted though I was. June only made one trip through the line, which explained why she might weigh ninety-five pounds soaking wet and why she was less able to tolerate her numerous whiskey sours. She kept leaning against me, saying things like, "You're the smart one in this group," or "I wish I had your willpower." Thankfully, I didn't feel the need to drink at all or have any sense of missing something, but I didn't think this was the time to explain that to her.

It was after 1:30 in the morning when I dropped them off, parking Mel's Range Rover in its usual spot. The path to the Guest House was so familiar by now, I could make my way by the light of the moon. The air was still, and the sea was calm. In the city, I'd be jumpy, skittish to be out this late at night by myself, but here I felt a certain confidence. Maybe it was the newfound familiarity that made it seem like I was on the right track about something, but it felt good. Once inside, I realized how tired I was and rushed through my evening routine before falling gratefully into bed.

Movement. And that smell. Don't look. He's not real if you don't see him. But I heard him. Close by, too close. Smelled the alcohol on his breath when he spoke. "If you make a sound, I'll kill her."

How did he know I was awake? I tried to see through my lids and finally gave up, cracking open one eye as little as possible. I saw he wasn't talking to me; he was talking to Abby. Was that what really happened? His face was turned toward her, horribly near to where he held her uncomfortably in his big hairy arms.

But I couldn't have seen that much detail. How did I know his arms were hairy? Because I'd seen them before when my father had first brought him home for supper. And he was the one who'd been working in the garden for several days in a row, always watching when we came home from school. I knew him!

I gasped before realizing my mistake. I turned over, away from the open side of my bed and toward the side against the wall, still faking sleep. I couldn't see anything now and dared not look. Abby whimpered, and I cringed, certain at any second I'd feel his hands on my neck or a blade slipping between my ribs. How long did I lie there? How long before I found the courage to open both eyes and look? Abby's bed was empty, and the house was still. So terribly still. I screamed then because I knew I could. Screamed loudly enough so Abby, wherever she was, could hear me.

Screaming myself awake, I sat up in the Guest House bed, the covers tangled, and my face wet with tears. Who was I kidding? I wasn't on any right track. I was on the same goddamn loop I'd been on every day since that night.

"Fuck," I screamed. "Goddamn fucking shit." I didn't know why cursing made me feel better, but it always had. Maybe because everyone in my young life had disapproved of it, and I knew that, no matter how they tried to hide it, they also disapproved of me. More than disapproved. Condemned. And rightly so. Especially since I'd already condemned myself long before the police arrived, before the doctor came to give my mother something to make her sleep, leaving me feeling more alone than I'd ever felt in my life.

Father had come home from his retreat that next afternoon, ready to share all he'd learned about the wisdom of the Lord, but there wasn't anything he could do. I was already tried, convicted, and sentenced by the new judge who had taken residence in my mind. And God? God had gone out the door in the arms of that horrible man.

"I'm sorry, Abby," I sobbed for what must have been the millionth time. "Please, please forgive me." But no absolution was forthcoming. And it never would be.

Seeing the sky lighten, I knew there was no way I could pull myself together for the conversation I needed to have with Beck. I wrote a note and taped it to the door, apologizing for not being available after all. I wrote that we'd get together soon, though I knew "soon" should never come. It was laughable, really, the idea that I could have a different life simply by trying to write differently. And why should I encourage Beck to spend time here when the only thing she could expect from me was the same moral deficiency I'd discovered in myself when I'd let Abby be taken? No one with my failings deserved consideration from someone like her. My self-contempt deepened until I considered begging off from seeing Mel and the gang as well, but I knew if I tried, they'd be over here with food or aspirin or some hopeful cure for my imagined ailment.

After I heard Beck's scooter come and go, I showered and dressed. As I locked the door, I saw she'd added something to my note. "I'll be back tonight." I'd never seen her handwriting before. It looked like something out of the cursive writing manual.

I added a quick reply. "The rest of this week is crazy busy. Maybe I'll see you after the weekend." Perhaps if I put her off long enough, she'd get the hint. I knew she'd try again, but surely she'd see, eventually, that there were no prospects with someone shackled to the misery of the past.

Over at Reefside, everyone was still at the dining table in their pajamas drinking coffee. I joined them for a cup, avoiding Mel's curious scrutiny. But when June and the guys had gone to their respective bathrooms, she moved next to me. "Did you fall off the wagon last night, and I was too wasted to remember?"

"It wouldn't be a good sign for you if that was the case, but no," I said.

"Then why do you look like shit?" she asked in her usual tactful way.

"I had a hard time falling asleep. Wound up from being out with you party animals, I suppose." I tried, starting for more coffee, but she held my arm.

"Tell me the truth, Em. Did you have another nightmare?"

She'd heard me screaming one August when we'd had adjoining hotel rooms during my first book tour. I had to tell her something, so

I'd lied about a recurring nightmare where I was naked in front of an audience at a reading. "For fuck's sake, Em. You've got a great body. Why would you worry about that?" she'd asked.

I had to laugh. "The fact that I'm naked has nothing to do with my body. It's about feeling exposed, vulnerable, with strangers." All those years of therapy weren't for nothing, after all. But I still had no intention of discussing the worst moment of my life with someone I wasn't paying to listen, certain that anyone who found out what kind of person I truly was would want nothing more to do with me. And I wouldn't blame them.

She'd frowned. "I used to dream I was late for school, but there wasn't anyone in the house who could take me. It must have been, like, finals or something because it was very important for me to be there, but I wasn't, and it freaked me out really bad."

"What if you assume that dream wasn't actually about school?" I had been so grateful to change the focus of our conversation from me to her that I would have willingly conversed about NASCAR if she'd mentioned it. "What else could it mean?"

She'd been quiet for a time. "Maybe," she finally said, talking her way through it, "it was about me feeling alone, like, abandoned. And that it was important to me to have someone around for meaningful things."

She usually hid her more thoughtful side, and I hadn't been prepared for her to be so deeply introspective. "And do you?" I'd whispered.

Getting up from my bed where we'd been sitting, she'd yawned and stretched. "I didn't until you, kiddo." She'd winked and turned into her room.

"I bet you say that to all the girls," I called after her, surprised when she stuck her head back in.

"No, I don't." She'd blown me a kiss, and the door closed quietly.

Now, years later, she knew me well enough to see through any casual lie I tried to tell. "Yes," I said. "But I'm fine. At least I didn't get sick this time."

"This time?" Her voice rose. "How many of these dreams have you had?"

Shit. "A few over the years."

"Damn, Emily. Why didn't you tell me?"

"There's nothing to tell. It's only a dream, and it goes away." I stood and she didn't try to stop me but followed me into the kitchen.

When I felt the touch of her hand on my back, I stepped away and gave her a playful push toward her bedroom. "Go get ready and let's keep this party going."

Ignoring her skeptical look, I turned away and went out to the deck. Down the beach, a lone swimmer was wading out of the surf. I squinted, trying to see more clearly. A woman, I assumed, based on the sports bra. She shook herself and walked toward the dunes, returning a moment later with a towel, which she used to dry herself before laying it on the sand as a blanket. She settled onto her stomach, head on her arms, and I wondered how it felt to be free like that. I heard the screen door, and June joined me at the railing.

"Isn't that Beck?" she asked.

"Is it?" I squinted. I'd always been a bit nearsighted but was too vain to wear glasses.

June nodded. "She swims there almost every morning but usually much earlier." She gave me a little poke. "She has a nice body. Very athletic. Women like that usually have great stamina."

I laughed at that. "I wouldn't know." I looked toward the beach and felt June's gaze on me.

"But you'd like to find out, wouldn't you?"

"There's no point, June. I'll be gone in less than two months, and she's young and really sweet. I don't want to hurt her." *Again*.

"Have you discussed this with her?"

"God, no. I'd be totally embarrassed. I mean, what if she said she wasn't interested? Besides, I'd feel weird about making a move on someone I actually know." I hoped June wouldn't comment on how odd it was that I felt more secure having sex with a stranger, but it had always been the surest way I knew to control the ultimate outcome: leaving alone.

She looked as if she wanted to say something else, but the W's joined us, munching on sweet rolls. William handed me one. "What are we looking at?" he asked, peering onto the beach.

"That's Emily's crush," Walter said, and I glared at him, readying a retort when Mel yelled from the kitchen.

"Why is there only one fucking sweet roll left? Whose birthday week is this, for Christ's sake?"

Like guilty children, we all cut our eyes at each other and giggled. "Let's go," June whispered. "Maybe we'll hit a McDonald's on the way out."

I glanced down the beach again. Beck had turned over, head on hands, face to the sky. I imagined what it would be like lying beside her and closed my eyes to let myself be there for a few more seconds before I followed everyone into the house to start our day.

❖

While avoiding Beck physically, I couldn't shake the vision of her coming out of the water, gorgeous body gleaming in the sun. Was she working on her project? Were things okay for her at home? And did she suspect I was deliberately not seeing her? God, I hoped not. I wondered if I could make her understand I was trying to spare us both any further damage by avoiding emotional or physical entanglement. Or did she think I always ran hot and cold, and she'd finally had enough of it? Whatever the case, I spent the week torn between telling myself to keep away, ignoring the surprisingly painful image of her finding someone else to spend time with.

There had been much discussion regarding Saturday, Mel's actual birthday, but ultimately, June decided we should stay in town, returning to the Seagoer, where we'd eaten the night I'd seen Beck with her friends and Peyton with the town thugs. Windsom Edge seemed more crowded than usual, and most of the young people we encountered were very nicely dressed. It didn't occur to me until halfway through dinner that this was the night of the event Beck had mentioned.

"The college is having a dance," I blurted, interrupting whoever was talking at the time.

The W's looked at me with amusement. "Welcome to the party, Emily," Walter said. "We all came to that conclusion about three conversations ago."

I grinned sheepishly. "I'm sorry. I think you guys have worn me out." I took a sip of water, hoping to soothe my voice to a casual tone. "Did anyone happen to see where it was being held?"

"I think it's in that old theater," June said.

"Why?" Mel demanded.

"Well, dancing is one thing we haven't done this week," I suggested.

Mel squinted at me. "I thought you were tired."

But the W's were chattering excitedly about learning the latest steps, and June leaned over and whispered something in Mel's ear, causing her expression to change to a sly smile. "Okay," she said, mostly to June, but the rest of us took it as agreement.

Techno music was blaring at high volume as we neared the entrance to the theater. The admission was ten dollars for a single and fifteen for couples. To my surprise, Mel paid with a fifty and told the girl at the ticket window the keep the change. I was grateful, as this week of continuous birthday functions had depleted my scheduled entertainment budget for the next two months. The college had set up bistro style tables on the edge of the dance floor, and we found an empty one near the middle of the room. Mel went with the W's to get us drinks, and I tried to look for Beck without being obvious about it. She wasn't hard to find. All I had to do was look for the best dancer in the room.

Provocative and sexy as hell without being nasty, Beck infused every move with power and grace. She was dressed more formally than I'd seen, in tight black jeans and a starched white collared shirt with a bolo tie. She and a boy I thought was Brick were dancing together. Well, they were dancing in the same area of the dance floor but not exactly together.

"Do you see your friend?" June asked.

I nodded, gesturing casually with my head. June followed the direction of my gaze, and after a minute, she turned back, smiling. "She's really good. And she's hot."

I sighed. "Yes. To both." Stupidly happy to see her, I had to work to stop smiling.

The guys and Mel returned with our drinks, and during a break in the music, I cast a glance at some of the other tables. To the far left, I recognized Beck's other friend, Jonesy. I looked again and saw he was talking to Peyton. "Shit," I mumbled.

"What?" Mel asked.

"Peyton is over there talking to one of Beck's friends."

Walter gasped. "That bitch from the college?" I nodded.

"Who cares?" Mel scoffed. "The video's gone, and there's nothing she can do to us."

"Impersonating a police officer is a crime, even in North Carolina."

Mel paled slightly, and Walter asked, "What about impersonating a lawyer?"

His frightened expression made me laugh. "Only if you make money out of it. I think."

"We should get out of here," June said, nervously glancing at Mel. "I don't want you to get in trouble, baby."

Mel glanced in Peyton's direction. "I doubt she would recognize me. My hair was different, and I was wearing a uniform and shades."

But she would certainly recognize the guys, and seeing Mel with them would give it all away. The music started again, and a group of students walked past us heading for the exit, leaving an empty table on the far side of the room. "Let's move over there and see what happens," I said, and began leading our group to the far wall. I wouldn't be able to see Beck as clearly, which was probably for the best, but I wanted one last glimpse. Our movement must have drawn Beck's attention because she had stopped dancing and was staring in our direction. Even from this distance, I could see her eyes go wide with disbelief. As our group continued walking away, she began moving toward us, pushing past the other dancers. I hesitated, not sure what to do. I'd wanted to see her but not be seen by her.

She called my name, twice, and my friends stopped. I turned slowly to face her, not sure how she would feel about my being there, but the delight on her face made me let out a quick sigh of relief as she reached us.

"Emily," she said, somewhat breathless. "I can't believe you're here." She searched my face as if still not absolutely certain it was me. Her hair was slightly damp, and her body glistened with a light veneer of sweat. Would she look like that after sex?

"Hi, Beck." I tried to keep my tone casual. "We were in the neighborhood having dinner. I hope you don't mind if we crash your party."

"You're not crashing. I invited you. Remember?"

I could feel the stares of everyone else in our group. "Uh, yes, that's right. You did, didn't you?"

Her eyes never wavered from mine. "Dance with me." She took my hands and began pulling me onto the dance floor.

"No," I said, laughing as she walked backward without looking around, pulling on my hands alternatively, making me sway. "I can't dance to this music."

"What are you talking about?" she said, with a teasing grin. "You already are."

When I looked back, Mel and Walter were already making their way to the table I'd indicated. William and June had fond expressions on their faces, and he made a quick shooing motion.

"Okay," I said. "But let's move away some more."

Beck nodded and kept a firm hold on one hand as we made our way through the jumble of exuberantly moving bodies. Somehow, she was able to catch the attention of the DJ and raised two fingers, like a peace sign. The volume of the music decreased, and the frantic beat slowed. The DJ crooned something about taking it down a notch, and invited all the "friends, lovers, sweethearts, romancers, and wannabe couples" out onto the dance floor.

As the crowd moved around us, I cocked my head. "Were you thinking we could be one of those?"

The corner of her mouth crooked, but her gaze was intense. "I think that's up to you."

I was casting about for a reply when the chords of Christina Perri's "A Thousand Years" began playing. A sweet and terribly romantic song from one of the teen vampire movies, it had gotten so much radio play a few years ago even I knew the chorus.

I startled when Beck's hand enclosed my waist. She leaned toward me and murmured, "Don't be scared, Emily. It's only a dance."

Chapter Nine

She took my other hand in a classic dance pose and pulled me toward her as she stepped away. "We're doing this"—she guided me away and stepped forward—"and this." I blinked, and she added, "With an occasional turn or something." At my glazed expression, she laughed. "Ready?"

I realized the music had reached the first chorus, and other couples were already dancing around us. I took in a breath and squeezed my eyes shut as we began to move. I knew instantly this was more than a dance. It was like flying. And it was like foreplay. When Beck turned us for the first time, my eyes opened, and I stumbled.

"You're doing great, Emily. Don't think. Just feel it," Beck said, her lips brushing my ear.

My breath hitched as my body seemed to relax in her arms of its own accord. Her hand moved up my side and onto my back, bringing us closer. It felt so right that I closed my eyes again and did exactly what she said. I let myself feel. I felt the motion of her body and the warmth of her hand through the thin material of my shirt. I felt the pulse of the music and the way our steps matched it. For that brief moment, I welcomed the feeling of enchantment, of immersing myself in the romance of a dance with this wonderful woman.

At our next turn, Beck's touch firmed as we reversed direction to avoid another couple, and I followed willingly. Never had I let another person completely control my movements. The few other times I'd danced at a club, it had been as one of two people moving separately in different spaces. This was as if our bodies had merged, and we were one entity, one being, mind and heart, working together.

I shifted my hand from Beck's shoulder to her back before lightly caressing her neck. I heard her moan quietly, and it made my head spin.

"Thank you for this, Emily," she whispered, her cheek lightly touching mine.

"Since I saw you in the kitchen that first day, I wondered what it would be like to dance with you," I admitted, though in reality, I'd been thinking about something even more intimate. As I was now…again.

Her face lit with that dazzling smile, and we came to a careful stop as the music ended. A few guitar chords announced a new song. "Could we try one more?" she asked. The accompaniment sounded more country, and I shrugged uncertainly. "We're now gonna do three steps instead of two," she said. "I may twirl myself or you a time or two, but you keep going, no matter what."

"Okay," I said, sounding doubtful, and we were off.

She showed me how to shuffle my feet, and I realized she was wearing boots instead of her usual sandals or tennis shoes. That explained why we were eye to eye instead of me being a little taller as usual. I mimicked her steps, feeling how the rhythm seemed perfect for the music as my body found a natural sway.

We went from facing each other to dancing side by side before she pushed me gently away and twirled me into her arms again. We glided along for a few seconds, and then she was behind me, mirroring my steps.

"Beck?" I asked, ready to panic.

"Keep going," she said, pressing herself against me. She lowered her chin onto my shoulder, and I caught a whiff of some enticing cologne. I closed my eyes again, feeling where her hands crossed over my belly, directly under my breasts. That awareness made my nipples tighten, and I was sure she could see them. We swung out of that pose and came face-to-face again, but our pelvises touched briefly, and I lost count of my steps. She must have as well because she circled us out of the flow of dancers, and we stopped for a second. "Are you okay?"

"Yes, I…" I couldn't compose myself, but it wasn't the dancing. "Can we try this without moving around so much for a second?" We were on the side opposite of both groups of our friends.

"Absolutely," she said, pulling me to her. As much as I'd tried to avoid any physical connection with her in the past, I was now certain she wanted me, and that awareness sent my nerve endings into overdrive. We were barely moving, our bodies as close as they could be with clothes on. My mind was busily supplying me with images of remedying that situation when Beck put her lips against my hair. "I knew you'd feel like this," she whispered, and I tightened my arms around her neck.

Maybe just this once, I told myself, tucking my head against her. No one needed to get hurt if it was only one night. We'd both regain our senses in the morning, and things could go on the way they'd always been. Two seconds later, I barely managed to hold in an audible snort. *As if.* Instinctively I knew Beck wasn't the sort of person who would go back, especially from involvement like that. With me.

I raised my head, preparing to say the words that would bring us both back to reality, when a man's voice came from behind me. "Oh no, you fuckin' queer. You've gone too far this time." My eyes flew open as Beck was jerked from my arms and punched in the stomach. She doubled over, and I screamed.

Everything after that was a blur until we were all sitting in Mel's car. Well, not all. Beck's mother had been called to get her, and the local cops had all but thrown us out once order had been restored. I had refused to move until I saw Beck get to her feet, and then her buddies, Brick and Jonesy, insisted we should go.

"Famous authors sure know how to spice up an evening," William teased, but I wasn't in the mood.

"You and Beck looked amazing together," June said to me. I wasn't in the mood for that either, but she added, "I couldn't even get Mel out on the floor. She was about to get off on watching you two."

"Bullshit," Mel barked. "I was just making sure that cleaning chick didn't get carried away."

"Goddamn it, Mel. Stop calling her that," I said, oddly close to tears.

We drove the rest of the way home in silence. The plan was to have presents at Reefside, along with ice cream and cake and champagne, but no one was particularly interested after all the drama. We agreed on a post-birthday brunch tomorrow, and they dropped me at the Guest House. I was happy to be at my summer home again, but I wished Beck would come by. I wished she'd at least call and tell me she wasn't hurt. I wished...what? That she was older or lived in the city or wasn't so charming and sexy and such a good dancer?

"To hell with it," I muttered and readied myself for bed. Once there, I found myself still aroused with thoughts of her, and I rolled onto my back, letting my hand fall between my legs. I worked myself gently, without the usual rough insistence of bringing on an orgasm. I was slow and careful as I imagined Beck would be, and came easily, quietly. Afterward, I worried the violence I'd witnessed would trigger a nightmare, but instead I dreamed of music and flying.

A pulsing bell signaled the end of the flight. I was waiting for the announcement about putting my tray table away when I realized it was my phone, and I was at the beach, not in the air. I didn't even look at the caller ID before I answered, peering groggily at the gray light outside.

"I'm sorry to bother you, Mrs. Harris, but Beck wouldn't rest until I promised to call you first thing."

"Is she all right?" I asked, almost breathless.

After a slight pause, Mrs. Janser said, "She won't be able to come by today. But if there's anything you need, I can—"

"I'm fine, Mrs. Janser. But is she badly hurt?"

Another hesitation, this one shorter but still noticeable. "She'll be fine in another day or two, I'm sure. And you can manage until then?"

"Yes, whenever. I feel terrible about last night. Tell her…" Now I faltered. "She doesn't have to return to work immediately, but I'd like her to call me when she's up to it."

"I'll tell her," Mrs. Janser said, and I thought she was about to hang up. "Beck told us the fight was her fault for stopping on the wrong part of the dance floor," she added. "Apparently, the school had gotten those boys to agree they'd each stay on their own sides, and she violated that. Is that what happened?"

"I didn't know about an agreement, but if she said so, I'm sure that must be it. We were dancing, and I asked to stop. I wasn't aware there were sides, or I would have said something. I don't…I'm not normally much of a dancer, and I was somewhat winded, I guess." That wasn't far from the truth.

After another stillness, she said, "It was you dancing with her?"

Shit. Had I broken some implicit confidence between us? But I'd already spoken, so I forged on. "Yes, at that moment. I had dropped by with my friends from Reefside. We were going to all dance once or twice and leave. But I happened to see Beck on the floor with someone else, and she saw me and asked me to dance."

"I see," she said, and the tone of her voice made me think she actually might. I swallowed, waiting to see if anything else was forthcoming. "I'll let her know you asked about her," she said finally.

"Please have her call me." I repeated what I really wanted, figuring it was too late for subtlety.

"I'll ask her," she amended tersely and hung up.

It was before dawn early, but I'd never get back to sleep now. I made coffee and carried a cup out onto the deck. I would miss this, I realized, watching the day arrive to the soft breaking of the waves and the calling of the seabirds flying across my gorgeous view of the sunrise. There was a kind of peace here, some sense of comfort I could feel even through my worry and my confusion. As soon as Beck returned, I was going to have her take me to the beach. Perhaps I could live a little closer in, like life was at my feet instead of a safe distance away. I still questioned if that readiness should include any more of Beck or not, but I was certain this place, and the experiences here, had altered my perceptions. I hoped it was for the better. And along with my mixed feelings about my return to the city in less than two months, I wondered if these changes would be permanent, or if, like everything else good in my life, they'd vanish with the next sunrise.

By the evening of the second day, I was pacing impatiently, unable to write, read, or watch a movie on my computer. I decided I would call tomorrow, even if I had to talk to Beck's mother again. At the sound of her scooter engine at dusk, I rushed to the door but then stopped myself. *Cool it.* Yeah, I needed to be cool. Not cold, though. No. Relaxed. "Oh hi," I'd say. "I'm glad you stopped by."

But when five minutes had passed and she hadn't come up, I began to fret. What could she be doing? I peeked out the window, seeing the light on in the big garage. Of course, she was checking on the damn cats. What was I? Just the person who'd gotten so aroused by merely dancing with her, that I— I cut myself off when the light went off, and a shadowy form moved to the stairs. I had grabbed my laptop and was reclining on the couch, but I could hear her footsteps were heavy and slow. When she tapped on the door, I called for her to come in. She was wearing a hoodie, which wasn't her usual style, and the way she slouched made it cover half her face.

"Hi, Emily. I know it's kinda late, and I can't stay long. The thing is, I needed…I wanted to make sure you were okay." This all came out in a rush, though her voice was hoarse and almost hollow sounding.

"It's not that late, Beck." I stood and gestured toward the couch. "I'm fine, and I'm very glad to see you. Come sit."

She swayed slightly but didn't move. "No, I gotta go soon. But you…you got home okay…uh, after?"

"Yes, fine. Mel took me. They made us go, Beck. I wanted to check on you, but they wouldn't let me." I took a step toward her, but when she flinched at the movement, I stopped. "Are you hurt? Did you see a doctor yet?"

She coughed, and her eyes closed. When she opened them again, they were watery with pain. "I'll be okay. Needed to see…my phone got broken, so I had to come over."

"Oh, Beck. I'm sorry about your phone. Why don't you let me drive you into town tomorrow, and we can get you another one?"

She shook her head slowly and swayed again. Troubled, I took another step and another, close enough to reach her but stopped short. "I'm not supposed to leave the house. But you…I was worried…" She trailed off again.

"Would you like some water?" I asked, and she nodded carefully. As glad as I was to see her, it was obvious she was hurting and certainly shouldn't have driven that damn scooter, much less come all the way here. When I handed her the glass, she drank deeply, tipping her head back, and the hoodie shifted. I saw what looked to be a deep red welt on her cheek. I hadn't remembered her getting hit in the face. From what I recalled, she had fallen after the first punch and curled into a ball. That boy had kicked her once in the ribs before I'd thrown myself at him, knocking him off balance, and he'd stumbled and gone down, taking me with him. After that, it was pandemonium, but I suppose anything could have happened. I was on the floor trying to avoid getting stepped on until Walter lifted me up.

"Let me see that," I said, pushing at the top. She tried to jerk away, but the movement made the hood slip off, and I got my first good look at her. Besides the red welt on her face, her bottom lip was split, and the other eye was turning black. "My God, Beck. Oh, sweetheart, come here and have a seat."

Ignoring my own inner grimace at the repeat of that endearment, I pulled her toward the couch. I felt her resist for a second before she followed me, her head bowed. She settled herself with a shudder, biting her lip. I hated seeing her suffer, but I wanted, needed, to talk to her. "Tell me how this happened."

"Doesn't matter." She took another sip of water.

"It matters to me," I said, resting my fingertips lightly on her free hand.

She said nothing for a few seconds. Then the undamaged part of her mouth lifted slightly, making a crooked grin that almost resembled a leer. "That last dance was worth it."

"Beck." I shook my head but I couldn't help smiling. "Nothing is worth you being hurt like this."

"That's where you're wrong, Emily." Her voice was so quiet I could barely hear her. Abruptly, she began coughing and holding her sides. The hacking sound ended with a moan.

"What did the doctor say?" I asked, trying to control my panic. Her face went slack. It took me a few seconds to understand. She hadn't been. "Jesus, Beck. You need to see someone. You could have broken ribs or a concussion…or both."

She sighed, stopping just short of touching the side of her head. "Yeah, since my brain got hurt once before, Mama's kinda worried. They think I'm in bed, so I gotta get home before—" She stopped abruptly, giving me a quick sideways look. "Could you give me a hand up?"

But for that quick glance, I might have missed it. I replayed the previous sentence, crossing my arms as I regarded her carefully. "Home before what?"

Her brows drew into an angry look. "Mama was right. I shouldn't have come over here. Forget it. I have to go, and I can manage on my own." She pushed herself up, using the arm of the couch for leverage but stopped, bending over in obvious pain.

I stood, and when she straightened, I took hold of her shoulders from behind, pulling her against me. "Answer me. Tell me and I'll let go. Home before what?"

I expected her to fight, but she slumped against me. "Home before Erik wakes up."

I heard tears in her voice. I wrapped my arms carefully around her, caressing her chest, hoping it wouldn't hurt. "Why? Because you're not supposed to be out?"

She made a sound, but I couldn't tell if it was yes or no. I stopped moving. "Am I hurting you?" I detected a slight shake of her head, and a teardrop fell on my hand where it rested across her. Carefully turning her toward me, I felt her tremble as she buried her face on my shoulder. Her hair smelled different, musty and with the faint salty odor of blood. I tried to put it together, her unexplained injuries and her worry—or was it fear?—about getting home soon. *Oh no.* "Did Erik do this to you, Beck? Do you have to get back so he won't hurt you again?"

She gave a low moan, shaking harder. She might have nodded, but I couldn't be absolutely sure. No matter. I ran my hands gently across her back. "Listen. You're not going anywhere. You're staying here tonight and for as long as you need to. You're going to see a doctor tomorrow, and I don't want any argument about it."

"I can't," she managed croak. "My mama…"

"Does he hit her too?" I asked, keeping my tone as neutral as I could.

"I don't think so. Or not that I know of. But what if—"

"No. No what if. I'll call her in a minute and tell her you're here and you're staying. That's final."

She swayed again, and I carefully tightened my hold. She said something that might have been "hurts" but I couldn't tell for sure. And it didn't matter. I'd already decided to call the W's, who always had a pharmacy's worth of pills, and get some pain relief for her until I could get a doctor out here tomorrow. "I think you'd feel better if you could get cleaned up. Would you like to try that?"

She sniffed and drew away slightly, wiping her face. "Yeah, I would. At home I couldn't manage…" A flush rose in her cheeks. "You know, uh, undressing and all."

"I'd be glad to help you with that." I was sincere, but the words sounded suspect once they were out.

For the first time that night, I got a full smile that reached her eyes. "I'm glad you'd be glad."

I shook my head fondly and turned her toward my bathroom. "Come on, you." Once there, I turned on the water, listening but not watching as she unzipped her jeans and slowly pulled them off.

After a few more seconds, she whimpered. I turned to see her holding herself again. "Emily, I can't lift my arms enough to get this shirt off."

I stepped close to her. "Let me help. I'll try not to hurt you." She nodded hesitantly. I pulled one sleeve and then the other until she could pull both elbows in, arms close to her sides. Her face glistened with sweat from the effort, but I was able to pull the shirt off over her head.

She wasn't wearing a bra, and I caught a glimpse of small but nicely rounded breasts with pale pink nipples before I reached into the shower to check the temperature. Making sure to look her in the face when I turned back, I said, "Let me know if this is too hot for you. But I want you to breathe the warm air as deeply as you can."

She nodded again and stepped past me, groaning as the water hit her. I closed the shower door and stepped into the bedroom, rummaging around in my drawer until I found a long sleepshirt with a three-quarter buttoned opening. Beck called my name, her voice tinged with agitation. "I'm sorry to bother you, but I can't reach to wash my hair."

I blinked, considering my options. Should I get in clothed or naked? Either would be difficult, though in very different ways. Then inspiration struck. "Hang on. I'll be right there."

I pulled on the one-piece swimsuit I'd bought for the beach but had yet to wear. When I stepped in behind her, Beck looked around at me before shaking her head. "No fair," she said, her injured lip sticking out in a pout.

I tried to ignore how cute she was and forced myself not to look at her body. Instead, I grabbed the shampoo and squeezed some onto my palm. "This is a medicinal shower. You behave."

Beck groaned again when I began lathering her hair, carefully massaging the scalp as I went. My fingers found a raised, thick crease under the longer side of her hair. I figured that to be the old injury, but when I touched a swelling knot above her ear, she flinched. "Did this happen at the dance or after?"

She eased away from my touch, stepping under the water to rinse off. I noted the slightest tinge of pink to the water, confirming there had been blood. I ground my teeth, telling myself it didn't matter. The point was, she was here now and safe from any further violence. I began reaching for the conditioner before it occurred to me that her short, straight hair probably didn't need it. "I'll do a better job in a couple of days. Right now, I want to get you into bed."

Beck turned to face me, letting her gaze drift over my wet, low-cut suit. I felt extra heat on my face, and my self-control slipped. I followed the streams of water sluicing down her body, over her small breasts and into the darker tangle of hair between her legs. She was exactly as I'd felt when we were dancing—tight and solid. She looked strong, without the willowy, delicate build of some younger women, but I admired the distinctly feminine curves of her hips and breasts. Her tanned coloring was only a shade lighter where a swimsuit would have been. She grinned and leaned toward me. Then her eyes closed, and she swayed again. "You would say that now, when I'm kinda…" she murmured, swallowing before she trailed off and put her hand on the wall as if for support. "Under the weather," she finished, drooping slightly.

I reached for her, steadying her with my arms under hers. "Come on." We stepped out of the water, and I grabbed a towel for her, propping her against the counter while I dried her as best I could. I pulled the sleep shirt over her head. She roused herself enough to get her arms in while I quickly dried myself. As I walked her toward her bedroom, she apologized over and over again. "Please stop, Beck. You have nothing to be sorry for."

"I shouldn't have come," she mumbled. "Shouldn't be staying, making you take care of me."

"That's where you're wrong," I said, echoing her earlier comment. I sat her on the small guest bed and leaned over her as I eased her onto her side. "You are where you should be, and this is exactly what you should be doing." She coughed a little as I swung her legs over. "I'll get you something to drink in a second. Do you feel sick to your stomach?"

"Not much. Just really…tired." Her eyes were already closed.

"Good. Rest is the best thing for you."

I was closing the door when I heard her whisper, "You're the best thing for me."

I called William before I changed, giving him the least information possible while still asking him for some pain pills. I talked to Mel and repeated the same story with a different request. I'd barely gotten into my sweats when there was a knock on the door. Handing me a small bottle, William gestured. "The blue ones she can take now. They're anti-inflammatory. The white ones are stronger, and she'll need something in her stomach," he said, sounding very authoritative. "And they'll make her sleep."

"I appreciate it, Dr. Porter," I said, and he giggled.

"Who knew I'd come to the beach and become a lawyer and a doctor in one summer? Oh, and Mel says to tell you the real doctor will be here between ten and twelve o'clock tomorrow morning."

I kissed his cheek. "I mean it, William. Thank you. And please thank Mel for me."

"She'll want that kind of thanks in person, you know." He winked.

"Tell her I'll deliver tomorrow afternoon after I know more," I offered.

After I'd taken my own quick shower and gotten into my pajamas, I poured some milk and carried one of the blue pills into her bedroom. I managed to rouse her enough to swallow the pill while I adjusted the covers and tried to make her as comfortable as possible. Beck finished about half the glass. Satisfied, I helped her lie down. "A doctor is coming in the morning," I whispered. "I'll wake you in time to get ready."

A frown creased her face. "The doctor comes here? To the house?"

"Yes. Just for you." I smiled.

"Wow," Beck said softly, her eyelids closing.

Even though I'd insisted she stay, I'd been worried about having Beck there overnight. If I had a nightmare and screamed myself awake, what would she think? I hoped she'd be too tired to hear anything, and perhaps tomorrow, the doctor would give her some other drugs to help her sleep. I'd been asleep for several hours when a noise penetrated my consciousness. I thought it was the door to my childhood bedroom opening, the usual start to the horrors of my nights. When nothing more happened, I started to sit up before realizing it was the toilet flushing and filling in the other bathroom. I listened for any further sounds, but hearing none, fell asleep again.

I turned over in the bright morning light, feeling surprisingly well-rested. When I glanced at the clock, I understood why. It was nearly nine o'clock. I didn't bother with makeup but hurried to dress and make coffee. I decided Beck would want something fairly bland, so I made instant oatmeal and carried it in on a tray, along with the coffee and some orange juice. She was already sitting up, and she broke into a grin when she saw me. I was relieved to see her eyes looked clearer and less pain-filled.

"It's taken me a few minutes to figure out where I was," she said. "I was hoping this was the right guess."

I put the tray on the nightstand. "What gave it away? The smell of my fabulous cooking?"

She nodded. "There's something about coffee I associate with you," she said, running her tongue over her lips.

My face warmed from both the words and the gesture. "That might be the nicest thing anyone ever said to me."

She looked at me for a long moment. "Then you haven't been with very nice people."

"I haven't always been a very nice person," I said slowly. She started to shake her head before taking in a sharp breath. She was still hurt, and I needed to change the subject. After all, we were about to have a visitor. "Eat your breakfast. The doctor will be here soon."

I started to go, but her voice stopped me. "Thank you, Emily. Thank you for being so kind. I don't know how I'm going to repay you, but I'll think of something."

"You just concentrate on getting better. You have a contest to win."

❖

"Are you really a doctor?" Beck asked, a touch of awe in her voice that gave me an unpleasant sting inside.

The physician was admittedly nice-looking, with shoulder-length dark hair over dark eyes and that confident but not arrogant manner powerful women sometimes have. When I greeted her at the door I'd wondered too, thinking she might be a PA since she looked relatively young, though she had a solid build, similar to Beck's. However, the card she'd handed me clearly stated her MD credentials after her name, Leonor Bastos.

"Yes, I really am." She smiled. "Would you like one of my cards too?"

"Sure," Beck said excitedly. She was lying on her back as the doctor examined the bruises on her face. Dr. Bastos pulled another card out of her pocket and presented it with a flourish. "It's cool how you come to people's houses," Beck said, staring at the card as she ran her fingers over the embossed letters. "Do you do that for free?"

The doctor laughed lightly. "No, I'm afraid not. I charge a home visit fee to cover the cost of gas and wear and tear on my car."

"Oh." Beck fell silent.

"Don't worry about that," I said from behind the doctor where I was leaning on the doorjamb, but neither of them turned to my voice. "It's covered."

"Are you okay to stand up?" Dr. Bastos asked. "I need to check your ribs."

I'd given her a report on Beck's possible injuries before bringing her into the small second bedroom. When Beck winced as she pressed on a particular area, the doctor said something that sounded like "this sculpe," which I thought might be some medical term. But then Beck replied with some other foreign sounding phrase, and their expressions of mutual delight made me oddly uncomfortable.

The doctor warmed her stethoscope with her palms for a few seconds before listening to Beck breathe and watching her chest rise and fall. "*Primo*," she said, rolling the R. "Your ribs are bruised but not broken, though I know they're still painful. You must remember to keep breathing deeply, even if it hurts a little, because pneumonia is a worry with damaged ribs. *Compreendo?*"

The last word sounded like Spanish. Beck replied with another phrase that included what might have been the word *doctor*. I was about to ask what was going on when Bastos gestured for Beck to sit before joining her on the bed. "Your mother and father?" she asked.

"Just my papa. Vincente Reynolds, but everyone called him Vince. You?"

Dr. Bastos nodded. "Both parents. Very strict. At an early age, it was determined I would go into medicine. Luckily for me, I loved it."

"I would have been happy to fish like my papa did. But he died when his ship went down. My mama had to work, and I started working with her as soon as I could. We clean houses."

The doctor gently touched the top of Beck's head. "'A good mind possesses a kingdom,'" she said. "Speaking of which, you may also have a mild concussion. There was a previous injury as well?" Beck nodded. "Rest, ice the ribs and the face." She leaned in. "And try to stay out of trouble, *primo*."

"Yes, ma'am."

She patted Beck's uninjured cheek and stood. "See me out, please?" she asked me, and we walked toward the door together. "I think she'll be fine in a few days. Give her Advil or Aleve every few hours if the pain gets bad or before bedtime. She works for you, is that correct?"

"Yes, part-time. And it's fine for her to take some time off." I lowered my voice. "I'm sure most of her trouble is at home, so I told her she could stay here if she wants to, though I'll only be around for about six more weeks or so."

Dr. Bastos raised a brow. "That's very generous of you."

I shrugged, hoping I didn't look guilty. "I don't like seeing nice kids get hurt." Perhaps stressing the age difference between us would lessen any suspicion on her part.

She studied me for another few seconds. "This visit is on me," she said finally. "But I'll have to charge you if I need to come back."

"That's very generous of *you*, doctor."

"I feel the same way about nice kids." She opened the door. "Good luck, Ms. Harris."

Beck was lying down again when I came in. I sat on the bed where the doctor had been as if wanting to reclaim that space. "What language were you were speaking with the doctor?" I asked.

"Portuguese," she said. "My papa's parents were Portuguese, and he taught me some."

"What does *primo* mean? It sounds like it might be first or mainly, something like that."

"No, it means cousin. We all sort of claim each other."

An odd feeling of lacking swept over me. No one had wanted to claim me after Abby. As if reading my mind, Beck asked, "What about your folks? You never talk about your family."

My stomach constricted, and I heard the harshness in my voice when I answered. "My father was a minister. He lost his faith and left our family when I was ten. My mother was a minister's wife. She lost her mind after she lost her husband and couldn't take care of herself or anyone else at that point. Does that answer your question?"

Beck pushed herself to a sitting position. She reached over and took my hand. "I'm so sorry, Emily. It must have been really, really hard for you, losing both parents like that."

I looked over to see her eyes brimming with tears. For a wonderful few seconds, I let myself enjoy the warmth of her touch and the graciousness of her sympathy. It was surprisingly comforting, and I tried to imagine what it would be like to tell her about the most profound loss of my life. The one that precipitated all the others and even made me lose myself. The one that not another soul in my life—not Jackson, not Mel—knew about. God, how I hated thinking of those words as memories because it was tacitly acknowledging Abby was…

"Did you have any brothers or sisters?" Beck asked as if reading my mind.

I knew from parents to siblings was a natural progression of questions, but I still wondered at this young woman's willingness to ask the questions that few people did. Usually the callousness in my tone when the subject of family arose discouraged any further exploration. For a few terrifying seconds, I imagined trying to answer. Would there be any relief in saying, *I did, but she's...* Quickly I stood, pulling my hand away from her. There wasn't and would never be any consolation for me because I didn't deserve it. I lost that when I let someone take her. "I'd prefer not to go through any further interrogation, if you don't mind. I'll make some lunch if you're hungry. Otherwise, I think you should rest." I turned away and walked toward her doorway.

"I guess I'll rest first," I heard her say.

She sounded bewildered, but I couldn't bring myself to look around. "Fine. Call if you need anything."

"Okay." Her voice was rough, presumably muffled by the pillow. Or that was what I told myself.

Chapter Ten

Beck was up that evening, talking to her mother on my cell phone and helping me with—okay, mostly making—dinner. I kept urging her to take it easy while she insisted cooking *was* easy. "So is your mother okay with this?" I asked, gesturing around the place as we were eating another tasty casserole.

"Yeah, she's fine. She'll bring some of my stuff over in the morning if that's okay with you. She seemed to think it was a good idea for me to stay over, and she said you were sweet."

"Little does she know," I said, wiggling my eyebrows. Beck started to laugh, and then her hand went to her side and she groaned. I reached over and squeezed her shoulder. "I'm sorry. I'll try to contain my wonderful sense of humor until you're healed."

"No, don't," she said, forcing herself to breathe deeply. "I'd rather this hurt some if it means you're being funny instead of sad."

"I'm usually funny, aren't I?"

She fingered the cut on her lip. "No, I think you are usually sad, at least inside. But I'm not, and that's why we get along so well. The thing is, we both know there are sad times, and you help me remember you can let yourself feel them sometimes and still be okay, and I remind you that it's okay to not feel them sometimes too."

I stared, only vaguely aware my mouth was slightly open. "You…" I trailed off, not certain of exactly what I wanted to say. Before, I would have snapped something angry and defensive, like "You don't know anything about me." But now I wasn't sure how the Emily I wanted to be should react. Beck turned her head away momentarily as if anticipating a blow—verbal, if not physical—before quickly finishing the last of her dinner. She had this way of making life seem remarkably simple. Or maybe it actually was, and I had a tendency to overthink and therefore overcomplicate everything. I rose and collected my plate and silverware. She wiped her mouth quickly, gathered her utensils, and made to stand, but I put my hand on her shoulder.

"No," I said firmly, making sure I didn't use any force in my touch. "I'm doing dishes from now on, and that's final. You stay there or go sit on the couch." I leaned in, intending to buss the top of her head, but she lifted her face, and my lips touched the skin of her forehead. I pressed lightly and moved away. "You are a remarkable person, and I'm glad you're here." I meant it, I truly did, though the worrier in me wondered if that would still be true in a week or so, when she was healed and puttering around my house every day.

By the time I'd done the dishes and tidied up, she was sitting on the couch after going briefly to her room. "You've been busy," she said quietly, pointing to the found jar. I'd come to treat it like the visual diary she'd said it could be, adding mementoes from the various birthday adventures and the old lock from the second garage space. "Here," she said, and dropped in a torn dance ticket.

I joined her without comment, thinking to read or perhaps watch something on my laptop. As I thumbed through my options, she slumped against me, the weight of her head settling on my shoulder. Motionless, I forced myself not to color this with anything from my past or find a future for it. I just let myself feel like I had when we were dancing. Had I truly changed so much that I could enjoy a casual touch? Or was I unable to separate the fact that it was Beck, hurt but still trusting, who relaxed against the damaged woman she'd allowed to become her refuge?

For the next two days, Beck did little more than sleep and eat. Used to seeing her more active, I was ready to call the doctor again and wished I'd asked more questions. Like, how long before…or when should she…solely to know what was normal. I'd lost track of that marker some time ago. But the morning I woke to the smell of coffee, I knew she was going to be fine. I had no idea where such positive assurance came from, and though it was most uncommon, it was a welcome feeling.

Already dressed, Beck greeted my sleepy appearance with a shy curve to her lips. "I'm going back to work today."

I wanted her to take another day to recover, but I didn't want to challenge her. She needed to be the one to make the decision, even though I wanted to change her thinking. I let my face fall, pretending to study the floor. "Okay," I said, being sure to sound sad, not angry.

She took a step toward me. "I feel much better, honestly."

"Oh, I'm sure you do. But I was going to ask…" I let my voice trail off, feeling a tinge of guilt about manipulating her.

"What?" When I shook my head, she touched my arm. "Please, Emily. I owe you big time. I'll do anything for you that I can."

This was one of the things I liked about Beck. She didn't make wild promises like *I'll do anything for you*. It was *anything for you that I can*. "Well, it's just that I haven't spent any time on the beach yet, and I was hoping you'd be my guide."

Her eyes widened. "You haven't gone to the beach at all?"

"I told you, I'm not very adventurous. I wanted to go with a local authority." Before she could deny any level of expertise, I added, "And with a friend who wouldn't tease me about all I don't know. But listen, I don't want to get you in trouble with your mother for not working."

She went to the window and looked out. "It's a perfect day." She turned with a smile that made me believe something awesome was coming. "And now that I think of it, I believe you are currently on Mama's good side. So if I said you needed a favor…"

I held out my cell phone with a wink. "I need."

❖

After a quick bowl of cereal and fruit, Beck packed a picnic basket. I put my bathing suit on under my shorts and coverup, having no intention of anyone seeing me in it, though I recalled quite clearly that Beck already had. The look on her face—well, until she'd almost collapsed from her concussion—had been hard to forget. We started down a path that led directly to the beach, opposite my normal route to Reefside. She carried the basket in one hand, the other she had stuffed into the pocket of her tight cutoffs. Having already caught myself admiring her ass twice on the way to the beach, I gave myself permission to slip my arm through her free one once we reached the water. She turned to me with her eyes warm, and I realized how much I liked that expression. "Walk first, then eat. Okay?"

"Today, you're in charge, Beck. Whatever you say goes."

She took in a breath and lowered her gaze. "That's a big responsibility, but I'll do my best."

I brushed the long side of her hair from her face. "Don't worry. Show me this world that you know so well, and it will be wonderful."

"Because it is?" she asked carefully.

I nodded. "Because you see it that way, yes."

Looking out at the water, I thought it could be wonderful anyway, but seeing it as she did would make it all that much better. Already barefoot, she pulled a trash sack from the picnic basket and talked me out of my sandals. The sand was warm on my feet where we stopped, and she pointed out how the different textures had different temperatures, which was determined by the amount of moisture in each. The dark strip that looked like dirt from my deck turned out to be a variety of shells and other marine elements Beck referred to as the strandline.

I wasn't particularly surprised she also knew the names of everything that had collected there: distinguishing pieces of whelks from murex and olive shell from augers. I picked up several scallops of vastly different design and coloring, and when I glanced at Beck, she was smiling broadly. "This is exactly what your found jar is for," she said. "I think it's human nature to want to hold on to beauty, don't you?"

"And we hold on to pain as well," I responded almost automatically.

Her face dropped into a somber expression. "I guess that's true too."

We walked quietly for a time, seagulls flying past, while I mentally kicked myself for sounding so fucking pessimistic. I would have said realistic, but my words had sounded depressing even to my own ears against the backdrop of such a lovely day and such pleasant company.

Beck lifted a dark, rectangular shape with curled, whip-like strings protruding stiffly from each corner. Turning to face me, she said, "This is the egg casing for a skate, which looks a lot like a stingray, but it doesn't sting. Some people call it a mermaid's purse, some say devil's purse. I can imagine which you would prefer, but I think we should focus on the beauty today. What do you think?"

God, I wanted to kiss her. I wanted to hold her and thank her for giving me a chance to amend my negative ways, at least for the moment. I settled for squeezing her arm as I cleared my throat. "I think the mermaid's purse should go in the found jar too."

She gave me her incredible smile, and slipped her hand in mine. Farther along the beach, she gestured at the dunes. "Did you know those are manmade?"

Beck in the role of guide was surprisingly alluring, and I wanted to encourage it. "No, I didn't." We sat cross-legged, facing each other on the two towels she spread out, and quickly devoured almost everything in the picnic basket.

Beck gestured at the nearby waves while I finished the last cookie. "These are barrier islands, which means they're not anchored by rock like other types of islands. You're sitting on what started during the last ice age, when the sea level was lower, and the coastline was much farther out. The banks were real dunes then, but the sea level began to rise, and they became sand bars instead. At a lower sea level, the banks grew again, breaching the surface, and as rain leached the salt from the sand, beach grass and other vegetation took root, helping to secure and grow the land. The Outer Banks are only about four to five thousand years old."

I stared. "That's fascinating. I had no idea."

Beck wiggled a bit, clearly pleased I was interested. "And I'll tell you something else. We're moving."

"You're moving from Windsom Edge?" I asked, confused but not totally surprised by her apparent change of topic.

"No." She laughed. "The Outer Banks are moving. Using storms and winds, the ocean moves the sand, and it pushes us west. You can't feel it, of course, but folks can see the changes in their lifetimes. This place is very much alive."

I blinked. "How do you know all this?"

"My papa taught me. Once we had our catch in, he'd ring the bell for school and we'd have a lesson about where we live." Her expression lost some of its enthusiasm. "I learned much more from him than I ever did in school. Except maybe from Mrs. Parrish. And now Mr. Howell."

I lay on my back, taking stock as I stared at the wisps of clouds being blown across the blue sky. I was lounging on the beach, listening to the waves of the Atlantic Ocean break only yards from me, and I wasn't at all worried. The sun felt wonderful on my body, and the breeze off the water kept the temperature pleasant. An attractive younger woman was spending time with me. Had my life somehow gotten really good? Or was I merely getting better at pretending all the potential problems didn't exist?

When she reached over and took my hand again, it felt decidedly different from how it had when I barely knew her, when the kittens had just been born. I closed my eyes, unable to stop myself from thinking of all the things I wanted to know about her. And all I didn't want her to know about me.

❖

Beck's voice was soft and sweet. "You need some more lotion." Her hand smoothed up and down each of my legs. If she'd gone a bit higher, I might have come right then. When she touched my face with fragrant, slick fingers, I reached up, wrapping my arms around her and pulled her on top of me.

"I think I'm wet enough already." God, this was a great dream. It was like I could actually feel the wonderful body that had held me when we were dancing. So fine, so hot.

Beck coughed. "This is sunscreen. To make sure you won't get sunburned."

I pressed myself into her. "How could I get a sunburn in bed, silly?"

She made a quiet sound—half pleasure, half pain—and moved her mouth close to my ear. "Emily, you fell asleep on the beach. Much as I'd love to stay right here or repeat this in your bed, I think you'll be terribly embarrassed when you wake up. If you rub this lotion into your face, I'll move onto my towel, and we can pretend this didn't happen."

I'd come fully awake after the second sentence, but I kept my eyes closed as I moved my hands to my face. The promising, arousing weight of her body disappeared. Beck announced she was going for a swim, and I peeked enough to see her shed her T-shirt before she sprinted for the water. She dove through an incoming wave before her sure, measured strokes propelled her through the breakers like a sleek sea creature. I wished I had the courage to let the ocean cool my absurd desire. Was that what Beck did on her daily swims? I rubbed the rest of the suntan lotion on my face and arms, thinking it was like masturbating compared to having Beck apply it. God, I needed to get my mind off the topic of sex, specifically sex with the woman who splashed toward me at this moment.

"You doing okay?" she asked, flicking the sand off her towel and drying off.

Was I staring? Probably. I forced myself to look at the water. "It's been such a nice day, but I think I'm ready to go back to the house."

"Sure." She gathered the picnic supplies and my towel as I stood, brushing nonexistent sand from my clothes. "But the tide's going out. Let's walk by the water this time. Maybe we'll find a few more goodies for your found jar."

We were within sight of the house when the water retreated, revealing a carpet of gloriously bright, multicolored pieces. It looked like a beautiful abstract painting but shining and more distinct. There was no way to capture it all, and I was certain it would look completely different once it was dried and out of context of the sand below it. Beck saw my admiring gaze. "It's called a shell bed." She ran her hand softly along my arm. "Even broken things have beauty when they find their place."

I swallowed hard. Her gentle touch and profound words made me feel seen. And terribly vulnerable. I searched for some sharp retort, some way to rebuild the defenses that seemed to have been washed away like a child's sand castle. And found it. "But beauty fades." I gestured at the colorful bits. "These will get ground into smaller and smaller fragments, won't they?"

"Yes," she agreed. "And they'll eventually become part of the sand. And without sand, we'd have no beach. Everything has a purpose throughout its life cycle."

Everything had a purpose? That was too easy. To be able to write off all the misery of humanity with one simple sentence? "Maybe everything in nature, but people? The evil of criminals, the cruelty of tyrants, the maliciousness of bullies? You think there's a purpose for that?"

"I wouldn't pretend to know, Emily. But if that's something you need to understand, maybe part of your purpose is to figure it out."

I started toward the house, trying to keep my fury at the forefront of the pain. I knew from my time in foster care that falling into grief would only leave my deeper wounds exposed. "What crap. I've spent most of my life trying to understand pain. But the answer is, there's no answer. There's no reason, there's no purpose, and there's no point to any of it. Life is nothing but random fucking shit, and all you can count on is you'll suffer before you die."

Beck, trailing behind me, was silent. When we reached the stairs, I remembered the shells in my pocket. "See?" I all but shrieked as I held them out. "You said it yourself. When I go, I have to give these up. So what's the point of having them at all? And why should I keep even one? It would just be a reminder of what I don't have anymore." There was no recovering all the other things in my life I'd already lost. I hadn't been strong enough to save Abby, and when everything and everyone else around me had fallen apart, I'd held myself together with anger and driven myself with guilt. Maybe in Beck's world there was reason and meaning, but I knew such ideals were simple, transient illusions. Beck's presence might sometimes tempt me to believe otherwise, in those moments when I let myself enjoy her company and especially when I saw in her eyes that she wanted to be with me. But it only took the slap of reality—of the danger of losing what little of myself I'd been able to hold on to—to know how ridiculously perilous such feelings would be. Beck couldn't free me from the constraints of my past any more than I could rescue her from an uncertain future here, and neither one of us should have wasted time trying.

Beck looked away. "I'm sorry," she said quietly. "I hoped it could be a reminder of a nice day that you enjoyed."

"Well, it isn't," I snarled and flung the handful away. Beck's flinch at my sudden motion made me feel worse, which suited me fine. She needed to be fearful, to be second-guessing whatever feelings she might have for me. Our steps to the house matched the rhythm of the words my brain was chanting: *Nothing good will come of this. Nothing good will come. Nothing good.*

She showered first, letting me wallow in my misery which, of course, was generous of her, considering. After I'd finally given in to getting clean, I found a plate of food waiting in the oven and the door to her room closed.

I was too hungry not to eat, and by the time I finished, I felt ashamed enough to stand at her door, calling, "Thank you for dinner. I'll see you tomorrow." I'd asked for her time, and until I fell into the familiar despair of my life's failures, I'd truly enjoyed the day. It wasn't her fault that joy always led me to remorse. On my way to my room, I glanced involuntarily at the found jar. A single scallop shell, the one I'd thought was the prettiest, sat atop the growing collection of memories.

Beck returned to work with her mother, but during the time she was home, she was a perfect roommate: quiet, unobtrusive, thoughtful, and clean. But she also brought an intimacy to our shared domesticity that had been completely absent from my marriage, and her sense of order settled some agitation in me and gave me an unaccustomed contentment. We both pretended my terrible temper tantrum hadn't happened and established a routine that suited us both.

My next round of edits had come in, and I felt like a split personality since my two writing personas were very different. When

Beck was gone, it was easier to slip into the surly, fear-provoking voice I'd used in all my previous work. But when she came through the door, and her face lit up when she saw me, I could easily find my newly created romantic again. I'd been working on a masquerade scene in my new novel, and as I sifted through my memories of dancing with Beck, I recalled that her phone had been broken that night. Since she hadn't given me a new number, I was certain she hadn't replaced it, and I felt oddly disturbed by the idea that I wouldn't be able to reach her if I needed to. I did some online shopping and found an iPhone 6S for less than two hundred dollars.

Pleased with myself, I returned to work. A few hours later, I became aware of a tinny murmuring and went looking for the source. Beck was asleep on the couch in the small second living area, where she'd gone so as not to disturb me. She had a clunky, older model iPad, and I thought she might have been playing games, but instead, it was giving the local weather report. Her earbuds had fallen out, and the forecaster's voice reporting tomorrow's temperatures and tides was the sound I'd heard. I assumed her interest in the weather stemmed from her time going out on her father's boat, which I knew she'd loved.

Taking advantage of the moment to watch her relaxed in sleep, I thought her face looked younger but as always, striking. Impulsively, I reached down to run my fingers along the closely shaven hair, and her lips parted in response. The warmth beneath my hand was matched by a stirring inside my chest. And lower. How could she be so kind and so sexy at the same time?

Her beautiful amber eyes opened and she blinked at me. "Am I dreaming?"

"No, Beck. You're staying with me now, remember?"

She held out her hand, and I took it, thinking she must want help up. Instead, she pulled me closer while running her other hand along my arm. "You are real," she whispered, gently pulling me toward her. For one excruciating moment, I thought she was going to kiss me, and I was stunned by how much I wanted her to. *In real trouble.* But she turned her head slightly at the last moment, rubbing her cheek against mine, a caring and tender gesture that was unlike anything I could remember experiencing. "I think the world of you, Emily," she said. Too overwhelmed to make my typical, caustic reply, I pulled back slowly and announced I was going to bed.

That night, I tossed and turned with a restlessness unrelated to my nightmares. Trying to fit Beck with one of the easy labels I used for people wasn't working. Her role in my life had grown until she spanned too many places. Like the ocean she loved, Beck was constant and enduring and yet intensely dynamic and vital. Perhaps it was that profound substance that offered me glimpses of opportunity, reminders that possibilities existed. Even the possibility of change. Of having feelings for someone that weren't simply based on impulsive allure or selfish need. At moments like these, I felt an awakening in the heart I'd so often been accused of not having, and it provoked and innervated me.

I fought for distance against the unsettling reactions to her presence lately. Well before that, if I was honest with myself. But it seemed that as I worked on becoming more of a true romance writer, my own feelings became more romantic. The impulses I'd been willing to pass off as simple attraction had deepened into more. I respected Beck, and I admired the way she went about her life. She was the model of a good daughter and a wonderful friend. The joy with which she lived her life was inspiring, even to a confirmed cynic like me. She was open and willing but strong in her core beliefs. The one time we'd talked about the incident at the dance, she told me she hated fighting, and she'd gotten her pacifist streak from her papa.

After a quiet pause she'd added, "That's one of the things that makes Erik so mad. He wants me to fight anyone who insults me. He says I'm shaming the family by 'taking it like a pussy.'"

As much as it surprised me to hear her speak of her stepfather at all, it was more shocking to hear the sneer in her voice at those last words. "What does your mother say?"

"Oh, he never gets into these conversations with me when she's around. Except he did after the dance. I don't think she realized about his temper, not really. Not until..." She ran her tongue over the healing place on her lip.

I was bothered by the notion of Beck refusing to defend herself against bullies like him and the one at the dance. Was there some part of her that doubted her own worth, as I had for so many years? "Is there nothing you'd be willing to fight for?"

"There may be," she'd said thoughtfully. "But I haven't found it yet."

The next morning, I went out on deck to watch her swim, awed by the way her body sliced through the waves with such power and ease. At moments like this, I wanted to be her. I wanted to feel the courage of my convictions so deeply that I would sacrifice my well-being. I wanted to have confidence in my strength to survive, to endure, to flourish in the face of untold adversity. Then there were the other times when all I wanted was to be with her, to pull her on top of me or feel her body arching beneath my touch. I'd already reached a point where I could put aside our age difference, and I could probably have overlooked the fact that she, technically, worked for me. What I couldn't get past was that I'd be leaving in a fairly short time, and it wouldn't be fair to either of us to start something that would be over too soon. I almost laughed at that thought, since "over soon" had been my typical strategy with women until now. But that was the difference, wasn't it? Before, there had been no relationship, only sex. Now it was the opposite.

Too agitated to work, I walked over to Reefside. June and the W's were out on their deck drinking coffee. "Isn't that your girl out there swimming again?" Walter asked.

"She's not my—"

"Yeah, yeah, whatever," he interrupted. "She's here earlier than last time."

It was going to come out sooner or later. I took a breath. "Well, she's staying with me right now." I held up a hand, hoping to forestall the reactions I knew would be coming. "And it's not what you think. She had some trouble at home after the incident at the dance, and I felt like she needed to stay somewhere…safe for a while."

No one spoke for a few seconds, which was rather unusual in this crowd. Then June said, "I think you're doing a wonderful thing, Emily. We all know how important your privacy is to you. I hope Beck appreciates what a gift this is."

I didn't see any evidence of pretext in her face or hear sarcasm in her tone, so I hazarded a reply. "Thanks, June. It's been fine. She works with her mother all day, and she's been no bother when she's home."

"Home?" Walter asked, raising his eyebrows.

I made a face at him. "You know what I meant." They shared looks with each other, and I had a feeling there had already been a discussion on something to do with me. "What?"

William cleared his throat. "You've been acting…uh…different lately. And it's more than the weird diet and not drinking." He touched my hand in a sweet gesture of compassion. "You know we think of ourselves as your family, Em. If there's something you need to talk about, if there's something going on, we're here for you."

I was deeply touched. I knew he meant it. They all did. But I also knew I couldn't say anything about Beck. I don't know what I would have said in any case. So I went with my fallback position for anything behavioral I couldn't or didn't want to explain: my writing. I squeezed William's hand and wrapped the fingers of my other hand around June's arm, blowing Walter a kiss. "You know I adore you guys, I truly do." I sighed. "And this is going to sound kind of crazy, but bear with me, okay?" They all nodded solemnly, partly, I was sure, because none of us could recall me ever saying anything that honest in such a good-natured way.

"I'm working on a new book that's unlike anything I've written before. And to do that, to do it justice, I have to change parts of myself. I can't be the same inside and write something this atypical. It's like I have to become someone else, someone…different. I know it's hard to imagine, but trust me, it's true."

There was another uncharacteristic silence. June asked, "Will this change be permanent?"

I considered the question, then grinned. "I guess it depends on how well the book sells."

They all laughed at that. Mel's voice boomed from inside, "Who drank all the fucking coffee?"

Walter grimaced. "Our master's voice," he said in a stage whisper, but they all got to their feet.

"Wait," I said, stopping everyone's movement. "I really appreciate that you care." I made eye contact with each of them. "All of you."

"Aww. Group hug," William exclaimed, and we did.

Mel appeared at the screen door. "Hey. What did I miss?"

"Not much," Walter said, pushing past her into the house. "Just Emily's MIA heart returning from war."

I pinched him hard enough to make him flinch, while close behind him, William added, "Emily's working on a new book."

"Oh yeah?" Mel asked, yawning. I bowed my head slightly. "What kind?"

"Uh, it's more of a more traditional contemporary romance," I mumbled as I reached the stairs off their deck.

"Cool," she said, barely managing to sound vaguely enthusiastic.

I glanced back and saw exactly what I'd expected to see on June's face, a look somewhere between admonition and sadness.

❖

Beck returned and showered. I sat at my computer and pretended to work, finding it extremely difficult through thoughts of her naked under the streaming water. When she walked out of my room smelling fresh and clean with her hair damp and body flushed with heat, my own skin warmed. Not for the first time, I thought about how she would taste. I'd always imagined a delicious combination of sweet and salty. Passing by me, she brushed her hand across my shoulder, squeezing softly as she'd begun doing frequently. When I shivered lightly, she stopped.

"Would you rather I didn't do that?" She bent toward me, and her robe gapped enough to show the tops of her breasts. I swallowed but couldn't bring myself to look away. "Does it bother you for me to touch you?"

Bother me? Hot and bothered was one way to put it. I gazed into her eyes. "I guess I wonder why you do it. You never did before."

"I didn't live here before. You hadn't taken such good care of me, paying my doctor bills and nursing me. I can't even help with your rent since I still have to give my mama most of what I make to pay our mortgage." Her voice had risen slightly, and she straightened, taking a breath as she looked out the window at the ocean. "I've never stayed any place as nice as this, and I've never gotten to spend time with someone who is as incredible a person as you are. Since I feel silly saying 'thank you' over and over again, and I don't have anything else to give you, I thought…I mean, it seems like that sort of affection is something you don't know about or you don't get very often. So I just…touch you sometimes." She took a step away, searching my face. "But if you'd rather I didn't, please tell me, and I'll stop."

It might have been the consoling tone when she said affection was something I didn't seem to have. Or maybe it was how I hated thinking it was only pity or gratitude and not desire that made her reach for me. Whatever the case, I snapped, "If you want to do something for me, get to work on your art. If what you create means anything to you, it should be worth fighting for. At least try. Make something of yourself and your life instead of mooching off other people."

The second those last words were out of my mouth I regretted every syllable. How had horrible bitch Emily reappeared so suddenly? Was the image of myself as a romantic person a complete lie? Or was I so fearful of losing who I'd always been that I'd lash out at anyone who threatened me with transformation? Worse than any self-reproach was the expression on Beck's face and the way her eyes filled before she looked away.

"Hey, I'm sorry. That came out a lot worse than it sounded as I was thinking it." I tried to sound contrite.

She sniffed once and looked over, her face set differently than I remember ever seeing it. Her expression was almost hard. "No, you're right. Thank you for telling me the truth. For once."

Those last words went through me like a knife, but before I could formulate a reply, she went to her room. After stewing and pacing for five minutes, I stopped to get more coffee when the unmistakable rattle of the door opening and closing made me look around. At the sound of her footsteps on the stairs I ran to the windows and caught a glimpse of her going into the garage. Relieved she was only seeking solace with her cat, I finished pouring and had settled at my desk when I heard her scooter start up. Shit. I knew she wouldn't hear me calling—or she wouldn't listen—but I went to the deck railing anyway. She was already riding away.

At least I knew she'd be back at some point. Did I want that, or would I prefer a return to the solitary life I'd always insisted on? I needed to clear my head, and the pleasant little house felt oddly claustrophobic. I decided a walk on the beach was what I needed. Gathering my self-assurance from Beck's previous guidance, I made my way down the path she'd shown me.

I wasn't sure how long I walked, letting the surges of seawater wash over my feet and appreciating the sounds and smells and the feeling of my body moving confidently, before it occurred to me that the tide was coming in. Something resembling a snakeskin rolled toward me, and I dodged it, finding it too strange for the found jar. I watched as the waves pushed relentlessly toward the dunes, reclaiming the sand I'd walked on earlier. It dawned on me that the moon had been almost full last night. What cautions had Beck given me about these conditions?

I began walking higher on the dunes, trying to be careful about the plants and wildlife. Here and there, birds glided past, and when I saw a crab, I barely contained my scream. Wanting very much to give him or her a wide berth, I walked farther up, working to keep my balance on what seemed like an unusually steep slope. I'd no sooner reached the top than I slipped and half fell, half tripped down the other side. To my surprise, there was a small gap, and a second dune behind this one. I paid for not watching my feet by stumbling, and I tried to regain my balance by jumping toward the second dune. Certain I was doomed to the world's sandiest face plant, I slid until my foot hit something harder than sand or plants. I managed to right myself and came safely to a stop in the gap between the two dunes. I wasn't sure if I'd ever catch my breath again, and I held my hand to my chest to try to control my shaking.

"Shit," I gasped, turning to examine my situation. Staring at the back dune, I saw an edge of bright blue below a tuft of grass. I knelt to find a small opening containing a tarp supported by poles on the corners and in the center, forming the roof of a small, cave-like room dug into the sand. Driftwood and randomly colored boards of different lengths retained the walls. Indoor-outdoor carpet covered the floor, and a sheet was neatly folded in the corner. A battery powered lantern and an ancient transistor radio hung from the center, and alongside several small bags hanging from the poles was a small brass bell. Obviously, this was no temporary setup for a day at the beach. This could be a shelter for overnight or even several days, and someone had taken a lot of time and care to disguise it. When I stood again, my foot touched something unyielding. Brushing away the sand, I uncovered a small ice chest buried up to the lid. It contained a reusable water bottle and a withered apple.

Was a homeless person living here? Someone on the run from the law? And what was the purpose of that bell? In no time, my disturbed mind had supplied all kinds of frightening scenarios of an abduction and torture locale. Seized by the thought that someone might be watching, I looked around. Clearly, I needed to call the police and have them check the area as a possible crime scene. I tried to fix some landmark in my mind, but there were no houses in this immediate area and nothing civilized to use as a signpost. I only knew I'd be looking for the back-to-back dunes, something I hadn't seen anywhere else on my walk. I was certain Beck could help me find it again, assuming she was still speaking to me. I needed to get home.

Chapter Eleven

The sight that greeted me as I panted my way up the path was the last thing I was expecting, and it pushed the afternoon's find out of my head. The back garage door was open, and multiple pieces of Beck's work were arranged on the cement path that led to the house. Sugar weaved in and out of the metal, sniffing and occasionally meowing softly as Mel, clearly in agent mode, stood with her hands on her hips. Clearly smitten, her eyes glittered as she took it all in.

Turning to Beck, she gushed, "Damn, Spike. This is some amazing stuff."

Joining them, I cleared my throat. Neither acknowledged me, but Mel shifted uneasily. "Sorry, kid. Bad habit of mine, giving people nicknames."

Beck's expression didn't change. "It's okay, ma'am. Maybe I'll use that as my artistic alias."

I choked down a laugh at how much Mel would hate being called "ma'am." The two women eyed each other for a few seconds while I looked around. It was breathtaking work in various sizes and a variety of styles, from wall hangings to large kinetic sculptures to standalone shapes. I admired a freestanding wave that moved remarkably like the real thing and a series of seagulls in various stages of flight that stretched toward the sky. I didn't have time to take anything else in before Mel barked out a laugh.

"Okay, kid...uh, Beck. Shall I bring over a contract later today?"

"Does your family have a lawyer, Beck?" I asked. Mel shot me daggers while Beck looked at the ground.

"Not exactly. Erik had one appointed by the court once."

"Why don't you look it over, Em?" Mel suggested. "You know how these things work."

"No," Beck and I said together.

Mel cocked her head. "*Okay*," she said slowly.

"But I'll call my lawyer and see if she'd be willing to look it over," I said. "It'll be the standard form you use with me, so it should only take a few minutes, right?"

"Uh, yeah, pretty much."

Her answer was evasive enough that I knew I would call no matter what, assuming Beck went through with hiring her to do a showing and sale of her current collection. Mel wasn't blatantly dishonest, but she wasn't opposed to making money, especially from someone naïve about the workings of business, like Beck.

June wanted us to come for drinks, Mel said, but we both declined. I wanted very much to linger, to look at the various pieces over and over until I found the one I couldn't live without, but Beck had already begun putting them into the garage again, giving me quick, sideways glances that obviously meant I should leave. Obeying her wish seemed the least I could do since it was possible my snide remarks had led to this situation. I went quietly inside, hoping she'd be willing to let me see her work later. It occurred to me that her art was different from mine, in that I always had copies of my books available, but once she let a piece go, it was gone.

After what seemed like plenty of time, I went out on the deck to see what Beck was doing. The garage was closed and locked again. She was on the bottom step, Sugar cuddling alongside her, while they watched Xena and Gabrielle chase each other. At the sound of a loud, rattling vehicle coming toward the house, the cats scampered into the garage, and Beck stood. A UPS truck stopped, and I ran downstairs. The delivery guy handed me the box, and I gestured to Beck as I went by again. "Please come upstairs. I need you to help me with this."

I set the box on the kitchen table and went into my bedroom. When I heard her at the door, I called, "Open that up, will you, Beck? I'll be right out."

There was a pause. "You want me to open your package?" she asked uncertainly.

"Yes, please. I'll be out in a few," I said from the crack in my door where I was watching. I'd forgotten how much fun giving could be.

After slitting the sealing tape open with her pocket knife, she looked toward the bedroom, clearly hesitant to pull apart the flaps of the box. I ducked out of sight. "It's open," she called, and I muffled my voice with my hand over my mouth.

"Break the box down so we can recycle it, will you?" That meant she would have to take out the contents and cut the bottom section to flatten the cardboard.

When I peeked again, she was staring at the phone box with a puzzled expression. "I don't think I should, Em. I think there's been a mistake."

Wanting to be with her for the big reveal, I returned to the room. "What's wrong?"

She held out the phone. "You don't need this. You already have a newer model."

I covered her hands with mine, making sure she kept a grip on the box. "I don't need it, but you do. This is my belated birthday present for you." I held my breath, hoping her birthday wasn't tomorrow or any time in the near future. I hadn't prepared myself for her possible refusal and my anxiety built.

She blinked a few times. "My birthday was a long time ago."

I breathed out. "Exactly. I apologize that this gift is late. And I'm very sorry I was so ugly to you earlier. You've already made something of yourself, and you aren't ever a mooch. You are the opposite of a mooch. You are the kind of person who gives much, much more than she takes, and I don't want you to think otherwise." The timing was such that I hoped she wouldn't think I was trying to buy her forgiveness. But since she'd never seemed suspicious of my motives before, I waited hopefully.

She was alternating between looking at me and looking at the phone, an expression of disbelief on her face. "You got this for me?"

I smiled. "Yes, to replace the one that was broken." I didn't mention that I felt at least partly responsible for the whole incident at the dance too. "This way, you can take pictures of your art and make a website. Launch your own sale if you want to. You don't need to do business with Mel simply because she's a friend of mine. I want you to feel like this is right for you. The sale. Mel. All of it."

She swallowed and looked away. "I went and talked to Mr. Howell this morning. He thinks it would be good for me to sell some pieces. He says getting rid of them may help me clear the way to something new, like making room for whatever's next in my career."

"Including the PAFA competition?" I said gently.

She nodded. "That mainly. He knows I work best under pressure. He says it's time."

Relief washed over me until I realized I was still holding her hands. Then the relief turned into something warmer and more internal. I was struck again by how much I wanted to take her into my bedroom. Giving in to my physical desire for her would be the easiest part. I'd been trying hard to inhibit the growth of my deeper feelings for her by nipping them in the bud, but the fact that she was now staying here was making it much harder. Forcing myself to let go, I said, "I need to get back to work. Can you set this up by yourself?"

Those tiny frown lines had reappeared. "Emily, I don't think I should. These phones are really expensive."

"But what if I need you to get something at the store while you're out? I don't like not being able to get in touch with you," I said, surprised to hear the genuine need in my tone. "I'm sure your mother feels the same way."

She looked at the box again, and I could see a tiny grin forming at the corner of her mouth. "Well, there is that." Her tone suggested adding her mother to my sales pitch hadn't been completely convincing. She met my eyes shyly, keeping her hands flat on the table. "Again I...I don't know how to thank you."

I cringed, certain she was thinking of my earlier unkind words. "I should be thanking you. You are such a good person. You make me want to be better." I marched to the almost constant internal drumbeat of my flaws, and this much overt self-avowal was rare.

"I'm not always good. Sometimes I have these thoughts..."

I could see her blushing as she trailed off. I could see something else too. Something in her expression as she looked at me which looked very much like desire. I stepped closer. "What kind of thoughts?" I asked softly.

She swayed toward me, her eyes never leaving mine. "Thoughts about you. And not as a friend."

I wasn't sure if it was actually hearing her say the words or the way her body had moved closer that made everything inside me do a funny sort of stutter. I opened my mouth to reply when I heard footsteps on the stairs. I drew away from some automatic impulse, and Beck turned toward the door. Mel came in without knocking, as usual, carrying some papers.

"Here you go, kiddo," she said, thrusting them in Beck's direction. When I intercepted and carried them to my computer, Mel's tone became harsher. "I won't do anything more until I get your signature."

"Another few hours won't matter," I said, gesturing at Beck. "We'll bring this to you tomorrow or the next day."

"Oh, will we?" Mel asked sarcastically. "I didn't realize this was a three-way deal."

"She needs time to read this, Mel. Surely you don't object to that." I knew from experience that the legalese in a contract could baffle the most gifted intellectual, and I was concerned that Beck's injury might make such reading even more daunting.

"Whatever." Mel glared for a few seconds before turning to Beck. "Let me know when you're ready to make some money." When Beck merely nodded, she glanced at me. "I guess we'll see you when we see you."

"It will be sooner rather than later," I assured her. She merely grunted and left. Beck and I stood in an awkward silence, the physical space between us seeming impassable. Perhaps she was worried that my friendship with Mel would be jeopardized if anything more happened between us. I tried to think if I'd given her reason to believe that.

After a few seconds, she picked up the phone box. Turning toward her room, she said, "The first thing I'm going to do with the money from my sale is to pay you back for this."

"It's a gift," I called, but there was no answer, other than her bedroom door shutting quietly.

A while later, I heard her voice, and while I couldn't make out the words, the tone was one of excitement. I assumed she had gotten the phone working and was probably calling her mother. I moved from my computer, where I'd gotten nothing done, to the couch where I could more comfortably read over the contract. As my sales figures had grown over the years, Mel had taken a slightly smaller percentage, not that she took that much to begin with. The amount she'd be earning from Beck was considerably higher, and I didn't see where she would be doing much more work to earn it. Oddly, I didn't feel at all conflicted about siding with Beck on this matter. As important as Mel had been in what I thought of as the most recent chapter of my life, I knew she didn't need anyone else to protect her or her interests. Beck's situation was essentially the opposite. She had no previous experience in this type of business and no useful family involvement. I was likely the only person she knew who could help, and though it was completely unlike me to feel confident about looking out for someone this way, I told myself that it was what a friend would do. It wasn't until we were sitting down to eat that it dawned on me that offering this kind of care was also like something spouses did.

I was pleased to see her carrying the phone, and it remained within sight all through dinner preparation. She put it in her pocket before coming to the table, though, and I was pleased by the display of manners. It always bothered me to see two people staring at their phones instead of talking to each other during a meal, perhaps for the very reason that it confirmed what I'd concluded about the inevitable tedium of relationships.

Granted, interesting conversation was a rare thing. I was apparently desperate for it after spending so much time alone during my marriage, which was probably why my friendship with Mel developed so quickly. I was almost sad, recalling how the thoughtful talks we used to have had grown fewer and farther between. But as my writing career had grown, it increasingly consumed large measures of my time and considerable portions of my thoughts, so I was as much at fault for that as she was. In the past, I'd needed absolute quiet and total seclusion to sink into my imaginary worlds, but for some reason Beck's presence hadn't been a distraction. I was honestly glad she was here. Perhaps I'd reached my quota of alone time for now. Or maybe it was that Beck was always good at engaging me.

I cleared my throat and announced, "I hope you don't mind, but I read over the papers Mel brought."

She sat straighter. "No, that's great. What do you think?"

"I think you need to negotiate. Her percentage seems high."

She frowned and bit her lip. "I don't know what you mean."

I began to talk about the ins and outs of a contract, what she should expect from an agent. In about three minutes, I could see I'd lost her. "Maybe we need to have your mother in on this conversation," I suggested and saw immediate relief on her face.

"That would be great." After another second, she said, "She's going to ask Erik to leave. She said he's getting on her last nerve." Lowering her voice, she added, "It may be because she finally saw how he was with me."

"If that happens, will you go back home?" I asked, aware of my insides clenching. I watched her start to shake her head before she stopped and looked at me.

"Would you want me to?"

Totally unprepared for this question, I felt my mouth go dry, and I stalled by drinking some water. Then, in typical fashion, I punted, hating myself even as the words came out with forced nonchalance. "Whatever you need to do, Beck. I'm fine either way." Concerned that lie would be apparent if I looked at her, I rose to clear our dishes.

"I guess I'll see what happens," I heard her say. I was debating my reply when I heard the screen door close and realized she'd gone out to the deck. Standing at the railing, she was looking out toward the water. It must have been cloudy because there was no moon or starlight.

I joined her, and we stood quietly, side by side for a time. When she sighed, I was certain we must be feeling pretty much the same confusion and indecision, complicated by the underlying attraction that had been growing between us. I'd never minded being alone, so asking her to stay would have been admitting she was what I wanted. But how could she possibly feel the same about me? After spending years developing the verbal jabs that would keep people at arm's length, making sure they saw only what I wanted them to see, I was shamed by the sincerity with which Beck lived her life. Knowing I could never be open and caring like that, it made sense that I protect both of us by keeping my distance—which was why I couldn't tell her the truth.

The wind was picking up, and it carried the sound of crashing waves closer than usual. "Weather man says we'll have showers tonight and bigger storms tomorrow night," she said, obviously trying for some neutral remark.

I squeezed her shoulders, fighting the urge to press myself against her before letting go. "I think I'll turn in. Good night."

"Sleep well, Emily," she said, but I doubted that would be the case.

Fear gripped me so tightly, it was like being paralyzed. I couldn't see or catch my breath, and when the swell of panic hit me, it came with the certainty of having awakened too late. "Help! Please, somebody," I called as loudly as I could. "Stop. Stop him!"

A few seconds later, I heard the door to my bedroom open, and I put my face in my hands. He'd come back, just like he'd threatened, and now he was going to kill me.

"Emily?" a woman's voice asked. "Are you okay?"

"Mama?" I sat up, relieved I was able to move again. "Mama, we have to get help."

"I think you're having a bad dream." The voice moved closer. I blinked, staring into the dark, my mind clearing slowly. Of course it wasn't my mother. Like Abby, she was gone from my life, and it was all my fault. A roll of thunder sounded in the distance, and I flinched when a hand touched my arm. "You're here at the beach, remember?" Beck. "Oh no," I moaned. What would she think? What could I say?

"It's fine." Her hand moved soothingly on my bare arm. "You're safe. Everything is all right."

It wasn't, and it wouldn't ever be, but she couldn't know that. "Yeah," I tried to say but choked, and only a strangled sound came out. Trying to settle myself, I focused on the movement of her hand. Her touch was gentle and calming. God, how I wanted the comfort of it.

Involuntarily, I made a needy, whimpering sound. In response, her weight settled onto the bed, though she didn't move under the covers. She knelt, hands on both my shoulders, easing me onto the pillows. I turned toward her as she reached around me, hands warm as she caressed my back. I responded automatically, arching into her. *This must be how Sugar feels when Beck pets her.* I intended to laugh, but what came out was a half sob. I tried to stifle it, to focus myself on the cold lump of guilt and shame that never relinquished its hold on me. But Beck's presence was too humane, too merciful, and it was like a dam broke. I clung to her, unable to stop the tears, while she pulled me closer, cradling my face. She didn't ask what was wrong. She didn't try to quiet me or tell me how everything would be fine. She simply continued stroking my back while I cried for what was lost and for what I'd never had.

It felt like hours passed. Maybe they did. But at some point, my tears ran out, and I was reduced to ragged breathing. The rational part of my mind began forming a series of apologies and possible excuses for my embarrassing behavior, but one of Beck's hands moved onto my neck, and she massaged me softly, occasionally letting her fingers trail into my scalp. I couldn't remember anything ever feeling so relaxing, and logic escaped on a long, heavy sigh. My eyes were already fatigued from crying, and I couldn't seem to keep them open. How was it possible to feel blissful and empty at the same time?

Time passed, and Beck shifted onto one elbow, withdrawing her hand. "Think you can get to sleep again?"

"Please stay." The words I should have said earlier were out before I even knew I was thinking them.

She let out a breath and settled in. "I was hoping you'd say that."

❖

The smell of coffee woke me from the deepest, most restful sleep I'd had in years. Gradually, I recalled the night: the dream, Beck's gentle comfort, crying myself to sleep. She was gone from the bed, but there were a few muted sounds from the other room. I rehearsed a few possible starters for what was bound to be an awkward morning. "I shouldn't have asked you to stay," and "I'm sorry for acting like such a child," were primary among them. A quick check of the time indicated it was already later than she usually went off to work, so perhaps the discomfort of seeing her wouldn't be prolonged. Mostly, I hoped she wouldn't expect some explanation of my emotional upheaval. Her back was to me when I entered the kitchen, but she turned upon hearing me clear my throat, and that beautiful smile flashed across her face.

She walked to meet me, taking my hands as I said, "Listen—"

"Emily," she interrupted, which was unusual for her. "I know you have some practiced speech you want to give me, but could I say something first?" Stunned, I could only nod. "Last night was the first time I ever slept through the night and woke with someone, and I wanted to say it was very, very nice. And also, I'm glad it was with you."

Moved, I couldn't remember a thing I was going to say. I slipped my arms around her waist, and she embraced me, much like she had in the dark. We stood like that for a time until I murmured, "Thank you." I couldn't bring myself to tell her that—other than my husband—it was the first time for me as well.

She sighed and stepped away, saying, "I have to go. I'm late now, but I wanted to be here when you woke up. Breakfast is in the oven. Will you be home for dinner?"

My chest clenched with an unfamiliar sensation of yearning for a life like this, where someone cared about my reactions and considered my needs. Especially someone like Beck, who somehow challenged me and comforted me at the same time. But I had less than nothing to give in return. I had a deficit of worth, and it would be pure selfishness to think otherwise. I did. I wanted to consume her, to take her vitality into my blood and let it restore me. But that would bring her too close, make us both exposed to more hurt, particularly from each other. Better to keep any contact on the uncomplicated carnal level. I could envision ripping her shirt off and putting my hands on her breasts. I wanted to feel her mouth on me. Yes, those desires were much easier to control and should plainly be the limit of my reactions. Still almost dizzy with greed, I took in two shallow breaths. "I think so."

"Good." She winked, and I wondered for a second if she'd somehow read my mind. "I'll see you later. Have a great day." She opened the door as I reached for my coffee mug. "Sugar's out here," she called. "Can she come in and say hi to you?"

"Uh, sure," I said, still trying to steady my breathing.

"You can toss her out when you're tired of her. Or if she starts to cry."

"Right."

Beck lingered at the door for another few seconds, her gaze on me while the white kitten made its way cautiously inside. I couldn't help smiling, oddly pleased that she didn't seem keen to leave. "Wow," she said smiling back. "A hug and a smile. I'm set for the day now."

Those last words had the slightest hint of self-satisfaction, so I decided to tease her. Sighing as if terribly bothered, I shook my head. "I suppose next you'll be asking for a kiss too."

To my surprise, she shook her head. "I don't kiss good-bye, Emily, and I don't kiss hello. I only kiss *yes*."

Closing the door quietly, she left me to ponder that. I'd never been much for kissing either, finding it much too intimate for my usual intentions. I wondered if Beck's motivation was the same or if her meaning of yes was something completely different. I sipped my coffee and watched Sugar make her way across the room toward me. She sniffed thoughtfully at every piece of furniture, running the side of her face along the couch as if to mark it for a return visit. She stopped about a foot away, and I knelt, holding out my hand like Beck had shown me. "Good morning to you."

She came the rest of the way and rubbed against my fingers, a surprisingly deep purr rumbling from her small form. "I need to talk to somebody," I told her. "Do you have a few minutes?"

Luckily, she did. I freshened my coffee and carried her out to the deck, where she sat on my lap while I told her about last night. We discussed our feelings, and she was quite certain Beck only had eyes for her. I knew differently. Remembering how Beck held me made me feel almost giddy with a sense of well-being different from anything I'd ever known. Though there had been nothing sexual in her caring touch, more closeness like that would take us from the edge of friendship and into an entirely different relationship. Which, unfortunately, was not a safe place for either of us to venture. There was too little time and too much risk. I sighed, and Sugar rubbed against my stomach, secure in her victory.

"Just promise me you'll take care of her," I said when the green eyes looked up at me. "She deserves it."

❖

I'd intended to present a middle ground between Emily the swooning wannabe girlfriend and Emily the bitch, but Beck didn't come upstairs after she arrived late that afternoon. At first, I thought she was playing with the kittens, but when more time passed, curiosity got the better of me, and I went downstairs. When I saw the back garage door open and saw two of the rusted car doors that had been set outside, I couldn't suppress the thrill that went through me. *Beck is working again.*

The heavy drag of metal pieces across the ground and a clang that sounded like a muffled bell was followed by a thud and "Dang." Torn between wanting to help and not wanting to interrupt, I waited. When Beck appeared in the doorway, we both startled.

"Oh, Emily," she said after a second, hand at her heart. "I didn't hear you come down. I was, uh…"

When she trailed off, I took a step away. "I didn't mean to interrupt. I heard your scooter, but I didn't see you so I…"

For a few seconds, the awkwardness between us was almost palpable. Then, as if by some unspoken signal, we both started laughing. Beck shook her head. "I had this idea, and I wanted to talk to Mr. Howell about it. But I needed to refresh my memory about what was in here." She looked into the garage again briefly before gesturing in my direction. "And, um…would you be willing to help me?"

"Of course." I couldn't keep the warmth from my voice, and when she smiled, I knew she'd heard it too. *Back off. She's asking for a professional favor, not for you to rock her world.* "I mean, I'll do what I can." At least I'd been careful not to say "anything I can."

"Great," Beck said. "I have to make some calls, but would you be free for a few hours next Thursday? Available to come to the campus with me, that is?"

"I…I'd have to check." What had I gotten myself into?

She nodded, obviously trusting me. "If you're about ready for dinner, you can put that dish in the oven." I retreated up the stairs as she began putting everything back in the garage. It seemed that no matter what I planned or how I told myself to act, every day with Beck seemed to draw me in deeper. In a short time, our vague acquaintance had transitioned into living together, and now she needed me? That thought was like crashing into an emotional ceiling. I followed her instructions for dinner, but as soon as I heard her in the shower, I called Mel.

My hastily scribbled note to Beck was not a total lie. *A minor crisis at Reefside, and friends need my attention. Sorry.* That was at least partially true. *Please don't expect me any time soon.*

I'd let myself be entertained by a rousing game of Cards Against Humanity to the point where I hadn't noticed the change in the weather. When Mel came in from a vape break, she commented on the wind, but we were all impatient for the next round and basically ignored her. It wasn't until a rattling clap of thunder followed close on a bright flash of lightning that we realized a storm was upon us. A few seconds later, there was another crash, and the power winked out. The W's sprang into action, reappearing with two battery powered lanterns, two umbrellas, and two flashlights.

"Is everything in pairs with you guys?" Mel asked, but June was delighted with the lanterns, pronouncing them "darling." I borrowed an umbrella and stepped out onto the deck, trying vainly to shield myself against the driving rain that had already begun to fall. The Guest House appeared dark as well. Surely Beck would be all right. When I ducked inside, shaking water off like a dog, Mel was watching.

"Worried about your houseguest?" she said, practically sneering. I assumed she was still miffed about the contract.

"I was checking on the house," I replied, keeping my cool despite the growing need to already be there. "Looks like my power is out too."

"I think you should stay here tonight," June offered graciously. "Beck will be fine by herself, don't you think?"

"I'm sure she would, but there are some things I need to do."

"Like what?" Mel challenged, clearly in one of her antagonistic moods.

"Shut down my computer, for one," I shot back, pleased I'd thought of something so quickly.

"Why don't you call Beck, tell her you'll be staying here, and ask her to do it?" June suggested.

It was all very reasonable, but I couldn't for several reasons. To begin with, I didn't want to admit I'd left home in such a rush that I'd forgotten my phone, and like most people, I didn't bother to memorize phone numbers anymore, relying on the automated choices on my screen. "I have files open, and I don't want to risk anything happening to them," I said, hoping that would be the end of it. I pointed at the umbrella. "Could I borrow this for tonight?"

Mel crossed her arms, and I braced myself, knowing from that pose I probably wouldn't like what was coming. "I don't see why you don't just fuck her and get it over with." And that was even worse than I'd expected.

June swatted at her arm, but she laughed too, and I could hear the W's snickering by the dining table. Apparently, this was the consensus of opinion as to my best course of action. It pissed me off they'd been talking about me behind my back, though it was something we all did with each other from time to time. The "get it over with" part was even more offensive, though they couldn't know that. I folded my arms, mirroring Mel's stance. "It's not like that, Melanie. Though I'm sure you couldn't possibly understand."

As expected, my use of her real name made the W's look at each other, humming with a slight rising tone that suggested trouble. "I'll tell you what I understand," Mel began, but June intervened.

"Take the umbrella, Emily," she said, practically pushing me out the door. "And be careful."

I wasn't ten feet up the path before my jeans and shoes were heavy with moisture. As I tried to adjust the angle of the umbrella, a gust of wind caught it, and I staggered sideways with the force of it. The umbrella turned inside out, useless. I continued to carry it anyway. Wind pushed my hair into my face, and rivulets of water ran into my eyes. With the power out, darkness was absolute. Slightly disoriented, I stumbled into a shrub and realized I had drifted off the path. Lightning flashed again, too bright and brief to help me, and the boom that followed hurt my ears. I paused, cowering and shivering. Shouldn't beach rain be warm? I started moving again, noticing after another minute that I'd dropped the umbrella. I looked around but couldn't make it out amid the dark, streaming plants. Shit. The path was all sand. I was definitely off track.

I peered ahead, hoping to at least see a shape that might be my home. House, I corrected myself. Not home. Home was the city, which was probably warm and dry right now. Unfortunately, my mind chose that moment to associate warm and dry with an image of Beck. I envisioned her cozy on the couch, possibly with Sugar on her lap, having no idea of my situation. Cutting off the scene before I could put myself in the kitten's place, I continued trudging uphill, winding around the soggy dunes and vegetation. If Mel hadn't been so mean, I might have thought to borrow a flashlight too. The satisfaction I felt at blaming this disaster on her was short-lived, however, because after the next lightning-thunder combo, the rain began to fall even harder, something I wouldn't have thought possible.

My clothing was growing heavier by the second, but I was too exhausted to take something off and lighten my load. Besides, water was running off every limb and into every crack and crevice in my body, which felt increasingly chilled. But I had to be close now, didn't I? The two houses were maybe half a mile apart, and it felt like I'd already covered twice that distance. Complete darkness made the world appear infinite, and my heart hammered as I tried to ignore the possibility that I was really and truly lost. If I kept climbing, I'd reach the road eventually, but what kind of person would stop to help a soaked, panicky, woman alone? And if someone did, could I even direct them to my house, assuming I felt it was safe to do so with a stranger?

I tried to fight against my anxiety, reasoning that if I couldn't find the Guest House, I should be able to find my way to Reefside again. But retracing my steps would be difficult, given the darkness compounded by the rain. And if I failed, I'd end up at the ocean. I could envision the force of this wind pushing me into the surf where I'd be swept away as easily as a piece of driftwood.

A stronger gust of wind pushed me like a self-fulfilling prophecy, and I stumbled into some more vegetation. Losing my balance, I barely avoided going sideways into the sand, sitting squarely on my ass instead. Perfect. Self-pity surged through me, and I felt the prick of hot tears. Maybe I'd sit here until morning, wet and miserable, and everyone would be sorry when I died of pneumonia. At my funeral, Mel would break down, filled with regret for all the cruel things she'd said to me.

A church scene came into my head, but the memorial wasn't for me. It was Abby's. After a year and a half, my mother had wanted a casket, but I'd come out of the shell I'd began to inhabit and put up such a fight that she'd relented. "She's not dead," I'd screamed over and over. "The police will find her. She'll fight him off. She's coming back." Of course, none of that had proven true, and after the service she'd so carefully planned, my mother had found it impossible to continue with any parenting responsibilities. Father was already gone. I had failed to save Abby, and no one else had rescued her either. Just like no one was going to rescue me now. And death wasn't beautifully tragic. It was fucking terrible and I didn't want any part of it.

Chapter Twelve

I stood, pushing aside one of the many heartbreaking memories that never left me. When I caught a glimpse of another flash of light, I cringed, waiting for the boom, but it didn't come. Strangely, this light seemed to sweep from side to side, and it came with a different sound… like a voice. Like a voice calling my name. It happened again, and I turned in a slow circle, trying to find the source of what was likely a hallucination induced by my continuous trembling.

But as the light moved closer, I called, "Here!" as loudly as I could. The voice came again, and I thought I could make out the shape of a figure. I yelled again, and the light swept toward me. I waved my arms, and in another few seconds, Beck's face under her bright yellow slicker hood appeared out of the darkness.

She pulled me to her side, supporting me with her body and an arm around my waist. "Come on," she yelled over the din of the storm. No foolish questions like *What are you doing?* or *Where have you been?* She kept her pace steady as we moved uphill, and before long, I could make out the shape of the Guest House looming in the night. It looked nearly as good as Beck had.

She stopped us inside the doorway. Propping me against the small washer-dryer, she quickly peeled off her slicker jacket and rain pants. "Take off everything. Everything," she said. "I'll get some towels and your pajamas."

I fumbled with buttons until she came back. Teeth chattering, I stuttered, "I'm not having much luck here."

"If I promise not to look, will you let me do it?" she asked with the slightest twinkle in her eyes.

"Look, don't look." I waved, well beyond such modesty. She didn't…much. I used one towel to dry my torso while she worked on my arms and legs. Once I was in my pj's and robe, she handed me another bath towel and directed me to start on my hair, but I was still shaking so hard I could barely hold it.

"How about a nice hot shower?" she asked, but I shook my head. I didn't want anything involving water falling on me. "I was going to sit you down with some hot tea, but your lips are almost blue. I think I need to get you in bed."

"You would say that," I teased, imitating her remark from our shower when she'd been hurt, "now that I've been out in the weather."

"If I'd known you were going out, I would have warned you," she said, touching my face.

"Last-minute thing," I said, not meeting her gaze.

She took my hand and led me to the bedroom without another word. Once I was tucked in, she went in search of blankets. I heard her muttering about needing to fix the non-functioning fireplace and something about "moth-eaten," and then she appeared at my bedside again, laying the wrap from the couch on top of me. "How are you feeling?"

"Better," I said, though I couldn't hide the quiver in my voice.

"Still cold, though," she said, laying a hand on my forehead. "And here's the thing, there's not a decent heavy blanket in the house. I know this is a summer rental, but still…cool fronts like this come through sometimes, especially later in the season."

If I was honest with myself, I knew what I wanted. I wanted her in bed with me. I wanted that solid warmth pressed against me.

"Emily?" she said softly. I'd closed my eyes, forcing myself not to ask. "If you wouldn't mind, I could warm you up by, uh, you know… getting close to you, like before."

"Yes." I nodded without looking, but when she settled in next to me on top of the bedspread, the way she'd been last night, I shook my head and patted the bottom sheet. "Right next to me. Please."

I turned to face away, but I suspected she heard me moan when her small round breasts pressed into my back. She wrapped an arm around my waist and pulled me close, lining our bodies bend for bend and curve for curve. In no time, I felt safe, warmed, and totally reassured. Was this what heaven felt like? I drifted for a moment, my body thawing. The thought occurred to me that Beck had done the same thing to my emotions. I should have been worried, but I couldn't seem to make myself care. Instead, my mind willingly supplied images of sleeping with Beck every night…naked…and I breathed slowly with the delightful sensation of caring and being cared for. How sweet it would be to…a distant throb began between my legs, and I quickly reined in my imagination. No, I definitely didn't need to go there. I switched my thinking to Mel and how angry I was at her. After a few more minutes, I felt almost normal, so I decided to follow that line of thought.

Clearing my throat, I asked, "How did you know to come look for me?"

"I was about to go to bed, but your phone starting buzzing like crazy. I decided to take it into your bedroom to make sure you'd see the messages when you got home. It buzzed again while I was carrying it, and I glanced at the screen." She sighed. "I know I shouldn't have looked. It was none of my business, but it was someone asking if you'd made it home yet, in all caps. I figured it was one of your friends from Reefside, and I was worried. I used my phone to call the house phone there, and one of those guys answered. He seemed really upset when I told him you weren't here, and I said I'd go look for you." I started to sit up, thinking I should call and let them know I was safe, but Beck wrapped a warm hand around my arm. "He gave me his cell number, so when I was getting your pajamas, I texted to let him know you were safe. I said you'd call him tomorrow." She paused for a few seconds. "I know I invaded your privacy, but I'm not sorry because if I hadn't, I wouldn't have known you were in trouble."

I wasn't sure how I felt about the matter of my privacy, but Beck was nearly vibrating with apprehension. "Let's talk about that tomorrow," I said finally, turning to face her and moving onto one elbow. "But there is something else I want to tell you." She leaned away slightly as if preparing for another of my terrible verbal onslaughts. I put a hand on her shoulder to steady her and leaned in, kissing her softly on the mouth. "I remember what you said about not kissing hello or good-bye, but that was a thank-you kiss. Thank you for caring enough to come look for me. All right?"

I couldn't read the expression on her face, and when she didn't answer, I began to second-guess myself. Why had I done that? And what did I mean by it? After a few more seconds she cleared her throat and turned over, her back to me.

"That's the thing, Emily. Friends take care of each other."

It was best she saw it that way, as only a friendly gesture. But I wasn't sure if I was relieved or sorry. I lay down again, unconsciously spooning her as she had me. It felt just as wonderful this way, which was more than a little unsettling. When I stretched my arm across her middle, her breathing hitched.

"You do make it problematic for me to remain chivalrous sometimes."

I started to laugh and make some sarcastic comeback, like "Is that what this is?" when it dawned on me: that was it, exactly. Beck was virtuous in a way that few people were today. Whether her code of conduct matched the medieval knights or not, she had one, and it guided her words and her deeds. Those beliefs were what made her dependable and generous and perhaps explained why I had this near compulsion to try to even the playing field for her since I lived in a world where very few people had or demonstrated those qualities. I felt like I had cracked some kind of cypher. "I don't mean to be so…difficult," I said slowly.

"I know," Beck said, and patted my hand where it lay on her stomach. "Get some rest now."

Oddly, as if obeying her command, I did.

❖

I was just managing to breathe underwater, but someone was shaking me gently from behind. "Emily, I have to go soon. How are you feeling?"

Beck. Trying to answer, I took stock. Scratchy throat, stuffy nose, achy body. I thought about how chilled I'd gotten last night. Yep, I had gotten a cold. I coughed, and a hand rested on my forehead before steps hurried away. Then she was helping me sit up. "You need to take this, and I'll get you some tea and toast."

Pills were in my hand, and I looked over to see a glass of juice. "What…" I croaked, forcing myself to swallow.

"It's aspirin. I think you have a low-grade fever. I'll bring you some cold medicine later. Do you have a preference?"

"Anything that will knock me out. I feel like shit."

"I'm sorry," she said, stroking my hair.

"God, Beck, it's not your fault. If it weren't for you, I'd probably have pneumonia." I closed my eyes again, surprised I could tolerate her contact. Usually when I was sick, the last thing I wanted was someone else around, especially someone who might touch me. It seemed none of my previous rules applied to Beck.

"Still, I'm sorry you feel bad." She propped another pillow behind me. "I'll be right back. Eat, then you can sleep some more."

I'd barely settled in after a trip to the bathroom when she appeared with the pretty tray, putting it carefully on my lap before leaving me with a soft squeeze on my shoulder. The tea soothed my throat, and I managed to eat most of the toast as well.

"Would you like more of anything?" Beck seemed pleased when she returned. "I think mama will let me work a half day today, and I'll go by the store on my way home. Text me if you think of anything special and especially if you start feeling worse. Should I call your friends and have them check on you?"

I shook my head. "I'll call them if I need to. At the moment, I only want to sleep."

"Good. That's the best thing for you."

I reached for her hand. "Maybe the next best thing."

She blushed, the color adding to her allure. I closed my eyes again, unexpectedly struck with melancholy at how long it was going to take to get over her. And with that thought, I sneezed. "Sorry."

"No more 'sorry' and no 'thank yous.' You take care of yourself till I get home, okay?"

I nodded, and after a moment, her footsteps faded away.

❖

The next day passed in a blur. All I knew for sure was that any time I woke up, Beck was there. For a while, she was in bed with me. I'd woken myself snoring—and probably drooling—to discover I was wrapped around her, my head pillowed on her shoulder. Her arm was around me, making lazy patterns up and down my back. I wanted to pretend like I was still asleep so she wouldn't stop, but my breathing must have changed because she shifted, and I could feel her looking at me.

"Oh," I rasped, scrubbing a hand over my face. "You're not working today?"

"I took the day off," she said, putting aside her iPad. "Can I get you something?"

"Tea?" I asked, regretting it in the next second when she got out of bed. Cuddling the pillow where she'd been was not at all the same.

I was sipping the hot liquid, and Beck was still puttering in the kitchen when I heard the door open.

"Oh, hi." It was Mel's voice.

"Hi, Mel. Emily's not feeling well. She caught a cold after being out in the rain the other night." I grinned at the slightly accusatory tone in her voice.

"Bummer," Mel said, typically unconcerned. "But I actually came to talk to you."

"Oh." I could tell Beck was nonplussed. "Can I get you something?" Mel must have declined because Beck said, "Would you like to sit down?"

Evidently, they did. I was glad Beck had left the door open, letting me hear most of what was being said.

"I hadn't heard from you. Is there some problem with the contract I sent over?" Mel asked, forgoing any other niceties.

I held my breath. It wouldn't be prudent for Beck to mention my name or use my concerns as an excuse. After a few seconds, Beck said, "You seem to be taking a pretty large percent. I'm not sure I'm getting my money's worth."

I would have given a lot to see Mel's face. She tended to flush when she was questioned, and often what followed was something very close to rage. Could Beck stand up to it?

"Okay," Mel said, obviously making an effect to stay calm, though I could hear the tension in her voice. "Let's talk about that. What do you think would be fair?"

"I know I'm new to this, but I have every reason to think I'll do well. A lot of people know me, and there are still lots of summer visitors here who have money. If we get enough publicity, I think we'll have a good turnout. What I need your help with is the pricing. Do you have any ideas on that yet?"

If Beck was stalling, she was doing a hell of a job at it.

"Well, like I told you, I'm not doing anything more until we have a contract. At that point, I'll make some calls to some art dealers I know, and I'll do some online research as well. But amounts will vary by piece, depending on size and quality."

It was quiet for a moment. Finally, Mel said, "Okay, I understand, my getting seventy percent seems like a lot. Seeing as how you're a friend of Emily's, I'm willing to go down to sixty-five."

"Fifty-five," Beck said, and I almost choked on my tea.

"Listen, kid. I don't know what Emily told you about our deal, but—"

Beck cut her off. "She didn't tell me anything about her personal business with you. If you know her as well as you say, you'd know that."

I was so proud of Beck my toes were curling. And Mel must be purple by now.

"Now look—" she started, but Beck interrupted again.

"Sixty this time, but if we do better than one hundred thousand, you'll drop it to fifty-five next time."

I clapped my hands silently. Beck had maneuvered Mel over a barrel. If she said no, that meant she didn't expect to do very well. If she said yes, Beck had the best deal of anyone Mel worked with, other than me.

"If you'll bring over that change, I'll sign it in front of you," Beck added. "And we can start on pricing tomorrow."

Holy shit. Pressure and a promise. I'd never heard or read of anyone negotiating better than that. It was quiet again for a long pause. "You'd better make me a hell of a lot of money, Spike," Mel muttered.

I heard their footsteps going away. Beck said one other thing I couldn't make out. The door closed hard, just short of slamming. I waited all of ten seconds before I called for her.

At my bedroom door, she ran a shaking hand through her hair. "That was Mel," she said.

"I know. Come here." I sat up and patted the bed. When she perched hesitantly beside me, I pulled her into my arms. "I am so proud of you. No one could have done better than you did."

"You heard?" she asked, her voice muffled against my body.

"Yes, all of it except the last thing you said."

"Oh, that." Beck seemed embarrassed. "I reminded her of my name. 'Cause the thing is, she never uses it." I laughed until I started to cough and reluctantly had to let her go. "Would you feel like coming to the table for dinner?" Beck asked. "It would do you good to move around if that cold is going to your chest."

I nodded, still warmed by her triumph. I stayed awake through dinner, then apparently fell asleep on the couch while we were watching an *American Experience* program on my computer. I wasn't aware that Beck had eased my head onto her lap, but the next thing I heard was Mel's voice.

"What the hell?"

"Shh," Beck said quietly. "Emily's asleep."

"Is that what you call it?"

Mel sounded increasingly upset. I tried to rouse myself, but Beck had placed her hand on my shoulder and held me gently in place.

"Did you bring the new contract?"

"Yeah, but I'd like to know what the hell you think you're doing." Mel's voice sounded louder, and I wondered if she'd come closer. "Emily is much more to me than a client. So whatever shit you're trying to pull, you can give it up right now."

"I'm not pulling anything. And please keep your voice down."

"Don't tell me what to do, you fucking little creep."

I could hear Mel's fury building. Being challenged on money was bad enough, but she'd always needed to claim first place in our friendship. This wasn't going to end well. I opened my eyes and pushed myself into a sitting position. "Mel, stop. I'm fine. I fell asleep is all."

Mel stared at me, huffing out a breath. "It didn't look fine. Do you realize this punk was pushing your face into her crotch?"

"I didn't push," Beck replied calmly. "When she first fell asleep, her neck was in an awkward position. I was making her comfortable."

It might have sounded more feasible if Mel knew we'd slept together—literally slept—twice. But I wasn't going to tell her. Not now. I stood. "I think I'll go to bed. You two finish your business."

After one step, I felt dizzy. When I stopped and stretched out a hand for balance, Beck was already beside me. "I'll help you," she said softly.

Mel stalked over. Standing in front of Beck, she pronounced, "*I'll* help her. You sit your punk ass down on that couch."

I felt Beck tense, but I was counting on her pacifist nature to not escalate the situation. "Thanks, Beck," I squeezed her hand quickly and let go. "Mel will be right out."

Once Mel had me settled on the bed, I grabbed her arm. "I want you to apologize to Beck. She's been nothing but nice about me being sick."

Mel scowled as she eased away from me. She'd never liked being around any kind of infirmity. "I don't like the way that girl looks at you. She's after something. You have to think of your artistic reputation. I don't trust her."

"Well, I do. And I want you two to work well together. Tell her you're sorry for being overprotective. She'll understand."

"Hmm."

"I mean it. Besides, you owe me."

To her credit, Mel didn't pretend like she didn't know what I meant. "You got medicine and everything? I can send that doctor again."

"No, I'll be fine. And yes, I have everything I need." I decided not to mention that Beck had bought three different cold formulas for me and refused payment.

"I'm going to check on you tomorrow," she announced loudly, standing at the doorway. I knew this was for Beck's benefit.

"Fine," I said because I knew she meant well. Even though we sometimes drove each other crazy, she was my friend.

I didn't even try to listen in to the murmur of conversation from the other room. I woke to a hand on my forehead.

"I think your fever is about gone," a voice said.

"Beck?" I'd been dreaming of a wind that had taken my umbrella and was carrying it away down a New York street.

"Yes. Would you rather I called Mel back?"

"Not for a second." I reached for her hand and held it to my chest. "You're staying, aren't you?" I could feel myself drifting off to sleep.

"For as long as you want me to," she answered in her quiet way.

How wonderful would that be? I asked myself, pretending I didn't know the answer.

❖

I was finishing my tea and the breakfast quiche Beck had left for me when Mel arrived. She began complaining about Beck's insistence that the sale would be next weekend. "I'm having to order a rush job on those posters, and that's going to cost extra," she groused. "Plus, I'll have to spend this weekend posting them all over the coast."

"I'm sure she just wants to get it over with," I said. "Besides, she needs the space to work on her PAFA project."

"Shit. I forgot to mention that on the poster." Mel pulled out her phone and began a conversation with the print shop in town, her tone verging on offensive at times. I wanted to tug her sleeve or make a face, but I knew it wouldn't help. I'd heard her dealing with other vendors and sales people before, and she could swing from charming to ill-mannered in a matter of seconds. That was simply how she worked. I realized I'd put much of that same behavior into my new character and cringed at the thought that I was like that too, only more so with the people I was close to. Or those who got too close to me.

As I often did, I let thoughts of work override any reformation I could apply to my own conduct. Instead, I considered that it had been a few days since I'd done anything on my new story. I felt like I might have an hour or two in me, so when Mel finished her call, I told her I needed to write.

"But remember, you've got friends here," she said. "You don't have to depend on your houseguest for everything."

I nodded, figuring that was about as nice as she was going to get about Beck. "Thanks, Mel. You know I appreciate it. And be sure and thank June and the W's too."

An hour later, I'd read over my last few days' work. It was so different from my usual style that I had to keep reminding myself that I'd written it. I couldn't decide if that was good or bad and ultimately decided I'd let my editor figure it out.

Beck was a firm believer in the healing properties of menthol rub, which meant I spent every day slathered in it. At night, she made me wear socks to bed after putting some of the aromatic ointment on the bottoms of my feet, claiming it would help with my cough. I wondered how she could stand lying close to me, but she claimed to like the smell. That or time and regularly provided cups of the echinacea tea she'd bought seemed to do the trick, and by Wednesday, I was all but well. The problem was, the better I felt, the hornier I got, and sleeping next to her—even in pajamas and socks—was not helping. That evening, after I'd gotten ready for bed, I told her I'd be fine to go with her to campus tomorrow. Her brilliant smile faded at my next words. "And I think I'm okay to sleep alone again."

"Oh." She looked into my face, but I quickly became busy, fiddling with the tie to my robe.

"I can't thank you enough for the comfort and care you've given me." I was forcing every word, but I had to. I couldn't let myself become accustomed to this, to her, to us. None of those things existed outside of this private dream world that the beach had become. "But I don't want...uh, we shouldn't, that is...I can't..."

"It's okay, Emily. You don't have to explain." She shrugged and turned away. "You're the boss."

That hurt, but I couldn't think of a single fitting reply. The door to her room closed quietly.

I stirred, slowly becoming aware of Beck in bed with me, close and warm, holding me with that intoxicating combination of strength and femininity. I was so glad, I didn't care how or why she'd come to be there. But an unexpected sound had awakened me, and I couldn't shake the feeling something was wrong. The bedroom door opened, and a figure stepped in. In a rush of panic, I shook Beck roughly, and she sat up.

"What?" she said, startled into speaking overly loud.

"I knew it." It was Mel's voice.

At least it wasn't the man of my nightmares, though it certainly wasn't the way I wanted Mel to find out about Beck and me. What there was of us. I sat up too. "It's not what you think."

"You know what I think? I think you didn't give me what I wanted for my birthday."

"Uh, okay. I mean, I'm sorry. What was it you wanted?"

She was next to the bed, though I hadn't heard her move. But now I could smell the alcohol on her breath. "I wanted a three-way with you and June. But you know what? I'll take on you and baby Spike here instead. Some butch-on-butch action might be an amusing change, once we're through."

I felt Beck rise and knew she was going in Mel's direction. Quickly, I sat up. "Mel, I think you've had way too much to drink. Let's go in the other room and talk about it."

"Why don't we talk about it here?" Her hand fondled my breast.

I gasped. "No, Mel." We'd established that boundary a long time ago, and for her to cross it now, so unexpectedly, was even more creepy than it was shocking.

I saw Beck's form engage with Mel, crowding between us and forcing Mel to step away from me. "Back off, Mel. Nothing like that is going to happen." Her voice was grim and almost harsh.

Mel laughed, but it didn't sound like any laugh I'd ever heard from her. It was maniacal. "That's what you think, you sorry fucking asshole."

I saw it. Mel had a weapon in her other hand. Like a bat but thicker. A club of some kind. Something metal. A piece of Beck's work maybe? Before I could think beyond that, she swung it at Beck's face, hitting her squarely on the jaw. I heard a terrible crack, and Beck staggered, holding her face as she landed hard against the wall.

"Mel, no. Stop!" I called, trying to get up, but she was beside me,

pushing me back onto the bed. I was powerless, just as I'd been with the man who'd taken Abby.

"Why don't you assume the position, and I'll be right with you." Mel leered.

Beck came forward again, reaching for the weapon, but it was like she moved in slow motion. Mel turned and swung, hitting her squarely on the side of the head. There was another sickening crack, and Beck went down and didn't move. Was she even breathing?

"Let me finish this," Mel said conversationally, "and then we'll get started." She raised the club again over Beck's fallen shape.

"No," I screamed. "Somebody help. Help me!" Mel started her downswing, and I kept screaming. "Beck, get up. Oh God, no. Please stop. Help!"

The door opened, and a figure stood on the threshold. "Emily? Did you call me?"

It was Beck. I inhaled sharply. The smell of alcohol had disappeared. Mel wasn't here.

"Beck? Are you okay?" I rubbed my eyes. All the hideous sounds and sights had seemed so tangible, I was having trouble believing it was all a dream.

"Am I okay?" Beck asked, clearly puzzled. "I'm fine. Are you?"

"Come here, please. Come here and let me see you." At that moment, needing the solid presence of her didn't seem nearly as threatening as the possessive violence of my nightmare.

She walked to the side of my bed where Mel had stood. I didn't like that. Beck and Mel were about as different as two people could be, and I was struck by the thought that they would always have distinctly separate places in my life. "Over here." I patted the bed beside me. She went around and got on top of the covers. I didn't care at this point. I touched her face, her hair. I ran my hands over her neck and down to her shoulders. "You're really all right? You're sure?"

She laughed quietly. "I'm sure, Emily." Her voice sobered. "Did you have another bad dream?"

"Yeah, I...I guess so. It...it seemed so real."

She reached out and smoothed my hair. "Sometimes the scariest ones are like that."

I leaned in a bit, breathing in her scent. God, I could recreate everything about the serenity of this place by the way she smelled. Her touch was slowing my pulse, and my breathing was close to normal.

"You have them too?"

"Sometimes. Sometimes I dream I'm aboard ship with my papa, and we're caught in the storm where he died. The bell is making a terrible racket as the boat pitches and I know we're going down. That's the worst one." I shivered at the very thought of a boat disaster dream. "Other times, I'm still in high school, having to talk in front of the class. I realize I didn't do the assignment, and I don't know what I'm supposed to be talking about."

"Are you naked?"

"Now?"

I still had my hands on her arms, so I could feel her T-shirt. I tugged at it. "No, silly, in the dream."

"Oh." She sounded embarrassed, and I felt bad. "No, not in the dream either. Why?"

"Never mind." I yawned. I didn't want analysis or reasoning. I just wanted her exactly where she was. But she moved away enough to separate us.

"I should let you get back to sleep."

"Could I…" Was I brave enough to ask this? "Could I exercise a woman's prerogative and change my mind?"

"What are you going to exercise?"

Don't be clever. Say what you want. "Could I ask you to stay?"

She shifted slightly. "Only for tonight?"

I owed her the truth, even if it meant risking her rejection. Somewhere, I found the fortitude to say, "I don't know, Beck. I'm… I'm trying to find my way on this. I want you here tonight. I don't know what I'll want tomorrow."

She didn't answer right away, and I was fairly sure she'd go, telling me that wasn't good enough. And I truly couldn't blame her. Why should she put up with an inconsistent, bad-tempered, sometimes pitiful woman with a permanent stain on her past? Half of me wanted to admonish her to get the hell out, but when I felt her pull down the covers and ease in beside me, the other half was almost overwhelmed with relief.

"Could I please hold you for a little while?" I asked, and she put her head on my shoulder. My arms went naturally around her. Before it had always been her holding me. This was different, but I felt an enchanting sense of certainty when her arm slipped around my waist.

It was part desire, but it was also part...perfection. "Thank you," I whispered.

"Sleep, Emily," she directed, and like before, I did.

Chapter Thirteen

My assistance with Beck's project turned out to be letting three art department students make a plaster cast of my face while I formed an expression of terror. Giving that look wasn't difficult, since I'd seen them make hers first, and she looked as though she was crying. Watching her interact with her peers was enjoyable, but the experience of having alginate harden on my face before having it covered with plaster-impregnated strips of cheesecloth wasn't my idea of a good time. I'd pretended that my dread of unfamiliar situations and unknown people was claustrophobia, and of course, Beck was wonderfully understanding and supportive, giving me an out at every turn—which meant I had to go through with it.

Though I was breathing much easier once we reached my car, there was still a slight tremor in my hands, and I asked Beck to drive. Once we'd left the campus area, she asked if I was hungry. My throat was so dry from breathing through my mouth that what I really wanted, for the first time in a long time, was a drink, but I told myself food would do. We pulled into a small storefront restaurant off the main drag, the type of place only locals would know or chance. The moment we entered, the scent of something familiar and warming made my stomach growl.

"Something smells divine," I murmured as we waited to be seated.

Before Beck could reply, a robust man with a fringe of hair appeared from the back, beaming at us, his arms open. "Good people," he all but shouted. "Let me take you to our best table."

Beck grinned. "Thanks, Dag."

Once we were seated, I smiled at her. "Do you know everyone in Windsom Edge?"

"Don't be overly impressed," she whispered. "He says that to everyone."

The Found Jar

I couldn't help laughing. Beck's total lack of pretentiousness was wonderfully refreshing. A few of the women I'd been with would have taken credit for getting a close parking space. Beck seemed to take my laughter as a positive sign. She covered my hand where it rested on the table with her own.

"You were amazing today. And your cast was absolutely perfect. I'd very much like to buy your dinner. Not as a date," she added quickly. "But as a thank you." Would I have preferred it if she'd made it a date? Beck seemed to misunderstand my hesitation. "Please," she added. "It would mean a lot to me if you'd say yes." Abruptly, she blushed and looked down. "I mean, if you'd let me treat you tonight."

I felt my own face heat up, remembering what she'd said about kissing for yes. If I'd had any doubt as to exactly what she meant, I certainly knew now. *Be gracious.* My Aunt Sharon's voice. What had made me think of her? "Thank you," I said, stopping myself before I said *yes.* "You're sweet to offer, and I accept."

She beamed, and I wished, for the millionth time, that she weren't so damned appealing. Luckily, my attention was diverted by a young waitress with a bored expression who approached our table. Her disinterested tone as she recited the special for the evening didn't reduce my distress when she mentioned chicken and dumplings. I hoped to cover my sharp intake of breath with a long drink of water, but Beck noticed.

"Could you give us a few minutes, please?" she asked politely, and the young woman sighed and left. I suspected we wouldn't see her for a while.

Once we were alone, Beck turned fully toward me, her expression focused. "What's wrong?"

I thought of dozens of possible answers, none of them true. My stomach twisted as I pondered telling her something so intensely personal. If I opened this door to my past even a tiny crack, could I control what came out? Once I started, would I be able to stop? I swallowed, hoping my voice would sound normal. "It's nothing, really. Chicken and dumplings was my favorite when I was young. My mother made them for special occasions or when someone was sick." *But never again, once they were gone.* I fought off my memory of that last time: Abby with the sniffles but smiling at me from across the table as we both enjoyed the delicious treat. Feeling Beck's eyes on me, I forced myself to breathe normally. "Later, when I was first living with my aunt, I asked her to make them for me." Realizing why she'd been on my mind moments ago, I managed a small laugh. "They were terrible. Absolutely awful. Before long, I learned she simply wasn't a good cook, but at the time I thought..." What had I thought? That she'd made them bad on purpose? I was angry, stupid, young, and scared. All I could recall now was the terrible fight we'd had about it, the first of many, as it turned out.

The press of warm fingers on my arm brought me back to the present. "The chicken and dumplings are great here, but I can understand if you'd rather not try them," Beck said quietly. "And if it bothers you, I won't get them either. Or we can go somewhere else."

It's only food. Did I truly need to guard this memory as if it was something precious? "No. It's...it's fine." I straightened my shoulders, taking courage from her tender touch. "And I should try them. I mean, they can't be any worse than my Aunt Sharon's."

Beck grinned and waved the waitress over. The girl clucked her tongue as if it couldn't have been more obvious when we both ordered the chicken and dumplings. Once we were alone again, Beck asked, "How old were you when you moved in with your aunt?" She was watching me carefully while trying not to seem too concerned.

"I'd just turned twelve. She was what my mother used to call an old maid. Unmarried, childless, and—from all appearances—perfectly happy that way. She'd moved across the country to have her own life and unexpectedly having the responsibility of a hostile, frightened preteen certainly wasn't in her plans. I see that now, but at the time... let's say it wasn't an ideal situation."

"How long did you stay with her?"

I wanted to finish this conversation but not appear overly defensive. This was the most I'd ever said to someone outside of therapy, but the fact that I hadn't lashed out at Beck for asking in the first place gave me some gratification. I told myself that if I handled this now, we'd never have to talk about it again. "Until I went to college. We managed to be civil to each other at least half the time, which is probably about average for most parent-teen relationships, don't you think?"

"I guess I'm below average, as usual." Her voice was glum, but she met my gaze steadily. "I get along really well with my mama."

"That's because you're practically perfect." I smiled at her blush, glad I hadn't gone with my first impulse, which was to mention her stepfather to prove my point. Instead, I tried for a casual change of subject. "So...will you tell me what you're going to do with those casts we made today?"

"Nope." She shook her head emphatically. "You'll have to find out along with the rest of the world when the PAFA committee makes its decision."

"You're not going to show me your work before you ship it?" I was only half teasing and more than a little disappointed when she shook her head again.

Our salads arrived, and I began eating. Then I noticed she was studying her greens with a face so serious, she almost looked sad. "What's wrong? Is your food not all right?"

She looked at me as if surprised by the question. I guess I hadn't often asked about what she was experiencing. "Oh no, it's fine." She resolutely took a bite, looking more cheerful as she chewed. But after a few more seconds, she put her fork on the plate again. "Could I talk to you about something else that has to do with my work?"

I put my fork down too, wanting her to know she had my full attention. "Of course. Anything."

She cleared her throat. "I'm nervous about this sale coming up. I mean, like, scared nervous. Maybe no one will come. Or what if they come, and they don't like my stuff? What if Mel loses what miniscule patience she has with me after the first night and quits, losing the money she's already spent? I won't have any way to pay her back." She looked away, but she was worrying at her lip. "There's a thousand ways for this to go wrong and only one way for it to go right. That's not a good situation."

She was about as upset as I'd seen her, and taking hold of her hand seemed like the thing to do. "I honestly believe you have nothing to worry about. Mel will be fine in any case, but I know people will love your work, and I think you're going to make lots of money."

I could feel her trembling under my grip. She looked at me, her honey brown eyes wet. "You're gonna be there, aren't you?"

"Every minute."

"You promise?" Her voice was weak, but her look was intense.

I knew this wasn't a cursory question, and I wasn't one to give my word carelessly in any case. There were things between Beck and me that I hadn't yet made up my mind about, but this wasn't one of them. She deserved my support, and I would act as a buffer between her and Mel. Enclosing her hand with both of mine, I smiled. "I promise."

The tension in her posture eased, and she added her other hand. "Thank you."

"You don't have to thank me, Beck. I told you I wanted to be able to say I knew you when."

"When what?" she asked, and we smiled at each other, leaving our hands clasped until the waitress appeared with our meals.

❖

It was still dark when I awoke. Somehow in the night, I'd positioned myself with one leg thrown over Beck's thigh. It must have been the heat between us, combined with the way my center fit against her, that had woken me from—or might have been the cause of—a very pleasant dream. I shifted somewhat, and the sensations intensified. I closed my eyes again, giving myself an extra moment to revel in her scent, in her warmth, in the firm smoothness of her skin. How, after sleeping alone for every night of my adult years, had I become so readily accepting of another body beside me? Accepting? I was practically dependent at this point.

I thought of how she had stood shyly at my bedroom door earlier, already in those boy boxers I'd come to know and one of the oversized T-shirts she regularly slept in. I'd known her uncertainty was based on my near muteness once we'd gotten in the car. The fact that a raging debate had been going on inside me had kept me from external conversation, other than a quick yes or no. Beck had taken the hint, and we'd made most of the drive in silence. Then she'd waited to be invited in or pushed away, doubtlessly unable or unwilling to guess what I might want from her, since I'd never given her any kind of measuring stick to help determine my mood or my desires. Probably because it had been years since I'd found a reliable one myself.

In the debate, one side of me had wanted her to stay, had wanted to kiss her yes and make love all night, and manage whatever happened next whenever we got around to it. The other side told me I needed to be responsible, to let her go, to tell her to return to her own bedroom, to prepare us both for the inevitable leave-taking that was only weeks away. Whatever the repercussions would be of sleeping alone again, I needed to deal with them as I always had. But after taking a few seconds to openly admire the look of her slightly tousled hair and browned body, I'd simply said, "I'm nearly ready. Make yourself comfortable," and disappeared into the bathroom like the weakling I was. When

I'd turned off the light after many minutes of self-recrimination, her presence in my bed drew me as if by gravity. "Thank you for dinner," I'd whispered, in case she was close to sleep.

"Thank you for you," she'd replied, causing me to smile.

We'd dropped off without another word, and that had been all I'd needed until this moment. Now my body insisted I deal with the swelling urge that pulsed where we touched. I moved slowly against her, rocking almost imperceptibly. God, she felt good, so fucking good. I moved some more, holding my breath as I listened for any change in her breathing, any indication she might be waking. I heard none. Would she notice the dampness from my panties coating her leg where I pushed against her? Could she sense the way my flesh was opening, the way my clit grew harder with each brief stroke? Apparently not, and I took advantage, as I'd done throughout our relationship. I pressed closer, increasing both the pressure and speed. The sensations increased, and I tried to hold back my rising moan. Increasingly desperate for release, I convinced myself Beck was a sound sleeper who, if she had any awareness, might think she was dreaming. And me? I just wanted to come. I needed to come. And I was going to come if I could get a little more pressure, move a little faster.

In a way, it all happened so quickly, I couldn't have done anything differently. In a way, it happened very slowly, deliberately, and with delicious purpose. Beck bent her leg, and I fully mounted her thigh. The added friction increased the sensation of my impending climax. At the same time, she cupped my buttocks, moving with the rhythm I'd set, pulling and releasing, pulling and releasing, before taking me to exactly the pace I needed. Any semblance of control shredded, and I whimpered with pleasure, unable to help it and, at that exact second, unwilling to try. Her touch, along with the added stimulation of our new position and momentum, pushed me over the edge, and I shuddered and spasmed against her, breathing erratically with an almost soundless "oh" of release and satisfaction. Her hands remained in place, letting me determine when the final thrust had milked the last of my indulgence, at which point, my body stilled alongside her, though I could still feel the beat of fading excitement in my throat.

She hummed quietly and kissed the top of my head, her hands drifting to my back where they encircled me with the same loving care she always showed. My mind prepared dozens of possible reactions, mostly various configurations of embarrassment or the total pretense of some ridiculous version of sleepwalking—sleep sexing?—but I opted to luxuriate in the fading sensations and the absurd relief that Beck hadn't said anything to indicate she was aware of what had happened, even though it was quite obvious she knew.

I didn't realize I'd fallen asleep until I felt a slight movement of the bed. How much time had passed? Was it morning, and Beck was getting up? I took stock, trying to determine the situation without completely waking up. I was on my side, facing Beck, who was on her back beside me. The subtle shaking continued, and I focused on her body. There was a tension in her torso that was new, different from her normal sleeping posture. The arm that usually held me close wasn't around me; it was resting between us. Well, not resting exactly. It lay between us while the other warm hand that had become the soothing companion to my rest now dipped between her own thighs. As I listened to her irregular breathing, everything became clear. Beck was touching herself, quietly masturbating next to me. Was this in response to my earlier loss of control, or had it happened before, and I'd slept through it?

Everything in my awareness seemed to sharpen. I could feel her muscles tightening in anticipation as I sensed the wet glide of her fingers and caught the rich scent of her arousal. In the next second, I imagined replacing her hand with my own, and the urge to touch her became so strong, I opened my mouth, ready to whisper, "Let me." I could only force myself to hold off by pressing my lips to her neck. At the same time, I reached across her chest, cupping her breast. I was certain her nipple would be erect, but I didn't touch it yet, gently massaging the full base of her instead. She arched, making a small sound somewhere between surprise and delight, and I felt her pace increase. I matched it with my own hand, and each of us worked our way toward the peaks we sought. I kissed her neck again, and when her higher-pitched breath sounded a warning, I bit gently, finding the hard tip of her breast and working it between my fingers. Her hips rose slightly, and she grunted a long, low sound. I could detect the waves of her pleasure even through the fabric of her nightclothes. After she stilled, and her breathing slowed, I pulled her onto my shoulder, running my fingers through her hair while she settled against me with a sigh.

It must have been the light. Beck startled and struggled to sit up. "It's late. I'm late," she mumbled, throwing off the covers and stumbling out of bed. I had barely gotten to a sitting position and was still rubbing the sleep from my eyes when she reappeared in her usual cutoffs and sleeveless tee. "I'm sorry, I'm so sorry, Emily." I might have frowned at that because she quickly added, "I don't like leaving you like this. It's just...there are four jobs today, and yesterday Mom said she was worried we wouldn't get everything done. Otherwise, I'd—"

I stopped her with a hand on her cheek, a gesture that felt more intimate than I'd intended. But then, everything between us seemed to be moving in that direction. "It's fine. I understand." I moved my hand away, but she caught it and held it to her chest. I swallowed.

"I think I understand something too," she said. I couldn't bring myself to ask what, but she went on anyway. "I understand about kissing good-bye. I'd really like to."

I stood and put my mouth to her ear. "I think we should talk about that tonight."

She shivered lightly before her expression turned worried. "You'll be here?"

I put my other hand to my chest. "I promise."

She seemed reluctant to let go but nodded. "Okay."

Less than two hours later, when I looked at the readout on my ringing cell phone, my upbeat mood dropped like a stone, its dead weight coming to rest in my gut. In the last twenty-four hours, I'd made two promises to Beck. Now I'd be breaking them both.

❖

"Girl, where in blazes are you?" William's voice was hushed, and I suspected he'd stepped away from the others to answer.

"In Blazes, Arizona." I tried for levity as I answered, unable to keep the weariness from my tone. "But I'll be back late tonight." His stunned silence gave me time to ask, "How did it go?"

"Fabulous, of course." He didn't pretend not to know what I meant. "Those twinkle lights we used looked way better than the tiki torches Mel wanted. That horror in Charlottesville ruined those for our lifetimes." The party to launch Beck's sale had been Friday night, with the sale going on through Saturday evening. It was close to noon on Sunday, and I wanted to call before I checked out of the motel. William's voice dropped even lower. "Mel can't seem to decide if she's happy or not. Apparently, the sale made a lot of money, but there was some other deal..." He trailed off, probably hoping I'd fill in the blank. But the money wasn't what I'd wanted to ask about.

"And Beck?"

He was quiet for a few seconds. "I think she's doing okay now."

I didn't like the sound of that. "What about during the party and the sale?" Another pause, followed by a sigh. "Tell me, Will."

"Em, we didn't think she was going to make it at first. She was frantic when you weren't home that first night—"

"I left a note," I said, hearing the defensiveness in my voice. Granted, it was deliberately vague and very brief, but I hadn't simply disappeared.

"Evidently, it fell onto the floor under the table, and it took Mel and June coming over and helping search the house before they found it."

Okay, that was bad, but not entirely my fault. "So then?"

"Beck wanted to call the whole thing off, but Mel wouldn't hear of it. I think I heard them yelling from here. Luckily, June calmed everyone down. She really saved the day, Em. She told me later how Beck was practically catatonic on Thursday. While we were all running around, trying to get stuff ready for the sale, she was sitting on your deck, staring out at the water and petting that white cat. She wouldn't talk beyond a syllable or two. Mel was getting pissed again, but June went over and talked to her for a while. Finally, Beck came downstairs, mumbled an apology to everyone, and started pitching in to help. Friday night, June acted as Beck's date."

"Date?" I asked, trying to tamp down the unpleasant taste in my mouth.

"You know, walking her around, hanging on her arm while they talked to people, bringing her drinks and making sure she ate something." He giggled lightly. "Beck was stiff as a board at first, but by the end of the evening, they looked pretty cozy. You should have seen Mel's face. I wouldn't be surprised if she asks June to marry her or some other crazy thing just to make it clear who rules that roost. She wouldn't want Beck getting any ideas."

Beck didn't usually drink. I wondered if June was the one who'd been getting ideas. She'd always said how cute she thought Beck was. William took advantage of my silence to ask, "What about you, Em? Are you okay? What made you take off for Arizona, of all places? And why now?"

It was my turn to sigh. "It's too complicated, Will. I can't go into it on the phone. And please, don't tell anyone you talked to me."

"Not even Beck?"

The question was completely sincere. Despite the fact she'd been on my mind almost constantly, I answered, "No, especially not Beck." A secondhand conversation was not what she and I needed.

His sniff conveyed immense disapproval. "You're the boss."

That phrase made the unpleasant taste edge toward the same scream that had been threatening to emerge ever since the phone call four days ago. When it tried again to force its way out of my throat, I swallowed vigorously. "Thank you, William. I'll see you soon."

After spending three days in the desert in the company of people like me, people whose lives had already been shattered and whose broken hearts hoped only for some imperfect conclusion, I wanted nothing more than to return to the fresh, cleansing scents of sand and sea. I'd met a wide sampling of humanity over the years at similar scenes, huddled together as we watched distant lights at night surrounding shallow graves in the woods or standing isolated in the unbearable brightness of morgues in cities large and small. Some of us knew each other's stories. All of us knew each other's pain. Once, the familiarity of their anguish would have brought me some small measure of comfort, but this time I'd found myself wanting distance from it.

Detective O'Malley, whose cop instincts still worked though he was retired, had eyed me over coffee at the airport. "You look different," he said. "You seeing someone?"

"Not really," I'd hedged. "Some friends talked me into a vacation, and it's been…a nice break."

He gave me a shrug. "Maybe you need a break from this too. You want me to not call for a while?"

"No," I said emphatically, shaking my head to show there was no question. "I want to know. I need to—"

"Okay, okay," he cut me off. "I just asked because things can change. The way people feel about what they're doing in their lives can change. But sometimes, they don't realize it until someone else points it out to them."

His words echoed for the entire flight to Norfolk.

❖

It was late, and the Guest House was totally dark. It took me two circuits of every room, turning on lights and calling softly, to convince myself I was truly alone. I couldn't imagine where Beck could be at this hour. No, I didn't *want* to imagine, but as I wheeled my bag into the bedroom, a most unwelcome series of ideas presented themselves. Was she sleeping with June or reunited with Peyton? Injured in a scooter accident? No longer at risk from her stepfather, had she moved back home?

After confirming that her things were still here, I kicked off my shoes and flopped onto the bed. The previous cool spell had evidently passed, as the air felt heavy and oppressive. I'd practiced my return speech in my head dozens of times, and it still wasn't good enough. But having to wait, not knowing when I'd see her or how she was feeling would make me crazy if I thought about it anymore. In no time I was dozing, relieved by the now familiar scents and sounds of the ocean. I opened my eyes again when a faint, unfamiliar sound broke through my lethargic mind. When it came again, I stood and walked slowly into the main room.

"Beck?" I asked hopefully.

The answer was another faint cry from the door. I opened it to find Sugar waiting expectantly. She darted in, making her move before I could react, trotting quickly toward the bedroom.

"She's not in there either," I called, and the little cat looked back at me as if to say, *whose fault is that?*

Two days later, there was still no sign of her. Or rather, I hadn't sighted her physically. Wandering around the house on the first morning after my return, my stomach lurched when I noticed the found jar. Cleanly shifted sand covered all the trinkets we'd collected. One shell and a piece of a ticket stub were still visible as they clung to opposite sides of the tall container, but everything else was completely covered over. Certain this was Beck's doing, I tried to puzzle out what it meant. Could it signal we had a chance to start over? Or did she mean it as the end of everything we'd known together?

Head spinning, I'd gone to Reefside, thinking they would know where she was. But everyone denied any knowledge of Beck's whereabouts, so I let it go, despite thinking June looked a tad guilty. They insisted I eat breakfast with them, and since I owed them for all they'd done to help Beck with her show, I tried to be as sociable as my mood would allow.

When I returned to the Guest House, my shower had been used, and Sugar, who I'd left sleeping on the couch, had been let out. I thought it was an indication Beck knew I was there and she'd be home that evening, but I was wrong. Though there was a thawing pan of lasagna on the counter when I awoke from my nap, there was no note, and my houseguest—as Mel had called her—did not return. Similar occurrences repeated at odd hours when I was gone or sleeping until, on the morning of the third day, I lost patience. I left a note for Beck, requesting her to stay until I returned or at least contact me in some way.

Storming down to Reefside, I ignored everyone else and marched straight over to June. "I know you know where she is."

June shook her head. "I don't."

"But you've been in touch with her, haven't you?" I countered. When she didn't reply, I snatched the phone from her hand. Of course there was a passcode, so it was a vain gesture, but I knew I was on the right track when Mel locked eyes with June and inclined her head in my direction.

June reclaimed her phone but didn't look at it. "We've texted a few times, but I honestly don't know where she is. She won't tell me."

"Do you think she's at her mother's house?" I asked, my temper cooling.

"I asked. She says not."

Mel stepped up beside me. "Never mind all that. We're leaving before the storm gets here, and you need to come too."

I frowned. "What storm?"

Walter jumped in as if he'd been offstage waiting for a cue. "Girl, haven't you been watching the weather?" Ignoring my exasperated expression, he explained, "There's a hurricane a few hundred miles off the coast. It's already a category three, and they think it will continue to strengthen until it reaches land."

He waited for my reaction. Finally, I asked, "It's expected to hit here?"

"They're not sure yet, but there's a chance it will. And even if it doesn't hit here directly, there will be strong winds and heavy rain, probably for days. Food shortages, gas shortages, terrible traffic." Mel and June were nodding like bobbleheads. "We think it makes sense to go back to the city now. We'll lose our deposits, but it's better than possible damage to our cars or other property." He lowered his voice dramatically. "Never mind us risking our lives if we try to ride it out."

I could have pretended to give it some thought, but what would be the point? As unusual as it was for me to disregard something that was potentially dangerous, I knew I wasn't leaving. Not yet. At this moment, the idea of having something else in my life cut short was achingly unacceptable, and I was determined to do the right thing this time. "I'm not going until I hear from Beck."

Mel and Walter both started talking at once, but June pulled me out onto the deck, shaking her head at them as she closed the deck door. "I don't think she wants to talk to you, Emily. After you came by on Monday, I told her you were asking about her, and she's stopped texting me since. You know, it would be best if you came home with us. You always told me things were never going to work out between you two anyway."

I'd said that, true, but the idea that Beck was avoiding me because she'd reached the same conclusion stung in a place I couldn't remember hurting before. Besides, my feelings toward our future had changed. But there certainly was no chance for us if Beck wouldn't speak to me. Anger rising, I stepped into June's space. "That's not the point. The point is, I need to talk to her before I go. You don't understand. There are some things I need to…" I stopped myself, aware I'd closed the distance to her and was dangerously close to losing my temper.

June's expression was difficult to read. I couldn't tell if there was sympathy or pity in her look. She waited a beat to see if I would finish. "We won't be ready to leave until tomorrow," she said. "I hope you'll reconsider."

Not wanting to watch the discussion between her and the rest of my friends, I left quickly. The house had been cleaned and the dishes done. A single word had been added by way of reply to my note. "No," was all it said.

By the next morning, most forecasts had Hurricane Harper veering off to the north, though it did seem likely we'd get hit by several outer bands of rain and wind from the storm. Still, my friends were as determined to leave as I was to stay. Mel's objections rose in volume until she was practically shouting, and even William chimed in, but I simply refused to go. I spent the next day helping them with the last of the packing and loading after having left a new, very short note for Beck. It simply said, "Why not?"

Mel initially insisted on hourly reports from me, but after we watched the latest storm track report, I was able to convince her that twice daily contact would be sufficient. Saying good-bye to everyone took almost as long as the round of car Tetris we'd played to get everything into Mel's Range Rover. I kept offering to bring some things when I came, but as I couldn't give a specific date as to when that would be, no one seemed willing to take me up on it. Watching them drive away gave me a strange feeling that was part relief and part panic. I felt worse when I returned to the Guest House and saw the words responding to my latest note: "I can't count on you."

Beck had said those words to me the last time I'd hurt her. I understood how she must feel, but how could I get her to forgive me if she wouldn't let me near enough to explain? I closed my eyes, revisiting a major decision I'd made while in Arizona. I wanted to tell Beck yes because I found I no longer cared about our age difference or her working for me or about what limited time we might have. Not anymore. After being forcefully reminded how life could be all too brief and was often brutally cruel, why wouldn't I choose to make love for hours before falling into an exhausted sleep next to someone who wanted the same? Why not have Beck and give myself to her if doing so could block out our individual pain and sadness for a time? It wouldn't be the first time I'd used sex to help me forget something, though now it felt like a kind of surrender I'd never tried before. The echo of Detective O'Malley's words had gelled into a realization in the skies over Oklahoma, jarring me to the point where I'd seriously contemplated ordering a Bloody Mary before settling for a second cup of coffee. Something in me had indeed changed, and Beck had been primarily responsible, either for the transformation itself or at least for helping me become aware of it. Now, pondering not being able to ever take that next step in our relationship left me hollow, with an emptiness that threatened to devour whatever was left of my feelings.

Chapter Fourteen

Sugar and I were equally restless as we watched the rain batter the windows. Under other circumstances, the sound might have been pleasant or perhaps exhilarating, but not knowing where Beck was in the storm was making me increasingly anxious. I suspected Sugar was missing Beck as well, but when the little white cat stopped at the door, meowing loudly for the third time, it occurred to me she might need to do some kitty business. I had no intention of installing a litterbox, which meant she'd have to go outside eventually. I peered out, noting we seemed to be in a lull between bands of rain. I put my hand on the doorknob, and she shifted restlessly.

"You have to come back as soon as you're finished," I warned her. "I'll get a towel to dry you off, okay?" Apparently, I'd come to this, talking to a cat as if she'd understand both a present caution and a future plan. Like so much else that was different, this was certainly Beck's doing. I rolled my eyes at myself and opened the door. Sugar shot out into the misty half-darkness of the stormy afternoon, darting away as if she feared I'd change my mind and chase her. I tracked her movements, surprised to see her making her way down the path and across the dunes. I knew nothing about feline bathroom habits, but shouldn't she prefer to go around the garage, or somewhere closer to the house…and drier? There were two more houses in the direction she was going, and then only sand and water. Squinting at the vanishing white speck, I recalled walking that way, something I would never have done on my own had not Beck taken me out to the beach that first time and showed me around. At the sting of memory, I cursed myself for all the time we'd lost and for what we might never have. As I was about to turn away from the window, I was struck by another recollection from that solitary walk, the small encampment I'd found. And the bell. It had seemed so incongruous in a place so carefully hidden...unless the occupant had some maritime background. I stood very still, thinking it through. Beck had twice spoken of the bell on her father's ship, ringing for her school lessons and in her nightmare. Could she be there, even in this weather?

I put on my slicker and grabbed a flashlight—having learned my lesson from my last venture out in the rain—and ducked out into the storm. I wanted to start calling the second I got out the door, but I was too far from my destination. Besides, the force of the wind coming off the ocean would blow my voice all the way into town rather than letting it travel along the shore as I would have wanted. My next thought was it might be best not to announce my presence ahead of time anyway. Though I wanted to tell her the things I'd been thinking and all my plans for our remaining time together, depending on Beck's chivalry rather than on her forgiveness was probably a better bet at this point.

The tide was much higher than I'd ever seen it, making it more unlikely I'd recall the vague location, but I'd already decided I was going to keep looking until I found her...or found the place I now thought she was. I made my way along the dunes, trying to follow the path Sugar had taken. I could hear the waves crashing angrily, and it seemed to be getting darker the farther I got from the house, but that might have been fear. Water streamed off the top of my hood, at least half of it going into my face, dampening the collar of my shirt. Turning my back to the wind, I walked sideways for a time, hunched away from the ocean and the weather it pushed toward me. I was glad I'd substituted rain pants for my jeans this time.

But slogging through the storm got harder, prompting my mind to supply me with thoughts of all the things I'd quit on in my life. I'd let anger and resentment sever any connections with my mother and Aunt Sharon, and numerous friendships from my early life had been left behind in my wish to be someone else. Understandably, I'd left my marriage, and I'd long ago abandoned the idea of love. Without Mel's pushing, I probably would have even given up on my writing. So was I going to lose this chance with Beck, disregard my best intentions, forsake my greatest chance to transform this moment in my life? As if in answer, my flashlight swept across a dune with another behind it, revealing a startling swath of blue against the soaked sand. I hurried toward it, knowing she wouldn't hear me approach over sounds of the storm. A board had been placed across the gap like a barrier to keep the rising water out, and the tarp had been spread out to make a kind of storage area in front of the sand cave. I climbed over the board and approached, listening for any sign of life. I thought I heard the faint rise and fall of a weather forecaster's voice.

"Beck?" I called. "Beck, it's Emily. I need to talk to you."

The sound stopped, then nothing. I was about to call again when I heard her say, "Go away."

The voice was flat and hard, and God, that hurt. I understood why she was upset, but for once in my life, I wasn't going to quit so easily. "Please, Beck. I want to explain what happened. I never, ever intended to hurt you. If you'll listen to me for five minutes, I'll go."

Another long silence. "Tell me from there." I took a breath, trying to determine if I was ready to tell her the whole story. As if reading my mind, I heard her add, "And don't lie to me again, Emily."

I nodded slightly, though I knew she couldn't see me. It was time. "A police detective I've known for a long time called me unexpectedly. A child's remains were found in Arizona, and I had to go and see if it might be my little sister. She was kidnapped from our house when I was ten, and there's been no sign of her since."

I heard no reply other than the roar of the surf for a few seconds. Then the tarp lifted enough to reveal Beck's face peering up at me. "What was her name?"

Beck had often surprised me, but this question gave me extra pause. I didn't like hearing her ask it in the past tense, but given what little I'd told her, I understood. "Abby."

She studied me. "I've heard you say that name in your sleep. I thought she was a girlfriend." She looked down for a few seconds before fixing on my face again. "Will you tell me everything?"

"Yes." I pushed away the tightness in my stomach. "If you want to hear it." Since I'd made the decision that everything was what I wanted, it made sense that to get it, I'd have to give it. And if "everything" for us lasted until the end of the month, it would fit perfectly with what I believed about anything good.

She lifted the tarp higher. "Come in."

I crawled into the shelter. We sat facing each other, our heads mere inches from the roof of Beck's hideaway. If we'd been in the bedroom on one of those warm, sultry summer nights, I don't know if I could have gone through with it. Being in a similar location in the same weather as the night it happened would have thrust me too forcibly back to that place and time. But today's weird mid-afternoon dimness, howling wind, and the smell of damp sand were almost otherworldly as they filtered through the blue plastic above us.

Her expression was still somber, but when I met her eyes, I saw only compassion in them. "Was it her?"

"No, it was a boy. But they couldn't tell at first, so the detective who worked on her kidnapping called me, just in case."

Beck nodded solemnly. Okay, that wasn't bad. Maybe I could do this. I took a breath, aware of a hammering in my chest. I opened my mouth, but nothing came out. Instead, I was replaying the one of many conversations I'd had with Detective O'Malley concerning Abby's case, this one after I'd reached adulthood. O'Malley had reacted with some frustration of his own at my complaints. "Emily, do you realize the numbers involved here? A child goes missing every forty seconds. There are more than thirty-two thousand names of children under the age of eighteen in the National Crime Information Center's Missing Persons File. Twenty percent of the children reported to the National Center for Missing and Exploited Children in nonfamily abductions are not found alive." Which had brought me to the big question: Did Abby fit in all of these categories or only the first two? Would I ever know?

"Think of it like a story, like someone else's story," Beck said softly.

"Once upon a time…" I began, and she stroked my hand one quick time.

I held on to that touch like a lifeline, even after it stopped. Thankfully, telling of my cowardice in the face of Abby's abduction didn't take long. But eventually, reliving the weight of my family disintegrating despite my childish and inept attempts to save it, made my head bow. Eyes closed, I bumped into something warm and solid. Beck's shoulder. Had she moved to me, or was there so little room that physical contact was inevitable? I started to straighten, but her hands rested on the back of my head, and I couldn't move. Didn't want to move. She hadn't said a word the whole time I'd been talking, and now she didn't need to. I'd heard plenty of useless platitudes along with well-intended sentiments during my time with various therapists. What I'd never gotten was this kind of comfort, this quiet support. It was all I wanted.

Time passed. We breathed together. Her fingers moved lightly through my hair, pausing for a few seconds when I rested my hand on her thigh. The plastic above us rattled as the wind picked up, and

I became aware it was raining hard again. "Would you...would you please come home with me?" I spoke without looking up.

Before she could reply, an odd sound—like a groan and a rip simultaneously—sounded above us, and water and sand began to pour in. "Go!" she yelled, pushing me abruptly out of the opening and into the gap before I could even get my hood up. I rolled a few feet away before stumbling to my feet and working to fasten my rain jacket. Horrified, I looked over to see the whole cave appearing to collapse in on itself. I screamed Beck's name and jumped in, pulling ineffectively at the torn plastic for a few seconds before falling to my knees and digging at the mound of sand. I'd heard it said certain sounds were so loud you can't hear yourself think, but I could hear my own thoughts clearly above the storm. *No.* That was all I was thinking, over and over. *No.* She'd be fine. *No.* It was not like that dream where she suffocated. *No*. This was not how this was going to end. *No. No!* No!

When tarp and sand fell away and Beck appeared, rearing up and sputtering like some prehistoric sea creature, I felt a rush of something I hadn't felt in years: joy. She barely had time to tilt her face to the rain as she shook the sand off before I flung myself onto her, knocking us both to the ground. "I have something else to tell you," I announced from atop her as she coughed and turned her head to lightly spit sand out of her mouth.

"I guess I'll have to hear it," she half grunted while not making any effort to dislodge me. We were both soaked already, and the sounds of angry surf seemed to be getting closer. The board groaned dangerously. "But you better hurry before we wash away."

Her words might have been only half-serious, but her expression was unsmiling. Somehow, I knew if I didn't say it now, I wouldn't get another chance. *This is what people mean when they say now or never.* "Yes," I said.

There was a pause. She wiped her mouth with her hand, using the rain to rid herself of another layer of grit. "Yes, I'll have to hear it, or yes, we're about to be washed away?"

I almost laughed. How perfect that I'd just taken the biggest leap of my adult life and been totally misunderstood by the woman with whom I'd been prepared to risk it all. It seemed so simple when I'd planned it in my mind. *Tell Beck yes and kiss her.* Oh yeah, I'd forgotten the second part.

"When I said *yes*, I meant *yes*." I took her face in my hands and kissed her on the mouth, getting a taste of salt and sand for my efforts.

Not exactly the way I'd imagined that either, but it wasn't her fault. I pulled away to look into her face. Beck had that look she had when she was trying to figure something out, eyes narrowed with a slight frown causing the space between her brows to crease. She squirmed, and I realized she might be uncomfortable. I struggled to my feet and offered my hand to help her up. We climbed the board gate and began moving in what I assumed was the direction of the Guest House.

"Beck?" I asked, as we trudged through the weather. "Did you understand me?"

The wind pushed my words away so fast I almost couldn't hear them. She shook her head and shouted, "Home." Having this conversation indoors suited me more than fine. I nodded and put my arm around her. I leaned in, more for reassurance of her presence than for protection from the storm. After what seemed like hours, we reached the small garage door, and she looked in.

"Where's Sugar?" she shouted.

"She was in the house until I came to look for you," I answered, trying not to sound guilty. "I'm sure she'll be back soon. Come on." I had started up the stairs when I felt her move away. When I saw she was heading out into the storm, I ran four quick steps and caught her arm. "Beck, no! The weather is getting worse again." I tugged at her sleeve. "Please don't go now, not by yourself. If she's not here in an hour, we'll both go look for her." I started to add "I promise" but didn't think it was the time to remind her of the ones I hadn't kept. Instead, I pulled her toward the house, saying, "I need to explain something to you, but we've got to get inside."

She moved reluctantly inside. Once there, I waited until we'd both stripped down to our panties and bras since everything else was well beyond damp, and we both toweled off enough to be able to walk without dripping. When Beck handed me her towel, I let it drop to the floor and stepped closer to her. "When I said *yes*, I meant yes to you. Yes to trying. Yes to this." I cupped her neck and pulled her mouth to mine. She tensed with shock for a few seconds but then relaxed and gave the kiss her full attention, her soft lips tasting me as if I were something delicious. Fittingly, in about thirty seconds, my legs were jelly. I wrapped my other arm around her shoulders, tightening my grip to steady myself. When her arms encircled me, one around my back and the other sliding slowly toward my ass, I did something I'd never done while merely kissing. I moaned.

Beck must have taken that sound as encouragement because she shifted into another gear, adding a sense of urgency to the things her mouth was already doing to my pulse rate. And with no say-so from my rational mind, I went with her, pressing my body closer to hers. At that, Beck kissed me as if we were already lovers, and what she ignited inside made me panic, afraid this was something I didn't know how to do. I couldn't match her intensity, not now, not yet, so I pulled apart for a second, breathing shallowly.

Beck looked into my eyes for a few seconds before murmuring, "Shower."

"What?" I made no attempt to hide my confusion.

She grinned. "I need a shower. I was already dirty, and now I'm totally gritty too." She moved her hands around to my waist and leaned away, giving me more space. "Would you like to join me?"

I tried not to look as if I was examining my feelings on the matter. I'd never taken a shower with another person—other than the time I'd helped Beck when she'd been hurt—and since I'd been wearing a bathing suit, it didn't seem like that should count. I swallowed. "Why don't you get started, and I'll join you in a minute?"

She stroked my cheek. "You don't have to, Emily. Just tell me if you don't want to, and I'll be sure not to use all the hot water waiting on you."

There it was. Admirably uncommon kindness and pure decency. The type of qualities I clearly lacked. "If I were you, I'd walk away from me now and never come back," I said, trying not to choke on the warning.

Beck shook her head. "Not until after my shower." I blinked, watching as a smile lightened her serious expression. "You must know I'm joking. I wouldn't let you get rid of me that easily." She leaned in and kissed my forehead gently. "Especially not now, after you said *yes*."

I lowered my head to hers, wanting to keep that contact. "Oh, Beck." I sighed.

She jerked back and straightened abruptly. "Unless really kissing me has changed your mind."

"Not at all, I—" The phone I'd left on the table rang, interrupting what I didn't know how to say anyway. I glanced at the readout and shrugged apologetically. "It's Mel. If I don't answer, she'll keep calling." I brushed at a patch of sand on her neck. "Why don't you go take your shower, and I'll meet you in the bedroom."

Watching those adorable, slightly damp boxers clinging to her tight butt as she walked away, I knew this time I'd be there as promised. My conversation with Mel was short and not particularly sweet. I told her I'd found Beck, and she was cleaning up at the moment.

"Putting her to work already, huh?" Mel asked.

"No, cleaning herself from being out in the storm," I explained. "And afterward, we'll take some time to talk about our situation."

"Your fucking situation?"

I was so tired of Mel and her endless jabs at me and Beck that I answered honestly. "Yes, among other things." I was gratified by the pause that followed.

"Em, you need to stop and think very carefully about this." Mel's tone was as sober as I'd ever heard. "That girl knows who you are, personally and professionally."

"So?"

Her voice lowered. "She could make trouble for you. Go public with salacious details of your affair once you're back here and it's over. I've got a line on some movie people, and they'll be looking at your sales figures, so this is not the time to freak your readers out with news of your young lesbian lover." I sighed, but she kept talking. "This is when you need to follow your usual pattern. You're horny? Fine. Go find a stranger to fuck. And if you suddenly think you're ready to come out with a real relationship, wait till you're here in the city to find Ms. Right. She could be down the block, for all you know. But the main thing is, Spike isn't her, okay?"

I was aware that Mel's tone hadn't returned to her usual insistent confidence. She sounded genuinely concerned, bordering on apprehensive. I heard the shower shut off and decided I wasn't going to question that or anything more just now. "Here's what I know, Mel. You asked me to check in, and I'm checking in. *Beck*," I stressed her name as deliberately as I could, "Beck and I are going to talk. And this conversation is over."

"But you'll call me tomorrow?" Mel asked quickly.

"Yeah, yeah."

I hung up, briefly weighing the legitimacy of Mel's warnings before dismissing them. She had never bothered to know Beck like I did. If she had, she wouldn't think those things. Besides, the movie deal seemed an improbable daydream, especially when compared to my much more tempting present. A plaintive cry caught my attention as I wavered in the kitchen. Rushing to the door, I caught Sugar as she dashed inside, drying her as best I could with the same towel Beck had used. She squirmed in my arms, and when I had gotten her coat drier than dripping, I let her go. She trotted toward the bedroom, but I dashed ahead of her. "Yes, she's back. But I've got first dibs this time." I shut the bedroom door behind me.

When Beck emerged from the bathroom wearing only a towel, everything inside me tightened in anticipation. She took one tentative step before asking, "Should I put on sleepwear?"

My residual annoyance at Mel combined with Sugar's competition had given me the courage to get under the covers naked, and I couldn't help smiling at Beck's considerate question. I patted the bed the way I'd done before when I wanted her next to me. "No, just bring yourself."

Smiling shyly, she kept the towel on until she got to her side of the bed. "Don't expect to be impressed," she said softly. "I'm kinda small up top and kinda big on the bottom."

And perfect in your heart, I wanted to say, but it sounded much too serious, as if we were actually starting a relationship. As much as she'd pissed me off, Mel had reminded me of one thing—this would simply be an affair. "Small or big is a matter of degree. Proportion is what makes someone beautiful." I watched her think about what I'd said, letting her understand it for herself.

"I'm not sure about that," she said, but when she dropped the towel, I almost stopped breathing. I'd already known about the solid sturdiness of her, but I'd pushed the particulars of the nude form I'd seen when she'd been hurt out of my mind. The broad shoulders and narrow waist of her swimmer's body didn't overwhelm the delicately feminine curves of her breasts and hips.

"You're gorgeous," I whispered, and she blushed as she quickly joined me in bed.

Turning to face me, she lifted the sheet, looking beneath. When I gasped and held it back down, she grinned. "If you'd been wearing a bathing suit, I was going to call BS."

Between the differences in our ages and in the amount of exercise we got, I was relieved we weren't going to have an "I'll show you mine if you show me yours" kind of evening. I laughed.

"I love it when you laugh. When your face relaxes, your true beauty shines through."

Beck's statement was deeply sincere, and my mirth faded. "We should talk for a minute."

Her expression darkened. "That sounds serious."

"No, I..." I trailed off, uncertain about how to put it. In the stillness, Beck moved closer, placing one hand on the curve of my waist.

"Don't be afraid, Emily. I would never hurt you."

"I know, Beck. But I'm honestly not sure I can say the same." Gathering myself, I added, "I don't know why you want to do this with me. I'm an awful bitch with a mean temper. And I'm a coward who doesn't know the first thing about real intimacy. I've avoided this sort of closeness all my adult life because I know I'll be terrible at it. Probably because I'm certain that ultimately, something bad will happen. I've always thought that, and I've always been proven right. Or maybe I'm afraid to care about someone because it could end up being a waste of time. So I just don't. Care, I mean. For years, I haven't cared about any of the women I've slept with." Well, that might have been a tad more honest than I'd intended, but I owed it to her.

Beck's brow creased. "But you care about me, don't you?"

The truth was much easier this time. "Yes, I do."

"Good. Did any of the women you had sex with before care about you?"

"I don't know. Maybe some, but I doubt it. It wasn't about that for either of us, I think."

Her kiss was soft as a caress. I rested my hand on her waist, and she smiled. "We're kind of alike in that way. But you know I care about you too, don't you?" When I nodded, she brought her arm fully around me, bringing us so close our breasts brushed. "Maybe that's what we've both been missing." I felt myself heat up. "Do you know I've wanted to be with you like this for a long, long time?"

"It can't have been that long," I protested, making sure my tone was teasing. "We've only known each other this summer."

"Every day and every night. Waking or sleeping, weekdays and weekends. Sun or rain or wind. All of those added together make for a lot."

"I suppose they do." God, she was damn cute and sexy at the same time. I simply had to kiss her. I'd meant to keep it light, but when I moved one hand from around her waist to her hip while stroking her chest, she hummed approval and pushed herself against me. At that, the kiss got hotter, while I reached her shoulder, pulling her closer. Feeling her skin under my fingers and making my way along the length of her body was about to set me off. I couldn't remember ever burning for someone like this, and when I felt her hand teasing along my thigh, I moaned and pressed against her. "I've wanted you too," I confessed, my voice weak with need. "But I've tried to fight it."

"Stop fighting," she growled. "Start feeling."

It was like I had permission to let go. And I did. "Okay" was all I said and all I needed to say. She kissed me, rolling me onto my back as she did. Her body followed mine while she brushed the already damp hair between my legs. "Okay," I said again, and she went a little deeper, groaning as she moved gently through my wetness.

"God, Emily. You feel wonderful." She brushed my swollen clit, and I shuddered with pleasure.

This kind of surrender was easy. "That's it." I grabbed her ass and thrust myself against her while I kissed her neck hard.

"Maybe this is the *yes* we've both been waiting for." With that, she moved her mouth to my breast, closing her lips on my nipple. The insistent caress of her tongue matched the movement of her hand between my legs, and I felt the first hint of orgasm along my spine. It had been so long since I'd come by someone else's hand, and I wanted it to take a long time. I wanted her to do the things to me I didn't do to myself.

"More, Beck," I moaned in her ear. "Please."

She switched her mouth to the other breast and increased her pace as she pressed harder against me. I was wet, and we moved easily together. I wanted to tell her to come inside, to put her mouth on me, to do a dozen other things I'd thought to try but hadn't been with anyone I liked enough, but I was too far gone already. I bit my lip, tilting my head back as the pleasure built. Beck kissed my neck as her other hand palmed my breast. I could hear her breathing heavily, and I tightened my grip on her, almost afraid this was more than I could handle, something I'd always feared.

"I've got you, baby. You can come now."

Beck's voice, tender and full of feeling, pushed me over the edge. "Oh. Oh. Oh!" I hadn't realized I was speaking aloud until I heard the last word, which came out more like a scream, high and long.

Seconds? Minutes? Sometime later, my body calmed, and Beck moved carefully from my center before pulling me over, onto her shoulder. My leg fell weakly across hers, and I felt her lips curve against the side of my head. "God, Beck." My voice sounded fragile, even to my own ears, so I cleared my throat. "Sorry."

Beck carefully lifted my chin, looking into my eyes. "Please, Emily. Don't ever apologize after sex. It's like, the worst thing you can do because no matter what you meant, it can be misinterpreted in many ways."

She had a point there. Embarrassed, I teased, "Is this the voice of experience talking?"

Beck blushed. "I also think commenting on your history is something else you shouldn't do at certain times."

I laughed. "You're very wise for a young one, grasshopper."

She brightened. "I know that show. My papa loved it." Her gaze grew distant. "I think you must miss Abby like I miss him. They never found his body, you know. Only some wreckage they said came from his boat. I used to believe he was still going to come back, like he'd been rescued by someone, but for some reason, he just hadn't been able to make it home yet."

I knew how that kind of waiting felt. "I used to think that man had kept her alive, and she'd get away from him somehow and show up at our door," I said, my voice quiet. "I'd sneak out of my bedroom at night and turn the porch light on after mom had gone to bed, so she would be able to tell we were waiting for her." That was another thing I'd never told another living soul. I considered what an odd coincidence it was to have met someone who'd suffered a similar loss. Beck must have thought the same thing because she cuddled close to me, rubbing her cheek across my hair. I'd always felt uncomfortably smothered when my bed partner for the evening had tried any similar moves, but now it felt comforting, reassuring even.

"When did you stop?" Beck asked after a while.

I was drifting, and quickly blinked myself awake. "Stop what?"

"Leaving the light on."

"Oh. After my mom gave me up, and I had to go into foster care. I wasn't living there anymore, so…"

She moved enough to look at me, and my voice trailed off at the admiration in her eyes. "I can't get over how strong you are, how resilient. You've not only survived, you've thrived. You're an amazing woman, Emily Harris."

I usually reacted badly to compliments like that. Normally, I would have snapped off some awful comment to push her away, like "I guess there's some lingering brain damage from that injury," but I knew how much those words would hurt her, and I couldn't bring myself to do that again. Not yet. "Oh, Beck. You're sweet to say so, and I wish all that were true, but it's not."

"You see yourself through the lens of the past. I see you as you really are." She kissed my forehead. "But let's not argue about your wonderfulness. Not right now."

As I smiled at the word *wonderfulness*, it occurred to me we'd been lying there for a while, and I hadn't made a move on her yet. Very unlike me to have been talking instead of taking advantage of her fine body and way too much like what she'd told me about her former bed partners. I moved from her arms and straddled her waist. "Let me show you what I'd like to do," I said, making sure my voice had a low, suggestive tone to it. "Right now."

Her mouth opened slightly, and she reached to cup my breasts. "You look like a goddess, sitting there like that."

Though her comment was silly, the arousal I felt at her touch momentarily distracted me. Then I leaned forward, and as I stretched full length against her, her hands moved around to my back. I kissed her, slowly at first, but soon I was ready to devour her. Which was exactly what I intended to do. Moving down her body, I parted her legs with my shoulders. She made soft whimpering sounds as I kissed across her belly. This moment of being in control, of making a woman tremble at my touch, was what I'd most savored in the past. But this time, it felt different. More than wanting to make her come, I needed Beck to feel how special she was. Because she wasn't some woman I'd picked up for the night, someone I'd just met and would never see again. This was someone I knew to be decent and talented and patient enough to have saved me from myself, more than once. I nuzzled the soft hair between her legs, catching the scents of soap and her arousal. Tracing the tip of my tongue along the inside of her thigh, I reached to massage her breast. At my touch, she arched toward me, whispering, "Being with you is even better than I imagined."

At the sound of her voice, I could feel my own desire building again, but it could wait. Judging by Beck's breathy tone, her rapid breathing, and the way her hips flexed, she was almost beyond waiting. The thought that she wanted me this way, that she was as desperate as I was to have her, made me move more forcefully than I'd intended. I pushed my mouth against her center, running my lips around the slick heat there. When I dipped my tongue out to taste her, she was as divine as I'd imagined. She moaned again as I kissed along her firm clit, and the sounds made me pull her fully into my mouth. Her hands bunched in the sheet as I sucked slowly, wanting to make it last, to be the lover she would always remember. Before I could analyze that last thought, I felt her shudder, and she jerked once against my mouth, her hands coming to rest on my shoulders where her fingers beat lightly, like the raindrops falling against the windows.

I lay with my head on her thigh as her breathing slowed. When I reached to pull the covers over us, she caressed my shoulder.

"Come up here," she murmured, her voice husky. When I settled next to her, she leaned over to kiss me. "You taste a little different."

I licked my lips, getting a remaining hint of her essence. "I wonder why."

Beck's eyes squeezed shut, and she blushed. "I can't believe I said that. I'm so—"

"Beck." I cut her off quickly, anticipating that sentence would end with something negative. "Remember when I asked you not to be so hard on yourself?"

Looking at me, she licked her lips and nodded. "June said something bad about herself once when Melanie yelled at her while we were getting ready for the sale. I told her what you had said, and she thought you were right."

I stiffened at the mention of June. "I honestly intended to be there, Beck. I never meant to break my promise."

She was quiet for a while. "I didn't think I'd ever be able to understand why you weren't there. But if someone had called and told me they might have found my papa, I'd have gone." She took my hand. "And if I'd known why you were leaving, I would have wanted to go with you, and that would have ruined everything here. Is that why you didn't tell me?"

Sighing, I shook my head, though my mind jumped to the very foreign notion of having someone who'd react with sympathy to another of those dreaded phone calls. Someone who'd pack and make travel arrangements for us both while I let myself fall apart. No, it was impossible to imagine such a trip with someone loving and supportive by my side. It had never happened, and I didn't believe it ever could. I made my way through that world of violence and loss alone, and it would always be that way.

Beck tightened her hold. "We don't have to talk about this now. Or ever again if it hurts too much." Her gentle tone made me move to take comfort in her strong, warm body. I burrowed closer to her, letting those thoughts fade, replacing them with the physical satisfaction I felt. "I just want you to be happy."

I closed my eyes, assessing my mood. Was that what I was feeling? Would I even know happiness if it was lying next to me?

Chapter Fifteen

I must have fallen asleep because it was pitch black when I looked around. The sound of deep breathing awakened me, and I pushed away from the body nearby. "You're hogging the bed again, Abby."

A vaguely familiar voice—though certainly not Abby's—answered me. "Emily. Baby, it's me."

I blinked, coming fully awake as my vision adjusted. Abby would never be hogging the bed again. Tears pooled in my eyes. *Pull yourself together.* "Sorry, Beck. I must have been sound asleep."

Beck brushed the wetness off my cheek with a touch so tender it made me feel like melting. "It's okay. I'm just glad I know you're not calling for another girlfriend."

I smiled but resisted the urge to lean into her. "You can rest easy about that. I haven't had a girlfriend, really. Only…uh…temporary amusements."

"Before," Beck added.

I stood and stretched again, heading for the bathroom. "Before what?"

"You've never had a girlfriend before. Before now."

Shit. This kind of entanglement was one reason why I hadn't wanted to get involved in the first place. I didn't answer and started on a new subject when I returned. "Are you hungry at all?"

Beck grinned and hopped out of bed. "Yeah, I am. Meet me in the kitchen?"

I nodded and watched her stroll casually toward her room. Parading that naked body in front of me when I was trying to get some distance simply wasn't fair.

Five minutes later, Beck was busy at the stove, and I was setting the table. We were both in our usual sleepwear, and I was feeling much better, not just because her cooking smelled delicious but also because it meant we were resuming our usual roles. But when she kissed my cheek before putting my plate down and moved her chair closer to mine before sitting, I knew things weren't exactly like normal.

"This looks fantastic." I tried for some neutral comment before risking a glance over. Beck wore an ear-to-ear grin. The warmth in her eyes made me reconsider if normal was even what I wanted. I was in completely new territory, having never gotten up in the middle of the night to have a snack with a sex partner before. It felt strangely agreeable.

"I think you look fantastic." She put her hand on my leg. "In fact, I've never seen you look more beautiful."

Having recently been in the bathroom, I had a pretty good idea of what she was looking at. And while I could admit I was more relaxed, I was far from beautiful. "I've heard that too much sex can make you blind, but you must have a very low threshold."

It wasn't the worst thing I could have said, but it certainly wasn't the best either. Beck frowned and moved her hand off my leg. I looked away from her and took a few bites. She truly did have a way with eggs, and I searched for something nice to say, something to ease the growing tension between us. "What time is it anyway?" Okay, not particularly nice, but at least neutral, wasn't it?

She gave the clock behind me a quick glance before turning her chair to face me head-on. "I think it's time for you to tell me what's going on in that head of yours."

I'd never heard her tone sound quite like that. Not aggressive, but strong, almost forceful. In typical fashion, I reacted timidly. "I don't know what you mean."

"If you wanted a one and done, we could have had that weeks ago. You need to tell me why you're acting as if you barely know me or like I'm only someone who works for you."

Okay, that landed pretty close to home. "I'm not," I protested. She cocked her head slightly with an expression that would have been amusing if I hadn't been so busy defending myself. "That is, I don't mean to." I put a hand on her face, and her expression softened. "I told you, I'm not good at this relationship stuff."

Beck leaned in and kissed me. Not being much of a kisser, I didn't have much to go by, but no one's lips had ever affected me like hers. In seconds, all my discomfort melted away, and I had no idea why I'd ever been worried. My hands found the back of her neck, and I pulled, needing to be closer. She shifted me onto her lap, and I slid one hand under her shirt and cupped her breast. The sound in her throat made me want to be in bed with her again. Now. I broke the kiss to whisper in her ear, "Have you had enough?"

"No," she answered. The way her eyes traveled down my body, I knew she wasn't referring to the eggs. I shivered, imagining what that mouth of hers could do to the rest of my body. "I'm ready for the next course."

Back in the bedroom, Beck fed my every need without me having to ask. She didn't move her mouth away after my shattering orgasm. As soon as the throbbing began to slow, she eased into me gently. The incredible feeling of being filled when I was so open and wet made me cry out with pleasure. Immediately, she froze and looked up. "Is this okay? Emily, baby, did I hurt you?"

I felt her start to withdraw and grabbed her wrist. "No. Don't… don't leave. I want this. Want you exactly where you are."

She rested her head on my stomach, and I felt the tension leave her shoulders. "It feels amazing to be inside you, but I was afraid that I'd—"

"You didn't. Please believe me." She moved hesitantly, and I arched, pushing myself against her. "Yes. Like that."

Oh God. When she moved in deeper and curled her fingers slightly, I'd never felt anything so right. Her lips caressed my clit, and I totally lost control. I called out her name, something I'd never done with any of my previous lovers—probably because I wasn't sure I knew it—and clutched frantically at her shoulders as her pace increased. The sensations gathered strength until I could no longer hold them back. Heat and light rushed through me like a blissful inferno, and my scream of release echoed around the room.

Beck kissed her way up my body, her fingers still inside me. "Stay," I whispered.

"Always," she answered.

Did she know my sex-addled brain was only referring to her physical position at that moment? When she turned us so we faced each other, her free hand on my back and my breasts at the level of her mouth, I quickly decided it didn't matter. My insides pulsed around her, and when her knuckles grazed my clit, I knew I wasn't through. She lifted her head, her mouth pressing softly over my shoulders and my neck. I eased a leg over her hip, opening myself to her in a whole new way. I'd intended that openness to be physical, but something inside—something that felt like the heart I'd always denied having—told me it wasn't. In the next instant, my body was too far gone to hear my mind's warnings about what that might mean.

❖

"Wanna go out?" It was such a simple question, and Beck asked it with such enthusiasm. I tried to calm my stomach and ease the panic in my limbs. If I'd known we'd end up at the marina, I would have absolutely refused to leave the house, especially since the past two days had felt more like a honeymoon than anything I'd ever experienced. This morning, Beck had us eating breakfast in bed, and we'd giggled about having "crumby" sheets. Once she'd finally gotten me up, I'd been unusually pliable, initially having no qualms about her surprise. Now I was resolutely shaking my head.

"Come on," Beck urged. "It's easy. You don't have to do a thing but enjoy it."

I hadn't even wanted to walk out on the pier, but she'd taken my hand in hers and was pulling me along so excitedly, I'd had no choice but to follow. Now Beck was pointing at one of the few moored boats. There had been a series of calm, sunny days after the storm had passed, and all the others were fishing, I supposed, or simply out enjoying the weather. But I didn't intend to be one of them.

"No," I said, crossing my arms for emphasis. "I don't like boats."

She widened her stance and pointed both thumbs at her chest, grinning broadly. "Because you haven't been out on one with me."

The truth was, I'd been on one boat in my life. My inexplicable aversion to them had spared me until I'd accompanied Jackson on a business trip to Chicago early in our marriage. We'd started the day with a breakfast of Bloody Marys and mimosas to the point I'd been tipsy enough to go along. From the moment I'd stepped aboard, I'd felt unbalanced and desperate to escape. Afterward, I had only a memory of my own nausea and sounds of disgust from the other passengers.

I tried to cover the embarrassing memory with a cough.

"You're late, Reynolds," a gruff male voice said behind me.

I watched the grin disappear from Beck's face. "I'm sorry, Mr. Avery."

"I should take out extra for my wasted time."

Beck ducked her head, her gaze fixed on the ground. I turned, taking in the speaker's weathered face and the worn cutoffs and dirty T-shirt. He scratched at his belly while his eyes ran lazily over my body, eventually making their way back to my face. "So who's this pretty lady?" he asked.

Beck's head snapped up, and she took a step closer to me. "This is the lady who's renting the Guest House. I clean for her and thought she might enjoy a ride around the Outer Banks."

I noted she didn't use my name or suggest any relationship between us, other than employer and employee. "It's my fault we're late," I said, using my most imperious tone. "I'm visiting from the city and am not accustomed to these early hours." Most of that was true, though today we'd gotten a late start mainly because I'd been unwilling to let Beck out of bed, and she'd been equally unwilling to go. "And I'm afraid there was a misunderstanding. We're going to have to cancel," I added. "Please let me know the fee, and I'll cover it."

When Mr. Avery squinted hesitantly, Beck filled in. "There's no fee," she said. "You said I could have her all day after I fixed that throttle last month and cleaned her up, remember?"

His face darkening, Avery snarled, "Yeah, I remember. I'm not a retard like you."

I turned to Beck, whose face had gone slack as she focused on her feet. "Send him a bill for whatever your work would normally cost and let's go. I'm not going to stand here and have my employee insulted."

The corner of Beck's mouth curved up slightly. "Yes, ma'am," she said softly, following me as I strode down the pier.

"That wasn't our deal," Avery protested, his voice rising. "Hey, wait a minute."

I paused, looking over my shoulder. "Yes?"

"Look, I...I didn't mean nothing. It's just something to say." I gave him a skeptical look, and he took a step toward us. "How about I put it on your account, Beck?"

I cocked my head at her. "You have an account here?"

She nodded. "I'm saving to buy a boat of my own. Mr. Avery keeps a balance of what I've put in so far, though it's not much." She looked toward the man, asking, "Barely over five hundred, isn't it?"

He shrugged. "Something like that."

"I'd like to see your accounting system," I said. "And get a receipt for today's addition."

Over Avery's sputtering, I glanced at our intended ride. Rust showed in places, and it had all sorts of ropes and netting hanging off it. How could Beck even get near a pulley after what had happened to her? I suppressed a shudder. "What kind of boat is that, anyway?"

"It's a trawler," Beck said, looking at the water beyond. "Specifically, a wet fish trawler. Our boat was a lot like it."

I swallowed. She wanted a boat like the one her father had died on? "Do you know how to drive one of these?"

Beck's head bobbed eagerly. "I could do it with my eyes closed."

I frowned. "Don't you dare."

"Does that mean you'll go?"

The adorably excited look on her face was almost impossible to resist. Almost. "No. But maybe when you get your own boat."

Her face fell. "We might both be old and gray by then."

"So much the better. I'll need some excitement to get my heart going at that age."

I knew Beck was trying to hide her disappointment, so when she asked, "Will you at least come aboard and let me show you around? I promise she'll stay docked," I had to agree.

The boat rocked slightly as we climbed on, and my stomach protested immediately. Beck was in her element, though, pointing out the various functions of the assorted pieces of equipment on board, all designed for some kind of fishing. We went down some narrow stairs to the living quarters underneath. The area was remarkably clean, with a faint, antiseptic smell. Beck's work, I imagined. That thought made me settle enough to ask, "Could you make a living doing this? By yourself?"

She shrugged. "Probably not by myself, no. And it's getting harder and harder to do, even for the bigger operations. Those huge commercial ships have just about fished this area dry. It's sad." She stared at the water. "This is the ship I know from being out with Papa, but I'd need a smaller one to run by myself. When I talk to Mama, she acts like she agrees, but I think it's because she knows I'll never have the money to buy one."

Her expression was grim, and I moved to her without thinking. Holding her, I felt the gentle rocking of the water rippling beneath us. It was somehow soothing and romantic at the same time. Both sensations were nice, but I wanted to steer her away from this pursuit for several reasons, the main one being my own fear. "Maybe there's something else you're supposed to do first. Like become a world-famous artist by winning the PAFA."

I felt her nod against me. "There's amazing prize money too. First place, along with the money I made from the sale, would get me close to buying this." I sighed. "What?" she asked.

"Maybe I'm being selfish right now." *Right now? How about 99.9 percent of the time?* I brushed aside cynical Emily and went on. "But I'm afraid for you out on this thing by yourself. When I told you I don't like boats, what I should have said is, I'm afraid of them. I don't know why, but I've always had this deep-seated dread."

Beck met my eyes. "But you came here with me because you knew I wanted to. That's not selfish." She kissed my forehead and led me off the boat. A truck started in the distance. "There goes Mr. Avery. Guess you won't be doing any accounting today." We walked slowly down the pier. "Did you know the word *calculus* comes from a Latin word for pebble because the Romans used stones to calculate things?"

I did know, but I loved that she knew too. I loved how she thought of things like that. I loved... *No, no, no, Emily. We're not going there.* "Hey, how about you give me a ride on your scooter instead? Take me around the island and show me some of your favorite spots?"

Beck was giving me her "trying to figure something out" look. "Do you really want to, or are you just trying to make me feel better?"

"Both," I answered, and her face lit up. "But don't laugh if I fall off or something."

"I wouldn't laugh at something like that, Emily." It was true. Beck wasn't the type of person to be amused by someone else's misfortune.

I took in a breath. "Okay. Let's do it. Only...you'll bring me back if I don't like it, won't you?"

She stepped closer. "Absolutely, I will. You trust me, don't you?" When I nodded, she added, "And thank you for standing up to Mr. Avery. Mom always thought I should go to work for him in his engine shop, but he's so mean I never wanted to, even if I could make more money."

We were at the car, but I stopped her with my hand on her chest. "I would say the extra money wouldn't be worth the possible damage to your sweet heart."

She put her hand over mine. "You call me that, sometimes."

"Yes. And that's a first for me, you should know." I could feel that same heart beating powerfully through her shirt.

She smiled, and I wanted to melt into her. "We're going to have an amazing day."

And it was. Though initially, I pressed myself close and held on tight strictly out of nerves, my confidence in Beck's riding ability grew by the moment. Before long, I was able to relax my death grip and enjoy the feel of the wind, the warmth of the sun, and the wonderful views. She turned to ask if I was hungry, and at my nod, we pulled into a small restaurant that fronted the sound and had a view over to the mainland. A few heads turned as we entered, and Beck's strut had me feeling like a girl from the '50s who was the envy of all the kids at the malt shop because she had the coolest date.

We rode on after lunch, farther than I'd been before, and came to an area devoid of any houses, business, or people, for that matter. "This is the Cape Hattaras National Seashore," Beck announced, pulling off the main road at the beginning of a sandy trail. A small, deserted cove lay below us. "If you want some beach time, we can ride down, but you'll have to help push it up. And it may be a little rough."

"Sometimes rough is fun," I teased, reaching around and pinching her nipple.

Beck flinched, the bike jerked, and I—predictably—lost my balance and slid off. Thankfully, the sand was soft, and I landed squarely on my ass, which I could only think served me right for being one. At that, I bit my lip, trying hard to hold in a laugh. Beck, however, gave a cry and dropped the scooter, kneeling beside me on the sand. "Oh God, Emily. I'm so sorry. Oh God, are you hurt?" She ran her hands over my sides, quickly pulling them off when she felt my barely suppressed chuckle. "Don't let me hurt you. Oh God. Shall I call 9-1-1?" Her eyes were wide and wild, and I'd never heard her so upset or panicked. The motor coughed and died.

"I'm okay." I tried to reassure her, but laughter choked my voice, and she began fumbling for her phone. I reached to touch her hand. "Honestly, Beck. I'm fine. Please. Don't call anyone. Just help me up."

"Are you sure you should move? You might make things worse. Maybe you have a concussion or something, and you think you're okay, but you're really not."

The somber expression on her face made me want to laugh all over again. "Trust me, if I've concussed anything, it's my pride. And it, like my ass"—which I paused to rub strategically—"could certainly use some deflating." Beck looked at me warily. I rubbed her arm. "I promise, I'm fine."

It took me another ten minutes to convince Beck I didn't need to go to the hospital. She would only be mollified when I promised she could conduct a "thorough examination." We might have differing ideas of what that would entail, but I was certain I could make her see things my way. After walking the bike down, Beck produced a large towel from the storage compartment under the seat and insisted I lie on it. She stripped me to my bathing suit before brushing her fingers lightly over every part of my body. She bent each of my joints as she repeated things like, "Does this hurt?" or "Is this sore?" Finally, tired of the nursey routine and more than a little turned on, I took her face in my hands.

"Look at me, Beck." When her gaze settled on mine, I said, "I am fine. Do you hear me? I promise I'm not hurt. I landed where I have the most padding, and I may have a butt bruise tomorrow, but there's nothing else wrong. Okay?" She frowned, and I added, "Now, you promised me an amazing day, and it has been one so far. Would you please come here with me, and we can continue with that?"

She fidgeted. "I…I don't know what I'd do if you got hurt, Emily. You're…you're very important to me."

I ignored the sentiment. Here was an opening, and I took it. "The way you feel now? That's how I worry about you getting out on that boat, Beck. I'd be terribly upset if something happened to you."

Beck blinked and said, "Oh." After a few seconds, she took off her T-shirt and flopped beside me on the towel, staring at the sky. For once, I didn't push, letting her consider my remark.

After several minutes, she reached over and took my hand, rubbing her thumb across it softly. It felt nice, but I needed more. I rolled onto my side, onto my elbow, and kissed her softly.

"I guess I never had anyone care about me like that," she mused. Then her body turned to meet mine, and we kissed slowly, savoring each other in this beautiful, private setting. Things began to heat up even more when she pulled a small tube of suntan lotion from her pocket and began rubbing it on my exposed parts. My skin was considerably more healthy-looking than it had been when I arrived, but we'd been in the sun for several hours, and Beck was being her usual, considerate self. I decided to returne the favor, though she probably didn't need it. I had her sit and knelt behind her, making sure she could feel my breasts pressing against her back as I applied the lotion with long, sensuous motions.

"You have such nice arms. And legs. And I'm quite fond of all your other parts too."

By way of response, Beck turned and brought me onto the towel, easing herself between my legs.

"Is this okay?" she asked, obviously as aroused as I was. "I'm pretty sure we're alone here."

At this moment I might not have cared, but by way of answer, I cupped her breast and thrust myself against her. She growled, and I wrapped my legs around her ass, bringing us closer. I'd never come like that before, but the way we fit made it easy. Afterward, we lay quietly, facing each other again as we touched lightly with random strokes on arms or backs. I reached to run my hand down the thin braid, the memory of the first time I touched it much less painful now. "Did your hair used to be this long all over?" I asked.

She nodded, rolling onto her back, her eyes closed. "From the time I was little my papa never wanted me to cut it. I usually kept it tied up or wore a ball cap. But one year we were having a really hot summer, and I just couldn't stand it anymore. I'd seen this hairstyle in a magazine, and I took the picture to the salon where my mom went. I had them leave this back part long so he couldn't say I cut it all off. Mama was the one who put it in a braid. But Papa was still angry at me." After a deep sigh, she added. "So angry he banned me from going out on the boat with him for a week. Mama told me he'd get over it, but two days later, he got caught in the storm. If I'd been with him..."

Beck trailed off, but not before I heard the tremor in her voice. Turning to her, I saw her face was wet with tears. In her mind, I was sure, she would have saved her father by bringing them in sooner and avoiding the storm, but I was equally certain it would have been the other way. She would have been killed too. Taking a breath, she ran a hand over her face. "We don't ever talk about it, Mama and me. But we know. We're the only ones who do." She turned toward me again. "And now you."

For one of the few times in my life, I thought very hard about what to say. Should I argue with her about her belief that she could have saved her father? Encourage her to speak with a professional about it? Or take this for what it was—the sharing of an intensely private shame or guilt or remorse, similar to my own. With that understanding, I did what she'd done when I told her about Abby. Without offering any platitudes or absolution, I reached for her. At my touch, she went rigid for a few seconds before letting me hold her. A surge of relief and protectiveness rushed through me. Even before we'd taken the risk of moving from friends to lovers, Beck had always made me feel secure, and I relished knowing she felt the same with me.

Effortless as my solution was physically, it was emotionally unsettling. I felt like I was standing on the threshold of a place I'd never been before, and she was beckoning me in. But before I could consider what it might be like inside, it dawned on me that my time here was running out. That door would close forever once I returned to the city, and I'd be left on the outside, alone, exactly like I'd been before I met her. I closed my eyes, forcing myself not to count the days.

A breeze began to cool the coming evening, and Beck stirred. "We'd better get going," she said, helping me to my feet.

I touched her arm, stopping her from moving away. "I'm not saying this to make you feel bad again, Beck. I swear. But do you understand how I feel about boats?"

She nodded solemnly. "I've been thinking about that. How about if neither of us goes out on one for as long as you're here?"

It was a fair offer and probably the best I was going to get. I kissed her cheek. "Deal."

I held on to her hand as we pushed the scooter to the road. After starting it up, she gestured to me to get on behind her. Looking down at the small cove, I leaned close to her ear and whispered, "I want you to know, I had a wonderful day. And I guess if anyone could make a beach person out of me, it would be you."

Beck's smile seemed sad, and she didn't answer, focusing intently on the road ahead of us.

That night, I had trouble falling asleep. I leaned over to study Beck's face as she slept, trying to understand why it felt so good when we were together. How had she opened me to her world and inched her way into mine? And what was I going to do when our worlds were no longer in the same place?

The bedroom was so bright, I thought it might be morning before I remembered the moon had been almost full the night before. I turned to Beck, eager to tell her that I'd noticed such a thing. But her side of the bed was empty. I waited, listening to see if the toilet might flush in the other part of the house, but it didn't. After a few more moments of silence, I put on my robe and went out into the kitchen. When I didn't find her there, I went to check in the other bedroom. Empty. Trying not to worry, I glanced toward the deck and saw her standing naked in the moonlight, looking like a statue I should fall to my knees and worship.

I caught my breath as she ran a hand across her eyes, and I realized she was crying. With no regard for the privacy she might have been seeking, I threw open the screen door. She must have heard it, but she didn't turn. I stopped myself, taking one long, slow breath, trying to make sure I didn't sound upset or angry.

"Beck? Sweetheart, what are you doing out here?"

It took a moment for her to answer. I walked slowly to join her while I waited. "Have you ever felt like your life was coming together and falling apart at the same time?" she asked, a slight quiver in her voice.

"Usually just the falling apart one," I said. She sighed. Neither of us spoke for a while. "Do you want to tell me more about it?"

She continued staring at the water. "I don't think that's a good idea right now."

Perhaps she meant now as in the middle of the night, but something in her tone made me wonder if she ever would. I wanted to pry, to tease it out of her, to make her feel guilty for not saying, any number of techniques that had been tried on me when I didn't want to talk, all to no avail. Keeping that in mind, I simply said, "Will you come back to bed? Please?" Playing on her soft heart, I added, "It seems that lately, I can't sleep without you."

Her gaze remained fixed on the ocean, and she whispered something so softly that I had to replay the sounds twice to understand the words. But as soon as I did, I knew what was wrong. She'd said, "Then how will you sleep after you go?"

I remembered my vision of the door into the new place and wondered how our thoughts had gotten so in sync. Perhaps my remark about becoming a beach person had started her thinking about me leaving. Whatever the case, there wasn't a damn thing I could do about it. I began to walk away as I had done dozens of times before when other women hadn't given enough or wanted more than I was offering.

As my hand touched the door handle, Beck said, "I'll be in before long."

I took in her form, standing so still, and considered how different my time here would have been without her. I admitted to myself that, from the beginning, I'd been the one asking too much and giving too little. I returned to her side, wanting very much to make her believe me.

"It's not just the sleeping part or even the sex. I wish I could stay here with you, Beck."

Her head turned, her eyes still liquid. "You do?"

Something inside me twisted at the doubt in her expression. "Very much." The words resonated in my gut. God, I genuinely meant it, even while I knew it was impossible. I reached for her hand, but she pulled me into an embrace.

"I was feeling sad, and it started because I have to go back to work tomorrow. It's like Harper gave us some extra time off while the island recovered, and now I've gotten spoiled being around you all the time." She squeezed me and added, "And then I started thinking about how it will feel when you're not around at all. And I…"

She trailed off, lowering her head to my shoulder. I stroked her hair. "I know, Beck. I really do. But I've decided—and this isn't at all like me—but I think we simply have to make the most of the time we have and enjoy each other while we can." I didn't admit this absurdly Pollyanna approach was the only thing keeping me from grabbing on to her with both hands and not letting go. That and believing I'd surely become more my old self, with barbs and shields at the ready, when I returned to the city. I felt for Beck, who didn't have that kind of old self to return to but would always be this gentle, well-intentioned person, even when I was gone. I'd already decided to dip into my savings and pay her rent here at the Guest House for two months, hoping that would give her time to adjust to our separation without worrying about where she would live.

She sniffed. "But that's less than three weeks."

"Yes, but that's nearly three weeks we wouldn't have if we'd never met."

Okay, I was going off the deep end now, but she lifted her head. "That's true, isn't it?"

I nodded, and moving my arm around her waist, I tugged lightly. "Come on. You have to work tomorrow. You need your rest."

What good could it possibly do to discuss how ridiculously poignant parting was going to be? Perhaps if we had a little more time together, we'd begin some depletion or reach a culmination point that would smooth the way forward. Despite feeling like a total fake for refusing to admit that the next three weeks could well be the second hardest of my life, I cuddled against Beck and fell asleep almost immediately.

❖

Even before I reached the coffee pot the next morning, my first words to Beck were, "What would you think if I stayed through October?" I poured a cup and sipped, smiling at her astonished expression. "It came to me this morning. The only reason I was leaving the weekend after Labor Day was because that was when the rest of the gang was going. But they've already left, and I don't have anything going on until my new book release in November, when Mel's scheduled a reading and signing."

"Oh, Emily." She flung her arms around me, and when I felt her trembling, I stretched to put my cup on the counter so I could return the embrace. "I...I couldn't be happier."

"I know your weekends are busy, but I'd like to take you out for dinner next week." I tightened my hold for a few seconds before pulling back to add, "Someplace nice. To celebrate. And yes, this will be a date."

To my great relief, she smiled. "Where? Is what I wore to the dance okay?"

"It's a surprise. And yes, that outfit would be fine. In fact, it looks very sexy on you."

Beck blushed before her expression shifted. "Oh, I forgot. I couldn't get the bloodstains out of my white shirt. I gave it to Mom to use as a rag."

I touched her arm. "Then let's go into town a little early and shop for you." When her frown didn't change, I reminded her, "You have money of your own now, from the sale. You can spare the cost of one new shirt."

She worried at her lip, speaking almost to herself. "While I was still homeschooling, we did a unit on budgeting and also on writing checks. But I can't remember..,"

I put my hand on her chest, bringing her face back to me. "We could talk about opening a checking account and figure out your budget when you get home tonight."

"My budget." She mulled the words over while I suppressed my amusement. She was so competent at the things she knew how to do, I sometimes forgot how the injury had affected her, especially in terms of doing new things. "Maybe I'll decide about the bank after we talk."

"Perfect," I assured her, and she beamed.

Turning to look outside, she studied the sun. "I need to go, but I'll be home by four." She pulled me to her, kissing me tenderly. "You're the exception to the kissing rule," she said, grinning at my shocked expression. "Like you, I've figured out what we have is more than sex, and it makes me want to kiss you all the time. So I decided I just will."

Speechless, I watched her go, hearing the scooter gradually fade into the distance. I'd hoped an extra four weeks would be enough time to calm things between us, but the warm softness of her mouth echoing through me made it seem unlikely. "Damn it, Beck," I fussed. *Damn it, Emily.*

As we returned to our routine, plus benefits, I gradually relaxed into the idea of having something entirely new: a physical and emotional relationship with someone who genuinely cared about me. Released from the inner turmoil of not being able to touch her, and without the pressure of counting the days we had left, I found myself enjoying our time while feeling a sense of self-determination I'd never known. Telling Beck everything about Abby seemed to have freed me from being quite as constrained by experiences in my past. I felt free to react to each moment as it came. I spent more time outdoors, and the ocean no longer seemed a threatening presence.

Beck's tender affection became ever more familiar and reassuring and right. Increasingly, I was less self-conscious as I returned her touches and kisses. My sense of the change was not exactly like a switch being thrown, but more like the intensity of a dimmer switch being gradually turned up.

Despite the improvements in my romantic side, my cowardly streak remained firmly intact. It was June I called to inform the gang—well, mainly Mel—of my change in plans. June giggled enthusiastically, and I knew the W's would be happy for me too. But Mel's protective side could come off as bordering on volatile, and while I'd appreciated it when she'd shielded me from an overzealous fan, her dislike for Beck had me expecting a furious phone call questioning my motives and my sanity. I proofed the final version of Leigh's novel while I waited for the proverbial shoe to drop. When it didn't happen, I felt increasingly edgy during the quiet of the days, but at Beck's late afternoon greeting, my world seemed to settle. She'd made my time here nearly perfect, and I started thinking of ways to repay her. Date night would be my first real test.

Chapter Sixteen

Our shopping episode resembled a cross between a debate and a game show. I never dreamed the simple purchase of a shirt could involve such intense negotiation. What should have been a simple, fifteen-minute visit to the clothing department of a moderately priced store turned into an hour of diplomacy and concession. I sighed, now aware that buying clothes was one of those things Beck didn't do often, and therefore wasn't particularly good at. After briefly wondering what sort of person she would have been if not for that brain injury, I decided I liked her exactly as she was.

As we began walking toward the restaurant, I thought about having a drink. But when Beck slipped her hand into mine, the urge faded. "Thank you," she said. "I know I'm terrible at getting new clothes, but you made it easier." She looked at me almost shyly. "You make everything better. I love—"

She paused as I raised my hand to her lips to stop her from finishing the sentence. My heartbeat had tripled, but I wasn't sure if it was due to discomfort or elation at what she might say. At that same moment, my phone rang, and my motion switched to removing it from my jacket pocket.

As Beck said, "I love spending time with you," I breathed out in relief, thankful I hadn't recognized the number and could put my phone on mute while feeling oddly conflicted about what Beck had said…or hadn't said.

Our only conversation about love had been so long ago, we both seemed like different people now. But Beck never seemed to expect or need a reply to her remarks, no matter how personal. I squeezed her hand, and she looked at me with that smile I'd been drawn to from the start.

We arrived at the restaurant, and I opened the door with a flourish. "Wow," she said, looking around, wide-eyed. "I've lived here my whole life and never eaten at the Seagoer." I slipped in and gave my name to the hostess. As we followed her to our table, Beck said, "You know that girl Peyton I used to see? My friend Jonsey told me he got her a job here."

Well, shit. "As a waitress?"

"Oh no. She busses tables."

Once seated, we sipped our water as we studied the menu. "Emily," Beck whispered. "This place is really expensive."

"I told you, this is my treat," I answered as she shook her head. I touched her arm. "Your cooking has saved me a fortune, and I want to do this. Please, enjoy yourself."

She sighed. "I don't know what half of this is. Would you order for me?" she asked, loosening her tie.

I liked how she'd asked. It did feel like a date, except we already knew each other. Maybe this was what longtime couples did? "Tell me what you're in the mood for."

"I already have what I'm in the mood for," she said, looking at me intently.

I felt myself blushing. "Me too," I answered, reaching for her hand.

The meal was delicious, and Beck was wonderful company, as always. After we'd finished, I excused myself to visit the restroom before starting for home. This outing felt decidedly different from any previous visits to such places. I hadn't overeaten, and I wasn't at all tipsy. And what had been a lovely evening had the promise of being an even more enjoyable night—together.

Returning to the dining room, I was greeted by the unexpected sight of Beck standing by the bar, faced by Peyton, who was clasping her arm. Beck was leaning away and looking rather uncomfortable, but I couldn't stop the churning in my gut nor the roaring in my head. Jealous, yes, but I also felt terribly possessive. Starting toward them, I had no plan except to get my lover away from that woman's clutches.

When Beck turned, something in her eyes eased both my anger and my steps. Maybe it was the lighting or that she was looking directly at me, but I could read her expression clearly. I saw uneasiness but not guilt, and a stunning depth of delight at my appearance. I'd never seen a woman look at me quite that way before, but still, I knew exactly what it meant. One, Peyton's presence didn't mean a damn thing, and two, Beck Reynolds was in love with me.

My phone buzzed again, but I ignored it. I'd meant to check it in the restroom but now was glad I hadn't. What if I'd missed that look? And what was I going to do about it? *Nothing. You can figure this out later.* Peyton must have seen it too, because she departed quickly.

At home, Beck held out a bowl of the last strawberries of the season. "Would you be my dessert?"

"If you'll be mine." We ate the fruit off each other's bodies until we were sticky and satisfied. Or so I thought until we showered.

"I don't think I'll ever get enough of you," she murmured, her voice hoarse as we dried each other off, having both experienced a steamy third orgasm.

We got into bed, and I whispered, "I love spending time with you too."

The last thing I remember before drifting off to sleep was Beck sighing happily and kissing the top of my head.

❖

It was midday before I thought to check my cell. Beck and I had such a nice morning that I began wondering what it would be like to honestly say how I felt about her, assuming I could put it into words. Not love, surely, but possibly something close to it. I'd been pondering that concept since she left for work, and I'd totally forgotten my phone was on mute. When I looked, I was shocked to find twelve missed calls, all from the same unfamiliar number. There were also ten texts and five voice mails, but I hesitated to look at them, fearing some pesky solicitor or deranged fan had somehow found my number. As I held the phone, it buzzed again, and a strange thought entered my mind. What if it was Abby? What if she'd escaped after years and years of captivity and had finally found all that was left of her original family? I clicked on the most recent text. An obviously irate message popped onto the screen.

Goddamn it, Emily. If you don't write me back in the next five minutes, I'm getting in the car and driving there, I swear to God. This is Mel, btw. Again. Still.

Whose phone are you using? I replied.

Answer this call or else.

The phone vibrated, and I picked up.

"Where the fuck-all have you been?" she demanded.

"I've been right here, but I put the phone on mute since I didn't recognize this number."

"You could have looked at one of the texts or listened to the voice mail to find out."

I sighed. "Just tell me, Mel."

She took a breath, obviously trying to calm herself. "June and I broke up, and I have a new number."

I nodded, though I knew she couldn't see me. That was Mel's routine ever since an irate ex had tried to get revenge by giving her cell to every unlikely charity and oddball company she could think of. Now it was good-bye, girl, hello, new number. "You and June broke up? When? Why?"

"About two days after you called with news of your new schedule. She hadn't bothered to tell me until I expressed some concern that you weren't here yet. It made me mad, and I said some things. Then she got mad and said some other things. Plus, she'd started bringing those damn cats over all the time, and they were always getting into stuff. It was what I needed to do."

I felt a flash of guilt. "Oh, Mel, are you sure you can't work it out? I really like June."

"Well, good, you can start dating her when you get back to the city. Which needs to be in, like, three days."

My stomach turned. "What do you mean? I don't have anything scheduled until November."

"You didn't, but now you do. Some execs from Saga Films in LA are flying here. I'll do the negotiating, but they want to meet you too, just to make sure you're on board so there won't be any trouble getting the rights. This could be it, Emily. Our big break."

I couldn't speak. I couldn't even swallow. Seconds ticked by. Finally, I forced out two words before I stopped. "Mel, I…"

She didn't wait for me to finish. "You what, Emily? Don't tell me this cleaning butch has some golden pussy that has you in its spell. You can't give up this deal for a little tail. There's plenty of that here. I'll drive down tomorrow and help you."

"No, Mel. Not tomorrow. I need a day at least."

"You've got today. And I wouldn't be in until late tomorrow. In the meantime, say what you have to say or do what you have to do and start packing."

She hung up. I knew there was nothing to be gained by calling her back. I felt the tears on my face before I realized I was crying. I hadn't felt so undone since Abby disappeared. And this wasn't going to hurt only me. Envisioning Beck's reaction to this news made me sob out loud. At length, emotionally exhausted, I forced myself to abandon any belief in the possibilities of this relationship once and for all. This was simply another place, and Beck was just another woman. Life was exactly as I'd always known. Anything good was fleeting and always ended in despair. Wiping my face, I went to get my suitcase.

But I couldn't tell her I was leaving. Not so soon. As I packed everything that wouldn't be obvious, the budding romantic in me had bargained with the confirmed cynic for a few last hours of the way it had been. I tried to keep my voice level and not lie to her, desperate to hang on to the feelings I knew would soon disappear forever. But after our greeting, she obviously sensed something was wrong. She checked me for fever after I told her I hurt all over, which was true. I said I didn't want anything to eat—also not a lie—and suggested she do something on her project. She kissed me softly on the cheek and went to change. To keep from crying again, I bit my lip so hard I almost drew blood. When she came out with a heavy apron over the ripped jeans and torn T-shirt she worked in, I realized the last thing I wanted was to be apart from her.

"Can I watch? Please?"

"No, baby. I'm using the welding torch right now, and I don't have any extra eye protection." At my pleading look, she said, "I'll go by school tomorrow and get some for you, okay?" How could I tell her there wouldn't be a tomorrow for us? I turned away, and she moved behind me, resting her hands lightly on my shoulders. "Is it possible a walk on the beach would make you feel better?"

Turning to her, I nuzzled into her chest and nodded. I hated thinking about all the "lasts" we were now having, last walk on the beach, last evening with the two of us at the house, and certainly the last time to sleep together once she found out what I'd been keeping from her. During the brief intersection of our lives, I'd felt so much more for her than I'd even imagined possible, but I'd also known that it would end. Such good things always did, the only question was how and why. For us, despite the closeness we'd found, the distance between us was too great to bridge, our lives too different to reconcile. Hers was here, grounded in the dependable diversity that the sea offered, while mine was in the city where I was fed by my antagonism toward the hustle and bustle of humanity and the stability of my friends that balanced the precariousness of my inner world. I wondered if I'd ever be able to explain it to her in any way that made sense, when it barely made sense to me.

She changed back into her shorts, and we made our way to the water's edge. The tide was out, and we had lots of room, but I stayed as close as I could to her. Instead of walking hand in hand or arm in arm as we sometimes did, I pulled her against me by the waist. She took hold of my shoulders but stopped walking as she looked into my face.

"You have that worried line here," she said, touching my forehead between my eyes. "Are you sure you don't have something to tell me?"

"Remember last week when you were out on the deck, and you were sad about something but said it wasn't a good idea to tell me?" She nodded, her face solemn. "That's how I feel right now. I don't want to talk about it. I just want to be here with you."

"Okay."

After a while, the silence between us started to feel like distance, something else I wasn't ready to deal with. "Are we anywhere near your hideaway?" I asked.

"It's about fifty yards farther." She pointed down the beach.

"How can you tell? It looks like more sand and dunes to me."

"I lived there sometimes. It's like how you can tell one house from another when you live in a big neighborhood."

I thought of a dozen arguments of why that wasn't a valid comparison, but instead I asked, "Did you ever repair it, after the storm?"

"No." She grinned. "I found somewhere much nicer to live."

"Is that so?" I teased.

"Yep. And the scenery?" She held me at arm's length. "I've never known anything more beautiful."

Shit. Now I really was going to cry. Instead, I pulled away and ran up the dune beside us. "Let's find it," I called.

She was beside me in an instant. "Race you," she said and darted away. By the time I joined her at the remains of her sand cave, I'd had time to collect myself. She was digging through the sand, pulling out objects from where they'd been buried when the shelter collapsed. I watched until she sat back on her heels, holding the small bell. "I made this to commemorate my papa's ship. It's what got me into metalwork. I'm so stu—" She cast me a sideways glance, and I gave her a meaningful look. "I mean, I forgot about it since the storm, but I'd have been upset when I realized I'd lost it."

I knelt beside her, putting my arms around her neck. "I'm proud of you for not saying something bad about yourself. Because you know what that proves?" She shook her head. "Only smart people can do what it takes to break a bad habit. And don't you forget it."

"It's easier since I have you around to remind me."

She couldn't have known what a stake through my heart that was. I had to do something to get my mind off leaving. Tightening my grip, I kissed her fiercely. "Have you ever gotten naked and made love out here on the beach?"

She grinned, brushing at my hair. "No. And there's one good reason why." When I cocked my head, she said, "Sand. It gets in the worst places."

"Is this the voice of experience again?"

"Experience, yes, but not that kind. From, you know, playing as a kid."

"Uh-huh. Well, the advantage of being with an older woman is that we're more resourceful when it comes to these things." I stood up, pulling off my shirt and stripping off my shorts and underwear. Ignoring her stare as I pushed her onto her back, I knelt, positioning myself above her face. "Is this okay?"

She swallowed and brushed at her mouth. "Uh, yeah."

I slowly settled onto lips, groaning when I felt her tongue slip into me. "Beck," I whispered. "You're the one who's beautiful."

Her hands slid onto my hips, and I whimpered as she pulled me more firmly against her. Oh God, this was going to be over much too quickly. As if reading my mind, Beck slowed her movements, molding her hands to my breasts. She fondled me through my T-shirt, lightly squeezing my nipples as they hardened under her fingers. I wanted that mouth on my breasts, on my body, and wished we were in bed so I could have her inside me. At the next surge of bliss, I lost any rational thought, only wanting that warm wetness against mine, wanting it to never to end almost as badly as I wanted to come. "Suck me," I begged, settling the matter as I pushed against her. She ran her hands up my thighs and around to my ass. I rocked against her, crying out as waves of pleasure crashed inside. Once my breathing had slowed, I realized my predicament. I didn't have the strength to stand. Well, fuck the sand, I decided, rolling off Beck and onto my side.

"Oh, Emily," Beck said with alarm. "I was going to pick you up."

"No need." I grimaced, trying in vain to rid myself of the scratchy granules on my skin before I dressed. As we walked toward the house holding hands, I said, "I don't know why I sometimes fail to trust you on matters of beach life."

"That's okay," Beck said, "as long as I can trust you on matters not related to beach life."

Tell her. Tell her now. I swallowed. "Beck, I—"

"Hey, you know what?" She interrupted, pointing at a box-like structure under the stairs. "We should fix that outdoor shower. I've been thinking about it since the storm. Most houses along here have one. It keeps things cleaner inside if you avoid tracking in the first layer, at least. And I bet you could use it right now." She grinned. "What do you think?"

"I don't—"

"Yeah, I don't think it would take much work, either. Possibly the diverter and maybe some washers. A few pipe pieces at most. I'll see if Mr. Guest would pay for it. Or at least half."

"Beck!" I said, much more sharply than I'd intended. At her shocked expression, I brushed at my skin again. "Could we please stop talking about showers of the future and let me get one now?"

She covered her mouth with her hands, but I could see her eyes were teasing. "I'm sorry, Emily. I didn't think older women like you ever run out of resources for dealing with common beach sand." I huffed and started up the stairs. "Hey," she called after me. "Would you like me to wash your back?"

"I really want to wash my…my front, thank you."

Her laughter followed me into the house, and I wasn't at all surprised when my shower door opened a minute later. Beck stepped in behind me, soaped her hands and ran them over my butt. "You know I've never once thought of you as older," she whispered in my ear, touching me in that tender, loving way she had. "I just think of you as my wonderful, amazing Emily."

I wanted to scream my frustration at the change in plans, and tell her to never touch me again because it changed the way everything else in my life felt. I needed to find the anger that had been part of my emotional life for so long and unleash it on her again. I was certain I could find the words—I could feel them forming in my mouth—words that would hurt her enough to make her go, find a place to lick her wounds, leaving me to sneak away like the horrible person that I was. I was certain that for me to survive this, she would have to hate me. But when I felt her small breasts hardening against me, and her lips on my neck, all the horrible reality that was waiting for me washed away, and I melted into her. *It's okay.* I'd allowed myself this last night, hadn't I? I turned, and pressed myself into her, holding her face in my hands. "I want to take you to bed."

Her eyes went a bit hazy. "Did you want dinner first?"

"I want you. First, last, and—" Oh God, I'd almost said "always." I coughed to cover my faltering. "First, last, and right now."

She'd noticed. I felt her body tighten, and she put down the soap. Barely touching me, she leaned over to rinse her hands and face again. "I'm done. Do you need another minute?"

I'd teased her before about being the fastest showerer on the island, but this wasn't the time to repeat my witticism. "Yes, thanks."

A sandwich, chips, and grapes were waiting for me on the bedside table. It had obviously taken longer than I realized to collect myself.

Beck came in from the kitchen and handed me a napkin. I patted the bed next to me, but she shook her head. "Emily," she said. "I know there's something bothering you, and I understand you don't want to talk about it now. But I hope...I hope you'll be able to tell me soon."

"Yes." My mouth was so dry, I couldn't manage the sandwich. I ate a few grapes. "Soon, I promise."

I hadn't made Beck any promises since the time I'd broken two at once. I wished I could break this one as well, but tomorrow would come all too quickly.

❖

All night, my mind played out multiple scenarios and wrote script after script featuring tomorrow's conversations. I'd seen the gray sky of morning before falling into a hard sleep, to the point I didn't even feel Beck stir, although I missed her warmth immediately. I groaned, and she settled beside me, kissing my forehead. "I think you should stay in bed for a while longer this morning. You had a rough night."

"Will you stay with me?" I pleaded.

She yawned. "I can't, baby. I have to go to work."

"No." I clung to her, my own voice sounding unfamiliar. Since when had I turned into such a needy infant? *Since you fell for Beck, and now you're leaving her.* Unable to ignore that explanation, I countered my own mental reply. Fell for her? Ridiculous. I didn't fall. No, I thought she was too kind and sweet for her own good. For example, who else but Beck would tell me to stay in bed when it was obvious that my tossing and turning had given her a rough night too? Ridiculous.

Sometime later, I smelled coffee and tried to remember when she'd left the bed. Left? "Beck!"

There was no answer. I ran to the window, ignoring the fact I was naked, and looked out. No scooter. My God, had I slept through the one morning when I really needed to say good-bye? And not just the "have a great day" good-bye, but a "have a nice life" good-bye? "Fuck me!"

Fuck you indeed.

A bad day was made worse when Melanie Daniels drove up in a small sedan about an hour later.

"How did you get here so soon?" I demanded when she burst through the door.

Her lips curved into that cocky smirk, and she strode across the room, pulling me into a tight hug and rocking us both until I thought I was going to be sick. "Good to see you too, Em." I managed to lean back enough to give her a look, but it didn't help. "Goddamn, girl, you look great." She pulled at the front of the oversized T-shirt of Beck's I was wearing, trying to look down it. "You've got a tan."

I slapped at her hand and stepped away. "Seriously, Mel, I'm not in the mood."

She bussed my cheek. "Aw, Em. Was your baby butch sad about your departure?" I ignored her and turned away. She followed me into the kitchen where I began making more coffee. "I flew into Norfolk last night and drove here this morning. We can go home the same way, and I'll return this piece of shit rental." She gestured at the car parked outside. "Then we can drive the rest of the way together in your car. Sweet, huh?"

At the moment, I couldn't think of anything worse. I took a breath, reminding myself about the film deal, and that the timing wasn't Mel's fault. Mel was my friend, though she was annoying as hell sometimes. And I'd have to figure out a way to get rid of her for an hour or so when Beck came home because the tension between the two of them would make it impossible to have a reasonable conversation. I was pouring coffee when I realized she had gone into my bedroom.

"You haven't done shit in here," she called and poked her head out the door. "Your stuff is still all over the place, Emily. What the hell did you do all day yesterday?"

"Did you want some coffee?" I asked calmly, ignoring her question.

"I guess I better," Mel grumbled, joining me again. "Since we'll obviously be working all day." She took the cup I held out to her and sipped absently. "Seriously, Em, I wanted to get going ahead of the traffic. Do you realize it's Labor Day weekend?"

I crossed my arms but kept my tone neutral. "First, the date on the calendar is not my fault. You insisted on coming now instead of waiting a few days for the traffic to lessen. Second, griping about it won't change the situation. Let's get started and see where we are at lunchtime."

She was staring at me like I was a stranger. "What is that attitude, the Tao of Spike?"

"Mel?" I said sweetly, and she cocked her head. "I know this upcoming meeting is important, possibly life-changing, and something both of us have been working toward. That's why I'm giving up the remainder of the most restful and...meaningful...vacation I've ever had." I darkened my tone. "But I swear to God, if you don't call Beck by her name—and I mean every goddamned time—I'm driving by myself, and you and that POS rental can make your own way home. Alone. Clear?"

"Crystal."

By noon, nearly everything was done. My suitcases were by the door, and I'd washed the sheets and towels to get them ready for Beck. When Mel questioned why I was remaking the bed and putting the clean towels out, I told her someone else would be here after I left, and I was making sure the place was decent for them. She, wisely, did not comment. She had started into Beck's room once, and when I'd told her everything in there stayed, she probably knew exactly who "someone" was. I stepped out on the deck to fix the beautiful setting in my mind as it put on a show for me—soft, warm breeze and cloudless azure sky over the sparkling calm water. At one time, I would have returned to the city eagerly. Now I knew I'd never forget this place or the woman who was embedded in every memory of it.

Mel joined me. "You sure did have a nice view here. And we had fun, right?"

My throat tightened at her use of the past tense, and I only nodded.

"So," she said after another moment. "What else is left to do?"

"I need to back up my files before I put away the computer. Shouldn't take long."

"Would you mind if I took a shower? I didn't take one this morning, and it would be nice to get rid of the travel."

"Sure," I said absently, reminded of my last shower with Beck. "Would you please use a towel from the small bathroom and toss it on the washer when you're done?"

She squatted beside me. "I'm sorry to ruin the last of your time here. I can see it did you some good. But I'll do everything in my power to make this deal happen, and it will all be worthwhile."

That was an unusually sensitive comment for Mel, so I smiled, possibly for the first time since she'd arrived. She gave my shoulder a squeeze and walked toward the small bathroom.

Between the running water and my intense concentration on composing my note for Beck, I didn't hear her scooter. I was on my fifth draft when she burst through the door, her face glowing with excitement.

"Mr. Guest wants to sell you this house!"

I turned from the desk, mouth agape. Beck was bouncing on her toes, the rest of her body quivering with excitement. She looked jubilant. "He called Mama with a question about two extra months' rent. Two extra months? And whose car is that, anyway?"

"I was going to tell you about all of that," I said weakly. In fact, I was going to explain in the note since I hadn't expected to see her before I left.

"Well, here's the thing." I hid my pleasure at her familiar saying as she paced in small circles. "He said he'd consider any reasonable offer. He's tired of trying to maintain this place from a distance." She walked over, resting her hands softly on my arms. "I'll give you half of what I made at my sale, and if I do well enough at PAFA to get a cash prize, there'd be more right away. I'm covering what Mom lost from not getting Erik's disability any more, but I'll pay whatever rent I can."

"Beck…" I needed to cut her off now, because the more she dreamed, the worse the reality nightmare would become. But she wasn't listening.

"Just think, in a year or so, folks would start calling this the Harris House. I'll fix the outside shower and get the fireplace working before winter. We can make the back living area your office, and you'll have better privacy and more room. Like for a bigger desk and more bookshelves and stuff. Whatever you need."

"Beck, listen—"

She stopped talking abruptly, staring over my shoulder toward the master bedroom, her mouth open as her expression turned grim. Oh God. Mel. I turned, and sure enough, Mel was moving into the room, her hair still damp, and wearing only a towel. She also wore what could be referred to as a "shit-eating grin." "Hey, Beck," she said jovially. "How's it going?"

Beck, speechless, turned away, her gaze searching. "Where's June?" she finally said.

"They broke up," I answered quietly. At that, I could see her forming and discarding questions in her mind while Mel, either oblivious to her distress or happily overlooking it, had no such problem directing her next words to me. "Emily, babe, could you spare a T-shirt? I forgot to pack an extra, and I'd like to start home clean."

"Start home?" Beck's voice was faint, but the question was clear.

Before I could explain, Mel began speaking in her best imitation of a North Carolina drawl, which wasn't particularly authentic. "I come to take my girl back to the city. But I guess you knew that."

Beck didn't look at me. "No, I didn't."

Mel had no such constraints. She pointed at me while she snorted with delight. "You haven't told her? OMG, that's harsh, even for you, Emily. What were you going to do, write her a Dear Jane letter?"

Our eyes all turned to the paper in my hand. I quickly crumpled it into a ball and threw it at her. "Shut the fuck up, Mel. You don't know what you're talking about."

"Then why don't you explain? To both of us."

Beck's voice was barely restrained anger under an extremely cool tone. I could see her hands were in fists at her side and willed myself not to flinch when she took a step toward me. "Tell me this is all a big misunderstanding. Tell me what's really going on." She lowered her voice, but I was sure Mel still heard it. "Tell me you're not her girl."

As I'd envisioned this conversation, I'd found myself secretly wishing she would hurt me somehow. I wanted her to be angry enough to shake me hard or even hit me. At least that way, I could claim some moral high ground. But I knew she wouldn't, just as I knew I'd never had any such ground in that department, and I never would. "I was going to tell you this morning, but I accidently slept in."

"How long have you known?"

Mel cut in. "We talked yesterday around noon. See, we have this—"

"Excuse me," Beck said, her voice louder and so firm Mel actually stopped talking. "I wasn't asking you."

Very few people got away with speaking to Mel that way, and Beck certainly wasn't one of them. I couldn't have this escalate any further. "Mel, why don't you finish getting ready?"

Beck met Mel's fierce stare with one of her own, but she said nothing, thank God. After what felt like hours, Mel nodded in my direction. "Okay, Emily. I'll be out in a few minutes. Finish your business here. We need to get on the road."

I walked out onto the deck and motioned Beck to follow. The door hadn't finished closing before she asked, "Is that what I am to you? Business?"

"You can't possibly believe that." I tried to sound disappointed rather than upset.

"I don't know what to believe anymore. Five minutes ago, I could see us living here together, maybe for a long time. Now I think I won't ever see you again." She looked directly at me for the first time since Mel had appeared. "Which one is it, Emily?"

"There's a chance that one or maybe more of my books could be made into a movie. That's why I'm going back sooner. To meet with some executives from a studio who are flying in from LA. Mel and I have been working on this for a while, but I had no idea it would happen now. I'm sorry, Beck. I never meant—"

"Sure. You never meant to hurt me, like you always say."

"Yes. Yes, that."

"But you couldn't bring yourself to tell me you were going until we'd had one last fuck." She continued as if I hadn't spoken, her voice rising. "And you were going to leave me a note? Again?"

"I...I didn't know where you were."

"Bullshit. Remember that phone you bought for me? You have my number and my mom's number. You could always find me when you needed something from me."

God, that was true. I had simply been my usual, chickenshit self about it. Perhaps she was well on the way to being angry enough to hate me, just as I'd planned. But somehow, that wasn't what I wanted anymore. "You're right," I admitted, and she slumped. "I didn't know how to tell you. I've never known how to tell you how I felt."

"Tell me now."

That request sounded more normal. I debated briefly about explaining how our lives weren't compatible, even though I'd enjoyed my time here, or how I didn't believe a long-distance relationship would ever work out. All of that sounded weak, even to me. Worse would be to tell her how much she meant to me, and how badly I wanted to stay. Better to just cut it off. "I still can't. Because now it wouldn't be fair to either of us. But I paid the extra months' rent so you can stay on here until after the PAFA decision. I know you'll win, and afterward, you can find somewhere else to settle if you want. Other than that, let's leave things as they are."

Her face hardened. "Well, I'm glad I found out you're one of those people who thinks money solves everything. A few dollars to ease your conscience, and it's okay to run out. Fine." She pulled the cell from a pocket of her shorts. "Should I leave this to pay off my conscience?"

"No, Beck. That was a gift. It's yours to do with as you want."

She stared at the object in her hand as if it was her mortal enemy. Then she took three quick steps and heaved the phone over the railing, out toward the ocean. We both watched it land nearly halfway to the water. She continued to stare at the waves as if willing them to come and claim it. "That's what I want. For all of it to go away. Everything I ever thought or felt about you."

Chapter Seventeen

Beck fled into the house, grabbing the found jar on her way out the door. I heard her on the stairs and listened for the scooter. Instead, I heard the barely audible slide of the garage door opening.

Mel joined me. "I take it that didn't go too well. But hey, that was a hell of a throw, wasn't it?"

"Mel—" I began, warning in my tone.

"I know, I know." She waved her hands, turning to go. "I'll shut up and start carrying the bags to the car."

"I'm going to take a quick shower too," I called, wishing I could truly cleanse myself. If all the mistakes in my life were dirt, I'd be caked ten feet deep.

Mel started down the stairs. I stared at the neatly made bed. Would Beck sleep in here or in her old room, or would she refuse to stay at all? The outside door slammed, and Mel shouted, "Goddamn it."

"What's wrong?" I asked, hurrying toward the main room.

"I have two flat tires. Two! Both on the driver's side, front and back. What are the odds of that? I swear, if your little butch—"

Could Beck really have…? "Mel, she's clearly not my little butch any more, as if she ever was, and secondly, there's a lot of construction out on the highway and more in town. You could have gotten nails in either of those places."

Grumbling, she punched in a number on her cell phone. AAA certainly had a fire lit under them by the time she finished her conversation. I showered quickly and was barely dressed before their flunky arrived. After a brief examination, he pronounced both tires unfixable. Mel's face got so red, I thought she was going to have a heart attack. She called the guy an assortment of unpleasant names before calling the rental company. Apparently, tire replacement had to be done at the rental facility. After going through one clerk and two supervisors, they agreed to bring her a new car...tomorrow. Despite her pleas and threats of a lawsuit, there was apparently nothing more that could be done. I pulled one of Beck's casseroles out of the freezer, trying hard to ignore the ache in my chest as I did so. When I told Mel to put her overnight things in Beck's room, she acted shocked.

"Are you kidding? You're gonna make me sleep on that tiny bed?"

"Well, you're sure as hell not sleeping with me," I countered.

Mel came up behind me in the kitchen. "Are you sure?" she crooned. "I could make sure your last night here was a really fine memory." She ran her hands down my arms and reached around my waist. "If I'd known you were into butches, I'd have made my move a long time ago."

"I'm not into butches. And the answer is still—" Before I could finish my sentence, a roaring sound came from below.

Mel jumped. "What the fuck?"

I was about to say that it was Beck working but stopped myself. Instead, I lied. "We thought there was a gas leak last week, but Beck showed me how to check it."

"Gas?" Mel shuddered, sniffing. "Isn't that dangerous?"

"Not as long as you don't vape around it," I assured her. "But let me go see."

In the garage, Beck was standing with her back to me, legs spread wide. Sparks flew as she handled the cutting torch, her face hidden by a welding helmet. I looked away from the flame, watching that tight butt and the muscles in her arms flexing instead. My gut fluttered the way it often did around her, but it was the tender way she caressed the metal, examining it lovingly, that was thoroughly Beck. The found jar was in front of her foot, and I noticed some sand had spilled out, though most of the contents seemed intact. The torch shut off abruptly, and I gasped. She turned, raising the mask on her helmet. Neither of us spoke for a few seconds.

"I hate this," I said softly. "I hate the way I've made you feel, and my suggestion that we just leave it like this was asinine. I don't want to leave it. I don't want to leave you. Is it possible for us to keep in touch and for me to come back and visit you, maybe after my book launch?"

I hadn't planned to say any of this, but I couldn't seem to stop once I'd started. It was certainly wishful thinking on my part, along with some feeble attempt to make things right with Beck with another empty promise. My most recent therapist had told me I needed to focus my vision for living on the future. When I argued that I'd never returned to places of my past, she said that mentally I'd never let go of them, especially Abby. Would lingering memories of Beck become a part of my psyche and nothing more?

Beck removed the helmet, placing it on the bench where she was working. "You know, donkeys have an unjustified reputation for being stubborn." I tried to process the point of this nugget of knowledge but failed. Beck was watching me, and when I looked at her searchingly, she said, "You said *asinine*. It literally means *like an ass*, and I think they were referring to the donkey as opposed to someone's behind. Don't you?"

I fought hard against tears and approached her slowly. "I am going to miss you so much," I whispered, reaching out to lay my hand on her cheek.

She closed her eyes but didn't shy away from my touch. "I'm sorry I got angry. I do better when I have time to understand things, and I think I understand now. I mean, I know it's important to have enough money to live, and I apologize for what I said to you about that. You've been very generous this whole summer, and now you have a chance to make lots of money, so you need to try to do it. For your future. Is that right?"

"First, you have absolutely nothing to apologize for. I deserve a lot worse than I got. And yes, I don't know if things will work out for this movie deal, but I have to try."

"I understand." Beck looked at me with a sly expression as she covered my hand with hers. "And at least you're not leaving today after all."

At her touch, I knew everything between us was as good as it could be. I'd never understood the concept of grace, but I felt it now. As was her way, she'd forgiven me for no reason other than she was a decent person. "And how would you know that?" I couldn't keep the tease out of my voice, still wondering if she'd been responsible for the delay.

Beck leaned toward me. "I don't think Mel has a low volume option."

I tried to restrain my amusement, but in the next second, Mel shouted, "Is everything okay?"

I managed to choke out "Fine," and then Beck and I were almost hysterical with suppressed laughter.

"Do you need some help?" she called. I didn't want another

confrontation between her and Beck, so I answered, "No, I'll be right up."

Beck joined me outside, and we both stood for a moment, breathing in the cooling air. I turned to face her again. "I hope you know, of all I've experienced here and all the memories in the found jar, you are what I'd most like to keep, if I could. I wish..." I couldn't finish. There was too much to say and no way to say it without ruining everything.

"Yeah," she said softly. "I wish too."

I sighed. "Will you come in for dinner? Or to sleep?"

"I don't think I'll be in tonight, Emily. There's something very important I need to finish."

I wondered if that was true or if she was avoiding Mel. "Well, if that should change, there's room in my bed for you. The other room will be occupied." Something flashed in her eyes, and she nodded. "And please, please don't leave before I have a chance to see you in the morning, okay?"

She looked away. "I don't think I can promise that. I don't want to...I can't watch you leave, Emily."

I couldn't stand it another minute. I threw my arms around her neck and pulled her close, savoring it all, the rough texture of the protective apron, the smoky scent from the torch, and the fiery odor of hot metal. Combined with the tang of her sweat and the salt air, it was all too special to let go of. Why was I leaving when nothing else had ever felt this fulfilling or this right? The reality of how much I would miss Beck was more fearful than anything I'd ever written or dreamed. How would I manage? How would she?

"You can't text or answer my calls without a phone," I murmured sadly into her neck.

I felt her smile against me. "Well, I do have this one." She held up a newly cleaned phone, the one I'd gotten for her. "My mama would have called that toss 'cutting off your nose to spite your face.'"

I could only imagine what Mrs. Janser and all Beck's friends would think of me disappearing without a word. "Please tell her and everyone else good-bye for me."

I felt her tremble. "But you'll be back in November, won't you?" I nodded vaguely. "Then I'll tell them you said 'see you later,' okay?"

"Emily," Mel called. "I think this dish in the oven is burning."

"I need to go."

She squeezed me gently and turned away. "Just in case you ever want to know," she said, putting on her helmet and lowering the mask again. She finished the sentence while turning a knob on the torch, and it roared to life when she snapped the sparker below it. I shielded my eyes, and between that and the rumble of the flame, I couldn't be sure I heard her correctly. Did she say something about love?

❖

A commotion woke me the next morning, combined with heavy footsteps on the stairs. "Hey, Emily!" I heard Mel call. "Make coffee."

Any questions as to whether my days would be different without Beck were answered in that one moment. Of course, the coffee command was the least of it. I'd tossed and turned for another night, missing all the wonderful parts of Beck I'd come to know and regretting those I hadn't met yet. I glanced out the window as I shuffled to the kitchen, delighted to see her scooter was still there. I decided to bring her some coffee and get a few last moments with her. When the brew was done, I moved toward the door, jumping slightly when it opened, and Mel came in, pocketing her car keys and shaking her head. "I have to admit, that kid is something else."

At the sound of Beck's scooter, something twisted inside me. I looked out the window, and seeing her ride away felt like watching something precious being dragged into the depths by an unrelenting ocean current. I wondered if the Emily I'd become was disappearing with her. "What do you mean?" I asked absently.

"I hate that cocky side of her, but she's super creative and really talented. I can't wait to see what she makes for the PAFA. She could be famous if she put her mind to it. You'll see later." The Beck I knew was not cocky, but the two of them did seem to clash. Mel sniffed at the cup in my hand, and her face twisted in disgust. "Have you lost your mind? That's no way to drink coffee."

Our trip back seemed terribly long, yet not long enough. The time I had alone on the way to Norfolk was invaluable, as I worked on stifling my tears and stuffing thoughts of Beck into the same emotionally distant corner where I kept Abby. By the time Mel joined me, talking a mile a minute, I was almost able to drift into the blank emptiness I'd frequently inhabited before my time in North Carolina. But as we neared the city, my face must have shown my anxiety because Mel ran her hand soothingly along my forearm. "Don't worry, Em. Living here is like riding a bike. You never forget how."

But I'd been seeing it through Beck's eyes, which only reaffirmed my conviction that she would hate this place. She could never adjust to crowded roads, vast numbers of pedestrians, musty air, and random blowing trash everywhere. Not asking if she'd consider moving was probably the most unselfish thing I'd ever done. "I wish I could forget," I muttered, and at first it seemed snarky enough to be something old Emily would say. But it mainly sounded sad, and what I wanted to forget was unclear. It was going to take more practice to lose the thoughtful view of life I'd learned from Beck. Fuck, who was I kidding? It was going to take a miracle to forget anything about Beck.

As if in confirmation, a panel truck decorated with a beach scene passed me. For just a second, I could feel the warmth of sand under my feet and Beck's sensuous touch during the sultry nights…no, no, no! I was not doing this. I was not driving myself crazy in the first hour I was here.

Grateful to have a strong friend, I hugged Mel at my apartment as she brought in the last of my things. "You're really gonna love me when I show you this." She grinned, pulling out a large, paper-wrapped rectangle that must have been on the bottom of my trunk. My brow furrowed as she directed me to a chair and put the heavy object on my lap. "Open it. It's a farewell gift from your beach buddy." My heart began pounding as I tore away the paper. "I think she must have worked on it all night." I revealed what looked like bars on a jail cell, except they were horizontal. Between the bars were various pieces of welded metal. "See?" Mel said, taking it from me before I could protest. "This is what she got me up at the butt crack of dawn to show me. When you hang it on the wall like this"—she held it like a normal picture—"it's an abstract. But when you pull this thingamajig up…" She grabbed a hook, hidden on the bottom, and pulled. "It shows—"

I stood and walked closer, touching the piece reverently. The hinge I hadn't noticed shifted the bars, and the shapes on them into different positions. "Our view," I whispered. And it was. The beach grass and dunes, down to the distant waves, with objects from the found jar cleverly attached or recreated at strategic intervals. It was so perfect, I wanted to cry.

"Where do you want it?" she asked, carrying the piece around to different walls.

I knew exactly, but I didn't want to tell her. I wanted lots of time to examine the amazing detail, but it would live in my bedroom, becoming the first thing I'd see every morning. I yawned before rubbing at my eyes. "I'm too tired to decide," I told Mel. "Just leave it on that chair for now."

As I expected, she seemed pleased by my lack of enthusiasm. "Wanna get something to eat?" she asked, but I shook my head.

"I want to unpack and go to bed. If I get hungry enough, I'll order in."

"Yeah, I'm kinda tired myself. How about lunch tomorrow?"

"I don't know. When's the meeting?"

"What meeting?"

A warning bell sounded in my mind, and the sharp edge I had been known for returned. "The meeting you dragged me here for, Mel."

"Oh yeah, shit. I must be more tired than I thought." She edged toward the door. "I'll call you tomorrow with the details."

I took a step toward her. "I swear to God, Melanie Daniels, if you've—"

"No, no, there's a meeting. Honestly, Em. I'll call you, okay?"

She was out the door before I could say another thing, but I heard her yell, "Get some sleep!"

Not likely, I thought, though I was exhausted. Breathing shallowly in the dim, stale apartment with sounds of the traffic below, I did the one thing that might help. I called Beck. I mainly wanted to thank her for the wonderful gift of her work, but at the sound of her voice, I choked down tears. It seemed like she might be doing the same. Having even brief, long-distance communication was going to be way harder than I'd imagined. More like impossible, my cynical mind whispered. *Welcome back, New York Emily.*

The meeting, when it finally happened, was basically a cattle call for which Mel had been promised a private, five-minute spot. The Saga Films execs had been meeting in the morning with someone they'd already signed, and the studio ordered them to use the afternoon to do some scouting. Our reserved opportunity was at 4:30, by which time I was certain they would be tired and totally disinterested in anything but making their flight to California.

I shot daggers at Mel as we stood in the packed waiting area, unable to find a seat among the throng of hopefuls. At 4:45, after we'd been there for over an hour, a woman came out and announced the meetings were over. She offered to pick up our proposals, all of which, I was certain, would never leave this room alive. If anyone was looking for ideas, they only needed to check the trash after everyone was gone. Mel sidled over and surreptitiously pressed a bill into her hand. After a quick glance, the woman murmured something, finished collecting the pitches, and disappeared.

Mel stood by my side. "Act like we're leaving too. Fumble in your bag or something."

Eventually, after the room cleared, we sat. "Are you sure they'll see us?" I asked.

Just then, the door opened, and the woman gestured nervously. "Two minutes."

We walked in, facing a table where three men sat, briefcases packed and suit jackets on. "Whatcha got?" the man on the right asked.

"Horror, suspense, romance," Mel answered. "Love and murder."

The middle of the three regarded Mel suspiciously. "Boy-girl romance? Or something else?"

"Male-female," I answered, stepping forward. "I'm the author. The titles I've already published and their one-liners are on here." I handed him a business card.

The third man stood. "Great. We'll be in touch."

"We've been in touch," Mel said shortly, obviously still smarting from middle man's question. "I've spoken with Gerry Chambers on several occasions."

The men glanced at each other. I couldn't tell if they were looks of respect or indifference. "Your proposal?" the right side guy asked.

Mel pulled a copy from her leather portfolio. The man on the left looked at his watch. "We'll read it on the plane and get back to you." He must have seen my glance drift to the overflowing trash can because he slowly and deliberately placed it in his briefcase.

"Just to give you a heads-up, we already have another meeting scheduled in three weeks with one of your competitors," Mel said, offering her hand. "If we get a favorable offer from you first, we'll cancel it. We won't play you off against each other, but this is a damn good property, so don't lowball us if you want a shot at it."

I didn't know if this was true, and at that moment, I didn't care. All I wanted to do was sit on the deck and hold Beck's hand. Without that option, the vision that came to me was of a cold glass of white wine and the seclusion of my apartment. I wondered how much longer I'd resist the former, especially since all I had was the latter.

❖

Mel had scheduled the book signing in a wonderful location. A former office building on the edge of the Village had been bought by an artists' collective and made available for various kinds of performances. The area that had once held workers' cubicles was now a big open space, although a few office rooms with doors remained on one side.

Much to Mel's dismay, I'd invited June to attend our setup, and she quickly made herself useful by arranging tables for snacks well away from the area where I would be signing, while the W's set out the chairs where my adoring fans—I inwardly jeered at the optimistic numbers—would sit to hear my reading. It was like old times, and everyone was going out of their way to be upbeat and helpful, including me. My cheeks hurt from almost constant smiling, it was all I could do to keep the sun from shining out of my ass and blinding us all.

We all knew the truth, of course. After our unsatisfactory movie meeting, I'd answered Mel's first three calls but declined any further contact, insisting I wasn't mad at her but simply felt like having some time alone. In reality, I felt like I was mourning, very much like I had when I'd first lost Abby. Food lost its taste, and I had trouble sleeping. I ached all over, and sometimes it felt like I couldn't catch my breath. When Mel resorted to informing the W's I was home, they each took a turn at bugging me, but after the first time, I hadn't answered additional calls or texts from them either. I had resigned myself to finding my NYC mode again, but it was proving even harder than I'd imagined. Just as I'd told Beck, it had done me no good to become a beach person because leaving there had made me more miserable than I'd ever been.

At first, she was the only person I spoke to regularly. But after one or both of us ended our phone conversations in tears, I suggested we try communicating by text or email, not initially aware of how much more difficult the brain injury had made writing for her. I knew she was busy, while unpacking had been my biggest task. She asked briefly about the city and about my work, telling me she was glad the end of summer rush had finally slowed because she worried about her mom's health. She said she spent most of her free time working on her project, which I was glad to hear. One thing I had done since my return was to google the PAFA contest, so I knew the deadline was coming up soon. I tried not to let it bother me that my messages outnumbered hers by two or even three to one. I never referred to missing her—missing us—but let my longing pour out in wistful comments about her town, the Guest House, and the sights and smells of the ocean. The connection we'd developed was the most meaningful of my life, and though I couldn't stand the idea of losing it, I knew I would, if I hadn't already. Returning to Windsom Edge was a dimming dream, and the thought that I'd be breaking my word yet again made me almost immobile with sorrow.

Finally, Mel all but broke in my door, and after pointing me toward the shower and picking out an outfit, she announced we were going to dinner. By the end of the evening, I'd fallen off the wagon nearly as hard as I'd fallen for Beck. Mel grinned like the Cheshire Cat all night, and when I finished the fifth drink of the evening, she pumped her fist in triumph and proclaimed "our Emily" was back.

So began an all too familiar pattern in my life. Late in the afternoon, about every second or third day, Mel would appear, uninvited, and push me toward the shower. I moved automatically as I prepared myself. After our fourth outing, when Mel again found herself holding my hair in an alley behind a bar as I puked my way to some semblance of reality, I wondered how she could be truly happy about the reappearance of the nasty drunk she called her friend. Each morning left me increasingly disgusted with myself, especially when I recalled Mel's oddly attentive behavior. The more I withdrew emotionally, the more touchy-feely she became, more than I would have been able to tolerate before my time with Beck. It was like my body had been reconditioned, and not even the oblivion I sought in drinking was fully returning me to what I sought—the colder, more remote version of "our Emily."

However, between my long nights out and my mornings-afternoons recovering from them, my communications with Beck grew fewer, shorter, and less meaningful. She asked if something was wrong on more than one occasion, and I put her off with banalities about catching up with things in the city or being busy getting ready for the signing. Beck was no fool, and she proved it again with a deliberate change in her communication. She began sending photos. None were selfies or group photos of her in social settings. Many were of Sugar; some featured the house or the beach or a particularly beautiful sunset. There was a blurry picture, probably taken quickly or in secret, of her mother and Barbara at the diner, coffee cups in front of them and their heads close together. The concerned looks on their faces made it easy for me to imagine they were worried about Beck.

Typically, New York Emily avoided sentiment for these scenes by just looking at each one for a few seconds before clicking off, sending nothing but a smiling emoji or thumbs-up in reply. I tried not to think about how fittingly this communication summed up our separate worlds. Hers was filled with natural color and the authentic texture of life. Mine conveyed imitation emotions by way of garish cartoons and simulated symbols.

I found my anger, though. By the time I actually saw the W's, my first words were an apology for the things I'd said before hanging up on Walter when he'd called me the previous day before eleven o'clock. On a good day, I would have been awake and working long before then, but there hadn't been any of those days lately, and I'd taken it out on him in no small measure. I couldn't recall any details of the conversation, but June had phoned me that evening, confronting me in her easy way. She'd already come by my apartment one afternoon, at my request, because she was the only person I could talk to about Beck.

We spent the first hour and a half finding the floor under layers of discarded delivery containers, empty wine bottles, and dirty clothes. At least the process saved us from any painfully obvious conversation about how I was doing. When the kitchen table was clean enough for me to put out some snacks I'd purchased for the occasion, I sipped white wine while she opted for tea, explaining she was following my example—my earlier example—and not drinking for a while.

Maybe it was because we'd run through most of our small talk during the cleaning frenzy, or maybe it was the loosening effects of alcohol, but I admitted I couldn't seem to get myself together, and I was genuinely sorry all the raggedy pieces were falling on my friends. She nodded her understanding, after which I surprised myself by saying, "I miss her so goddamn much, June. Nothing feels right anymore. I don't know what to do."

She sighed dramatically. "I think you're in love, Emily. And honestly, I didn't expect you to come back here at all. You should be following your heart. But first, you have to be okay for the book event. You owe that to all of us and to your readers. Then you'll be free to do what you need to do for yourself and for Beck."

Eventually, she convinced me to demonstrate the sincerity of my regret by not drinking before the signing and having William act as my babysitter. At least he would know I didn't want sympathy. My dominant yearning was the kind I'd previously ascribed only to heroines of sappy romance novels: what I wanted was gone and would never return again, and I didn't need anyone to remind me of that.

Instead I concentrated on preparing for my reading, since

professional reviewers usually attended these bigger book events. Gerry Chambers had called, apologizing profusely for the "mix-up" and the meeting and assuring us we were very much on Saga's radar. Assuming this book was well received, Mel and I would fly out to California within the week to meet with two Saga producers—one of whom was a woman, thanks to my insistence—for negotiations on the movie deal Mel claimed could expand to something like the *Twilight* series.

The fact that I hadn't written a word beyond my texts and emails to Beck didn't seem to worry Mel. During our last outing, when I'd drunkenly confessed my inactivity, she'd put her hand on my thigh and rubbed encouragingly. "Everyone hits a slump every now and then. You simply need to find the FA state of mind." We both knew what she meant. I needed to get my thoughts off the woman I'd left behind. I was grateful she didn't resort to the cliché about getting over one woman by getting under another.

As William and I shared a quiet dinner, I was feeling almost human and nearly capable of managing tomorrow's tasks when he casually asked, "Are we ever going to talk about the cute butch elephant in the room?"

I half choked on my salad and reached for his wine. He pushed the water glass into my hand instead and waited while I sipped, grimaced, and sipped again.

"Emily," he said, using a tone similar to when we'd first broached the subject of our families, "not talking about her will not help you forget her." I gathered myself and fixed him with a glare I hoped would stop this line of questioning. I should have known better. "Assuming that's what you want," he added fearlessly.

In my mind, I saw Beck. I saw beautiful kind eyes and an incredible smile. I felt comforting arms around me and heard the way she said my name as she came beneath me. How could I forget the woman who'd brought me into her life as she'd taken residence in my mind and helped me discover my previously nonexistent heart? I took a breath. "It doesn't matter what I want. What matters is what is. I live here. She lives there. End of story."

"End of current chapter," he corrected, grinning. "People move, you know. They live in one place for a while and sometimes they find another place they like better. You can work anywhere." He leaned forward, his expression gentle. "I saw how you were with her. We all did. And since you've been back, you've been…well, terribly unhappy. Why not be where your heart is?"

It was odd hearing him and June, two of my favorite people, both making reference to my heart. "Are you trying to get rid of me?"

He grinned. "You know it. But besides that, we all want to see you happy. Well, all except for Mel. She just wants to see you naked."

I laughed. "Now I know you're joking. Mel and I got past that point in the first week we knew each other."

"Hmm." He took a sip of wine while I pondered the noncommittal sound he'd made.

❖

Walter escorted me to the reading-signing. I stopped in the doorway, astonished by the turnout. I didn't know what kind of promotion Mel had done, but it had certainly paid off. When my agent-friend stepped out from the crowd and began clapping, I tried to wave her off, but soon the whole room was applauding. The scene made me feel like a former Broadway star who'd recently completed a stunning comeback performance.

"This is your moment, Famous Author," Walter whispered. "Make the most of it."

But it wasn't mine, really. It belonged to these true friends of mine and to my audience. Still, I responded to the greeting with an elaborate curtsey, and the ovation changed to laughter.

"I want to welcome you here tonight," I said when I reached the podium, "and thank you for choosing to spend your evening with me and your fellow readers. Before we go any further, I need to acknowledge the wonderful team that supports me, encourages me, and sometimes gives me a swift kick in the pants when I need it. June, Walter, William—my thanks are absolutely insufficient, but still, you have them. And to Mel, our *capo dei capi*—that's boss of bosses for those of you who don't watch Mafia movies—thank you for riding herd on me." I blew her a kiss, and she blew one back. "So, if you haven't had a chance to grab some of the wonderful refreshments over there…tough. You'll have to wait until I'm finished because the story I'm going to tell might make you lose it." More muted laughter, and the audience stirred with anticipation.

After a brief introduction, I read from a suspenseful section early in the novel. I heard a few gasps along the way, and when I finished, there was absolute silence. About the time I thought, uh-oh, and looked toward Mel, the whole room burst into applause. My relief must have shown on my face because a few people in the first three or four rows laughed too. Waving, I moved toward my signing table, and the line began forming.

After signing what felt like my hundredth book, my hand began to cramp, and I took an extra moment to flex it. I heard some commotion and looked to see William was working his way down the line. I cocked my head in puzzlement, and he smiled. I felt Mel stiffen behind me, and I turned. "What's the matter?"

"Listen, Em—" she began, but I heard a book hit the table. Apparently, someone was impatient.

I took a breath, mentally preparing a mild rebuke, but before I could look up, I heard her voice. "Hi, Emily."

Heart pounding, I raised my eyes hesitantly, praying I'd heard right. "Beck." She smiled hesitantly. "Oh God. Beck." I started to stand, but Mel's hand fell on my shoulder.

"Emily, you need to finish signing."

I couldn't stop looking at Beck, lest she disappear. "No, Mel." I pushed against her. "I need to greet my…" I couldn't think what to call Beck, but it didn't matter. I leaned across the table, my arms awkwardly around her neck, I touched my forehead to hers. "I can't believe you're here," I whispered.

"Me neither. If it hadn't been for that friend of yours, William, I don't think I would have made it. Boy, do I have travel stories to tell you."

I felt a genuine smile on my lips. "I bet." I moved back, smiling even wider when I saw what she was wearing. Those black boots that made her my height along with the black jeans hugging every important curve, were topped by the maroon shirt with the leather tie I'd bought for her. She'd had her hair cut into a classic fade, short on both sides with the top longer and stylishly tousled as the same long thin braid trailed down her back. Cupping her face, I said, "You look absolutely amazing. How long can you stay?"

She blushed before putting her hands over mine. "I so much wanted to see you at your book event. And it was wonderful. But I'm catching the last train tonight in about…" She looked at her wrist, and I was astonished to see a watch there. "Two and a half hours. I have to work tomorrow."

"No," I said, surprising myself with how unequivocal I sounded. "Let me finish here and I'll drive you. We can take turns driving and talk all night on the way home. You can tell me everything."

Her face lit up. "Really?"

This feeling I got in her presence, I recognized it then. Having done without it for what felt like years, seeing her and touching her again made me fully aware of what I'd been missing. All the empty, heavy, and aching parts inside me were overflowing with gladness and lightness, along with the physical urgency that was only for Beck. The previous time we'd been apart, when I'd gone to Arizona, I'd come to the realization that I was willing to risk being with her. This time, I thought I knew something more.

Tell her. "I'm incredibly happy to see you," I said softly, rewarded by the curve of that beautiful mouth as I pushed my chair back, bumping into Mel, who reluctantly stepped away. Speaking to her without looking, I said, "Please tell everyone I'm going to take a short break. Encourage them to eat more or at least pull a chair over and take a seat." I turned to Walter, who was still at the sale table. "Give everyone who buys a book while I'm gone a ten percent discount." That took a chunk out of my profit, but I didn't care. I heard Mel huff with displeasure as I rounded the corner of the table, taking Beck's hand and pulling her into the nearest office room. She turned on the lights, and after a quick glance where I observed nearly every soul in the place looking this way, I hastily closed the door. Perhaps if they read Emily Harrison's novel, they'd understand.

I pressed myself into her, arms around her waist, and she pulled me closer, holding my shoulders. "Oh," I breathed, closing my eyes as I fell into her, burying my face in her neck. She smelled a little different, presumably from traveling. But she felt right, as always. I could stay like this forever. Or in any one of various horizontal options, as long as they were with her.

I felt her take a deep breath. "I want you to know my life isn't the same without you, Emily," she said. I wanted to engulf her. Or have her pull me onto the floor and make love this instant. Instead, I searched her face, ready to tell her all those things, when her expression changed. "But I think I see now what you have here. This city, it's like the opposite of the beach. Loud and busy and…exciting, I guess. I mean, I get it. All you get in Windsom is a small beach house and some poor folks' casseroles. And wow." She gestured, indicating everything beyond the door. "This is like a TV show. You really are famous, aren't you?" She lowered her voice. "That story you read? It scared me. But I'm going to buy that book anyway and have you sign it. So I can say I knew you when," she added, smiling sadly.

"Beck—" I began, but she interrupted.

"You're supposed to say 'when what?'"

This was such a typical Beck conversation that I laughed. "Yes. I'm sorry. When what?"

"Yeah, so I have to say that your offer to take me home was sweet, but…"

She seemed to have talked herself out of it, and I thought I recognized the behavior. "Did your mother make you promise not to be a pest?"

When she looked down, not answering, I knew I was right. I leaned and kissed her on the mouth. I meant it to be just a sweet, reassuring kiss, but it had been too long for both of us. I was hungry for her in a way I hadn't been since the first time between us. Then, I'd been more nervous than needy. This was me wanting Beck to know what I felt and what I knew. With her mouth and her hands, she told me she understood, and she felt all those things too. When she moaned and broke the kiss, whispering my name and kissing down my neck, I pushed harder against her, running my hands across her back, feeling that delicious connection I never wanted to be without again.

A brief knock sounded, and Mel was in the room. I didn't let Beck move away, although she would have. "Oh, for fuck's sake," Mel said in her most disgusted tone, glaring. "Emily is working, okay? Do you think you could find some measure of self-control?"

I held on to Beck with one arm, turning slightly toward Mel. "It's my fault, though I don't think fault is exactly the word. But anyway, I'll be out in a moment." An idea occurred to me. "Is June still here?"

I tried not to be bothered by the way Beck brightened, reminding myself June had been friends with both of us. Mel shook her head. "She left about fifteen minutes ago. Right before Spike here showed up."

"Please tell her I'm sorry I missed her," Beck said to me in that wonderfully sincere way.

I squeezed her hand as I plotted how to get even with Mel for the Spike comment. "Well, are the W's both busy?"

"They're getting swamped since you're giving away all your profits."

I turned to Beck. "Would you mind taking a taxi to my place? I'd rather you wait there than get bored staying here." I touched her cheek and smiled. "Or keep distracting me. It probably won't be more than another forty-five minutes."

Beck paled. "A taxi?"

Mel shifted impatiently. "I can take her." My face must have shown some concern because Mel cleared her throat. "Look, I'll get her there safely, and then I'll come help with cleanup, okay? Unless she's scared to ride with me through the big city."

Beck clearly knew a challenge when she heard one. "I'm not scared."

"Mel—" I began, but she waved dismissively.

"Don't worry. I'll take care of her."

Something in her tone made me frown as they moved toward the door, but I was sure it was only anxiety about letting Beck out of my sight again so soon. Preparing for my return to the public eye, I smoothed my clothes and pushed my hair away from my face. Beck looked back at me from just outside the doorway and asked, "See you soon?" Before I could answer, Mel slammed the door with a finality that made me cringe.

Chapter Eighteen

It was almost two hours before I got away. Mel hadn't returned for what seemed like forever, mumbling something about "Spike" wanting to see more of the city by way of excuse—which earned her the silent treatment from me—and it seemed to take inordinately long to clean up. Beck might be worried about making her train, but there was no answer when I tried to call her. Perhaps she'd put her phone on mute and was taking a nap, trusting me to wake her when I came in. But I was determined to drive her home and ran two very pink lights while speeding every chance I got on the way.

I opened the door to a quiet apartment. Beck was usually a light sleeper, but I was sure she was exhausted by the unfamiliar stress of traveling. I walked toward the bedroom, whispering her name as I approached. "Beck? Sweetie, we have to get—" The bed was untouched. My apartment was smaller than the Guest House and made for a quick search. Every time there was no reply when I called her name, my heart cracked a little more. I was about to phone Mel when my eye fell on what looked like toilet paper draped across a rail of the artwork Beck had created. I held it with trembling hands, surprised to see the words written in block printing instead of her schoolbook cursive.

Dear Emily,
Mel told me about the two of you, and it explains a lot, like why she always acted jealous and why you didn't mind the way she treated you. I never heard of an open relationship before, and I wish you had been the one to tell me, but Mel explained that's not how you do. So instead you fooled me good, I guess, because I would have acted real different if I'd known. I'm not sure I'll ever understand how you two

> see this as a way to live, but all I know is, I couldn't ever share you like that, even though Mel invited me to be a part of it. I'm sorry, Emily, but getting to be with you sometimes wouldn't be enough to make me willing to be with Mel or let her watch us.

The next line was struck through, but I made out, "I once believed you were everything I ever wanted and seeing you again was…" Then it continued.

> Sorry for that. There's no point crying over spilt milk, as my mama says. But it feels like it's gonna take me a long time to clean this spill up. Maybe if one of us was a different kind of person, we could work things out. But we're not, and I don't suppose we ever will be. I came here to fight for you, but you know I'm not much of a fighter anyway, plus I sure don't know how to fight this. Mel explained to me about how she changes her number when she leaves her girl, but how you're always the first person she calls afterward. Though I don't exactly see it as I'm the one who's leaving, I guess I'll change mine too, cause I don't think I can talk to you again anytime soon. They announce the PAFA results tomorrow, and if I get any of the money, I'm going to buy a boat and live the life I used to dream about before we met. I guess you and Mel will be doing the same for yourselves.
> Good-bye and good luck.
> Beck
> P.S. Excuse the printing, but I'm writing this in the bathroom cause Mel don't want you to know she told me. She kept talking about your reputation, but I hope you know you don't have to worry about me saying anything. The thing is, I have to press harder to make my hand do cursive right, and I didn't think even this nice 2-ply would stand up to that. Ok, bye.

I was so angry I was shaking. I was going to kill Mel. And then I was going to fire her. I knew she was capable of lying and I knew she'd never approved of Beck, but I hadn't expected this. Melanie Daniels had played me, and she was going to live to regret it. But before anything else, I was going to North Carolina to find Beck. I packed carefully, fairly sure I wouldn't be in the city again for some time, if ever. Mel could go to California by herself, or the whole deal could go to hell. I honestly didn't care. The last thing I put in the trunk of my car was Beck's artwork. I didn't want to leave it, though I'd be looking at that view live if everything worked out. But I wanted to show Beck how much it meant to me, just after I showed her how much she meant to me.

It was getting late by the time I got outside of the city, and I began to worry about how dangerously impulsive this trip was. Leaving in the middle of the night to take a very long drive alone was totally unlike me. When the people in my stories did things like this, it never ended well. I could easily write of the horrors faced by a woman with a broken-down car on a lonely road or about the aging, lovestruck driver, seizing a last chance for romance, who dies in a fiery, asleep-at-the wheel crash. I saw the ghost driver following her intended lover out to sea, where a storm takes them both to the bottom, together at last.

I shook my head to clear it. Shit, how sick. What kind of person thought of these things on a trip to make up with her sweetheart? Especially that ending. Oh God, Beck had said she would buy a boat if she could. I'd developed some appreciation for the beauty of the ocean, but the idea of Beck out on a boat, knowing her father had died on one, made me press the accelerator a little harder. I needed to get there before she made that purchase, knowing my nerves would never settle any time she was out on that contraption. And if she wanted me to go, that would lead to a whole new round of difficulties.

I passed the car I'd been following, taking a position closer to the front of the line. As I eased back into the lane, the romantic Emily who had taken over my body kicked in her two cents worth. *What about what Beck wants? She said this was her dream. Couldn't you manage your own baseless anxieties to give her some happiness?* I supposed I could, but only if she would always return safely. Always.

In my mind I ensconced Beck's ship in a Disney-like protective bubble, assuring serene travel through any rough seas or mechanical problems. The twist in my stomach relaxed somewhat. *All right. Done.*

Glancing in my rearview mirror, I watched the car which had been behind me earlier pull in after me again. The headlights had a distinctive shape and looked increasingly familiar as I studied them. I fumbled for my purse to look for my phone. After unearthing my sunglass case and my hairbrush, I found it…completely dead, of course. I plugged in the charger I'd thrown in, wondering how much power it would take to call 9-1-1. I watched and waited. The car ahead of me took an exit. The one behind me didn't. I increased my speed, and it did too. I slowed, and it dropped back.

Okay, maybe I was overreacting, but maybe not. I passed a sign giving the mileage to the next service area and decided to stop there. They were brightly lit and popular places for travelers, even at this hour.

I checked the power on my phone and called William. It went to his voice mail, and after the beep I said, "Listen, I'm on the turnpike, and I think someone's following me. Or maybe I'm freaking out because I'm going to North Carolina, and I don't know how Beck will react to seeing me now. Oh, I'll explain that later. Anyway, if you don't ever hear from me again, tell the police to start their search at the Molly Pitcher Service Area." I hesitated only a second, not wanting the device to cut me off. "And thanks for everything, Will. You've always been a special friend, and I'll miss you, but maybe you and Walter can come visit."

When the car followed me off the exit toward the service area, I swallowed hard. After all these years of living with Abby's terror and writing stories of horrible things happening to other people, was something like that about to happen to me?

In the parking area, I squeezed past someone leaving their space. After an angry honk, they continued pulling out slowly enough that the car following me was delayed. I screeched into the next available slot and ran toward the lights and the people inside. I didn't look back.

I needed the restroom but didn't want to go into a confined space until I was certain about what was happening, so I joined the queue at Starbucks where I could watch the door. Four or five other people came in, but I wasn't sure what I was watching for. None of them looked like killers. Mostly they looked tired.

Sipping my coffee, another thought came to me: my stalker might be out in the parking lot, hiding by my car, waiting for me. I took another lap around the facility as I finished my drink, deciding it was safe to empty my bladder. I began another scan as I exited the bathroom. Someone approached on my left, and when I heard my name, I turned quickly.

Melanie Daniels moved toward me. "I've been looking all over this place for you. Goddamn woman, you can drive like a bat out of hell when you want to."

The rage that flared in me was like nothing I'd ever experienced. Before Beck, the strongest feelings I'd had were about Abby, sadness and regret, along with guilt, of course. But seeing Mel standing there with that smirk on her face made me think of all the hurts she'd inflicted, all the snide remarks and cutting looks. Part of my anger was at myself, and how I'd been too much like her until I met the kindest person I'd ever known. Now, knowing she'd deliberately lied to send Beck away from me, blithely dismissing our feelings for each other, made something in me snap. I slapped her as hard as I could, which was apparently much harder than either of us would have expected. She staggered and nearly fell while I shook out my stinging hand.

"How dare you?" I hissed. "How dare you come up to me like we're friends after what you did?"

Mel had her hand on her cheek and was working her jaw. "Okay, now that you got that out of your system, can we talk about this calmly?"

"No, we can't fucking talk calmly. Why are you following me?"

The restrooms were at the rear of a small hallway, but everyone in the vicinity, male or female, could hear us, and more than a few heads turned.

"I'm trying to keep you from making the biggest mistake of your life," Mel said.

I stepped closer, poking my finger in her chest. "You are the biggest mistake of my life." I felt a strange satisfaction when she flinched. "You're fired. And I don't ever want to see you again."

"Come on, Emily. You don't mean that. We've got way too much history to call it quits." She lowered her voice. "And I meant what I said about us having an open relationship. If you'll think about it for a minute, you'll see it would be perfect. You can have some fun at the beach for a few weeks here and there, and I'll do the same with whoever. Then come back and we can play house together." Taking advantage of my open-mouthed shock, she moved a step closer. "You know I've always had a thing for you. We could live nicely on my trust and what you make writing. Give me a try and I'll make you forget all about your beach buddy. You'll realize you never had it so good."

She reached for my arm, but I stepped away. Typically, Mel was rejecting anything that didn't fit with what she wanted. "No, Mel. I meant what I said. I'll consider whatever termination fee you think you're due, but we are finished, professionally and personally. And if you follow me again, I'll call the police." She started to reply, but I held up a hand. "We're done here. And I still have several hours of driving to do."

As I walked away, I heard Mel's distinctive voice, obviously on the phone. "Lisa? Hey, baby. Change of plans. I'll be home tonight after all. Why don't you come by about…"

Her voice faded away as I hit the door.

The sun was well up by the time I reached the Guest House. I hadn't given back my key from before and breathed with relief when it still worked. The air had a nip in it that hadn't been there before, but the scene was as beautiful as I remembered. Home. I felt that certainty in my newly awakened heart. The house was spotless, of course, and Beck's things were still in the second bedroom. The indication that she wasn't sleeping in the master bed struck me with an emotion I wasn't sure how to name.

Sugar appeared at the door as I was unpacking, and we took some time to get reacquainted. I showered off the road grit and familiarized myself with the kitchen again while making some eggs. The results weren't too bad, though not nearly as tasty as Beck's. After cleaning up, I wandered into the smaller living area, envisioning it as my writing space. It was as she had said; there was room for a good-sized desk and some bookcases. This could definitely work if only Beck would take me back, and I practiced on making my case for that scenario.

But she didn't return. Not that night or the next day. By the second evening, I was pacing as I held long conversations with the cat. Had she gotten hurt somehow? I considered moving my car in case she'd seen it and was avoiding me, but I didn't want our first conversation to begin with deception. After another restless—but thankfully nightmare-free night—I decided to call Beck's mother.

"Hello, Mrs. Janser, it's Emily Harris," I said when she answered on the third ring. "I was just calling to see how Beck was doing."

"Oh." There was a pause. "That's very nice of you, I'm sure. I gather you left that cat here, and now I'm stuck with taking care of it for a time." That haughty, sarcastic tone had returned in spades. I said nothing. "But Beck is doing fine, thank you. Of course, she's kinda disappointed, but there's enough, so she'll be all right, I suppose."

I took a few seconds to process this odd reply. Then it hit me. The PAFA! In my travel-weary and self-absorbed mind, I'd forgotten all about it. I rushed to end the call, knowing I could look for the results online. "Please tell her I called. Thank you."

She'd won second place. I sighed. Her piece, called *Hit and Run*, featuring the likeness of a car body split in half, the fiercely dented, crumpled parts interspersed with multiple copies of our tormented faces in delicate plaster of paris positioned behind cracked or missing windows. It was a stunning, disturbing, brilliant work, which held more meaning for me than the obvious. I studied the photo for a long time before glancing over the other submissions. I knew I was biased, but I genuinely felt hers was superior to the winner's. Reading between the lines of the judges' comments, I gathered there was a point penalty for her use of mixed media. I wondered if Beck knew this or if she simply hadn't cared.

I glanced through the rest of the information. Beck's share of the prize money was seventy-five thousand dollars. I knew immediately where it, and she, had gone. I threw on some warmer clothes and headed to the marina.

Unfortunately, Mr. Avery was the first person I saw. Though he was the last person I wanted to talk to about Beck, I approached him. "Mr. Avery, good morning. I don't know if you remember me, but I'm Beck Reynolds's employer and I—"

He laughed. "Not anymore, you ain't. Or did I hear wrong?"

Knowing the way small town people talked, I decided to stay close to the truth. "Well, I've been gone for a time, yes, but I'm back, and I need to let Beck know."

His thin sneer revealed uneven teeth. "She's been gone three, four days." He gestured out toward the expanse of water and I steeled myself for my next words.

"Yes, well, I need to rent a boat and find her. Is there one available?"

He climbed onto the pier, standing much too close for comfort. "Were you planning on piloting it yourself?"

I would have laughed if I wasn't getting desperate. "Heavens, no. I'll need a, uh, pilot also."

"Then you want to charter something. What size?"

Scanning the few remaining boats bobbing in their slots, I decided I needed something that was as safe as possible if I was actually going to do this. I pointed to a pretty white one that looked like it was made to cut through the water, with a high—and therefore more protected—enclosed area. "How about that one?"

Avery snorted. "Figures. A snooty broad like you would want a yacht for your little day jaunt."

I frowned, ignoring his insult. Something about the look of that boat was vaguely familiar. "Well, it seems like it could handle the waves in relative comfort."

"Oh yes, ma'am, it's an excellent choice. If you've got the four hundred and fifty for half a day. And if Captain Saro is on board."

Had my sarcasm ever been that annoying? I gestured for Avery to go ahead, thinking I'd worry about the money if the boat and captain were available. When he reached the side of the boat, he called, "Hey, Miguel. You open for business?"

A muffled reply asked, "Who wants to know?"

"This lady here may want to go out for half a day."

A stocky, handsome man emerged from the enclosed area. When he saw me, he smiled and came down the narrow walkway that led from his deck to the pier, wiping his hands on a small towel. "How can I help you, ma'am?"

Relieved by his professional greeting, I said, "I just need you to take me one way to someone who's already out on the water. But if I need to pay for half a day, I'm sure I could manage."

He nodded, appearing to consider the options. "Do you have the coordinates for his location?"

Avery stepped in. "Becka Reynolds used to work for her. That's who she's trying to find."

Saro's eyebrows went up. "Beck? Didn't she buy that pocket trawler, the Nordhavn 40?"

"Yeah. She's already been out for a few days and didn't file a float plan, so no telling which way she went."

Even someone who didn't speak boat could figure out that a float plan was something like a flight plan for a plane. I turned to Captain Saro. "Is there any other way to know where she is?"

"It's a mighty big ocean when you're looking for one small boat," he said. "I guess we could try to hail her."

I shook my head vigorously. If I could see Beck, be with her, I was certain I could make her understand what had happened. "I need to speak with her personally. It's rather urgent."

He rubbed the back of his neck and looked at Avery. "Wasn't that the ship that did both an Atlantic crossing and a circumnavigation? Wouldn't the previous owners have had an AIS for all that serious cruising?"

I was surprised by Avery's thoughtful expression, and they went on talking in boating lingo until Captain Saro returned to his boat and started the engine while Avery trotted off in the direction of his office. I stood there, trying to decide if what was happening was good or bad. I heard the radio crackle, and Avery's tinny voice said, "*Almost Heaven.*"

Saro appeared again after a few seconds and waved. "Come aboard. I'll have to go by the pump and gas up. She's a ways out."

That last sentence echoed in my head as I approached the walkway to his boat. It looked much, much smaller now that I was going to be on it. I glanced out at the water. Was I really going through with this? Couldn't I wait until Beck came ashore again and talk to her then? Sighing, I reminded myself Beck thought I was a liar and a cheat, and she might never come back.

I put one foot on the walkway and Captain Saro stretched out his hand. "Don't look down," he advised, so of course, that was exactly what I did. The calm water of the marina wasn't too far away. I'd probably survive the fall if I didn't die of fright. My feet had stopped until he took my arm and pulled me along, cautioning me to watch my step onto the deck. I was increasingly queasy as the boat bobbed under me.

He pointed toward a set of stairs. "Why don't you go below and have a look around? The easy ride to the pump will be a perfect time to get acclimated. The rest of the trip may seem bumpy, so you can stay down there if it feels more comfortable."

I tried to imagine a bumpy trip a ways out. "Listen, I might change my mind." The words were out before I could stop them. "But I'll pay for your trouble. Whatever you think is fair."

"Normally, I ask for a deposit," he said after studying me. "But I'll trust you on that since I know who you are." At my quizzical expression, he added, "My sister-in-law is Dr. Leonor Bastos. We had dinner not long after she went to the Guest House, and she told us you were giving Beck a place to stay while she recovered from some injuries. She said you seemed like a kind, protective person."

"I'm usually not," I confessed. "But something about Beck just made me...care." But had she made me braver, too? Could I overcome this irrational fear of boats, the source of which I'd never tried to understand? I thought again about how something about this boat looked familiar, like something from a dream. Or a nightmare?

Smiling at my petrified expression, Saro gestured. "Feel free to look around."

"Below" was like a small apartment, with gleaming polished wood and tidy compact furnishings. There was a small, well-designed kitchen and a comfortable-looking sitting area. Was Beck's boat this nice? I passed a good-sized, beautifully appointed bedroom, and a smaller room with bunk beds sat across the room from each other. If they'd been twin beds, the arrangement would have been like mine and Abby's bedroom.

I noticed a child's book had been left on one of the top bunks. Looking closer, I saw a smiling cartoon boat on the worn cover. A long-buried memory hit me with such force I had to sit down. I had read to Abby the night that man had come in and stolen her away. She'd gone to sleep with the book in her arms while I had hidden under the covers with my flashlight and my "grown-up" chapter book. I couldn't remember any details of my book, only that hers had to do with a terrible storm where people had to be rescued by a brave boat.

God, could it be I had subconsciously associated boats and the ocean with something bad after that horrible night? My throat tightened as I remembered how much Abby had loved stories about people who acted valiantly when they were in danger. I knew she would have become one of them—a firefighter or a police officer or one of those everyday heroes who did something magnificent for someone they didn't even know—while the lesson I'd taken from the heartbreak of my early life was to become callous, apprehensive, and often unpleasant. Yes, my family had fallen apart, but I'd compounded that tragedy by letting my rare and reluctant concessions that I would never see Abby again turn me into her exact opposite.

Until I'd met Beck. She'd made me feel the goodness of being alive in a way I wouldn't have believed possible and had given me the courage to try romance, both in writing and in real life. Thinking of her alone and hurting, I held the book to my chest, certain Abby would urge me to run up those stairs and sail boldly to the person I loved. Could I take on Abby's courage and finally face my fears and my feelings?

❖

Luckily for me, Captain Saro was enough of a gentleman to turn his head while I puked over the side of the ship—again. I couldn't have said which unnerved me more, the rolling of the vessel as it cut through the huge expanse of water ahead or the nagging worry that since Beck's dream had come true, maybe she was done with me, with us, for good. Between my bouts of nausea, the captain asked me to call him Miguel, and explained how the Automatic Identification System could search for boats by name. *Almost Heaven* was the name under which Beck's boat had been sold, and she hadn't renamed it yet. He was probably talking to get my mind off where I was and what I was doing, but I couldn't stop thinking about that name. Was that what we'd had? Could we ever get it back?

After what seemed like hundreds of hours, I stopped grabbing desperately for the handholds every time we hit a swell. I fought the terror of endless water by pretending I was in my car, riding on a rough road. Eventually, I opted for mimicking the way Miguel adjusted his stance to keep his balance, which made me feel a little less unstable.

"There," he shouted suddenly, and I peered out the window at the tiny speck on the horizon. He grabbed the microphone from the radio, but I caught his hand.

"What are you doing?"

"I'm going to hail her. If we can see her, she can see us. I need to let her know who we are and what we want."

I grimaced, unable to envision any situation where Beck wouldn't start her engine and speed away when she found out I was aboard. "Can't we wait until we're closer? She might not...uh, I need the chance to talk before..." I couldn't seem to explain without sounding like a stalker.

He studied me for a few seconds before asking, "This isn't just employer business, is it?"

I shook my head and closed my eyes, wishing I didn't have to face the question or the worst possible outcome. When I opened them again, we were getting close enough to make out the shape of Beck's boat. It looked bigger than I had imagined.

Miguel was nodding. "She used to come around the marina all the time, but she hadn't been around for a while until the other day when she stopped by to ask about the Nordhavn 40. She seemed... different. Older. And since you know her, you know she's the type who always seems to bounce back from the knocks in her life. This time, there wasn't any bounce." He looked seriously at me. "Are you the reason for that?"

I tried for an innocent expression. "There was a misunderstanding. Someone else told her something that wasn't true, so I need some time to explain that I do want this. I want to be here with her." I managed a half-smile. "Well, not here like out here on the water, but here on the island."

"Like a lot of folks from here, she's got the ocean in her blood."

His intent expression matched his tone. "Were you expecting that to change?"

"Well, this boat part, yes. It's too dangerous," I countered. "Her father—"

"I know. But over thirty-five thousand people a year are killed in car accidents, while less than seven hundred die in boats."

As I pondered my response, Miguel's radio crackled. Avery's voice announced, "I'm getting transmission from *Almost Heaven*. She wants to know who's approaching. I'm assuming it's you."

"Affirmative," Miguel replied. "We're in sight. I'll hail her shortly." He turned to me. "Well? Moment of truth here. Are you going to make her choose between you and her boat?"

Was I? I let out a breath, trusting the bubble of safety I'd put around her in my mind. "No," I said slowly. "Just between having me and not having me. After that, we can work everything else out."

He pushed a lever forward, and the boat picked up speed as he spoke into the microphone. "Captain Reynolds, this is Captain Sora. Are you receiving me?" Winking, he said to me, "I'm going to try to stretch this out until we're right on her. Hang on."

We closed the distance while Miguel exchanged small talk with Beck about her new boat and the weather, intermittently clicking the microphone button and varying his speaking voice from very low to shouting, all the while complaining about his radio being on the fritz. By the time Beck repeated her question about his destination for the third time, I could make out someone behind the windows at the top level of her boat. When the figure lifted a set of binoculars, I ducked below, hiding.

Miguel gave me a look. "I have a passenger who's interested in your boat," he practically whispered into the mic. "We'd like permission to tie on for a few minutes."

I'd been so excited about being able to talk to Beck that I hadn't considered what the process of getting from one boat to another would entail. "Tie on?" I hissed at Miguel.

"That's how it's done out on the water. It's not hard. You'll step over."

Even without experience with such things, I could tell Beck's boat was taller than Miguel's. I tried to stop thinking about what came next as he repeated every second or third word of his previous message. I felt and heard the engine slow. I had to believe this crazy idea would work. That everything would work out.

I stayed out of sight until Miguel's engine was barely running, and I could hear Beck's voice clearly. "But there's not another boat like this for sale right now."

"Actually, I don't think it's the boat she's interested in," Miguel said, motioning to me.

When I stepped onto the deck, the confused expression on Beck's face flattened. "You lied to me," she said, but I wasn't sure who she was talking to. I moved toward the walkway they'd set up, which was tilted to accommodate the height of Beck's boat.

"Beck, please. Please give me a chance to explain. Mel is the one who lied. None of what she said is true."

But she was already walking away toward the front of the boat. "Go!" Miguel urged me, giving me a hand up so I could grab on to the flimsy railing on the walkway. "If she fires her engine, we'll have to turn loose."

It was a damn good thing my stomach was already empty. I couldn't remember the last time I'd been as scared. Well, I could, but I didn't want to. Not now. Now I needed to concentrate on what it would take to make Beck give me another chance. A large wave rolled both boats, and I screamed. Unplanned, it nevertheless did the trick. Beck stopped and looked toward me. As I flailed senselessly, she started in my direction. Encouraged, I called out, "God, Beck. Please help me. You don't have to take me back, but please don't let me fall."

Intent on watching what she was doing, I failed to notice a wet spot on the walkway where the bigger wave had splashed. My foot slipped, and I almost lost my balance. Crying, I lurched forward, closer now to her boat than to Miguel's. Beck stood at the other end of the walkway with her arms outstretched. "Jump, Emily. Jump and I'll catch you!"

If this wasn't a leap of faith, then I didn't understand the phrase. I righted myself to the point I could push off and did. Our bodies collided. The force of my movement knocked her to the ground, and she took me with her. We lay stunned for a few seconds until Miguel called, "Everyone shipshape over there?" Beck groaned. I wanted to laugh with relief but could only cough. "I'm going to tie off," he called, and Beck sat up, dumping me off her.

"Wait! What about Emily?" she asked as he pulled the walkway back onto his boat and secured it with the rope he'd used to tie us together.

"What about her?" he answered.

"How will she get to shore?" Beck stood and brushed herself off.

"Talk to her about that." He revved his engine and pulled away from us. By the time I'd gotten to my feet, his boat had turned and was already getting smaller in the distance. I sighed, a tiny part of me wishing I was going that way too. But first things first.

"Thank you for catching me," I said, looking at my feet.

"I guess you're welcome. But what are you doing here? Why aren't you in New York City with Mel?"

Beck's voice had an unfamiliar, gruff tone to it. Was it because she hadn't spoken much lately or because she was angry at me? I looked into her eyes, mustering all the sincerity I had in me. "Beck, I swear nothing she told you is true. Since I got to my apartment that night and saw your note, all I wanted to do was find you. I fired Mel since I can't count on her, but you can count on me. I've already made plans to buy the Guest House."

"You did?" Beck looked stunned. "Why?"

Since I wasn't sure which statement she was asking about, I just nodded as my first reply. Taking her face in my hands, I answered the real question. "Here's the thing. I love you."

Epilogue

On the first warm spring day, Beck insisted we take the boat out. Our found jar had been nearly overflowing for more than a month, and so, according to the established lore, we each got to keep one thing before returning the rest to the sea. I rarely took Bonine anymore, especially since she always chose the calmest days to take me out. I'd never be an old salt, but at least I didn't spend all my time at the rail, under the weather. Beck had taught me lots of nautical terms, and our word games now included expressions with origins in sailing history, such as *scuttlebutt* and *hunky-dory*.

My life was full and joyous in a way I'd never imagined, to the point that many memories of life in the last decade felt like sleepwalking by comparison. Most people in town had begun referring to our place as the Harris House, especially after the town paper covered the story of the house changing hands—"Author Buys Original Windsom Family Home"—accompanied by a picture of Mr. Guest giving me the keys. My smile was for Beck, who was standing out of camera range, making faces at me.

I sent copies of the article to June and to the W's, each of whom promised a summer visit. I sent nothing and heard nothing from Mel, which suited me fine. I'd cooled off to the point I could have spoken civilly to her, but I really had nothing to say, and apparently, neither did she. I'd concluded that in life, people came and went like characters in novels. A very few stayed with you after that last chapter ended, but mostly you found yourself ready for something new. Without Mel to drive it, though, my movie deal had fallen through the cracks. The woman producer had called, asking if I was agreeable to a TV miniseries. I told her she had my permission to pitch it and to let me know if anything came of it. So far, there had been no word. But I was anticipating a whole new reading audience with the publication of my first actual romance novel.

    I'd teased Beck about being a traditionalist in terms of her found jar routine, but I had a conventional practice of my own in mind. I just had to make sure to retrieve the ring I'd bought for her from the jar before it went into the ocean and get my proposal out without tears. Beck was the one thing I wanted to hold on to, day after day and year after year, like a favorite story that I'd never tire of returning to. And what I'd found that summer was not only Beck but the best of myself.

About the Author

Jaycie Morrison recently made the move to Colorado, trading the heat of her lifetime big city home of Dallas, Texas, for the cool beauty of the mountains in a small town. Her previous three novels, set during World War II, make up the Love and Courage series. *Basic Training of the Heart*, *Heart's Orders*, and *Guarding Hearts* combine Jaycie's love of the written word and of history. *The Found Jar* is her first foray into contemporary romance, but quite likely not her last. When not writing or reading, Jaycie may be hiking, traveling, experimenting with gluten-free cooking, or pretending to be a rock star.

Contact her at jaycie.morrison@yahoo.com. She is also on Facebook at https://www.facebook.com/jaycie.morrison.

Books Available From Bold Strokes Books

16 Steps to Forever by Georgia Beers. Can Brooke Sullivan and Macy Carr find themselves by finding each other? (978-1-63555-762-6)

All I Want for Christmas by Georgia Beers, Maggie Cummings & Fiona Riley. The Christmas season sparks passion and love in these stories by award-winning authors Georgia Beers, Maggie Cummings, and Fiona Riley. (978-1-63555-764-0)

From the Woods by Charlotte Greene. When Fiona goes backpacking in a protected wilderness, the last thing she expects is to be fighting for her life. (978-1-63555-793-0)

Heart of the Storm by Nicole Stiling. For Juliet Mitchell and Sienna Bennett a forbidden attraction definitely isn't worth upending the life they've worked so hard for. Is it? (978-1-63555-789-3)

If You Dare by Sandy Lowe. For Lauren West and Emma Prescott, following their passions is easy. Following their hearts, though? That's almost impossible. (978-1-63555-654-4)

Love Changes Everything by Jaime Maddox. For Samantha Brooks and Kirby Fielding, no matter how careful their plans, love will change everything. (978-1-63555-835-7)

Not This Time by MA Binfield. Flung back into each other's lives, can former bandmates Sophia and Madison have a second chance at romance? (978-1-63555-798-5)

The Found Jar by Jaycie Morrison. Fear keeps Emily Harris trapped in her emotionally vacant life; can she find the courage to let Beck Reynolds guide her toward love? (978-1-63555 825 8)

Aurora by Emma L McGeown. After a traumatic accident, Elena Ricci is stricken with amnesia, leaving her with no recollection of the last eight years, including her wife and son. (978-1-63555-824-1)

Avenging Avery by Sheri Lewis Wohl. Revenge against a vengeful vampire unites Isa Meyer and Jeni Denton, but it's love that heals them. (978-1-63555-622-3)

Bulletproof by Maggie Cummings. For Dylan Prescott and Briana Logan, the complicated NYC criminal justice system doesn't leave room for love, but where the heart is concerned, no one is bulletproof. (978-1-63555-771-8)

Her Lady to Love by Jane Walsh. A shy wallflower joins forces with the most popular woman in Regency London on a quest to catch a husband, only to discover a wild passion for each other that far eclipses their interest for the Marriage Mart. (978-1-63555-809-8)

No Regrets by Joy Argento. For Jodi and Beth, the possibility of losing their future will force them to decide what is really important. (978-1-63555-751-0)

The Holiday Treatment by Elle Spencer. Who doesn't want a gay Christmas movie? Holly Hudson asks herself that question and discovers that happy endings aren't only for the movies. (978-1-63555-660-5)

Too Good to be True by Leigh Hays. Can the promise of love survive the realities of life for Madison and Jen, or is it too good to be true? (978-1-63555-715-2)

Treacherous Seas by Radclyffe. When the choice comes down to the lives of her officers against the promise she made to her wife, Reese Conlon puts everything she cares about on the line. (978-1-63555-778-7)

Two to Tangle by Melissa Brayden. Ryan Jacks has been a player all her life, but the new chef at Tangle Valley Vineyard changes everything. If only she wasn't off the menu. (978-1-63555-747-3)

When Sparks Fly by Annie McDonald. Will the devastating incident that first brought Dr. Daniella Waveny and hockey coach Luca McCaffrey together on frozen ice now force them apart, or will their secrets and fears thaw enough for them to create sparks? (978-1-63555-782-4)

Best Practice by Carsen Taite. When attorney Grace Maldonado agrees to mentor her best friend's little sister, she's prepared to confront Perry's rebellious nature, but she isn't prepared to fall in love. Legal

Affairs: one law firm, three best friends, three chances to fall in love. (978-1-63555-361-1)

Home by Kris Bryant. Natalie and Sarah discover that anything is possible when love takes the long way home. (978-1-63555-853-1)

Keeper by Sydney Quinne. With a new charge under her reluctant wing—feisty, highly intelligent math wizard Isabelle Templeton—Keeper Andy Bouchard has to prevent a murder or die trying. (978-1-63555-852-4)

One More Chance by Ali Vali. Harry Basantes planned a future with Desi Thompson until the day Desi disappeared without a word, only to walk back into her life sixteen years later. (978-1-63555-536-3)

Renegade's War by Gun Brooke. Freedom fighter Aurelia DeCallum regrets saving the woman called Blue. She fears it will jeopardize her mission, and secretly, Blue might end up breaking Aurelia's heart. (978-1-63555-484-7)

The Other Women by Erin Zak. What happens in Vegas should stay in Vegas, but what do you do when the love you find in Vegas changes your life forever? (978-1-63555-741-1)

The Sea Within by Missouri Vaun. Time is running out for Dr. Elle Graham to convince Captain Jackson Drake that the only thing that can save future Earth resides in the past, and rescue her broken heart in the process. (978-1-63555-568-4)

To Sleep With Reindeer Justine Saracen. In Norway under Nazi occupation, Maarit, an Indigenous woman, and Kirsten, a Norwegian resister, join forces to stop the development of an atomic weapon. (978-1-63555-735-0)

Twice Shy by Aurora Rey. Having an ex with benefits isn't all it's cracked up to be. Will Amanda Russo learn that lesson in time to take a chance on love with Quinn Sullivan? (978-1-63555-737-4)

Z-Town by Eden Darry. Forced to work together to stay alive, Meg and Lane must find the centuries-old treasure before the zombies find them first. (978-1-63555-743-5)

Bet Against Me by Fiona Riley. In the high-stakes luxury real estate market, everything has a price, and as rival Realtors Trina Lee and Kendall Yates find out, that means their hearts and souls, too. (978-1-63555-729-9)

Broken Reign by Sam Ledel. Together on an epic journey in search of a mysterious cure, a princess and a village outcast must overcome life-threatening challenges and their own prejudice if they want to survive. (978-1-63555-739-8)

Just One Taste by CJ Birch. For Lauren, it only took one taste to start trusting in love again. (978-1-63555-772-5)

Lady of Stone by Barbara Ann Wright. Sparks fly as a magical emergency forces a noble embarrassed by her ability to submit to a low-born teacher who resents everything about her. (978-1-63555-607-0)

Last Resort by Angie Williams. Katie and Rhys are about to find out what happens when you meet the girl of your dreams but you aren't looking for a happily ever after. (978-1-63555-774-9)

Longing for You by Jenny Frame. When Debrek housekeeper Katie Brekman is attacked amid a burgeoning vampire-witch war, Alexis Villiers must go against everything her clan believes in to save her. (978-1-63555-658-2)

Money Creek by Anne Laughlin. Clare Lehane is a troubled lawyer from Chicago who tries to make her way in a rural town full of secrets and deceptions. (978-1-63555-795-4)

Passion's Sweet Surrender by Ronica Black. Cam and Blake are unable to deny their passion for each other, but surrendering to love is a whole different matter. (978-1-63555-703-9)

The Holiday Detour by Jane Kolven. It will take everything going wrong to make Dana and Charlie see how right they are for each other. (978-1-63555-720-6)

BOLDSTROKESBOOKS.COM

Looking for your next great read?

Visit BOLDSTROKESBOOKS.COM
to browse our entire catalog of paperbacks, ebooks,
and audiobooks.

Want the first word on what's new?
Visit our website for event info,
author interviews, and blogs.

Subscribe to our free newsletter for sneak peeks,
new releases, plus first notice of promos
and daily bargains.

SIGN UP AT
BOLDSTROKESBOOKS.COM/signup

Quality and Diversity in LGBTQ Literature

Bold Strokes Books is an award-winning publisher
committed to quality and diversity in LGBTQ fiction.

CPSIA information can be obtained
at www.ICGtesting.com
Printed in the USA
LVHW011734071220
673553LV00003B/543